Capture Me
& Bind Me

Anna Zaires

♠ Mozaika Publications ♠

Published by Mozaika Publications, an imprint of Mozaika LLC.
www.mozaikallc.com

Cover by Najla Qamber Designs
najlaqamberdesigns.com
Edited by Mella Baxter

e-ISBN: 978-1-63142-169-3
Print ISBN: 978-1-63142-170-9

Capture Me

Capture Me: Book 1

PART I: THE ASSIGNMENT

CHAPTER ONE

❖ YULIA ❖

The two men in front of me embody danger. They exude it. One blond, one dark—they should've been polar opposites, but they're similar somehow. They give off the same vibe.

The vibe that makes me go cold inside.

"I have a delicate matter I'd like to discuss with you," says Arkady Buschekov, the Russian official beside me. His faded, colorless gaze is trained on the dark-haired man's face. Buschekov says it in Russian, and I immediately repeat his words in English. My translation is smooth, my accent undetectable. I'm a good interpreter, even if that's not my real job.

"Go on," the dark-haired man says. Julian Esguerra is his name, and he's a big-time arms dealer. I know that from the folder I studied this morning. He's the important one here today, the one they want me to get close to. It shouldn't be a hardship. He's a strikingly handsome man, his eyes blue and piercing in his darkly tanned face. If it weren't for that chill-inducing vibe, I'd be genuinely attracted to him. As it is, I'll be faking it, but he won't know.

They never know.

"I'm sure you are aware of the difficulties in our region," Buschekov says. "We would like you to assist us in resolving this matter."

I translate his words, doing my best to conceal my growing excitement. Obenko was right. There *is* something brewing between Esguerra and the Russians. Obenko suspected as much when he heard the arms dealer was visiting Moscow.

"Assist you how?" Esguerra asks. He looks only vaguely interested.

As I translate his words for Buschekov, I sneak a glance at the other man at the table—the one with blond hair cut in a short, almost military style.

Lucas Kent, Esguerra's right-hand man.

I've been trying not to look at him. He unnerves me even more than his boss. Thankfully, he's not my target, so I don't need to feign interest in him. For some reason, though, my eyes keep being drawn to his hard features. With his tall, powerfully muscled body, square jaw, and fierce gaze, Kent reminds me of a *bogatyr*—a noble warrior of Russian folk tales.

He catches me looking at him, and his pale eyes flash as they lock on my face. I quickly look away, suppressing a shudder. Those eyes make me think of the slivers of ice outside, blue-gray and freezing cold.

Thank God he's not the one I need to seduce. It will be much, much easier to fake it with his boss.

"There are certain parts of Ukraine that need our help," Buschekov says. "But, world opinion being what it is right now, it would be problematic if we went in and actually gave that help."

I swiftly translate what he said, my attention once more on the information I'm supposed to retrieve. This is important; this is the primary reason I'm here today. Seducing Esguerra is secondary, though likely still unavoidable.

"So you would like me to do it instead," Esguerra says, and Buschekov nods as I translate.

"Yes," Buschekov says. "We would like a sizable shipment of weapons and other supplies to reach the freedom fighters in Donetsk. It cannot be traced back to us. In return, you would be paid your usual fee and granted safe passage to Tajikistan."

When I convey the words to him, Esguerra smiles coldly. "Is that all?"

"We would also prefer it if you avoided any dealings with Ukraine at this time," Buschekov says. "Two chairs and one ass and all that."

I do my best to translate the last part, though it doesn't sound nearly as punchy in English. I also commit every single word to memory, so I can convey it to Obenko later today. This is exactly what my boss was hoping I'd hear. Or rather, what he feared I'd hear.

"I'm afraid I will require additional compensation for that," Esguerra says. "As you know, I don't usually take sides in these types of conflicts."

"Yes, so we've heard." Buschekov brings a piece of *selyodka*—salted fish—to his mouth and chews it slowly, looking at the arms dealer. "Perhaps you might reconsider that position in our case. The Soviet Union may be gone, but our influence in this region is still quite substantial."

"Yes, I'm aware. Why do you think I'm here right now?" Esguerra's smile is reminiscent of a shark's. "But neutrality is an expensive commodity to give up. I'm sure you understand."

Buschekov's gaze turns colder. "I do. I'm authorized to offer you twenty percent more than the usual payment for your cooperation in this matter."

"Twenty percent? When you're cutting my potential profits in half?" Esguerra laughs softly. "I don't think so."

After I translate, Buschekov pours himself some vodka and swirls it around the glass. "Twenty percent more and the captured Al-Quadar terrorist remitted into your custody," he says after a few moments. "This is our final offer."

I translate his words and sneak another glance at the blond-haired man, inexplicably curious to see his reaction. Lucas Kent hasn't said a word this whole time, but I can sense him watching everything, absorbing everything.

I can sense him watching *me*.

Does he suspect anything, or is he simply attracted? Either way, it worries me. Men like that are dangerous, and I have a feeling this one may be more dangerous than most.

"We have a deal then," Esguerra says, and I realize that this is it. What Obenko was afraid of is coming to pass. The Russians are going to get the weapons to the so-called freedom fighters, and the clusterfuck in Ukraine will reach epic proportions.

Oh, well. That's Obenko's problem, not mine. All I need to do is smile, look pretty, and translate—which I do for the rest of the meal.

* * *

When the meeting concludes, Buschekov stays in the restaurant to talk to the owner, and I exit with Esguerra and Kent.

As soon as we step outside, the frigid cold bites at me. The coat I'm wearing is stylish, but it's no match for the Russian winter. The chill goes straight through the wool and into my bones. Within seconds, my feet turn to icicles, the thin soles of my high-heeled shoes doing little to protect them from the freezing ground.

"Would you mind giving me a lift to the nearest subway?" I ask as Esguerra and Kent approach their car. I know I'm visibly shivering, and I'm counting on the fact that even ruthless criminals won't let a pretty woman freeze for no good reason. "It should be about ten blocks from here."

Esguerra studies me for a second, then motions to Kent. "Frisk her," he orders curtly.

My heart rate speeds up as the blond man comes up to me. His hard face is emotionless, his expression not changing even when his big hands travel over my body from head to toe. It's a classic patdown—he doesn't try to feel me up or anything—but when he's done, I'm shivering for a different reason, the chill inside me exacerbated by a surge of unwelcome awareness.

No. I force my breathing to even out. This is not the reaction I need. He's not the man I need to be reacting to.

"She's clean," Kent says, stepping away from me, and I do my best to control my relieved exhalation.

"Okay, then." Esguerra opens the car door for me. "Hop in."

I climb in and take a seat next to him in the back, giving mental thanks that Kent joined the driver at the front. I'm finally in a position to make my move.

"Thank you," I say, giving my warmest smile to Esguerra. "I really appreciate it. This is one of the worst winters in recent years."

To my disappointment, there isn't even a flicker of interest on the arms dealer's handsome face. "No problem," he says, pulling out his phone. A smile appears on his sensuous lips as he reads whatever message is there and begins typing a response.

I study him, wondering what could've put him in such a good mood. A deal gone right? A better-than-expected offer from a supplier? Whatever it is, it's distracting him from me, and that's not good.

"Are you staying here for long?" I ask, making my voice soft and seductive. When he glances at me, I smile again and cross my legs—the length of which is emphasized by the silky black tights I'm wearing. "I could show you around town if you'd like." As I speak, I look him in the eye, making my gaze as welcoming as I can. Men can't tell the difference between this and genuine desire; as long as a woman looks like she wants them, they believe she does.

And to be fair, most women *would* want this man. He's more than handsome—gorgeous, really. Women would kill for a chance to be in his bed, even with that dark, cruel edge I sense within him. The fact that he doesn't do anything for me is my problem, one I'll need to work on if I'm to complete my mission.

I don't know if Esguerra senses something off or if I'm just not his type, but instead of taking me up on my offer, he gives me a cool smile. "Thanks for the invitation, but we'll be leaving soon and I'm afraid I'm too exhausted to do your town justice tonight."

Shit. I conceal my disappointment and smile back. "Of course. If you change your mind, you know where to find me." There's nothing else I can say without raising suspicion.

The car stops in front of my subway stop, and I climb out, trying to think how I'm going to explain my failure in this department.

He didn't want me? Yes, that would go over well.

Heaving a sigh, I wrap my coat tighter around my chest and hurry into the underground metro station, determined to at least get out of the cold.

CHAPTER TWO

❖ YULIA ❖

The first thing I do upon arriving home is call my boss and convey everything I've learned.

"So it's as I suspected," Vasiliy Obenko says when I'm done. "They're going to use Esguerra to arm those fucking rebels in Donetsk."

"Yes." I kick off my shoes and walk into the kitchen to make myself tea. "And Buschekov demanded exclusivity, so Esguerra's now fully allied with the Russians."

Obenko lets out a string of curses, most of which involve some combination of fucking, sluts, and mothers. I tune him out as I pour water into an electronic kettle and turn it on.

"All right," Obenko says when he calms down a little. "You're seeing him tonight, right?"

I take a breath. Now comes the unpleasant part. "Not exactly."

"Not exactly?" Obenko's voice goes dangerously quiet. "What the fuck is that supposed to mean?"

"I offered, but he wasn't interested." It's always best to tell the truth in these types of situations. "Said they're leaving soon, and he was too exhausted."

Obenko starts cursing again. I use the time to tear open a tea bag, drop it into a cup, and pour boiling water over it.

"You're sure you're not going to see him again?" he asks after he's done with his cursing fit.

"Reasonably sure, yes." I blow on my tea to cool it down. "He just wasn't interested."

Obenko goes silent for a few moments. "All right," he says finally. "You fucked up, but we'll deal with that another time. For now, we need to figure out what to do about Esguerra and the weapons that will flood our country."

"Eliminate him?" I suggest. My tea is still a bit too hot, but I take a sip anyway, enjoying the warmth going down my throat. It's a simple pleasure, but the best things in life are always simple. The smell of lilacs blooming in the spring, the softness of a cat's fur, the juicy sweetness of a ripe strawberry—I've learned to treasure these things in recent years, to squeeze every ounce of joy out of life.

"Easier said than done." Obenko sounds frustrated. "He's better protected than Putin."

"Uh-huh." I take another sip of tea and close my eyes, savoring the taste this time. "I'm sure you'll figure it out."

"When did he say he was leaving?"

"He didn't specify. He just said 'soon.'"

"All right." Obenko seems impatient all of a sudden. "If he contacts you, let me know immediately."

And before I can reply, he hangs up.

* * *

Since I have the evening off, I decide to indulge in a bath. My bathtub, like the rest of this apartment, is small and dingy, but I've seen worse. I spruce up the ugliness of the cramped bathroom by putting a couple of scented candles on the sink and adding bubbles to the water, and then I get in, letting out a blissful sigh at the warmth engulfing my body.

If I had my way, I'd always be warm. Whoever said hell is hot was wrong. Hell is cold.

Russian-winter cold.

I'm enjoying my soak when the doorbell rings. Instantly, my heartbeat spikes and adrenaline blasts through my veins.

I'm not expecting anyone—which means it could only be trouble.

Jumping out of the tub, I wrap a towel around myself and run out of the bathroom into the main room of my studio apartment. The clothes I took off are still lying on the bed, but I don't have time to put them on. Instead, I throw on a robe and grab a gun from the drawer in my nightstand.

Then I take a deep breath and approach the door, aiming the weapon at it.

"Yes?" I call out, stopping a couple of feet from the apartment entrance. My door is reinforced steel, but the keyhole is not. Someone could shoot through it.

"It's Lucas Kent." The deep voice speaking English startles me so much, the gun wavers in my hand. My pulse jumps another notch, and a peculiar weakness seizes my knees.

Why is he here? Does Esguerra know anything? Did someone betray me? The questions blaze through my mind, making my heart race even faster, but then the most reasonable course of action comes to me.

"What is it?" I ask, doing my best to keep my voice steady. There's one explanation for Kent's presence that doesn't involve me getting killed: Esguerra's changed his mind. In which case, I need to act like the innocent civilian I'm supposed to be.

"I'd like to talk to you," Kent says, and I hear a hint of amusement in his voice. "Are you going to open the door, or are we going to continue talking through three inches of steel?"

Shit. That doesn't sound like Esguerra's sent him for me.

I quickly evaluate my options. I can stay locked inside the apartment and hope he won't be able to find his way in—or get me when I come out, as I will inevitably have to—or I can take the chance that he doesn't know who I am and play it cool.

"Why do you want to talk to me?" I ask, stalling for time. It's a reasonable question. Any woman in this situation would be wary, not just one who has something to hide. "What do you want?"

"You."

The one word, uttered in his deep voice, hits me like a fist. My lungs stop working, and I stare at the door, seized by irrational panic. I wasn't wrong then, when I wondered whether he might be attracted to me— whether the reason he kept looking at me might be as simple as human biology in action.

Yes, of course. He wants me.

I force myself to start breathing again. This should be a relief. There's no reason to panic. Men have wanted me since I was fifteen, and I've learned to cope with it. To turn their lust to my advantage. This is no different.

Except Kent is harder, more dangerous than most.

No. I silence that small voice and take a deep breath, lowering my weapon. As I do, I catch a glimpse of myself in the hallway mirror. My blue eyes are wide in my pale face, and my hair is messily pinned up, wet tendrils trailing down my neck. With the terrycloth robe wrapped carelessly around me and the gun in my hands, I look nothing like the fashionable young woman who tried to seduce Kent's boss.

Reaching a decision, I call out, "Just a minute." I could try to deny Lucas Kent entry to my apartment—it wouldn't be that suspicious for a woman alone—but the smarter thing would be to use this opportunity to get some information.

At the very least, I can try to find out when Esguerra's leaving and tell Obenko, partially making up for my earlier failure.

Moving quickly, I hide the gun in a drawer underneath the hallway mirror and unpin my hair, letting the thick blond strands stream down my back. I've already washed off my makeup, but I have clear skin and my eyelashes are naturally brown, so it's not too bad. If anything, I look younger, more innocent this way.

More like "the girl next door," as Americans like to say.

Confident that I'm reasonably presentable, I approach the door and unlock it, trying to ignore the heavy, frantic beating of my heart.

CHAPTER THREE

❖ YULIA ❖

He steps into my apartment as soon as the door swings open. No hesitation, no greeting—he just comes in.

Startled, I step back, the short, narrow hallway suddenly stiflingly small. I'd somehow forgotten how big he is, how broad his shoulders are. I'm tall for a woman—tall enough to fake being a model if an assignment calls for it—but he towers a full head above me. With the heavy down jacket he's wearing, he takes up almost the entire hallway.

Still not saying a word, he closes the door behind him and advances toward me. Instinctively, I back away, feeling like cornered prey.

"Hello, Yulia," he murmurs, stopping when we're out of the hallway. His pale gaze is locked on my face. "I wasn't expecting to see you like this."

I swallow, my pulse racing. "I just took a bath." I want to seem calm and confident, but he's got me completely off-balance. "I wasn't expecting visitors."

"No, I can see that." A faint smile appears on his lips, softening the hard line of his mouth. "Yet you let me in. Why?"

"Because I didn't want to continue talking through the door." I take a steadying breath. "Can I offer you some tea?" It's a stupid thing to say, given what he's here for, but I need a few moments to compose myself.

He raises his eyebrows. "Tea? No, thanks."

"Then can I take your jacket?" I can't seem to stop playing the hostess, using politeness to cover my anxiety. "It looks quite warm."

Amusement flickers in his wintry gaze. "Sure." He takes off his down jacket and hands it to me. He's left wearing a black sweater and dark jeans tucked into black winter boots. The jeans hug his legs, revealing muscular thighs and powerful calves, and on his belt, I see a gun sitting in a holster.

Irrationally, my breathing quickens at the sight, and it takes a concerted effort to keep my hands from shaking as I take the jacket and walk over to hang it in my tiny closet. It's not a surprise that he's armed—it would be a shock if he wasn't—but the gun is a stark reminder of who Lucas Kent is.

What he is.

It's no big deal, I tell myself, trying to calm my frayed nerves. I'm used to dangerous men. I was raised among them. This man is not that different. I'll sleep with him, get whatever information I can, and then he'll be out of my life.

Yes, that's it. The sooner I can get it done, the sooner all of this will be over.

Closing the closet door, I paste a practiced smile on my face and turn back to face him, finally ready to resume the role of confident seductress.

Except he's already next to me, having crossed the room without making a sound.

My pulse jumps again, my newfound composure fleeing. He's close enough that I can see the gray striations in his pale blue eyes, close enough that he can touch me.

And a second later, he does touch me.

Lifting his hand, he runs the back of his knuckles over my jaw.

I stare up at him, confused by my body's instant response. My skin warms and my nipples tighten, my breath coming faster. It doesn't make sense for this hard, ruthless stranger to turn me on. His boss is more handsome, more striking, yet it's Kent my body's reacting to. All he's touched thus far is my face. It should be nothing, yet it's intimate somehow.

Intimate and disturbing.

I swallow again. "Mr. Kent—Lucas—are you sure I can't offer you something to drink? Maybe some coffee or—" My words end in a breathless gasp as he reaches for the tie of my robe and tugs on it, as casually as one would unwrap a package.

"No." He watches as the robe falls open, revealing my naked body underneath. "No coffee."

And then he touches me for real, his big, hard palm cupping my breast. His fingers are callused, rough. Cold from being outside. His thumb flicks over my hardened nipple, and I feel a pull deep within my core, a coiling of need that feels as foreign as his touch.

Fighting the urge to flinch away, I dampen my dry lips. "You're very direct, aren't you?"

"I don't have time for games." His eyes gleam as his thumb flicks over my nipple again. "We both know why I'm here."

"To have sex with me."

"Yes." He doesn't bother to soften it, to give me anything but the brutal truth. He's still holding my breast, touching my naked flesh as though it's his right. "To have sex with you."

"And if I say no?" I don't know why I'm asking this. This is not how it's supposed to go. I should be seducing him, not trying to put him off. Yet something within me rebels at his casual assumption that I'm his for the taking. Other men have assumed this before, and it didn't bother me nearly as much. I don't know what's different this time, but I want him to step away from me, to stop touching me. I want it so badly that my hands curl into fists at my sides, my muscles tensing with the urge to fight.

"Are you saying no?" He asks the question calmly, his thumb now circling over my areola. As I search for a response, he slides his other hand into my hair, possessively cupping the back of my skull.

I stare at him, my breath catching. "And if I were?" To my disgust, my voice comes out thin and scared. It's as if I'm a virgin again, cornered by my trainer in the locker room. "Would you leave?"

One corner of his mouth lifts in a half-smile. "What do you think?" His fingers tighten in my hair, the grip just hard enough to hint at pain. His other hand, the one on my breast, is still gentle, but it doesn't matter.

I have my answer.

So when his hand leaves my breast and slides down my belly, I don't resist. Instead, I part my legs, letting him touch my smooth, freshly waxed pussy. And when his hard, blunt finger pushes into me, I don't try to move away. I just stand there, trying to control my frantic breathing, trying to convince myself that this is no different from any other assignment.

Except it is.

I don't want it to be, but it is.

"You're wet," he murmurs, staring at me as he pushes his finger deeper. "Very wet. Do you always get so wet for men you don't want?"

"What makes you think I don't want you?" To my relief, my voice is steadier this time. The question comes out soft, almost amused as I hold his gaze. "I let you in here, didn't I?"

"You came on to *him*." Kent's jaw tightens, and his hand on the back of my head shifts, gripping a fistful of my hair. "You wanted *him* earlier today."

"So I did." The typically masculine display of jealousy reassures me, putting me on more familiar ground. I manage to soften my tone, make it more seductive. "And now I want you. Does that bother you?"

Kent's eyes narrow. "No." He forces a second finger into me and simultaneous presses his thumb against my clit. "Not at all."

I want to say something clever, come up with some snappy retort, but I can't. The jolt of pleasure is sharp and startling. My inner muscles tighten, clutching at his rough, invading fingers, and it's all I can do not to moan out loud at the resulting sensations. Involuntarily, my hands come up, grabbing at his forearm. I don't know if I'm trying to push him away or get him to continue, but it doesn't matter. Under the soft wool of his sweater, his arm is thick with steely muscle. I can't control its movements—all I can do is hold onto it as he pushes deeper into me with those hard, merciless fingers.

"You like that, don't you?" he murmurs, holding my gaze, and I gasp as he begins flicking his thumb over my clit, side to side, then up and down. His fingers curl inside me, and I suppress a moan as he hits a spot that sends an even sharper pang of sensation to my nerve endings. A tension begins to coil inside me, the pleasure gathering and intensifying, and with shock I realize I'm on the verge of orgasm.

My body, usually so slow to respond, is throbbing with aching need at the touch of a man who scares me—a development that both astonishes and unnerves me.

I don't know if he sees it on my face, or if he feels the tightening in my body, but his pupils dilate, his pale eyes darkening. "Yes, that's it." His voice is a low, deep rumble. "Come for me, beautiful"—his thumb presses hard on my clit—"just like that."

And I do. With a strangled moan, I climax around his fingers, the hard edges of his short, blunt nails digging into my rippling flesh. My visions blurs, my skin prickling with heated needles as I ride the wave of sensations, and then I sag in his grasp, held upright only by his hand in my hair and his fingers inside my body.

"There you go," he says thickly, and as the world comes back into focus, I see that he's watching me intently. "That was nice, wasn't it?"

I can't even manage a nod, but he doesn't seem to need my confirmation. And why would he? I can feel the slickness inside me, the wetness that coats those rough male fingers—fingers that he withdraws from me slowly, watching my face the whole time. I want to close my eyes, or at least look away from that penetrating gaze, but I can't.

Not without letting him know how much he frightens me.

So instead of backing down, I study him in return, seeing the signs of arousal on his strong features. His jaw is clenched tight as he stares at me, a tiny muscle pulsing near his right ear. And even through the sun-bronzed hue of his skin, I can see heightened color on his blade-like cheekbones.

He wants me badly—and that knowledge emboldens me to act.

Reaching down, I cup the hard bulge at the crotch of his jeans. "It *was* nice," I whisper, looking up at him. "And now it's your turn."

His pupils dilate even more, his chest inflating with a deep breath. "Yes." His voice is thick with lust as he uses his grip on my hair to drag me closer. "Yes, I think it is." And before I can reconsider the wisdom of my blatant provocation, he lowers his head and captures my mouth with his.

I gasp, my lips parting from surprise, and he immediately takes advantage, deepening the kiss. His hard-looking mouth is surprisingly soft on mine, his lips warm and smooth as his tongue hungrily explores the interior of my mouth. There's skill and confidence in that kiss; it's the kiss of a man who knows how to please a woman, how to seduce her with nothing more than the touch of his lips.

The heat simmering within me intensifies, the tension rising inside me once more. He's holding me so close that my bare breasts are pressing against his sweater, the wool rubbing against my peaked nipples. I can feel his erection through the rough material of his jeans; it pushes into my lower belly, revealing how much he wants me, how thin his pretense of control really is. Dimly, I realize the robe fell off my shoulders, leaving me completely naked, and then I forget all about it as he makes a low growling sound deep in his throat and pushes me against the wall.

The shock of the cold surface at my back clears my mind for a second, but he's already unzipping his jeans, his knees wedging between my legs and spreading them open as he raises his head to look at me. I hear the ripping sound of a foil packet being opened, and then he cups my ass and lifts me off the ground. Instinctively, I grab at his shoulders, my heartbeat quickening as he orders hoarsely, "Wrap your legs around me"—and lowers me onto his stiff cock, all the while holding my gaze.

His thrust is hard and deep, penetrating me all the way. My breathing stutters at the force of it, at the uncompromising brutality of the invasion. My inner muscles clench around him, futilely trying to keep him out. His cock is as big as the rest of him, so long and thick it stretches me to the point of pain. If I hadn't been so wet, he would've torn me. But I *am* wet, and after a couple of moments, my body begins to soften, adjusting to his thickness. Unconsciously, my legs come up, clasping his hips as he instructed, and the new position lets him slide even deeper into me, making me cry out at the sharp sensation.

He begins to move then, his eyes glittering as he stares at me. Each thrust is as hard as the one that joined us together, yet my body no longer tries to fight it. Instead, it brings forth more moisture, easing his way. Each time he slams into me, his groin presses against my sex, putting pressure on my clit, and the tension in my core returns, growing with every second. Stunned, I realize I'm about to have my second orgasm . . . and then I do, the tension peaking and exploding, scattering my thoughts and electrifying my nerve endings.

I can feel my own pulsations, the way my muscles squeeze and release his cock, and then I see his eyes go unfocused as he stops thrusting. A hoarse, deep groan escapes his throat as he grinds into me, and I know he's found his release as well, my orgasm driving him over the edge.

My chest heaving, I stare up at him, watching as his pale blue eyes refocus on me. He's still inside me, and all of a sudden, the intimacy of that is unbearable. He's nobody to me, a stranger, yet he fucked me.

He fucked me, and I let him because it's my job.

Swallowing, I push at his chest, my legs unwrapping from around his waist. "Please, let me down." I know I should be cooing at him and stroking his ego. I should be telling him how amazing it was, how he gave me more pleasure than anyone I've known. It wouldn't even be a lie—I've never come twice with a man before. But I can't bring myself to do that. I feel too raw, too invaded.

With this man, I'm not in control, and that knowledge scares me.

I don't know if he senses that, or if he just wants to toy with me, but a sardonic smile appears on his lips.

"It's too late for regrets, beautiful," he murmurs, and before I can respond, he lets me down and releases his grip on my ass. His softening cock slips out of my body as he steps back, and I watch, my breathing still uneven, as he casually takes the condom off and drops it on the floor.

For some reason, his action makes me flush. There's something so wrong, so dirty about that condom lying there. Perhaps it's because I feel like that condom: used and discarded. Spotting my robe on the floor, I move to pick it up, but Lucas's hand on my arm stops me.

"What are you doing?" he asks, gazing at me. He doesn't seem the least bit concerned that his jeans are still unzipped and his cock is hanging out. "We're not done yet."

My heart skips a beat. "We're not?"

"No," he says, stepping closer. To my shock, I feel him hardening against my stomach. "We're far from done."

And using his grip on my arm, he steers me toward the bed.

CHAPTER FOUR

❖ YULIA ❖

My mind in turmoil, I sit on the edge of the bed and watch Lucas undress.

First, he pulls off his sweater, revealing a tight T-shirt stretched across his muscular chest. Next, he takes off his shoes and pushes down his jeans and black briefs. His legs are as powerful as they'd appeared through his clothes, thick with muscle and as darkly tanned as his face. His cock, already hard again, is jutting out from a nest of brownish-blond hair at his groin, and as he pulls off his T-shirt, I see sharply defined abs and sculpted chest.

Lucas Kent has the body of an athlete, beautiful in its uncompromising strength.

As I watch him, I become aware of a strange urge to touch him. Not in an effort to please him or because it's expected of me, but because I want to. I want to know how his muscles feel under my fingertips, whether his bronzed skin is smooth or rough. I want to lick his neck, tongue the hollow above his collarbone, and find out how that warm-looking skin tastes.

It makes no sense, but I want him. I want him even though I'm sore from his rough fucking, even though he should be an assignment, nothing more.

He steps out of his jeans and briefs and kicks them aside, then comes toward me. I don't move as he approaches me. I hardly even breathe. When he's next to me, he stops and sinks to his haunches. "Lie back," he murmurs, grasping my calves, and before I have a chance to realize what he's doing, he pulls me toward him, not stopping until my ass is partially hanging off the mattress.

"What are you—" I begin to say, but he ignores me, using one strong hand to push me down on the mattress. I fall onto my back, my heart hammering, and then I feel it.

His warm breath on my sex as he pulls my thighs apart.

My breathing quickens again, heat surging through my body as he presses a kiss to my closed folds, his lips soft and gentle. There's barely any pressure on my clit, but I'm so sensitive from my earlier orgasms that even that light touch sends my nerves zinging. I gasp, arching toward him, and he laughs softly, the low, masculine sound creating vibrations that travel through my flesh, adding to the growing ache within me.

"Lucas, wait." My voice is breathless, panicked from the need he's invoking within me. The ceiling blurs in front of my eyes. "Wait, don't—"

He ignores me once again, his tongue sweeping over my slit and delving into my opening. As he begins to fuck me with his tongue, I forget what I was going to say. I forget everything. My eyes squeeze shut, and the world around me disappears, leaving only darkness and the feel of his tongue dipping in and out of my soaked pussy. The fire burning within me is white-hot, my flesh so swollen and sensitized that his tongue feels as big as a cock. Except it's softer, more flexible—and as he moves that tongue higher, circling my clit, I tense, feeling like a string being wound tighter and tighter.

"Lucas, please . . ." The words come out in a begging moan. I don't know what I'm asking for, but he seems to—because he closes his lips around my throbbing clit and sucks on it. Lightly, gently, using only his lips as his tongue laves the underside of it. And it's enough. It's more than enough. My toes curl, the tension gathering into a pulsing ball in my sex as I arch up—and then I come with a choked cry, the orgasm blasting through me with stunning force. Every cell in my body fills with the pulsing pleasure of release, and my heart gallops in my chest.

Before I can recover, he flips me onto my stomach, bending me over the edge of the bed. Then I hear another foil packet ripping and a second later, he drives into me, his thick cock spearing me, stretching me once more. I gasp, my hands fisting the sheets as he takes me with a hard, fast rhythm, pounding into me so hard it should hurt—except my body is beyond that now. All I feel is need. I'm awash in it, drunk on the sensations he's wringing from my flesh. As he thrusts into me, his movements force my sex against the edge of the mattress, putting rhythmic pressure on my clit, and I explode again, screaming his name. But he doesn't stop.

He just keeps fucking me, his fingers digging into my hips as he drives into me, again and again.

* * *

I wake up tangled with him, our bodies glued together with sticky sweat. I don't remember falling asleep in his embrace, but it must've happened, because that's where I am now, surrounded by his powerful body.

It's dark, and he's asleep. I can hear his even breathing and feel the rise and fall of his chest as my head rests on his shoulder. My mouth is dry and my bladder is full, so I try to wiggle out from under his heavy arm—which immediately tightens around me.

"Where are you going?" Lucas's voice is hoarse, roughened with sleep.

"To the bathroom," I explain cautiously. "I have to pee."

He lifts his arm and moves his leg off my calves. "All right. Go."

I scoot away from him and sit up, wincing at the soreness I feel deep inside. I don't know how long he fucked me that second time, but it could've easily been an hour or more. I lost count of how many times I came, the orgasms melding together into one never-ending wave of peaks and valleys.

My legs are unsteady as I stand up, my inner thighs aching from being stretched wide. After fucking me from behind, he turned me over and grabbed my ankles, holding my legs open as he drove into me, thrusting so deeply that I begged him to stop. He didn't, of course. He just shifted his hips, changing the angle of his strokes to hit that sensitive spot within me, and I forgot all about the pain, lost in the overwhelming pleasure of his hard possession.

Inhaling deeply, I force myself back to the present, my bladder reminding me of another overwhelming need. Shakily, I walk to the bathroom and relieve myself. Then I wash my hands, brush my teeth, and splash cold water on my face, trying to regain my equilibrium.

Everything is fine, I tell myself as I stare at my pale face in the mirror. Everything is going according to plan. Great sex is a bonus, not a problem. So what if this ruthless stranger can make me respond this way? It doesn't mean anything. It's just fucking, a meaningless physical act.

Except with him it isn't meaningless.

No. Squeezing my eyes shut, I force that voice away and splash more water on my face, washing away the doubts. I have a job to do, and there's nothing wrong with treating this night as a perk of that job.

There's nothing wrong with letting myself feel pleasure—as long as I don't let it mean anything.

Feeling marginally more like myself, I make my way back to the bed, where Lucas is waiting for me. As soon as I lie down next to him, he pulls me against him, curving his body around me from the back and covering us both with a blanket. I let out a sigh of enjoyment as his warmth surrounds me. The man is like a furnace, generating so much heat that I instantly feel toasty, the ever-present chill inside my apartment forgotten.

"When are you leaving?" I ask softly as he arranges me more comfortably, settling my head on his outstretched arm and draping his other arm over my hip. This is what I need to know from him, what I owe Obenko for my failure, yet something tightens within me as I wait for Lucas's answer.

That pang of emotion—it can't be regret at the thought of him leaving.

That wouldn't make sense.

Lucas nuzzles my ear. "In the morning," he whispers, his teeth grazing over my earlobe. His breath sends a warm shiver through me. "I have to be out of here in a couple of hours."

"Oh." Ignoring the irrational twinge of sadness, I do quick mental math. According to the digital clock on my nightstand, it's a little after four a.m. If he has to leave my apartment around six, then their plane must be departing at eight or nine in the morning.

Obenko doesn't have much time to do whatever he plans to do to Esguerra.

"You can't stay longer?" I turn my head to brush my lips against Lucas's outstretched arm. It's the kind of question a woman who has feelings for a man might ask, so I'm not afraid it would raise his suspicions.

He chuckles softly. "No, beautiful, I can't. You should be glad of that"—his arm on top of me shifts, his hand sliding down to palm my sex—"given how sore you said you are."

I swallow, remembering how toward the end of that marathon sex session I pleaded for mercy, my insides raw from so much fucking. Incredibly, I feel a twinge of renewed sensation at the memory—and at the touch of that big, strong hand between my legs.

"I *am* sore," I whisper, hoping he would stop and at the same time, hoping he wouldn't.

To my relief and disappointment, he moves his hand back to my hip, even though I feel his cock stirring against my ass. The man is a sexual machine, unstoppable in his lust. According to the file I've been given, he's thirty-four years old. Most men past their teenage years don't want to have sex three times a night. Once, twice maybe. But three times? His cock shouldn't harden with so little provocation.

It makes me wonder how long it's been since Lucas Kent's had a woman.

"Are you going to return any time soon?" I ask, pushing that thought aside. It's ridiculous, but the idea of him being with other women—of him giving them the kind of pleasure he gave me—makes my chest tighten in an unpleasant way.

"I don't know," he says, shifting so that his semi-hard erection is wedged more comfortably against my ass. "Maybe one day."

"I see." I stare into the darkness, battling the part of me that wants to bawl like a child deprived of her favorite toy. This is not real, none of it is real. Even if I were truly an interpreter, I'd know this is nothing more than a one-night stand. But I'm not the carefree, easy girl I'm pretending to be. I didn't have sex with him for fun; I did it to get information—and now that I have it, I need to get it to Obenko right away.

As Lucas's breathing evens out, signifying that he's asleep again, I carefully reach for my phone. It's sitting on the nightstand less than a couple of feet away, and I manage to grab it without disturbing Lucas, who's still holding me against him. Ignoring the growing ache in my chest, I type out a coded message to Obenko, letting him know that Kent is with me and what time they're planning to depart.

If my boss is planning to strike at Esguerra, now is as good a time as any, since at least one man from Esguerra's security team is out of the way.

As soon as the text message goes out, I erase it from my phone and put the device back on the nightstand. Then I close my eyes and force myself to relax against Lucas's hard body.

My assignment is done, for better or for worse.

CHAPTER FIVE

❖ LUCAS ❖

I wake up to the unfamiliar feel of a slender body in my arms and the faint smell of peaches in my nostrils. Opening my eyes, I see tangled blond hair spread across the pillow in front of me and a slim, pale shoulder peeking out from under the blanket.

For a moment, the sight startles me, but then I remember.

I'm with Yulia Tzakova, the interpreter the Russians hired for yesterday's meeting.

Memories of last night rush into my brain, making my blood surge.

Fuck, it had been hot. More than hot. Scorching.

Everything about her had been perfect, the sex so intense that just thinking of it makes me hard. I don't know what I had been expecting when I showed up on her doorstep, but what happened last night wasn't it.

I had watched her all through the meeting, enjoying the way she translated so effortlessly, her voice smooth and unaccented. It wasn't a surprise that she caught my attention. I've always liked tall, leggy blondes, and Yulia Tzakova is as beautiful as they come, with her clear blue eyes and fine bone structure. She didn't really eat during the meal, just nibbled on a couple of the appetizers, but she drank tea, and I found myself staring at her pink, glossy lips touching the rim of her porcelain cup . . . at the smooth white column of her throat moving as she swallowed. I wanted to feel those lips closing around the base of my cock and see her throat move as she swallowed my cum. I wanted to strip off her elegant clothes and bend her over the table, to fist that long, silky hair as I drove into her, fucking her until she screamed and came.

I wanted *her*—and she seemed to have eyes only for Esguerra.

Even now, the knowledge that she came on to my boss leaves a bitter taste in my mouth. It shouldn't matter. Esguerra's always been a chick magnet, and I've never minded that. It amuses me, in fact, the way women throw themselves at him, even when they suspect what he's really like. Even his new wife—a pretty, petite American girl he kidnapped almost two years ago—seems to have fallen for him. It's only logical that Yulia would try for him—or at least that's what I told myself as I watched her eye Esguerra all through the meeting.

If she wanted him, she was welcome to him.

Except he didn't want *her*. It surprised me, that last part, even though over the past two years I haven't actually seen him hook up with any woman. He would just go to his private island all the time. It wasn't until a few months ago that I learned he kept his American girl there, the one he ended up marrying. The girl—Nora—must've been taking care of his needs all along. Must still be taking care of them exceptionally well, given that Esguerra didn't spare Yulia so much as a glance.

I was tempted to forget the interpreter as well—except he asked me to frisk her. She stood there shivering in her elegant coat, and I got a chance to feel her, to run my hands over her body in search of weapons. There were none, but her breathing changed as I touched her. She didn't look at me, didn't move, but I could feel a slight hitch in her breathing and see her pale cheeks brighten with a hint of color. Up until then, I didn't think she was aware of me as a man at all, but that moment made me realize that she was—and that she was fighting the attraction for some reason. So when Esguerra turned down her invitation, I made the impulsive decision to take her for myself.

Just for one night, just to appease the craving.

It wasn't difficult to get her address—all it took was one call to Buschekov—and then I showed up on her doorstep, expecting to see the same put-together, confident young woman who flirted with my boss.

Except that wasn't who greeted me.

It was a girl who looked barely out of her teens, her beautiful face devoid of any makeup and her tall, slender body swathed in a decidedly inelegant robe. She let me into her apartment after I explicitly told her what I wanted, but the look in her wide blue eyes was that of a hunted rabbit. For a minute, I doubted whether she wanted me there at all; she seemed as nervous as said rabbit confronting a fox. Her anxiety was so palpable, I wondered if I'd made a mistake coming to her, if I'd somehow misread either the extent of her experience or the level of her interest in me.

Just one touch, I told myself as she took my coat. Just one touch, and if she didn't want me, I'd leave. I'd never forced a woman in my life, and I didn't intend to start with this girl—a girl who seemed oddly innocent despite her corrupt Kremlin connections.

A girl I wanted more with every second.

I told myself I'd stop with that one touch, but as soon as I touched her, I knew I'd lied. Her creamy skin had been baby soft, the bones of her jaw so delicate they were almost fragile. My hand looked brown and rough against her pale perfection, my palm so big I could've crushed her face with one hard squeeze of my fingers.

She froze at my touch, and I could see the pulse beating at the side of her neck. When I'd patted her down earlier, she smelled expensive, like some fancy perfume, but that was no longer the case. Standing there in front of me, her cheeks colored pink, she smelled like peaches and innocence. Logically, I knew it had to be some soap from her bath, but my mouth still watered with the urge to lick her, to taste that clean, fruit-scented flesh.

To see what was hidden under her big, unsexy robe.

She said something about a drink, or maybe it was coffee, but I barely heard her words, all my attention on the strip of pale skin visible at the top of her robe. "No," I said on autopilot, "no coffee," and then I reached for the tie of her robe, my hands acting seemingly of their own accord.

The garment fell apart at a light tug, revealing a body straight out of my wet dreams. High, full breasts tipped by hard pink nipples, a waist small enough to span with my hands, gently curving hips, and long, long legs. And between those legs, not even a hint of hair, just the smooth, bare mound of her pussy.

My dick got so hard it hurt.

She pinkened even more, a flush appearing on her face and chest, and whatever self-control I still had evaporated. I touched her breast, flicked my thumb over her nipple, and watched her pupils expand, turning her blue eyes darker.

She was responding to me. Still scared, perhaps, but responding.

It wasn't much, but it was enough. I couldn't have walked away at that point if a bomb had gone off next to us.

"You're very direct, aren't you?" she whispered, staring up at me, and I told her I didn't have time for games. It was true—if only because the lust I felt was more intense, more violent than anything I'd known before. At that moment, I would've done anything to have her, crossed any line . . . committed any crime.

"And if I say no?" she asked, her voice shaking slightly, and it took everything I had to ask if she was, in fact, saying no. I managed to keep my tone calm, gently circling her nipple with my thumb as I slid my hand into her hair, but she didn't give me a straight answer. Instead, she asked me what I'd do in that case, whether I would leave.

"What do you think?" I asked, stalling as I tried to figure out the answer, but she didn't reply. She must've sensed the violent hunger brewing within me and decided to stop teasing me. I could see the acceptance in her eyes, feel the way she swayed toward me, as if granting me permission.

And so I touched her, felt the soft, warm heat between her legs.

Penetrated her tight pussy with my finger and felt the wetness there.

She did want me—unless that wetness wasn't for me.

Unless she was thinking of Esguerra at that moment.

The thought filled me with black rage. "Do you always get so wet for men you don't want?" I asked, unable to conceal my irrational jealousy, and she said she did want me. She'd wanted Esguerra before, and now she wanted me.

"Does that bother you?" she asked, and for the first time since my arrival at her apartment, she seemed like the experienced, confident woman from the restaurant instead of the scared girl who greeted me at the door.

The dichotomy both fascinated and aroused me, even as rage continued to burn in my veins. "No," I said, pushing another finger into her slick channel and finding her clit with my thumb. "Not at all."

Her eyes went soft, unfocused, and I could feel her pussy squeezing my fingers, getting even wetter at my touch. Her hands grabbed my arm as though she wanted to stop me, but her body welcomed my touch. I watched her carefully, observing every flicker of expression on her face, listening to every gasp and moan as I worked my fingers inside and around her pussy. She was responsive, so fucking responsive that it took me no time at all to learn what she liked, what made her cream around my fingers. I could feel her body beginning to tighten, see her breathing coming faster, and my cock got so hard it felt like it would burst.

"Yes, that's it." I pressed hard on her clit. "Come for me, beautiful, just like that."

And she did. Her gaze turned distant, unseeing, and her pussy rippled around my fingers. I held her until her contractions stopped, my hand still grasping her silky hair, and then I said with satisfaction, "There you go. That was nice, wasn't it?"

She didn't answer me at first, and for a moment, I wondered again if I'd misread her, if I was somehow forcing her into this. But then she reached out and boldly cupped my balls through my jeans. "It *was* nice," she whispered, looking up at me. "And now it's your turn."

It was all the invitation I needed. I felt like a beast unleashed, but somehow I managed to kiss her in a semi-civilized manner, tasting her lips instead of devouring them, as everything inside me clamored to do. Her mouth was delicious, like warm tea and honey, and for a minute, I was able to maintain some semblance of control, to pretend I wasn't a lust-filled savage.

Except I was—and when her robe fell off her shoulders, I snapped, pushing her against the wall. It was only by the habit of two decades that I remembered to put on a condom, and then I was lifting her and telling her to wrap her legs around me as I thrust into her, unable to wait even a second longer.

She was tight around me, so unbelievably tight and hot that I almost came right then and there, especially when her pussy clenched around me, her body tensing at my entry. Worried that I'd hurt her, I stopped for a moment, waiting until her legs came up to clasp my hips, and then I began fucking her in earnest, driven by a hunger more powerful than anything I'd experienced before. I wanted to be so deep inside I'd never come out, to take her so hard I'd leave my imprint on her flesh.

I watched her as I fucked her, and I knew the exact moment she reached her peak. Her eyes widened, as though in surprise, and then I felt her pussy undulating, spasming around my cock. The sensation was so intense I couldn't hold back my own orgasm. It washed over me uncontrollably, rocketing out from my balls, and I ground my pelvis into her, needing to be as deep as humanly possible, to meld with her in this explosive, mind-bending pleasure.

It was the best climax of my life. I felt high, consumed with her taste, her feel, and for a few moments, I thought it was the same for her—but then she pushed at me. "Please, let me down," she said, looking distressed, and it was like a bucket of ice water thrown over my head.

I gave her two orgasms, and she was looking at me like I raped her.

Like I fucking assaulted her in a back alley.

Something inside me twisted and hardened. Curving my lips in a sardonic smile, I said, "It's too late for regrets, beautiful." Lowering her to her feet, I forced my hands away from her firm, shapely ass. My cock slipped out of her as I stepped back, and the condom, filled with my seed, began to feel loose.

I pulled it off, dropping it on the floor. Her eyes followed the movement, and I saw a flush creep across her face again. She was embarrassed by what happened, I realized, and my anger intensified.

She invited me in, said she wanted me—*her body fucking told me she wanted me*—and now she was acting like it was all some big mistake.

Like she couldn't get away from me fast enough.

Well, fuck that, I decided, my blood boiling with a mixture of fury and renewed lust. If she thought I'd let her get away with that shit, she was very much mistaken.

And for the rest of the night, I dedicated myself to showing her just how mistaken she was. I licked her pussy and fucked her until she begged me to stop, until her voice was hoarse from screaming my name and my dick was raw from pounding into her tight flesh. I made her come half a dozen times before I allowed myself my second release, and then I had to restrain myself from taking her for the third time when she woke up to use the restroom.

I had to restrain myself because somehow, impossibly, I wanted more.

I still want more.

Son of a bitch. I told Yulia I might return one day, but if this insane hunger doesn't go away, I'll have to come back to Moscow sooner than planned—maybe as soon as we're done in Tajikistan.

Yes, that's it, I decide as I get up and start getting dressed.

I'll do my job, and then, if the Russian girl is still on my mind, I'll come back for her.

CHAPTER SIX

❖ YULIA ❖

I pretend to be asleep as Lucas gets dressed and quietly lets himself out of my apartment. When he closes the door behind him, I hear the automatic lock click into place. I'm grateful that he set it. In Moscow, it's not safe to leave the door open for even a few minutes. Criminals are bold, resourceful, and seemingly omnipresent.

I lie with my eyes closed for another minute to make sure Lucas is not coming back, and then I jump out of bed, ignoring the twinge of soreness between my legs. Automatically, my thoughts turn to the source of that soreness, and I'm once again cognizant of that strange pang of sadness.

Odds are, I'll never see Lucas Kent again.

Stop it, I scold myself. There's no reason to dwell on him. We had sex, nothing more. What I need to do now is find out if Obenko had a chance to strike at Esguerra while Kent was out of the way. If so, my gig here will finally be up. My cover is strong, but once the Russians realize there's been a leak, I'll fall under suspicion.

I call Obenko while I'm getting dressed. "Anything new?" I ask when he picks up.

"We have a plan," he says. "We were able to track down Esguerra's Boeing C-17—it's the only private plane of that size scheduled to take off in the next couple of hours. Our contact in Uzbekistan will take care of the rest."

I pause in the middle of zipping up my boots. "What do you mean?"

"The Uzbekistani military will fire a missile when they fly over their airspace," Obenko says. "Accidentally, of course. The Russians won't be pleased, but they won't go to war over one arms dealer. Our contact will get jail time and a demotion, but his family will be well compensated for his trouble."

"You're going to shoot down Esguerra's plane?" A cold knot forms in my throat. I don't care what happens to Esguerra, but the thought of Lucas dying in a tangle of crushed metal or being blown into bits . . .

"Yes. It would be too risky to attack him here. He has four dozen mercenaries with him. There's no way we can get to him otherwise."

"I see." I feel cold all over, as though someone walked over my grave. "So they'll all die."

"If everything goes according to plan, yes. We'll eliminate the threat in one shot and without any casualties on our end."

"Right." I try to inject a note of appropriate enthusiasm into my voice, but I don't know if I succeed. All I can think about is Lucas's big body burned and broken, his pale eyes staring unseeing at the sky. It shouldn't matter—he's nothing to me—but I can't get that gruesome image out of my mind.

"We need to exfiltrate you," Obenko says, bringing my attention back to him. "If the Russians begin really digging and our Uzbekistani contact decides to talk, it won't take them long to figure out how the information got to us. It's unfortunate, but we always knew this was a risk with this specific assignment."

"All right." I squeeze my eyes shut and rub the bridge of my nose. "Where do I meet the team?"

"Take the train to Kon'kovo. We'll have a car ready for you there." And the phone goes silent in my hand.

* * *

It takes me less than twenty minutes to pack. I've lived in Moscow for six years, but I've acquired few possessions I care about. Some makeup, a hairbrush, a change of underwear, my fake passport, my gun—that's all that goes into my large Gucci handbag. I also make sure that the clothes I'm wearing—designer jeans tucked into knee-high flat boots, a cashmere sweater, and a thick, well-fitting parka—are both warm and stylish. In case anyone sees me leaving the apartment, I'll look much as they'd expect: a young woman heading off to work, bundled up against the brutal cold.

After I'm done packing, I wipe down the entire apartment to erase my fingerprints and walk out, carefully locking the door behind me. I no longer care if thieves break in, but there's no need to make it easy for them.

Nobody seems to be watching the apartment as I exit onto the street, but I still keep a wary eye on my surroundings, making sure I'm not being followed.

As I approach the metro station, thoughts of Lucas intrude again, making me shiver despite my warm clothing. I should be happy—I've been looking forward to exfiltration for months—but I can't get my mind off Lucas's fate.

Will he die fast or slowly? Is it going to be the missile that kills him, or the crash itself? Will he stay conscious long enough to realize he's about to die?

Will he guess I had something to do with what happened?

The knot in my throat expands, making me feel like I'm choking. For one insane moment, I'm seized by an overwhelming urge to call him, to warn him not to get on that plane. I actually reach for the phone in my bag before I jerk my hand away, sticking it in my pocket instead.

Stupid, stupid, stupid, I chide myself as I walk down the stairs into the metro station. I don't even have Kent's number. And even if I did, warning him would mean betraying Obenko and my country.

Betraying Misha.

No, never. I take a steadying breath, ignoring the crush of Moscow commuters all around me. At this point, the operation is out of my hands. Even if I wanted to change something, I can't. Obenko and his team are in control now, and the best I can hope for is a speedy exit from Russia.

Besides, even if Lucas Kent wasn't affiliated with the arms dealer who just became Ukraine's enemy, there's no room in my life for romance of any kind. Whether Kent is dead or alive shouldn't matter—because either way, I won't see him again.

The approach of the train drags me out of my dark musings. The people around me press forward, pushing their way onto the crowded train, and I hurry to make sure I squeeze in before the doors close.

Thankfully, I make it. Grabbing onto a rail, I wedge myself into a space between two middle-aged women and do my best to ignore a leer from an old man sitting in front of me. Another couple of hours, and I won't need to put up with the Moscow metro system.

I'll be on my way to Kiev, where I belong.

I close my eyes and try to focus on that—on coming home.

On being near Misha, even if I can't meet with him in person.

My baby brother is fourteen now. I've seen his photos; he's a handsome teenage boy, his blue eyes bright and mischievous. In all the pictures, he's always laughing, hanging out with his friends and his girlfriends. He's social, Obenko tells me. Outgoing.

Happy with the life they've given him.

Each time I receive one of those pictures, I stare at it for hours, wondering if he remembers me. If he'd recognize me if I approached him on the street. It's unlikely—he was only three when he was adopted—but I still like to imagine that some part of him would know me.

That he'd recall the way I took care of him that one brutal year in the orphanage.

A crackling announcement interrupts my musings. Opening my eyes, I realize that the train is slowing down.

"We apologize for the delay," the conductor repeats loudly as the train comes to a complete halt. "The issue should get resolved shortly."

The passengers around me groan in unison. The middle-aged woman to my left begins swearing, while the one to my right mutters something about corrupt officials pocketing public funds instead of fixing things.

It's not the first delay this month; the extreme temperatures this winter have taken a toll on both roads and underground metro tracks, exacerbating the commuting nightmare that is Moscow at rush hour.

I suppress my own sigh of impatience and check my phone. As expected, I have zero bars. The thick walls of the tunnel block out all cell phone reception, so I can't notify my handlers of the delay.

Great. Just great.

I put the phone away, trying not to give in to my frustration. With any luck, this problem is something that requires a little welding, rather than something more serious. Last month, a burst pipe snarled traffic all over Moscow, causing metro delays of three hours or more. If it's something along those lines again, I might not get to my pickup location until late this afternoon.

Against my will, my thoughts turn to Lucas again. By late afternoon, his plane will likely be flying over the Uzbekistani airspace. He might even be dead by then. My stomach churns with acid as I picture his body torn into pieces, destroyed by the explosion and the crash.

Stop it, Yulia. The churning in my stomach intensifies, turning into an empty rumble, and I realize with relief that I forgot to eat breakfast this morning. I was in such a rush to pack and get going that I didn't have so much as a bite of an apple.

No wonder I'm feeling sick. It has nothing to do with Kent and everything to do with the fact that I'm hungry.

Yes, that's it, I tell myself. I'm just hungry. Once the train starts moving again and I get to my destination, I'll grab some food and everything will be fine.

I'll be safely in Kiev, and I won't think of Lucas Kent ever again.

CHAPTER SEVEN

❖ LUCAS ❖

By the time I get to the plane, the whole team, including Esguerra, is already on board and dressed in combat gear. The suits are bulletproof and flame-retardant—which makes them ridiculously expensive. I'm grateful Esguerra insists on them for every mission; they help minimize casualties among our men.

I'm the last one on board, and I'm piloting the plane, so as soon as I get suited up, we take off for Tajikistan, where the terrorist organization of Al-Quadar has its latest stronghold. Esguerra sniffed it out recently, and since the idiots fucked with him by kidnapping his wife a few months back, he's determined to wipe them off the map. The Russians granted us safe passage—that's what that meeting with Buschekov was about—so I'm not expecting any trouble. Still, I keep an eye on the radar as we get farther away from Moscow and closer to Central Asia.

In this part of the world, one can never be too careful.

Once we're at our cruising altitude, I put the plane on autopilot and check all of my weapons, taking each one apart to clean it before putting it back together. It's one of the first things I learned in the Navy: make sure your guns are good to go before every battle. Esguerra's equipment is top notch, and I've never had it malfunction on me, but there's always a first time.

Satisfied that everything is in good shape, I put the weapons away and glance at the radar again.

Nothing out of the ordinary.

Leaning back in my seat, I stretch out my legs. I can already feel it—the beginnings of the adrenaline burn, the buzz of excitement deep in my veins.

The anticipation that grips me before every fight.

My mind and body are already preparing for it, even though we still have a few hours before we get to our destination.

This is what I was made for, what I love to do. Fighting is in my blood. That's why I enlisted in the Navy right out of high school, why I couldn't stand the thought of following the path my parents laid out for me. College, law school, joining my grandfather's prestigious law firm—I couldn't imagine myself doing any of those things. I would've suffocated in that kind of life, choked to death in the stuffy, elite boardrooms of Manhattan.

My family didn't understand, of course. For them, corporate law—and the money and prestige that comes with it—is the pinnacle of success. They couldn't comprehend why I'd want to do anything else, why I'd want to be anything other than their golden child.

"If you don't want to go into law, you could try for medical school," my father said when I expressed my concerns to him in eleventh grade. "Or if you don't want to be in school for so long, you could go into investment banking. I can get you an internship at Goldman Sachs this summer—it would look great on your Princeton application."

I didn't take him up on his offer. I didn't know at that point where I belonged, but I knew it wasn't at Goldman Sachs, and it wasn't at Princeton or the prep school my parents paid through the nose to have me attend. I was different from my classmates. Too restless, too full of pent-up energy. I played every sport there was, took every martial art class I could find, but it wasn't enough.

Something was still missing.

I discovered what that something was late one night during my senior year, when I was stumbling home drunk from a party in Brooklyn. In an empty subway station, I was attacked by a group of thugs hoping to score some easy cash off a kid from the Upper East Side. They were armed with knives, and I had nothing, but I was too drunk to care. Whatever training I received in those martial art classes kicked in, and I found myself in the first real fight of my life.

A fight where I ended up knifing a man and seeing his blood spill over my hands.

A fight where I learned the extent of the violence living within me.

* * *

We're flying over Uzbekistan, just a few hundred miles from our destination, when Esguerra comes into the pilot's cabin.

Hearing the door open, I turn to face him. "We're on track to get there in about an hour and a half," I say, preempting his question. "There is some ice on the landing strip, so they're de-icing it for us right now. The helicopters are already fueled up and ready to go."

We need those helicopters to get to the Pamir Mountains, where we suspect the terrorist hideout to be.

"Excellent," Esguerra says, his blue eyes gleaming. "Any unusual activities in that area?"

I shake my head. "No, everything is quiet."

"Good." He enters the cabin and sits down in the copilot's seat. "How was the Russian girl last night?" he asks, buckling his seatbelt.

I feel a momentary stab of jealousy, but then I remember how Yulia responded to me all night long. "Quite satisfying," I say, smiling at the images filling my mind. "You missed out."

"Yes, I'm sure," he says, but I can see that he's not the least bit sorry. The man is obsessed with his young wife. I have a feeling the most beautiful woman in the world could parade naked in front of him, and he wouldn't so much as blink. Esguerra's been well and truly caught—and by a girl he's been keeping captive, no less.

The thought makes me grin. "I have to say, I never expected to see you as a happily married man," I tell him, amused by the idea.

Esguerra lifts his eyebrows. "Is that right?"

I shrug, my grin fading. I'm not exactly friends with my boss—I've never known Esguerra to be particularly friendly with anyone—but for some reason, he seems more approachable today.

Or maybe I'm just in a good mood, thanks to one gorgeous interpreter.

"Sure," I say to Esguerra. "People like us aren't generally considered good husband material."

In fact, I can't think of two individuals less suited to domestic life.

Esguerra chuckles. "Well, I don't know if, strictly speaking, Nora considers me 'good husband material.'"

"Well, if she doesn't, then she should." I turn back to the controls. "You don't cheat, you take good care of her, and you've risked your life to save her before. If that's not being a good husband, then I don't know what is." As I speak, I notice a flicker of movement on the radar screen.

Frowning, I peer at it closer.

"What is it?" Esguerra's tone sharpens.

"I'm not sure," I begin saying, and at that moment, a violent jolt rocks the plane, nearly throwing me out of my seat. The plane tilts, angling down sharply, and adrenaline explodes in my veins as I hear the frantic beeping of controls gone haywire.

We've been hit.

The thought is crystal clear in my mind.

Grabbing the controls, I try to right the plane as we plunge through a thick layer of clouds. My heartbeat is rocket fast, its pounding audible in my ears. "Shit, fuck, shit, shit, motherfucking shit—"

"What hit us?" Esguerra sounds calm, almost disinterested. I can hear the engines grinding and sputtering, and then the smell of smoke reaches me, along with the sound of screams.

We're on fire.

Fucking fuck.

"I'm not sure," I manage to say. The plane is nosediving, and I can't get it to straighten out for longer than a second. "Does it fucking matter?"

The plane shakes, the engines emitting a terrifying sputtering noise as we head straight for the ground below. The peaks of Pamir Mountains are already visible in the distance, but we're too far to make it there.

We're going to crash before we reach our goal.

Fuck, no. I'm not ready to die.

Cursing, I resume wrestling with the controls, ignoring the readouts that inform me of the futility of my efforts. The plane evens out under my guidance, the engines kicking in for a brief moment, but then we nosedive again. I repeat the maneuver, calling on all my years of piloting experience, but it's futile.

All I manage to do is slow our descent by a few seconds.

They say your life flashes in front of your eyes before your death. They say you think of all the things you could've done differently, all the things you haven't had a chance to do.

I don't think about any of that.

I'm too consumed with surviving for as long as I can.

Beside me Esguerra is silent, his hands gripping the edge of his seat as the ground rushes toward us, the small objects below looming ever larger. I can make out the trees—we're over a forest now—and then I see individual branches, stripped of leaves and covered with snow.

We're close now, so close, and I make one last attempt to guide the plane, directing it to a cluster of smaller trees and bushes a hundred yards away.

And then we're there, crashing through the trees with bone-shattering force.

Strangely, my last thought is of her.

The Russian girl I'll never see again.

PART II: THE DETAINMENT

CHAPTER EIGHT

❖ YULIA ❖

Seven and a half hours.

The train was stuck in that tunnel for seven and a half hours. The relief I feel as the doors finally open at the next station is so strong, I actually shake with it.

Or maybe I shake from hunger and thirst. It's impossible to tell.

Stepping out of the cursed train, I push through the herd of exhausted, stressed-out commuters and take the escalator upstairs. I need to call Obenko immediately; my handlers must be going mad with worry.

"Yulia? What the fuck?" As expected, Obenko's furious. "Where are you?"

"At Rizhskaya." I name the train station some twenty stops away from my destination. "I was on the Kaluzhsko-Rizhskaya line."

"Ah, fuck. You got stuck because of that idiot."

"Yeah." I lean against an icy wall at the top of the stairs as people hurry past me. According to the last update from the train conductor, the reason for the delay was a hostage situation two trains ahead of us. A Chechen national got the bright idea to strap on a homemade bomb and threaten to blow himself up if his demands weren't met. The police managed to subdue him, but it took them hours to do it safely. Considering the seriousness of the situation, it's a miracle we were able to get off the train before nightfall.

"All right." Obenko sounds a bit calmer. "I'll get the team to return to the pickup location. Are the trains running again?"

"Not the Kaluzhsko-Rizhskaya line. They said it'll resume running later tonight. I'm going to have to take a taxi." I shift from foot to foot, my bladder reminding me that it's been hours since I've had access to a bathroom. I need that, and food, with extreme urgency, but first, there's something I must know. "Vasiliy Ivanovich," I say hesitantly, addressing my boss by his full name and patronymic, "did the operation . . . succeed?"

"The plane was shot down an hour ago."

My knees buckle, and for a dizzying moment, the station blurs out of focus. If it hadn't been for the wall at my back, I would've fallen over. "Were there any survivors?" My voice sounds choked, and I have to clear my throat before continuing. "That is . . . are you sure the target's been eliminated?"

"We haven't received the casualty report yet, but I don't see how Esguerra could've survived."

"Oh. Good." Bile rises in my throat, and I feel like I'm going to throw up. Swallowing thickly, I manage to say, "I have to go now, find that taxi."

"All right. Keep us posted if there are any issues."

"Will do." I press the button to hang up and lean my head back against the wall, taking in gulps of cold air. I feel sick, my stomach roiling with acid and emptiness. I have a fast metabolism, and I've never handled hunger well, but I don't recall ever feeling this bad from lack of food.

Pale blue eyes blank and unseeing. Blood running down a hard, square jaw . . .

No, stop. I force myself to straighten away from the wall. I won't allow myself to go there. I'm just hungry, thirsty, and exhausted. Once I address these problems, everything will be fine.

It has to be.

* * *

Before trying to catch a taxi, I head to a small coffee shop next to the station and use their restroom. I also get a cup of hot tea and scarf down three meat-filled pirozhki—small savory pies. Then, feeling much more human, I go outside to see if I can find a taxi.

The streets around the station are a nightmare. The traffic appears to be at a complete standstill, and all the taxis look occupied. It's not unexpected, given what happened with the trains, but still extremely annoying.

I begin walking briskly in the hopes that I can get to a less trafficky location on foot. There's no point in getting into a car, only to crawl two blocks in two hours. Now that the plane has gone down, I need to get to my handlers as quickly as possible.

The plane. I suck in my breath as the sickening images invade my mind again. I don't know why I can't stop thinking about this. I'd known Lucas for less than twenty-four hours, and I'd spent most of that time being afraid of him.

And the rest of that time screaming in pleasure in his arms, a small voice reminds me.

No, stop.

I pick up my pace, zigzagging around slower-moving pedestrians. *Don't think about him, don't think about him . . .* I let the words echo in my mind in tempo with my steps. *You're going home to Misha . . .* I pick up my pace some more, almost running now. Moving this fast not only gets me to my destination quicker, but it also keeps me warm. *Don't think about him, you're going home . . .*

I don't know how long I walk like this, but as the streetlights turn on, I realize it's already getting dark. Checking my phone, I see that it's nearly six p.m.

I've been at it for two and a half hours, and the traffic around me is as bad as ever.

Stopping, I look around in frustration. I've been walking along major avenues to maximize my chances of catching a cab, but that appears to have been a faulty strategy. Perhaps what I should do is get away from the main zones of traffic and try my luck on smaller streets. If I find a car there, the driver may be able to take me out of the city via some more obscure routes. I'll pay him whatever extra money he demands.

Turning onto one of the cross streets, I see a park a block away. I decide to cut diagonally across it, and then go up one of the smaller avenues on the other side of it. I'll still be heading in the right direction, but I'll be away from the busiest area. Maybe I'll find a bus there, if not a cab.

There's got to be some way I can get to my destination in the next few hours.

My phone vibrates in my bag, and I fish it out. "Yes?"

"Where are you?" Obenko sounds as frustrated as I feel. "The team leader is getting nervous. He wants to be across the border by the time the Kremlin learns what happened."

"I'm still in the city, walking for now. The traffic is impossible." The snow crunches under my feet as I enter the park. They didn't bother to clear it here, so all the walking paths are covered with a thick icy layer.

"Fuck."

"Yeah." I try not to slip on the ice as I step over a pile of dog shit. "I'm doing my best to get there tonight, I promise."

"All right. Yulia . . ." Obenko pauses for a second. "You know we're going to have to pull the team if you don't get there by morning, right?" His voice is quiet, almost apologetic.

"I know." I keep my tone level. "I'll be there."

"Good. Make sure you do that."

He hangs up, and I walk faster, driven by increasing anxiety. If the team leaves without me and I get caught, I'm as good as dead. The Kremlin isn't known to be kind to spies, and the fact that our agency is completely off the books makes the matters ten times worse. The Ukrainian government won't negotiate to get me back, because they have no idea that I exist.

I'm almost out of the park when I hear drunk male laughter and the sound of shoes crunching on snow.

Glancing behind me, I see a small group of men some hundred meters back, with bottles clutched in their gloved hands. They're weaving all over the walking path, but their attention is unmistakably focused on me.

"Hey, young lady," one of them yells out, slurring his words. "Wanna come party with us?"

I look away and start walking even faster. They're just drunks, but even drunks can be dangerous when it's six against one. I'm not afraid of them—I have my gun and my training—but I don't need trouble this evening.

"Young lady," the drunk yells, louder this time. "You're being rude, you know that?"

His friends laugh like a pack of hyenas, and the drunk yells again, "Fuck you, bitch! If you don't want to party, just motherfucking say so!"

I ignore them and continue on my way, snaking my left hand into my handbag to feel for my gun, just in case. As I exit the park and step onto the street, the sound of their voices fades, and I realize they're no longer following me.

Relieved, I take my hand out of my bag and continue up the street at a slightly slower pace. My legs are aching, and I feel like a blister is forming on the side of my heel. My flat boots are way more comfortable than heels, but they're not made for three hours of speed-walking.

I'm in a more residential area now, which is both good and bad. The traffic here is better—only a few cars pass me on the street—but the streetlights are sparse, and the area is all but deserted. Distant male laughter reaches my ears again, and I force myself to go faster, ignoring the discomfort of tired muscles.

I walk about five blocks before I see it: a cab stopping next to a curb across the street some fifty meters ahead. A short, thin man is getting out. Relieved, I yell, "Wait!" and sprint toward the car just as he begins closing the door.

I'm almost next to the cab when I see lights out of the corner of my eye and hear the roar of an engine.

Reacting in a split second, I throw myself to the side, hitting the ground as a car barrels past me. As I roll on the icy asphalt, I hear the driver hooting drunkenly, and then something hard slams into the side of my head.

My last thought as my world goes black is that I should've shot those drunks after all.

CHAPTER NINE

❖ LUCAS ❖

Voices. Distant beeping. More voices.

The sounds fade in and out, as does the buzzing in my ears. My head feels thick and heavy, the pain enveloping me like a blanket of thorns.

Alive. I'm alive.

The realization seeps into me slowly, in stages. Along with it comes a sharp throbbing in my skull and a surge of nausea.

Where am I? What happened?

I strain to make out the voices.

It's two women and a man, judging by the differences in pitch. They're speaking in a foreign language, something I don't recognize.

My nausea intensifies, as does the throbbing in my head. It takes all my strength to pry open my eyelids.

Above me, a fluorescent light flickers, its brightness agonizing. Unable to bear it, I close my eyes.

A female voice exclaims something, and I hear rapid footsteps.

A hand touches my face, a stranger's fingers reaching for my eyelids. Bright light shines into my eyes again, and I tense, my hands bunching into fists as agony spears through me again. My instinct is to fight, to lash out at whoever this is, but something is preventing me from moving my arms.

"Careful now." The male voice speaks English, albeit with a thick foreign accent. "The nurse is just checking on you."

The hand leaves my face, and I force my eyes to remain open despite the pain in my skull. Everything looks blurry, but after I blink a few times, I'm able to focus on the man standing next to the bed.

Dressed in a military officer's uniform, he looks to be in his early fifties, with a lean, sharp-featured face. Seeing me looking at him, he says, "I'm Colonel Sharipov. Can you please tell me your name?"

"Where am I? What happened?" I ask hoarsely, trying to move my arms once more. I can't—and I realize it's because I'm restrained, handcuffed to the bed. When I try to move my legs, I can move my right, but not my left. There's something bulky and heavy keeping it still, and tugging on it makes me hiss in pain.

"You're in a hospital in Tashkent," Sharipov says, answering my first question. "You have a broken leg and a severe concussion. I would advise you not to move."

Tashkent. That means I'm in Uzbekistan, the country bordering our destination of Tajikistan. As I process that, some of the fogginess in my mind dissipates, and I remember what happened.

The screams. The smell of smoke.

The crash.

Fuck.

"Where are the others?" Abruptly enraged, I tug at my wrist restraints. "Esguerra and all the rest?"

"I will tell you in a moment," Sharipov says. "First, I must know your name."

The pounding agony in my skull isn't letting me think. "Lucas Kent," I grit out. There's no point in lying. He didn't seem surprised when I mentioned Esguerra—which means he already has some idea of who we are. "I'm Esguerra's second-in-command."

Sharipov studies me. "I see. In that case, Mr. Kent, you'll be pleased to know that Julian Esguerra is alive and here in the hospital as well. He has a broken arm, cracked ribs, and a head wound, which doesn't appear to be too serious. We're waiting for him to regain consciousness."

My head feels like it's about to explode, yet I'm aware of a flicker of relief. The guy is an amoral killer—some might say a psychopath—but I've gotten to know him over the years and I respect him. It would be a shame if he were killed by some stray missile. Which reminds me—

"What the fuck happened? Why am I restrained?"

The colonel looks at me steadily. "You're restrained for your own safety and that of the nurses, Mr. Kent. Your occupation is such that we didn't feel comfortable putting the staff here at risk. It's a civilian hospital and—"

"Oh, for fuck's sake." I clench my teeth. "I promise not to harm the nurses, okay? Remove these fucking cuffs. Now."

We have a stare-off contest for a few seconds. Then Sharipov makes a short, jerky motion with his head and says something to one of the nurses in a foreign language. The dark-haired woman comes over and unlocks the cuffs, giving me wary looks the whole time. I ignore her, keeping my focus on Sharipov.

"What happened?" I repeat in a somewhat calmer tone, bringing my hands together to rub at my wrists as the nurse skitters away to the other side of the room. The pounding in my head worsens from the movement, but I persist in my questioning. "Who shot down the plane, and what happened to the other men?"

"I'm afraid that the exact cause of the crash is being investigated at the moment," Sharipov says. He looks vaguely uncomfortable. "It's possible there was a . . . miscommunication."

"A miscommunication?" I give him an incredulous glare. "Did you shoot at us? You know we were to be granted safe passage through the region, right?"

"Of course." He looks even more uncomfortable now. "Which is why we're currently conducting an investigation. It's possible that an error was made—"

"An error?" *The screams, the smoke . . .* "A fucking error?" My brain feels like a drummer took up residence in my skull. "Where *the fuck* are the others?"

Sharipov flinches, almost imperceptibly. "I'm afraid there were only three survivors besides Esguerra and yourself. They're still unconscious. I'm hoping you can help us identify them." Reaching into his breast pocket, he pulls out his phone and shows me the screen. "This is the first one."

My guts twist. I know the man in that photo.

John "The Sandman" Sanders, a British ex-con. Handy with knives and grenades. I've trained with him, played pool with him. He was fun, even when he was piss-drunk.

He might not be as fun anymore. Not with half of his face cooked extra crispy.

"The plane exploded," Sharipov says, likely in response to my expression. "He has third-degree burns over most of his body. He'll need extensive skin grafts—if he survives at all. Do you know his name?"

"John Sanders," I say hoarsely, reaching up to take the phone. My body protests the movement, my temples throbbing with nauseating pain again, but I need to see the others. Bringing the phone closer, I click to the next photo.

This face is nearly unrecognizable—except for the scar at the corner of his left eye. He's a recent recruit, someone I debated bringing on this mission.

"Jorge Suarez," I say evenly before moving on to the next picture.

This time I can't even venture a guess. All I see is burned flesh. "He's still alive?" I glance up at Sharipov. I can feel the churning in my guts worsening, and I know it's only partially because of my concussion.

The colonel nods. "He's in a critical condition, but he might pull through. If you look at the next picture, it shows his lower body. It's not as burned."

Fighting my nausea, I do as he says and study the hairy legs covered by strips of torn protective suit. The explosion must've blasted through the protective gear; the material is meant to withstand a brief exposure to fire, not a plane blowing up. It's hard to say who the man is from just his legs. Unless . . . I narrow my eyes, peering closer at the picture, and then I see it.

A tattoo of a bird behind one of the ragged pieces of the combat suit.

"Gerard Montreau," I say with certainty. The young Frenchman is the only one with that tattoo on the team.

Lowering the phone to my chest, I look up at Sharipov. "Why am I not burned? How did I escape the explosion? And what about Esguerra? Is he——"

"No, he's fine," Sharipov reassures me. "Or at least, not burned. The two of you were in the pilot's cabin, which got separated from the main body of the plane during the crash. The back of the plane exploded, but the fire didn't reach you."

The throbbing in my head becomes unbearable, and I close my eyes, trying to process everything.

Five men out of fifty. That's all that remains of our group. The rest are dead. Burned or blown to bits. I can imagine their terror as the fire engulfed the back of the plane. The fact that there are any survivors is nothing short of a miracle—not that the three men in the pictures will see it that way.

An error. What fucking bullshit.

I'm going to get to the bottom of this, but first, I need to do my job.

Forcing my eyelids apart again, I squint at Sharipov, who's cautiously reaching for the phone I'm still holding. What the fuck does the man think I'll do? Strangle him while lying incapacitated in their hospital?

I won't—unless I learn he's responsible for this "error."

"You need to get some bodyguards for Esguerra," I say, gripping the phone tighter. "He's not safe here."

The colonel frowns at me. "What do you mean? The hospital is perfectly safe——"

"He has many enemies, including Al-Quadar, the terrorist group whose stronghold is right across your border. You need to arrange for protection, and you need to do it right now."

Sharipov still looks doubtful, so I add, "Your Kremlin allies will not be pleased if he's killed or taken while in your custody. Especially after this unfortunate 'error.'"

Sharipov's mouth tightens, but after a moment, he says, "All right. I'll have a few soldiers brought in. They'll make sure no one unauthorized comes near your boss."

"Good. Use more than a few. Forty or fifty would be good. Those terrorists have a real hard-on for him." My head is in absolute agony, and the leg that's in the cast is beginning to ache like only a broken bone can. "Also, you need to put me in touch with Peter Sokolov—"

"We've already talked to him. He knows where you are, and he's sending a plane to retrieve you and the others. Now, please." Sharipov extends his hand palm-up. "Give me back my phone, Mr. Kent."

I open my mouth to insist on speaking to Peter myself, but before I can say anything, I feel something sharp prick my arm. Immediately, a heavy lassitude spreads through me, dulling the pain. Out of the corner of my eye, I see a nurse step back, holding a syringe. "What the—" I begin, but it's too late.

The darkness descends, and I'm not aware of anything else.

CHAPTER TEN

❖ YULIA ❖

"I told you, I'm fine."

Ignoring the nurse's squawking protests, I remove the IV needle from my wrist and stand up. I'm dizzy and my head is aching, but I need to get moving. Judging by the sunlight streaming in through the hospital window, it's already morning or later. The exfiltration team likely left already, but on the off chance they didn't, I need to get in touch with Obenko right away.

"Where's my bag?" I ask the nurse, frantically scanning the room. "I need my bag."

"What you need is to lie down." The red-headed nurse steps in front of me, folding her arms in front of her massive chest. "You have an egg-sized lump on your head from bumping into that pole, and you've been out cold since you were brought in last night. The doctor said we're to monitor you for the next twenty-four hours."

I glare at her. My head feels like it's splitting at the seams, but staying here means signing my death warrant. "Where is my bag?" I repeat. I'm uncomfortably aware that I'm wearing only a hospital gown, but I'll worry about clothes—and the headache from hell—later.

The woman rolls her eyes. "Oh, for heaven's sake. If I get you your bag, will you lie down and behave?"

"Yes," I lie, and watch as she walks to a cabinet on the other side of the room. Opening the cabinet door, she takes out my Gucci handbag and comes back.

"Here you go." She thrusts the bag into my hands. "Now lie down before you fall down."

I do as she says, but only because I need to conserve my strength for the journey ahead. It's been less than ten minutes since I woke up here, and I'm shaking from the strain of standing. I probably do need to be under medical observation, but there's no time for that.

I have to get out of Moscow before it's too late.

The nurse begins to change the sheets on an empty bed next to mine, and I take out my phone to call Obenko.

It rings and rings and rings . . .

Shit. He's not picking up.

I try again. *Come on, come on, pick up.*

Nothing. No answer.

Growing desperate, I try his number for the third time.

"Yulia?"

Thank God. "Yes, it's me. I'm in a hospital in Moscow. I almost got hit by a car—long story. But I'm leaving now and—"

"It's too late, Yulia." Obenko's voice is quiet. "The Kremlin knows what happened, and Buschekov's people are looking for you."

An icy chill spreads through me. "So quickly?"

"One of Esguerra's people is well connected in Moscow. He mobilized them as soon as he learned about the missile."

"Shit."

The nurse gives me a dirty look as she gathers the sheets into a big pile on the empty bed.

"I'm sorry," Obenko says, and I know he means it. "The team leader had to pull his people out. It's not safe for any of us in Russia right now."

"Of course," I say on autopilot. "He did the right thing."

"Good luck, Yulia," Obenko says, and I hear the click as he disconnects.

I'm on my own.

* * *

I wait until the nurse leaves with the pile of sheets, and then I get up again, without any interference this time.

The panic circling through me is stronger than any painkiller. I'm barely cognizant of my headache as I walk over to the cabinet that held my bag and look inside.

As I'd hoped, my clothes are there too, folded neatly. I cast a quick look at the room entrance to verify that the door is closed, then strip off my hospital gown and put on the clothes I was wearing earlier. As I do so, I realize the lump on my head is not my only injury. The entire right side of my body is bruised, and I have scrapes all over.

That stupid drunk. I so should've shot him and his hyena friends when I had the chance.

No. I draw in a calming breath. Anger is pointless now. It's a distraction I can't afford. There's still a small chance I may be able to get out of Russia. I can't give up hope.

Not yet, at least.

I pull my hair up into a bun to make the long blond locks less noticeable, and then I do a swift check of the contents of my bag. Everything is there, except cash in the wallet and my gun. But that's to be expected. I'm lucky the bag itself wasn't stolen while I was unconscious. The lining at the bottom of the bag has some emergency cash sewn into it, and the thieves didn't find it, as confirmed by the lack of rips inside.

Gripping the bag tightly, I walk to the door and step out into the hallway. The nurse is nowhere in sight, and nobody pays me any attention as I approach the elevator. Well, one elderly man in a wheelchair gives me an appreciative once-over, but there's no suspicion in his gaze. He's just looking, likely reliving his youth.

The elevator doors open with a soft ding, and I step inside, my heart beating much too fast. Despite the ease of my getaway thus far, my skin is crawling, all my instincts warning me of danger.

My room is on the seventh floor of the building, and the ride down is torturously slow. The elevator stops on each floor, with patients and nurses coming in and out. I could've taken the stairs, but that might've drawn unnecessary attention to me. Nobody uses those stairwells unless they have to.

Finally, the elevator doors open on the first floor. I step out, surrounded by several other people—and at that moment I see them.

Three policemen entering the elevator on the opposite side of the hallway.

Shit. I duck my head and hunch my shoulders, trying to make myself look shorter. *Don't stare at them. Don't stare at them.* I keep my gaze on the floor and stay close to a tall, heavyset man who lumbered out of the elevator ahead of me. He walks slowly and so do I, doing my best to look like I'm with him.

They would be looking for a woman on her own, not a couple.

Thankfully, my unwitting companion heads for the exit, and there are enough people around us that he doesn't pay me much attention. His massive bulk provides some cover, and I use it as much as I can, maintaining my stooped posture.

Walk faster. Come on, walk faster, I silently beg the man. Every muscle in my body is tense with the urge to run, but that would destroy any chance I have of leaving this hospital undetected. At the same time, I know I need to be out of here within minutes. As soon as those policemen realize I'm not on the seventh floor, they'll put the entire hospital on alert.

Finally, the man and I are by the exit, and I see a cab pull up next to the curb.

Yes! I'm due for a little luck.

Leaving the man behind without a second glance, I hurry to the cab and get in just as the woman inside climbs out. "The Lubyanka station, please," I tell the driver as the door is closing. I say it in case the woman is paying attention. That way, if she's questioned later, she'll tell them my supposed destination and, hopefully, muddy the trail a bit.

The driver nods and pulls away from the curb. As soon as we're on the street, I say, "Oh, actually, I forgot. I'm supposed to pick up something at the Azimut Moscow Olympic Hotel. Can you please drop me off there instead?"

He shrugs. "Sure, no problem. You pay, I take you wherever you want."

"Thank you." I lean back against the seat. I'm too anxious to relax fully, but the worst of the tension drains out of me. I'm safe for the moment. I bought myself some time. There's a car rental near that hotel. Once I get there, I'll find myself a disguise and get a car. They'll be watching airports, trains, and public transportation, but there's a small chance I can make it to the Ukrainian border via some less popular roads.

The drive seems to take forever. The traffic is bad, but not nearly as horrible as yesterday. Still, with the driver braking and accelerating every couple of minutes—and the numbing effect of adrenaline wearing off—my headache comes back in full force, as does the pain from all the bruises and scrapes. On top of everything, I become aware of a gnawing emptiness in my stomach and a cottony dryness in my mouth.

Of course. I haven't had anything to eat or drink since yesterday afternoon.

To distract myself from my misery, I think of Misha as he was in the last picture Obenko sent me. My baby brother had his arm around a pretty brunette girl—his current girlfriend, according to Obenko. The girl was smiling up at Misha with adoration that bordered on worship, and he looked as proud as only a teenage boy can.

For you, Misha. I close my eyes to hold on to the picture in my mind. *You're worth it.*

"Well, that's not good," the driver mutters, and I open my eyes to see the cars coming to a complete stop ahead of us. "Wonder if there was an accident or something." He rolls down the window and sticks his head out, peering into the distance.

"Is it an accident?" I ask, resigned. It's like the fates are conspiring to keep me in Moscow. It's not enough that Russia has winters brutal enough to decimate its enemies' armies; now it has spy-detaining traffic, too.

"No," the driver says, pulling his head back inside the car. "Doesn't look like it. I mean, there are a bunch of police cars and all, but I don't see any ambulances. Could be a blockade, or they caught someone—"

I'm out of the car before he finishes speaking.

"Hey!" he yells, but I'm already running, weaving my way through the stopped cars. Whatever discomfort I was feeling earlier is gone, chased away by a sharp surge of fear.

A police blockade. Somehow they triangulated my location—or maybe they just blocked all the major roads in the hopes of catching me. Either way, I'm screwed, unless I can get out of this city.

My heart pounds in a heavy staccato rhythm as I sprint for the street, heading toward a narrow alley I spotted earlier. They'll have trouble following me there in a car, and if I'm lucky, I may be able to evade them long enough to find another cab.

Anything to buy myself more time.

Behind me, I hear shouts and the sound of running footsteps. "Stop!" a male voice yells. "Stop now! You're under arrest!"

I ignore the order, picking up my pace instead. The cold air hurts my lungs as I push my leg muscles to their limits. The alley looms ahead of me, narrow and dark, and I force myself to keep running at the same speed, to keep going without so much as a glance back.

"Stop, or I will shoot!" The voice sounds more distant, giving me a grain of hope. Maybe I'll be able to outrun him. I've always been fast, my long legs giving me an advantage over shorter people.

A shot rings out, the bullet whizzing past me and plowing into the building ahead.

Shit. He *is* shooting. I don't know why that surprises me. The Moscow police aren't exactly known for caring about the citizens they're supposed to be protecting. They're tools of their corrupt government, nothing more. It shouldn't shock me that they'd risk the welfare of innocent citizens to catch me.

Another shot, and the snow explodes off the ground a few feet ahead of me. I hear terrified screams and see people diving for cover on the sidewalk.

Ignoring the commotion, I sprint into the alley. Straight ahead are two large dumpsters, and behind them, a metal fire ladder going up the side of the building.

A third shot, and the bullet ricochets off the dumpster, narrowly missing me. The cop, or whoever's chasing me, has good aim.

I'm almost at the ladder, and I jump up as high as I can, managing to catch the bottom rung of the ladder with my hands. Then, using the momentum of my jump, I swing my legs up and catch the metal bar with my feet. Hooking my knees over the metal bar, I use all my strength to pull myself up high enough to grab the next rung of the ladder with my left hand. It works, and I pull myself up into a sitting position before starting to climb.

Another shot, and the wall in front of me explodes, shards of brick flying everywhere.

Shit, shit, shit. I scramble up the ladder as fast as I can without slipping on the icy metal bars. There are shouts and curses below me, and then I feel the ladder shaking as another person jumps on it.

I guess they decided to try capturing me alive.

I don't look down as I continue my perilous climb. I've never liked heights, so I pretend it's a training exercise and a thickly padded mat is waiting for me below. Even if I fall, I'll be okay. It's a complete lie, of course, but it serves to keep me going despite my heart trying to leap out of my throat.

Before I know it, I'm at the roof, and I jump off the ladder onto the flat surface. The building I'm on is shaped like a square with a hole for a large yard in the middle—a typical Soviet-era structure that occupies an entire block. I pause just long enough to spot another ladder on the other side of the square, and then I start running again, heading toward that ladder.

"Stop!" someone yells again, and I realize with a jolt of fear that they're already up here, right on my heels. Unable to resist, I cast a frantic glance behind me and see two men running after me. They're wearing police uniforms, and one of them is holding a gun. They're both big men, seemingly fast and strong. I won't be able to outrun them for long.

Changing my strategy, I put on a burst of speed and use the two-second lead I gain to zip behind a concrete smoke stack. Leaning against it, I gasp for air, desperately trying not to make any noise as I catch my breath.

Three seconds later, I hear the men's footsteps.

Time to go on the offensive.

As the first cop barrels past me, I stick my foot out. He trips, falling with a loud curse, and I hear the gun sliding across the icy roof.

The shooter's down and disarmed.

Before his partner has a chance to react, I jump out in front of him, my right hand balled into a fist. He automatically ducks to the left as I swing it at him, and I use the momentum of his movement to punch upward with my left hand.

My left fist slams into his chin, and he stumbles back, grunting. Without pausing, I dive for the gun, and see the other policeman doing the same.

We collide, rolling, and for a second, my fingers brush against the weapon.

Yes! I grab it, and as the cop attempts to pin me down, I pull the trigger.

He screams, clutching his shoulder, and I push him off me, the adrenaline giving me almost superhuman strength. I'm already up on my knees when the second cop throws himself at me, his hand brutally squeezing my wrist.

"Drop the weapon, bitch," he hisses, and at that moment, I hear more footsteps.

"You got her, Sergey?" one man yells, and I see five more cops show up, their weapons drawn.

There's no point in fighting anymore, so I let my grip on the gun slacken. It falls to the roof with a dull thud as Sergey spins me around and handcuffs my wrists behind my back.

I'm caught.

Now I can give up hope.

CHAPTER ELEVEN

❖ LUCAS ❖

"They did what?"

My voice is a low hiss as I sit up, ignoring the nurse's hands fluttering around me in an attempt to get me to lie still. The rage blasting through me chases away all remnants of wooziness from the drug she gave me earlier. I have no idea how long I was out, but it was clearly too fucking long.

"The terrorists attacked the hospital a few hours ago," Sharipov repeats, his face tense and tired. "It seems we underestimated their capabilities—and their desire to get at your boss. As we didn't find his body among the dead, we can only assume that they took him."

"They took Esguerra?" It takes everything I have not to leap out of bed and strangle the colonel with my bare hands—which are still unrestrained, I note with some corner of my brain. "You fucking let them take him? I told you to put security around him—"

"We did. We had several of our best soldiers standing guard—"

"Several? It should've been several dozen, you fucking idiots!"

The nurse flinches at my roar and jumps well out of my reach. Smart woman. At this moment, I'd gladly strangle her too.

Sharipov's jaw tightens. "As I said, we underestimated this particular terrorist organization. We won't make this mistake again. It was a bloodbath. They wounded dozens of patients and hospital staff on the way out and killed all the soldiers assigned to guard duty."

"Fuck." I punch the mattress so hard, the pillow bounces. "Were you at least able to follow them?" Majid wouldn't be stupid enough to take Esguerra to the Al-Quadar compound in the Pamir Mountains; he must know by now that we've sniffed out its location.

Sharipov prudently steps back. "No. The police were notified right away, and we sent for more soldiers, but the terrorists got away before we could get to the hospital."

"Son of a bitch." If it weren't for the cast immobilizing my leg, I'd be out of bed and punching the colonel's weary face. As is, I have to settle for slamming my fist into the cheap mattress again. My head throbs with the violent movement, but I don't give a fuck.

Esguerra was taken while I lay here, drugged and oblivious.

I failed at my job, and I failed badly.

"Give me the phone," I say when I'm calm enough to speak. "I need to talk to Peter Sokolov."

Sharipov nods and takes the phone out of his pocket. "Here you go." He offers it to me cautiously. "We already spoke to him, but you're welcome to do so as well."

Fighting the urge to grab Sharipov's hand and break his arm, I take the phone and punch in the numbers for a secure connection that takes me through a number of relays. To my annoyance, Peter doesn't pick up.

Sharipov is watching me, so I conceal my frustration as I try again. And again. And again.

"I'll be back in a few minutes," Sharipov says on my fifth attempt. "Feel free to contact whomever you need."

He departs, and I resume trying Peter's number, driven by increasing anger and worry. Esguerra's Russian security consultant always carries his phone with him, and I have no idea why he's suddenly out of reach. Could there have been an attack on Esguerra's estate in Colombia? The mere possibility makes me see red.

Just when I'm about to give up, the call connects. "Yes?" The faintly accented voice is unmistakably Peter Sokolov's.

"It's Kent."

"Lucas?" The Russian sounds surprised. "You're awake?"

"Fuck, yeah, I'm awake. Where are you? Why didn't you pick up?"

There's a short pause on the line. "I just landed in Chicago."

"What?" That's the last thing I expected to hear. "Why?"

"Esguerra's wife. She wants to be Al-Quadar bait."

"What?" I almost jump off the bed, the cast be damned.

"Yeah, I know. That was my reaction too. Turns out Esguerra, that obsessive bastard, implanted some trackers in her. If they take her to use as leverage against Esguerra, we'll have a fix on their location."

"Fuck." The plan is brilliant, and dangerous as hell. If the terrorists find those trackers in her, Esguerra's pretty little wife will pray for death. And if Esguerra somehow survives, he'll dismember Peter—slowly—for using the girl like that. "Nora came up with this?"

"She did." There's a hint of admiration in the Russian's cool voice. "I don't know what hold he's got over her, but she's pretty determined. I was against it at first, but she convinced me."

I inhale and let the air out slowly. I should be surprised—Esguerra did kidnap the girl, after all—but I'm not. However their relationship started, it's obvious that whatever's between them now is mutual. I'm tempted to rip into Peter for going against Esguerra's orders, but that would be a waste of time and energy. What he's set in motion can't be undone. "So what's the exact plan?" I ask instead. "Are you going to hang out in Chicago to make sure they take the bait?"

"No. I'm heading to Tajikistan right away. The rescue team is already on the way there. As soon as Majid's men bring her over, we'll come for her—and for Esguerra."

"You know they might not bring her to him. A video of her getting tortured would be just as effective as the real thing."

"I know."

Of course he does. Like me, he's used to life-and-death gambles. I could point out the risks from now 'til eternity, and it wouldn't change anything. The plan will either work or it won't, and there's nothing I can do about it.

"Did you figure out what happened?" I ask, changing the topic. "Sharipov said it may have been some kind of error on their part."

"An error?" I can hear Peter's derisive snort over the phone. "More like lax security. One of their officers has been in the Ukrainians' pocket for years, and the idiots had no clue until he fired a missile at your plane."

"Ukraine?" It makes sense; now that Esguerra's sided with the Russians, the Ukrainians would want to eliminate him. Except . . . how could they have found out about our conversation so quickly? Was the restaurant in Moscow bugged? Did Buschekov play for both sides? Or did—

"It was the interpreter," Peter says, voicing my next guess. "I had her detained in Moscow as soon as I learned what happened."

A loud beep sounds in my ear, and I realize I squeezed the phone so hard I nearly crushed one of the volume buttons.

"What the fuck—"

"Sorry. Pressed the wrong button." My voice is cold and steady, even as burning lava moves through my veins. "The interpreter is a Ukrainian spy?"

"It appears that way. We're still digging into her background, but so far at least half of her story appears to have been fabricated."

"I see." I force myself to unclench my fingers before I crush the phone completely. "That's how they were able to act so quickly."

"Yes. They somehow figured out exactly when you'd be passing through the Uzbekistani airspace and activated their agent there."

The phone emits another angry beep as my hand tightens involuntarily. I know exactly how they figured out the timing: I all but told the spying bitch our departure time.

"Lucas?"

"Yeah, I'm here." I can't remember the last time I've been so furious. Yulia Tzakova—if that's even her real name—had played me for a fool. Her initial reluctance, her peculiar air of innocence—it had all been an act. She had probably been hoping to get close to Esguerra, and when she couldn't get him, she settled for me.

"I have to go now," Peter says. "I'll contact you again when we land. Get some rest and heal up; there's nothing else for you to do right now. I'll keep you apprised of any new developments."

He disconnects, and I force myself to lie down, my headache worsened by my burning rage.

If Yulia Tzakova ever crosses my path again, she will pay.

She will pay for everything.

* * *

I'm still livid with fury when Sharipov returns to reclaim his phone. As he approaches my bed, I sit up and glare at him. "A fucking error, huh?"

Raising his hand, the colonel rubs the bridge of his nose. "We're questioning the officer responsible right now. It's not yet clear whether—"

"Take me to him."

Looking taken aback, Sharipov lowers his hand. "I can't do that," he says. "This is a matter for our military."

"Your military fucked up big time. You had a traitor in charge of your missile defense system."

The colonel opens his mouth, but I forestall his objections. "Take me to him," I demand again. "I need to question him myself. Otherwise, we'll have no choice but to assume that others in your military or your government were involved in the missile strike." I pause. "And maybe even in this terrorist attack on the hospital."

Sharipov's eyes widen at my implied threat. If the Uzbekistani government is found to have ties to a terrorist organization like Al-Quadar, that could be disastrous for the country. I wouldn't be surprised if the colonel is aware of our connections in the US and Israel. By denying me a chance to interrogate one treasonous officer, the Uzbekistani government might be making an enemy of the powerful Esguerra organization and getting a worldwide reputation for associating with terrorists.

"I have to discuss this with my superiors," Sharipov says after a second. "Please, let me have my phone."

I hand it to him and watch as he leaves the room, already dialing someone. I wait, confident of the outcome, and sure enough, he returns a few minutes later, saying, "All right, Mr. Kent. We'll have our officer brought here within the next hour. You can talk to him, but that's all. Our military will handle it from there."

I give him a grim look. The only thing their military will handle is the traitor's body, but Sharipov doesn't need to know that yet. "Bring him," is all I say, and then I lie back and close my eyes, hoping the throbbing pain in my skull subsides in the next hour.

I may not be able to lay my hands on the interpreter right now, but I can certainly get my pound of flesh here.

* * *

When the traitor arrives, the nurses give me crutches and lead me to another hospital room. It takes me a few minutes to get the hang of walking with the crutches—the fucking headache certainly doesn't help—and by the time I get there, they have the guy sitting on a bed, with Colonel Sharipov and an M16-toting soldier flanking his sides.

"This is Anton Karimov, the officer responsible for the unfortunate incident with your plane," Sharipov says as I hobble toward them. "You are welcome to ask him whatever questions you have. His English is not as good as mine, but he should understand you."

One of the nurses drags a chair over, and I sit down on it, studying the profusely sweating man in front of me. In his early forties, Karimov is on the plump side, with a thick black mustache and a receding hairline. He's still in his army uniform, and I can see circles of sweat staining his underarms.

He's nervous. No, more than that.

He's terrified.

"Who are the people who paid you?" I ask when the nurses leave the room. I decide to start off easy, as it might not take much to crack this man. "Who gave the order to shoot down our plane?"

Karimov visibly cringes. "N-nobody. Just a mistake. I clean the controls—"

I cut him off by lifting one of my crutches and putting the far end against his groin. Though I apply the lightest pressure to his balls, the man turns sickly pale.

"Who gave the order to shoot down our plane?" I repeat, looking at him. I can see that Sharipov is uneasy with my method of questioning, but I ignore him. Instead, I push the wooden stick forward, applying greater pressure to Karimov's crotch.

"N-nobody," Karimov gasps, scooting back to get out of the stick's reach. "I clean the—"

I lunge forward. He lets out a high-pitched squeal as I pin his balls to the mattress with the stick. "Don't fucking lie to me. Who paid you?"

"Mr. Kent, this is not acceptable," Sharipov says, stepping between me and the prisoner. "We told you, questions only. If you do not stop—"

Before he finishes speaking, I'm already on my feet, propping myself up on one crutch as I lash out at the armed soldier with another. He doesn't so much as lift his M16 before I hit him in the knee and he pitches forward, enabling me to grab his weapon. In the next second, I have the assault rifle pointed at Sharipov.

"Get out," I say, jerking my chin toward the door. "You and the soldier both. Get the fuck out."

Sharipov steps back, his face turning red. "I don't know what you think you're doing—"

"Out." I lift the weapon to point it between his eyes. "Now."

Sharipov's jaw clenches, but he does as I say. The soldier limps out behind him, shooting me a venomous look behind his shoulder. I have no doubt they'll come back with reinforcements, but it will be too late by then.

As soon as the door closes behind them, I turn my attention to Karimov. "Now," I say, my tone almost pleasant as I point the gun at the traitor. "Where were we?"

The man's eyes are wild with fear. "It—it was mistake. I said it before. Nobody pay me. Nobody—"

I squeeze the trigger and watch the bullets tear through his knee. The gunshots and the resulting screaming aggravate my headache, which adds to my rage. "I told you not to lie to me," I roar when the man's screams die down a notch. "Now, who paid you?"

"I d-don't know!" He's sobbing and clutching his knee as his blood soaks the hospital bed. "It was all email! All email!"

"What email?"

"M-my Yahoo! They transfer money to my bank for years and then they ask favors. S-small favors. I not meet them. Never meet them—"

"You don't know who they are?"

"N-no," he sobs out, trying to stop the bleeding with his pudgy hands. "I don't know, I don't know, I don't know . . ."

Shit. I'm inclined to believe him. He's too much of a coward not to give them up to save his skin, and they probably knew better than to trust him. We'll hack into his email, but I doubt there'll be many clues there.

Hearing shouts and running footsteps in the hallway, I press the gun to Karimov's sweaty forehead. "Last chance," I say grimly. "Who are they?"

"I don't know!" His wail is full of desperation, and I know he's telling the truth. He doesn't know anything, which makes him useless. I'm tempted to save him for Esguerra or Peter's amusement, but it'll take too much effort to get him out of the country.

That means there's only one thing left for me to do.

Squeezing the trigger, I pepper Karimov with bullets and watch his body slam against the wall, blood and bits of brains spraying everywhere. Then I lower the weapon and take a few deep breaths, trying to calm the pounding pain in my head.

When Sharipov's troops burst into the room a few seconds later, I'm sitting in the chair, the empty weapon lying at my feet.

"I apologize about the mess," I say, leaning on the crutches to stand up. "We'll pay for the clean-up of this room."

And ignoring the horror on everyone's faces, I start hobbling toward the door.

CHAPTER TWELVE

❖ YULIA ❖

"Which organization do you belong to?" Buschekov leans forward, his eyes trained on me with the intensity of a snake hypnotizing its prey.

I stare back at the Russian official, barely registering his question. I can't decide if his eyes are yellowish gray or pale hazel; whatever color his irises are, they manage to blend with the yellowish-gray whites around them, producing the illusion of a complete lack of eye color. In general, everything about Arkady Buschekov is yellowish gray, from his skin tone to the wispy hair plastered against his shiny skull.

"Which organization do you belong to?" he repeats, his gaze boring into me. I wonder how many people have caved from that stare alone; if I believed in x-ray vision, I'd swear he's looking straight into me. "Who sent you here?"

"I don't know what you're talking about," I say, unable to keep my exhaustion out of my voice.

It's been over twenty-four hours since my capture, and I've neither slept nor had anything to eat or drink. They're wearing me down this way, undermining my willpower. It's a standard interrogation technique here. The Russians consider themselves too civilized to resort to outright torture, so they use these "softer" methods—things that mess with your psyche rather than cause lasting harm to your body.

"You know, Yulia Andreyevna"—Buschekov addresses me by my name and fake patronymic—"the Ukrainian government has disavowed any connection with you." He leans even closer, making me want to shrink back into my seat. At this distance, I can smell the salted fish and garlic potatoes he must've eaten for lunch. "Unless some unofficial agency in Ukraine claims you, we'll have no choice but to presume that you're a Russian citizen, as your false background indicates," he continues. "You understand what that means, right?"

I do. If treason is the charge they levy against me, I'll be executed. That's no reason for me to talk, though. Obenko won't come forward to claim me, not even if I expose our off-the-books agency. One operative is nothing in the grand scheme of things.

When I remain silent, Buschekov sighs and leans back in his seat. "All right, Yulia Andreyevna. If that's how you wish to play it." He snaps his fingers at the wall-wide mirror to the left of me. "We'll talk again soon."

He rises to his feet and walks to the door in the corner. Stopping in front of it, he looks back at me. "Think about what I said. This can go very badly for you if you don't cooperate."

I don't respond. Instead, I look down at my hands, which are handcuffed to the table in front of me. I hear the door open and shut as he walks out, and then I'm alone, except for the people watching me through the mirror.

* * *

The hours drag by, each second more torturous than the next. The thirst that torments me is comparable only to the hunger that gnaws at my insides. I try to lay my head down on the desk to sleep, but every time I do so, an ear-piercing alarm blares through the speakers, startling me awake. The screeching noise is impossible to ignore, even in my exhausted state, and eventually I stop trying, doing my best to zone out for a few precious moments while sitting upright in my chair.

I know what they're doing, but that doesn't make it any easier to bear. People who haven't experienced prolonged sleep deprivation don't understand that it's genuine torture, that every part of one's body begins to shut down after a while. I'm nauseated and cold all over, and everything hurts—my stomach, my muscles, my skin, my bones . . . even my teeth. The headache from earlier is a blaze of agony in my skull, and my lips are cracking from lack of water.

How long has it been since Buschekov left me alone? Several hours? A day? I don't know, and I'm losing the will to care. If there's any silver lining to all this, it's that I don't need to use the bathroom. I'm too dehydrated, and my stomach is too empty. Not that this saved me from humiliation. Upon arrival, they stripped me and went over every inch of my body. Even now that I'm dressed in a gray prison jumpsuit, I feel horribly naked, my skin crawling at the memory of the guards' latex-covered fingers invading me all over.

I close my eyes for a second, and the screeching alarm blares to life, jolting me awake. Opening my eyes, I attempt to swallow, to gather what little moisture remains in my mouth so I can wet my throat. I feel as though I've been eating sand. Swallowing hurts even more than not swallowing, so I give up, focusing on just surviving from moment to moment. They won't let me die like this, not when they hope to get some information from me, so all I need to do is hang on until they bring me some water.

Until they return to question me again.

My mind drifts, going over the last few days. There's no reason not to think of Lucas now, so I let the memories come. Sharp and bittersweet, they fill me, taking me away from my aching, exhausted body.

I remember the way he kissed me, the way he fit against me and inside me. I recall his taste, his smell, the feel of his skin against mine. He'd looked at me while he was fucking me, his gaze possessing me with its intensity. Did it mean anything to him, the night we spent together? Or was I just a casual lay, a way to scratch an itch while passing through Moscow?

My dry eyes burn as I stare, unseeing, at the wall in front of me. Whatever the answer is, it doesn't matter. It never mattered, but now it has zero relevance. Lucas Kent is dead, his body likely blown into pieces.

The room blurs in front of me, fading in and out of focus, and I realize I'm shaking, my breathing shallow and my heart beating painfully fast. I know it's probably from dehydration and lack of sleep, but it feels like something within me is breaking, the pressure around my chest hard and crushing. I want to curl up into a ball, to shrink into myself, but I can't, not with my hands cuffed to the table and feet chained to the floor.

All I can do is sit and grieve for something I never had—and now would never know.

CHAPTER THIRTEEN

❖ LUCAS ❖

After my interrogation of Karimov, Sharipov assigns ten armed soldiers to stand guard over me and accompany the nurses when they take care of me. I know he's tempted to do more, like throw me in prison, but he doesn't dare. Peter's already worked some magic with his Russian connections, so everyone at this hospital is on their best behavior, the minor matter of armed guards excluded.

I don't mind my entourage. Now that I've had a chance to release some of my rage, I'm a tiny bit calmer, and I spend the time between Karimov's death and Esguerra's rescue learning how to move around on crutches. According to the doctors, it's a clean tibial break, so the cast should come off in six to eight weeks. That gives me a small measure of comfort, lessening my anger and frustration at being stuck in the hospital while others are doing my job.

Peter keeps me updated, so I know Al-Quadar took the bait. Now it's just a matter of waiting for Nora to be brought to wherever the terrorist cell is hiding Esguerra. Feeling cautiously optimistic, I make arrangements for the two of them to be brought to a private clinic in Switzerland after the rescue. I have a feeling they'll need it. I also strategize with Peter about the best way to extract Esguerra out of whatever hole they're keeping him in, and regularly check on the burned men, who are at this point stable but drugged unconscious to ease their suffering. They'll need multiple skin grafts—an expense Esguerra needs to authorize when he returns.

With all that activity, I don't spend much time resting in bed, which upsets the doctors taking care of me. They claim I need to lie still and not stress in order to let my concussion heal. I ignore them. They don't understand that I need to keep busy, that even the worst headache is better than lying there and thinking about *her*.

The Russian interpreter / Ukrainian spy.

Yulia.

Just thinking her name makes my blood pressure spike. I don't know why I can't put her betrayal out of my mind. It's not even a betrayal as such. Rationally, I understand she didn't owe me any loyalty. I came to her apartment to use her body, and she ended up using me instead. That makes her my enemy, someone I should want to kill, but it doesn't mean she betrayed me. I shouldn't give her any more thought than I give Al-Quadar.

I shouldn't, but I do.

I think about her constantly, remembering the way she looked at me and how her breath caught when I first touched her. How she clung to me as I drove into her, her pussy tight and slick around my cock. She wanted me—that much I'm sure of—and sex with her had been the hottest thing I'd experienced in years.

Maybe ever.

Fuck.

I can't keep doing this to myself. I need to forget the girl. She's in the hands of the Russian government, which means she's no longer my problem. One way or another, she'll pay for what she's done.

It's a thought that should comfort me, but it enrages me more instead.

* * *

"We got them."

At the sound of Peter's voice, I get up, too tense to sit still. "How are they?" It's a struggle to hold on to the phone while balancing on crutches, but I manage.

"Esguerra's pretty fucked up. They did a number on his face—I think he lost an eye. Nora seems okay. She took out Majid. Blew his brains out before we got there." Peter sounds admiring. "Gunned him down cold, if you can believe that."

"Damn." I can't form that picture in my mind, so I don't even try. Instead, I focus on the first part of his statement. "Esguerra's lost an eye?"

"Seems like it. I'm not a doctor, but it looks bad. Hopefully, they can fix it in that Swiss place."

"Yeah." If they can do it anywhere, the clinic in Switzerland would be it. It's known for treating celebrities and the obscenely wealthy of all persuasions, from Russian oil tycoons to Mexican drug lords. A stay there begins at thirty thousand Swiss francs a night, but Julian Esguerra can easily afford it.

"He wants you and the others transferred to that clinic, by the way," Peter says. "We'll send a plane for you shortly."

"Ah." I'd expected nothing less, but it's still nice to hear that. Recuperating at the ritzy Swiss clinic should be much better than being stuck in this shit hole. "He didn't rip into you for letting Nora get taken?"

"I didn't really talk to him. I'm keeping my distance."

"Peter . . ." I hesitate for a second, then decide the guy deserves a fair warning. "Esguerra's not very rational when it comes to his wife. There's a chance he'll—"

"Rip out my liver barehanded? Yeah, I know." The Russian sounds more amused than concerned. "Which is why I'm dropping them off at the clinic and leaving. They're all yours now."

"Leaving? What about your list?" It's no secret that in exchange for three years of service, Esguerra promised to get Peter the names of people responsible for what happened to his family.

"Don't worry about that." Peter's voice cools to arctic levels. "They'll get what's coming to them."

"All right, man." This is probably my cue to message the guards to detain Peter. Esguerra would undoubtedly praise me for that, but I can't bring myself to betray the Russian like that. Though we haven't been working together that long, I've grown to admire the man. He's a cold-blooded motherfucker, and that makes him excellent at what he does. And frankly, he's dangerous enough that I don't want to risk the lives of any more of our men. "Good luck," I say, and mean it.

"Thanks, Lucas. You too. Hope you and Esguerra heal up soon."

And with that, he hangs up, leaving me to wait for the plane and try not to think about Yulia.

* * *

We stay at the Swiss clinic for almost a week. During that time, Esguerra undergoes two surgeries—one to fix his cut-up face and the other to put a prosthetic eye into his left eye socket.

"They said the scars will be barely visible after a while," his wife tells me when I run into her in the hallway. "And the eye implant should look very natural. In a few months, he'll be almost back to normal." She pauses, studying me with her large dark eyes. "How are you, Lucas? How's your leg feeling?"

"It's fine." I've been refusing painkillers, so it actually hurts like a motherfucker, but Nora doesn't need to know that. "I got lucky. We both did."

"Yeah." Her slender throat works as she swallows. "What's the prognosis on the others?"

"They'll live until the next surgery." That's about the only positive thing I can say about the three burned men. "The doctors say they'll each need about a dozen operations."

She nods somberly. "Of course. I hope the surgeries go well. Please give them my best wishes if you speak to them."

I incline my head. There isn't much chance of that, since they're completely doped up, but I don't see any need to tell her that. The petite young woman in front of me is already dealing with enough shit. Esguerra said she's handling it, but I wonder. Not many nineteen-year-olds from the American suburbs blow open a terrorist's head.

I'm about to continue on my way when Nora asks quietly, "Have you heard from Peter?" Her expression as she stares up at me is hard to decipher.

"No, I haven't," I tell her honestly. "Why?"

She shrugs. "Just curious. We do owe him our lives."

"Right." I have a feeling there's more to this, but I don't pry. Instead, I incline my head at her again and continue hobbling to my room.

As I fall asleep that night, the blond spy invades my thoughts again, and my cock hardens despite my lingering headache. It's been like that every night for the past week. Random images from our night together come to me when my guard is down—when I'm too tired to fight them off. I keep recalling the tight clasp of her pussy, the cries that escaped her throat as I fucked her, the way she smelled, the way she tasted . . . It's gotten so bad I've considered getting a hooker, but for some reason, the idea doesn't appeal to me.

I don't just want sex. I want sex with *her*.

Furious, I get up, grab my crutches, and hobble to the bathroom to jerk off again.

If all goes well, tomorrow we'll be back in Colombia, and this chapter of my life will be over.

Maybe then I'll forget Yulia once and for all.

PART III: THE PRISONER

CHAPTER FOURTEEN

❖ LUCAS ❖

My fingers hover over the keyboard of my laptop as I stare at the screen, debating the wisdom of what I'm about to do. Then I take a deep breath and start typing. My email to Buschekov is short and to the point:

Esguerra requests to have Yulia Tzakova remitted into his custody for further interrogation.

I click "send" and get up, reveling in the freedom of moving without crutches. It's been two weeks since I've gotten the cast off, and I still feel exhilarated every time I stand up and walk unassisted.

Leaving my library/office, I head into the kitchen to make myself a sandwich. Cooking is a skill I've never been able to master, so my sandwich is beyond simple: ham, cheese, lettuce, and mayo between two slices of bread.

I sit down at the table to eat, so I don't overtax my leg. Though it's healing well, I still have to fight a tendency to limp. It's only been two months since the break, and the bone needs longer to mend completely.

As I eat, my thoughts turn to the Russians' probable response to my email. I can't imagine Buschekov will be pleased to lose his prisoner, but at the same time, I don't think he'll push back too hard. Esguerra's weapons are the best in the business, and with the conflict in Ukraine escalating, the Kremlin needs our covert deliveries to the rebels more than ever.

One way or another, they'll honor Esguerra's—but really, my—request. Which means that after two months of obsessing about her, I'm going to get my hands on Yulia Tzakova.

I can't fucking wait.

* * *

Over the next two days, I exchange half a dozen emails with Buschekov. As I'd suspected, he's not too happy, initially going so far as to say he'll only talk to Peter Sokolov about the matter.

"Sokolov is currently unavailable," I tell Buschekov when we get on a video call. The Russian official is once again using an interpreter—a middle-aged woman this time. "I'm the one speaking for Esguerra in all matters now, and he wants Tzakova in his custody as soon as possible, along with whatever information you've been able to uncover about her thus far."

"That's impossible," Buschekov retorts once the translator conveys my words. "It's a matter of national security—"

"Bullshit. All we require are the files on her background. That has nothing to do with Russian national security."

Buschekov doesn't say anything for a few moments after the woman translates, and I know he's considering how to best handle me. "Why do you need her?" he finally asks.

"Because we want to track down the individual or the specific organization responsible for the missile strike." Or at least that's what I tell myself: that I want to interrogate the girl personally to find the motherfuckers who shot down our plane.

Buschekov's colorless eyes are unblinking. "You don't need Tzakova for that. We'll share that information with you as soon as we have it."

"So you don't have it. After two months." I'm both surprised and impressed that they haven't managed to break the girl. Her training must've been top notch to withstand such lengthy interrogation.

"We'll have it soon." Buschekov folds his arms in front of his chest. "There are ways to accelerate information retrieval, and we've just received authorization to use them."

My stomach muscles tighten. I've been trying not to think of what they might be doing to her in Moscow, but every so often, those thoughts creep in along with memories of our night together. I want Yulia to suffer, but the idea of some faceless Russian guards abusing her stirs something dark and ugly within me.

"I don't care about your authorizations." I force my voice to remain calm as I lean closer to the camera. "What you'll do is remit her into our custody. If you wish to maintain our business relationship, that is."

He stares at me, and I know he's thinking this over, wondering if I'm bluffing. And I am—Esguerra didn't authorize any of this—but Buschekov doesn't know that. As far as the Russian official is concerned, I represent the Esguerra organization, and I'm about to pull the plug on what has been a mutually beneficial association.

"It wouldn't go well for you, you know," Buschekov says finally. "If you were to go against us like that."

"Maybe." I don't blink at the not-so-veiled threat. "Maybe not. Esguerra's enemies rarely fare well."

I'm referring to Al-Quadar, which has been completely decimated since our return. We've been at war with the terrorist group for a number of months, ever since they tried to get a certain explosive from Esguerra by kidnapping Nora. However, things have really escalated since we came back from Tajikistan.

We've gone after the terrorists' suppliers, financiers, and distant relatives; nobody even remotely connected to the group has escaped our wrath. The body count is coming up on four hundred, and the intelligence community has taken notice.

Buschekov doesn't respond for a few tense moments, and I wonder if he's going to call my bluff. But then he says, "All right. You'll have her within a month."

"No." I hold Buschekov's gaze as the woman translates my words. "Sooner. We're sending a plane for her tomorrow."

"What? No, that—"

"Should be enough time to get everything ready," I interrupt the translator. "Remember, we expect to get her *and* the files. You don't want to disappoint us, believe me."

And before he can voice any further protests, I disconnect from the video call.

* * *

The next morning, I train with Esguerra and the crew, as usual. Like me, he's almost back to normal, having kicked ass with our three new recruits. Since my leg is still healing, I'm sticking to boxing and target practice, and I'm more than a little envious that he's able to spar properly.

As we leave the training area, I fill him in on the latest developments with Peter Sokolov. Turns out the Russian somehow got his list from Esguerra, and is now going through the names and systematically eliminating them one by one.

"There was another hit in France, and two more in Germany," I tell Esguerra, using a towel to wipe the sweat off my face. This area of Colombia, near the Amazon rainforest, is always hot and humid. "He's not wasting any time."

"I didn't think he would," Esguerra says. "How did he do it this time?"

"The French guy was found floating in a river, with marks of torture and strangulation, so I'm guessing Sokolov must've kidnapped him first. For the Germans, one hit was a car bomb, and the other one a sniper rifle." I grin. "They must not have pissed him off as much."

"Or he went for expediency."

"Or that," I agree. "He probably knows Interpol is on his tail."

"I'm sure he does." Esguerra looks distracted, so I decide it's as good a time as any to bring up the Yulia situation.

"By the way," I say, keeping my tone casual, "I'm having Yulia Tzakova brought here from Moscow."

Esguerra stops and stares at me. "The interpreter who betrayed us to the Ukrainians? Why?"

"I want to personally interrogate her," I explain, draping the towel around my neck. "I don't trust the Russians to do a thorough job."

Esguerra narrows his eyes, his prosthetic eerily lifelike. "Is it because you fucked her that night in Moscow? Is that what this is about?"

A wave of anger makes my jaw tighten. "She fucked me over. Literally." That much I'm comfortable admitting. "So yeah, I want to get my hands on the little bitch. But I also think she might have some useful info for us."

Or at least I'm hoping she does, so I can justify this insane obsession with her.

Esguerra studies me for a second, then nods. "In that case, go for it." We resume walking, and he asks, "Did you already negotiate this with the Russians?"

I nod. "Initially, they tried to say they'd only deal with Sokolov, but I convinced them it wouldn't be wise to get on your bad side. Buschekov saw the light when I reminded him of the recent troubles at Al-Quadar."

"Good." Esguerra looks grimly pleased. In the world of illegal arms dealing, reputation is everything, and the fact that the Russians backed down bodes well for our relationships with clients and suppliers.

"Yes, it's helpful," I say before adding, "She'll be arriving here tomorrow."

Esguerra's eyebrows lift. "Where are you going to keep her?" he asks. It's a measure of his trust in me that he doesn't question my initiative. Ever since I saved his life in Thailand, he's been giving me tremendous leeway.

"In my quarters," I say. "I'll be interrogating her there."

He grins, and I know he understands. "All right. Enjoy."

"Oh, I will," I say darkly. "You can bet on it."

I'm literally counting down the hours until Yulia is on the plane. I considered flying to Moscow myself to get her, but after some deliberation, I decided to send Thomas, a former Navy pilot, and a few other men I trust. It would've looked strange if I'd gone; as Esguerra's second-in-command, I'm needed on the estate, not handling minor tasks like spy retrieval.

"If there's any trouble, notify me immediately," I told Thomas, though I'm confident there won't be.

In less than twenty-four hours, Yulia Tzakova will be here.

She'll be my prisoner, and nobody will save her from me.

CHAPTER FIFTEEN

❖ YULIA ❖

The heavy metal door at the end of the hallway clangs, and I jerk awake, conditioned to respond to that noise as if to an electric shock.

They're coming for me again.

I begin to shake—yet another conditioned response. As much as I want to remain strong, they're getting to me, breaking me down piece by piece. Every grueling interrogation, every humiliation great and small, every day that blends into night as I sit there without food and sleep—it all adds up, destroying my willpower bit by tiny bit. And I know they're only getting started.

Buschekov implied as much the last time he had me in that mirrored room.

Trying to control my breathing, I sit up on my cot, pulling a thin, dirty blanket around myself. Outside, it might be May, but in this prison, it's still winter. The chill here is everlasting. It permeates the gray stone walls and rusted metal bars, seeps in through the cracks in the floor and ceiling. There are no windows anywhere, so the sun never warms these rooms. I reside in fluorescent grayness, the cold walls around me pressing closer each day.

Footsteps.

Hearing them, I slide my sock-covered feet into my boots. My socks are dirty, as is the jumpsuit I'm wearing. I haven't had a shower in three weeks, and I undoubtedly stink to high heaven. It's one of those small humiliations designed to make one feel less than human.

"Yulechka . . ." A familiar singsong voice makes me shake even more. Igor is the guard I hate most, the one with the grabbiest hands and the nastiest-smelling breath. Even with the cameras everywhere, he manages to find opportunities to touch me and hurt me.

"Yulechka," he repeats, approaching my cell, and I see the glee in his beady brown eyes. He's using the most familiar form of my name, one that would normally be an endearment spoken by parents and other family members. On his thick lips, it sounds dirty and perverted, like he's a pedophile talking to a child.

"Are you ready, Yulechka?" Staring at me, he reaches for the lock on the cell door.

I fight the urge to shrink back against the wall. Instead, I stand up and throw off my blanket. He'd welcome any excuse to lay hands on me, so I don't give him one. I just walk over to the metal bars and stand there waiting, my stomach twisting with nausea.

"You're wanted out there again," he says, reaching for my arm. I almost puke as he grabs my wrist, his fingers thick and oily on my skin. He snaps a handcuff on that wrist and then grabs my other arm, stepping closer. "They said you won't be coming back here," he whispers, and I feel one of his hands squeezing my ass, his fingers digging painfully into the crack. "It's too bad. I'll miss you, Yulechka."

Vomit rises in my throat as I smell his breath—stale cigarettes mixed with rotting teeth. It takes everything I have not to shove him away. Fighting means he'll get to touch me even more; I know that from experience. So I just stand there and wait for him to release me. He won't rape me—that's one humiliation I've been spared, thanks to the cameras—so all I need to do is remain still and not throw up.

Sure enough, after a few seconds, he snaps the second handcuff on my wrist and steps back, disappointment darkening his features.

"Let's go," he barks, grabbing my elbow, and I gulp in air untainted by his stench, desperately hoping my stomach will settle down. I've thrown up once before, when they fed me greasy meat after starving me for three days, and they made me clean it up with the blanket that's still on my cot.

To my relief, my nausea recedes as Igor marches me down the hall, and I register what he said.

You won't be coming back.

What does that mean? Are they moving me to another facility, or did they finally decide it wasn't worth it, trying to get anything out of me? Am I about to be executed? Is that what Buschekov was hinting at when he said he was about to get some new authorization?

My heartbeat picks up, a fresh wave of nausea moving through me. I'm not ready for this. I thought I was, but now that the moment is here, I want to live.

I want to live to see Misha.

Except if I give the Russians what they want, I won't see Misha ever again. Obenko's sister and her family will be forced to go into hiding, and my brother along with them. Misha's happy life will be over, and it'll all be my fault.

No. My resolve firms again.

It's better that I die.

At least then I'll be out of this hellhole once and for all.

* * *

Despite my determination, my legs feel like gelatin as Igor leads me down an unfamiliar hallway. We're moving away from the interrogation room, which means the guard wasn't lying.

Something different is happening today.

"This way," Igor says, tugging me toward a set of double doors. As we approach, they swing open for us, and I blink at the sudden flood of blinding light.

Sunlight.

It's warm and pure on my skin, so unlike the cold fluorescence of the prison lights. The air wafting in through those doors is different too. It's fresher, full of scents that speak of city in the spring and have nothing to do with desperation and human suffering.

"Here she is," Igor says, pushing me through the doors, and to my shock, a woman's voice repeats his words in Russian-accented English.

Squinting against the overwhelming brightness, I turn my head to see a short middle-aged woman standing next to five men in a narrow courtyard. Beyond them is a thick wall with barbed wire at the top and several armed guards.

"Who are you?" I ask the woman in English, but she doesn't respond. Instead, she turns to look at one of the men—a tall, thin one who seems to be their leader.

"You can go now, thank you," he says to her, speaking American English without an accent, and I realize she must be an interpreter.

She nods at him and hurries toward the gate on the other side of the courtyard. The man steps toward me, and I see an expression of disgust cross his narrow face. He must've smelled my lack of showers.

"Let's go," he says, grabbing my arm and pulling me away from Igor.

"Where are you taking me?" I'm trying to stay calm. This is not at all what I was expecting. What could Americans want from me? Unless . . . Could they be with—

"Colombia," the man says, confirming my horrified guess. "Julian Esguerra requests the honor of your presence."

And before I can process this new blow, he drags me toward the gate.

* * *

I don't know at what point I start fighting—whether it's once we're beyond the prison gate or when we approach the black van. All I know is that a beast wakes up inside me, and I lash out at the man holding me with all my remaining strength.

I have no idea how the arms dealer could be alive, and at this moment, I don't care. The panicked animal inside me cares only about avoiding the terrible torment that awaits at the end of this journey. I've read the file on Esguerra, and I've heard the rumors. He's not only a ruthless businessman.

He's also a sadist.

My hands are cuffed, so I use my feet, kicking out at the leader's knee at the same time as I crouch and twist, breaking his hold on my arm. He cries out, cursing, but I'm already rolling on the ground, away from the five men. I don't get far, of course. Within a second, they're on me, two big men pinning me to the ground and then jerking me up to my feet. I continue to fight them, kicking and biting and screaming as they shove me into the back of the van. It's only when the doors close and the van starts moving that I stop struggling, exhausted and shaking all over. My breathing is harsh and loud, and my heart slams against my ribcage in a terrified tempo.

"Hijo de puta, she stinks," the man holding me mutters, and my cheeks flame with embarrassment, as if it's my fault I've been reduced to this disgusting creature.

They gag me then, probably to stop me from screaming again, and cuff my wrists to my ankles before throwing me in the corner of the van and sitting down a couple of feet away. They don't touch me beyond that, and after a few minutes, some of my blind panic recedes and I begin thinking again.

Julian Esguerra wants me delivered to him. That means he didn't die from the missile strike. How is that possible? Did Obenko lie to me, or did Esguerra somehow get lucky? And if the arms dealer survived, what about the rest of his crew?

What about Lucas Kent?

A familiar ache pierces my chest as I think his name. I'd only known him for that one night, but I've grieved for him, cried for him in the cold confines of my cell. Could he possibly be alive? And if he's alive, am I going to see him again?

Will he be the one who tortures me?

No. I squeeze my eyes shut. I can't think of that right now. I need to take it one minute at a time, same as I did in that interrogation room. It's likely that the next several hours are my last ones without extreme pain—if not my last ones overall—and I can't spend that precious time worrying about the future.

I can't spend it thinking about a man who's most likely dead.

So instead of Lucas Kent, I think of my brother again, of his sunny smile and the way his small, pudgy arms embraced me when he was little. I was eight years old when he was born, and our parents were afraid I would resent the intrusion of a new baby into our close-knit family. But I didn't. I fell in love with Misha from the moment I met him in the hospital, and when I held him for the first time and felt how tiny he was, I knew it would be my job to protect him.

"It's wonderful that Yulia loves her brother so much," my parents' friends would tell them. "Look how well she takes care of him. She'll make a wonderful mother one day."

My parents would nod, beaming at me, and I would redouble my efforts to be a good sister, to do whatever I could to ensure my baby brother was happy, healthy, and safe.

The van comes to a halt, bringing me out of my thoughts, and I realize with a jolt of panic that we've arrived.

"Let's go," the group leader says when the van doors open, and I see that we're on a landing strip in front of a Gulfstream private jet. I can't walk with my wrists cuffed to my ankles, so the man who complained about my smell earlier carries me out of the van and onto the plane, the interior of which is as luxurious as anything I've seen.

"Where do you want her?" he asks the leader, and I see his dilemma. The wide seats in the cabin are upholstered with cream-colored leather, as is the couch next to the coffee table. Everything here is clean and nice, whereas I'm filthy.

"There," the leader says, pointing to a seat by the window. "Diego, cover it with a sheet."

A dark-haired man nods and disappears into the back of the plane. He returns a minute later with what appears to be a bed sheet. He drapes it over the seat, and the man holding me deposits me there.

"Do you want the gag removed and her ankles uncuffed?" he asks the leader, and the thin man shakes his head.

"No. Let the bitch sit like this. It'll teach her a lesson."

And with that, they turn away, leaving me to stare out the window and try to keep my mind off what awaits me when the plane lands.

CHAPTER SIXTEEN

❖ YULIA ❖

"Come on, let's go." Rough hands lift me off the seat, startling me out of uneasy sleep. "We're here."

Here? My heartbeat jumps as I realize we've already landed. I must've fallen asleep at some point during the flight, my exhaustion outweighing my anxiety.

It's another man carrying me now—Diego, the leader called him. His grip on me is not especially gentle as he holds me in front of his chest. However, I'm glad they're not making me walk. After spending the whole flight with my ankles and wrists cuffed together, I'm not sure my cramping muscles would be up for the task. Not to mention that I'm so hungry I feel sick and dizzy. They took off my gag and gave me some water mid-way through the flight, but they didn't bother feeding me.

As soon as Diego exits the plane, a wave of warm humidity washes over me, making me feel like I just entered a Russian bathhouse—or maybe a rainforest. The latter is probably a better comparison, given the thick, vine-draped trees surrounding the air strip.

Despite the terror circling through my veins, I'm dazzled by the greenery around me. I love nature—I always have, ever since I was a small child—and this place appeals to me on every level. The air is rich with the scent of tropical vegetation, insects are chirping in the grass, and the sun is bright despite a few clouds in the sky. For a couple of blissful moments, I feel like I'm in paradise.

Then I hear a car approaching and reality crashes in.

The owner of this paradise is going to torture and kill me.

My empty stomach clenches. I don't want to give in to the fear, but I can't help the dread that spreads through me as the car—a black SUV—stops in front of the plane.

The driver's door opens, and a tall, broad-shouldered man steps out, the sun glinting off his short, light-colored hair.

I stop breathing, my eyes glued to his hard features.

Lucas Kent.

He's alive.

His pale eyes lock on mine, and the world around me recedes, blurring out of focus. I forget all about my hunger and discomfort, about the cuffs restraining me and my fear of the future.

All I'm cognizant of is the stark, irrational joy that Lucas is alive.

He starts walking toward me, and I force myself to breathe again. He's even bigger than I remembered, his shoulders wide and thick with muscle. Dressed in a sleeveless camo shirt and ripped jeans, with an assault rifle slung across his torso, he looks exactly like what he is: a ruthless mercenary working for a crime lord.

"I'll handle it from here, Diego," he says, approaching me, and I begin to shake as he reaches for me, his gaze sliding away from mine. Diego hands me over without a word, and my shaking intensifies as I feel Lucas's hands on me again, his touch burning me even through the rough material of my prison jumpsuit.

Stepping back, he turns and begins carrying me to the car, holding me flush against his chest. He evidences no disgust at my unwashed state, and a shudder ripples through me as I feel the heat of his body seeping into me, melting some of the residual chill inside. I should be terrified, but instead I feel that awareness again—that irrational attraction I've only experienced with him. At the same time, a pressure gathers behind my temples, and my eyes prickle, as though I'm about to cry.

Alive. He's alive.

It doesn't seem real. None of this seems real. My reality is a gray, smelly cell in a Russian prison. It's Igor's greasy hands and Buschekov's mirrored interrogation room. It's hunger, thirst, and longing—longing for the life I lost when my parents' car slid on black ice, for the brother I only saw in pictures, and for the man I'd known just one day.

For the man I thought I'd killed—the one holding me right now.

Could all of this be a dream? A fantasy concocted in my exhausted, sleep-deprived mind? Could I even now be passed out at the interrogation table, with that screeching alarm about to jerk me back to consciousness?

Lucas's face blurs in front of my eyes, and I realize I *am* crying, fat, ugly tears welling up and spilling down my cheeks. Embarrassed, I automatically try to wipe them away, but my hands, still cuffed to my ankles, can't reach that far. The motion ends up being jerky and awkward, and I see Lucas's face turn to stone as he glances down at me.

"You fucking bitch," he says so softly that I can barely hear him. "You think you can manipulate me with your tears?" His grip on me tightens, turning hard and punishing as he stops in front of the SUV and glares down at me, as if waiting for a response. When I don't give him one, his features harden further. "You're going to pay for what you did," he promises, his voice filled with quiet fury. "You're going to pay for everything."

And with that, he jerks open the car door and throws me onto the back seat. As my back hits the cushioned leather, I know that I was wrong.

This is not a dream.

It's a nightmare.

* * *

The ride takes only a few minutes. Lucas drives silently, not saying anything else to me, and I use the time to compose myself. Strangely, thinking of his threat helps me control my tears, my stunned joy turning into cold fear as I process the fact that Lucas Kent is alive—and that he will indeed be the one to make me pay.

Does that mean the plane crash happened after all? If so, how did he and Esguerra survive? I want to ask Lucas that, but I can't bring myself to break the silence, not when I feel his rage pulsing in the air like a malevolent force waiting to be unleashed. He took off his weapon, setting it on the front seat next to him, but that doesn't lessen the threat emanating from him.

He can kill me with his bare hands if he's so inclined.

As the car leaves the heavily wooded area, I see a big white house in the distance. It's surrounded by manicured green lawns that form a contrast to the untamed jungle behind us. Farther back, I see guard towers spaced a few dozen meters apart. The sight doesn't surprise me; Esguerra's file said that his Colombian estate is heavily fortified despite its remote location on the edge of the Amazon rainforest.

We don't go to the big house; instead, we turn and drive along the jungle to a cluster of smaller houses and boxy, one-story buildings. It must be where the guards and others on the Esguerra compound live, I realize as I see armed men—and an occasional woman—going in and out of the dwellings.

The car stops in front of one of the individual houses, the one with a front porch, and Lucas exits, leaving the gun in the car. He slams the door behind him, and I flinch, trying not to give in to the anxiety choking me from within. The fear is thick and bitter in my throat. It's worse somehow that it's Lucas who'll do those terrible things to me, that he'll be the one to rip out my fingernails or cut me open piece by piece.

It's worse because there were times in that Moscow prison when I used to imagine I was with him, when I fantasized that he was holding me and I was safe in his strong embrace.

Lucas walks around the car and opens the back door. Reaching in, he grabs me and drags me out, still not saying a word as he lifts me against his chest and slams the door closed with his foot. His hold on me is again harsh and punishing, and I know it's only the start.

My fantasies are about to shatter under the weight of reality.

He carries me up the porch stairs, walking as easily as if I weigh nothing. His strength is tremendous, only there's no safety in it. Not for me, at least. Maybe for some woman in the future, someone he'll care about and want to protect.

Someone he won't hate as much as he hates me.

As he pushes open the front door and turns sideways to carry me through the doorway, I catch a glimpse of curious faces staring up at us from the street. There are several men and a middle-aged woman, and for one absurd moment, I'm tempted to beg them for help, to plead with them to save me. The urge fades as quickly as it comes. These people aren't some innocent passersby. They're employees of a sadistic arms dealer, and they're fully complicit in whatever fate is about to befall me.

So I stay silent as Lucas carries me into the house and once again shuts the door behind him with his foot. He's not looking at me, so I use the opportunity to study him, noting the granite set of his jaw. He's still furious, the rage radiating off him like heat off a flame. It makes me wonder why he's so mad. Surely this sort of thing—making Esguerra's enemies pay—is routine for him. I would've expected cold detachment, not this volcanic anger.

Come to think of it, I would've expected him to take me to some warehouse or a storage shed, some place they wouldn't mind dirtying with blood and bodily fluids. Instead, I find myself inside a residential home, albeit one with only basic furnishings. One black leather sofa, a flatscreen TV, gray carpet, and white walls—the room he carries me through is not luxurious, but it's certainly no torture chamber. Could this be Lucas's house? And if so, why am I here?

I don't have time to dwell on it for long because he brings me into a large, white-tiled bathroom. There is a massive tub, a glass-walled shower stall, and a sink next to a toilet.

Definitely not a torture chamber.

"Why did you bring me here?" My voice is hoarse, scratchy from disuse. I haven't spoken since Esguerra's men stopped me from screaming back in Moscow. "It's your house, isn't it?"

Lucas's jaw muscle flexes, but he doesn't respond. Instead, he carries me into the shower stall, sets me down on the tiled floor, and pulls out a key. Grabbing my handcuffs, he unlocks them and detaches them from the ankle cuffs, which he unlocks next. Then he yanks me to my feet.

"You need a fucking shower," he says harshly. "Take those clothes off. Now."

My knees buckle, my leg muscles unable to bear the sudden strain of standing, even as my aching back weeps in gratitude at finally being straight again. My head spins from chronic hunger and exhaustion, and it's only Lucas's grip on my arm that prevents me from sinking back down to the floor.

A shower? He wants me to take a shower? Before I can process that odd demand, he lets out an impatient noise and grabs the zipper of my jumpsuit, pulling it down roughly.

"Wait, I can—" I try to reach for the zipper with one trembling hand, but it's too late. Lucas spins me around, flattening my face against the shower wall, and yanks the jumpsuit down to my knees, leaving me wearing nothing more than a pair of loose, high-waisted panties and a stretched-out sports bra—the only underwear allowed at the prison. Within a second, he rips those off me as well and spins me around to face him.

"Don't make me tell you twice." His fingers catch my jaw in a hard grip as he holds my upper arm with his other hand. "You'll do what I say, understand?" His eyes glint with icy rage and something more.

Lust.

He still wants me.

My heart pounds in a furious rhythm as the fact that I'm naked in front of him again sinks in. I should've expected this, but for some reason, I didn't. In my mind, what happened between us before was entirely separate from the punishment he's about to dole out, but I should've known better.

For men like Lucas Kent, violence and sex go hand in hand.

"Do you understand?" he repeats, his fingers digging painfully into my jaw, and I blink affirmatively, the only movement I'm capable of. Apparently, that's enough, because he releases me and steps back.

"Wash yourself," he orders, stepping out of the stall and closing the glass door behind him. "You have five minutes."

And crossing his arms in front of his massive chest, he leans back against the wall and stares at me, waiting.

CHAPTER SEVENTEEN

❖ LUCAS ❖

She reaches for the faucet, her entire body shaking, and I see the effort each movement is costing her. She's weak and thin, infinitely more fragile than the last time I saw her, and the fact that this disturbs me enrages me even more.

I expected to feel lust and hatred, to revel in her suffering even as I slaked my hunger on her deceitful flesh. I planned to treat her like my fucktoy until my obsession with her faded, and then do whatever it took to find the puppet masters pulling her strings.

I didn't count on this pale, bedraggled creature and how seeing her this way would make me feel.

Did they starve her? Apparently so, because I can see each of her ribs. Her stomach is concave, her hipbones are jutting out, and her limbs are painfully skinny. She must've lost at least fifteen pounds in the last two months, and she'd already been slender.

She manages to turn on the water, and I force myself to remain still as she reaches for the shampoo. She's not looking at me, all her attention focused on her task, and I feel a fresh wave of rage, mixed with lust and that disconcerting something.

Something that feels suspiciously like protectiveness.

Fuck. I clench my teeth, determined to resist the bizarre urge to step into the shower and gather her against me. Not to fuck her, though my body is eager to do that as well, but to hold her.

To hold and comfort her.

Infuriated, I shift against the wall, watching as she begins to lather her hair. Despite her extreme thinness, her body is graceful and feminine. Her breasts are smaller than before, but they're still surprisingly full, her nipples drawn into taut pink buds as she stands under the water spray. I can see soft-looking blond fuzz between her legs; after nearly two months of no razor or wax, her pussy must be back to its natural state. My cock, semi-aroused from stripping her naked, hardens fully, and I imagine myself stepping into that shower, unzipping my jeans, and driving into her tight heat with no preliminaries. Just taking her, like the fucktoy I intended her to be.

And there's nothing stopping me from doing that. She's my prisoner. I can do anything I want to her. I've never forced a woman, but I've never wanted and hated one at the same time either. How would fucking her be any worse than slicing up her delicate flesh to make her talk?

It wouldn't be. She's mine to hurt in any way I please.

Except hurting her is not what I want to do right now. The violence seething inside me is not for her. It's for those who hurt her. When I saw her in Diego's grip, her long hair lank and dull around her pale face, I felt a rage unlike any other. And when she began crying, it was all I could do not to cradle her against me and promise that no one will ever hurt her again.

Not even me.

The urge maddened me then, and it maddens me now. I have no doubt the witch knew what she was doing to me with those tears, just as she knew how to extract information out of me that night in Moscow. Her frail appearance is just that: an appearance. That beautiful blond exterior conceals a trained agent, a spy who's as skilled at mind games as she is at foreign languages.

"Your five minutes are up," I say, straightening away from the wall. She's washed her hair and her body, and is now just standing under the water with her eyes closed and her head tilted back. "Get out." My voice is harsh, reflecting none of the turmoil I'm feeling.

I won't let her fuck with me again.

At my words, she jumps, her eyes flying open, and reaches back to turn off the shower. She's still shaking, though not as badly as before, and I wonder how much of that is an act and how much is actual weakness.

Pulling open the shower door, I grab a towel and throw it at her. "Dry yourself."

She obeys, toweling off her hair and then her body. As she does so, I notice bruises covering her legs and ribcage and bluish circles under her weary eyes.

Damn her. She's not faking *that*.

"That's enough." Suppressing the illogical pang of pity, I yank the towel away from her and hang it on a hook. "Let's go."

Her eyes plead with me as I grab her arm, but I ignore their silent entreaty, my hold on her unnecessarily rough. I can't give in to this weakness, to this obsession that seems to be completely out of control. Over the past two months, I've come to terms with the fact that I can't stop wanting her, but this is something else entirely.

She stumbles as I tug her through the doorway, and I stop to pick her up, telling myself that it will be easier to carry her than to drag her. As I swing her up against my chest, I feel the soft press of her breasts and smell her scent, now clean and mixed with the aroma of my body wash. Lust surges through me again, pushing aside my awareness of her too-light weight, and I welcome it. This is exactly what I need: to want her and nothing else. And for that, I can't have her as this frail, pathetic waif.

I need her stronger.

The bedroom was my destination, but I change my course, heading for the kitchen instead. I can feel her breathing fast—she's probably afraid—but she doesn't struggle. She undoubtedly realizes how pointless it would be in her weakened state.

When we reach the kitchen, I set her down in a chair and take a step back. Immediately, she draws her knees up against her chest, concealing much of her naked body. Her eyes are big and scared as she stares at me, her wet hair plastered against her back and shoulders.

"You're going to eat," I tell her, approaching the fridge. Opening it, I take out turkey, cheese, and mayo, and place everything on the counter next to the loaf of bread sitting there. As I make the sandwich, I keep an eye on her, making sure she's not attempting anything—which she's not. She's just sitting there, watching warily as I smear the mayo on both slices of bread, slap on some cheese and turkey, and place everything on a plate.

"Eat," I say, putting the plate in front of her.

She runs her tongue over her lips. "May I have some water, please?"

Of course. She must be thirsty as well. Without answering, I walk over to the sink, pour a glass of water, and bring it to her.

"Thank you." Her voice is quiet as she accepts my offering, her slender fingers wrapping around the glass and brushing against mine in the process. A frisson of electricity races up my spine at that accidental touch, and my jeans become uncomfortably tight again, my cock straining against the zipper.

Her eyes flick down for a second before returning to my face, and I see her pupils dilating. She's aware of my lust for her, and it frightens her. Her hand holding the glass trembles slightly as she drinks, and her other arm tightens around her drawn-up knees.

Good. I want her afraid. I want her to know that I may want her body, but I won't show her mercy. She won't be able to manipulate me ever again.

While she's drinking, I sit down across the table and lean back in the chair, linking my hands behind my head.

"Eat. Now," I order again when she puts down her glass, and she obeys, her straight white teeth sinking into the sandwich with unconcealed eagerness.

Despite her obvious hunger, she eats slowly, thoroughly chewing each bite. It's a smart move; she doesn't want to get sick from eating too much too fast.

"So," I say when she's eaten about a quarter of her meal, "what's your real name?"

She pauses mid-bite and puts down her sandwich. "Yulia." Her eyes hold mine without blinking.

"Don't lie to me." I unlink my hands and lean forward. "A spy wouldn't use her real name."

"I didn't say it's Yulia Tzakova." She picks up the sandwich again and consumes another bite before explaining, "Yulia is a common name in Russia and Ukraine, and it happens to be my birth name. It's the Russian version of Julia."

"Ah." That makes sense, and I'm inclined to believe her. It's always easier to stick close to your real identity when going undercover. "So, Yulia, what is your real last name then?"

"My last name doesn't matter." Her soft lips twist. "The girl it belonged to no longer exists."

"Then there's no harm in telling me what it is, is there?" Despite myself, I'm intrigued. Whether it matters or not, I want to know her last name.

I want to know everything about her.

She shrugs and bites into her sandwich again. I can tell she has no intention of answering me.

My teeth grind together, but I remind myself to be patient. The Russians hadn't been able to get anything useful out of her in two months, so I certainly can't expect to crack her in the first hour. Priority number one is having her eat and regain her strength. Answers will come later. I'll get them out of her, one way or another.

For now, I mentally go through the information Buschekov emailed me on her. There isn't much that they were able to uncover. All she's admitted is that she's twenty-two, not twenty-four as listed in her fake passport, and she was born in Donetsk, one of the embattled areas in eastern Ukraine. The Ukrainian government refused to claim her as one of their own, so the organization she works for must be private or strictly off the books. Her degree in English Language and International Relations from Moscow State University is apparently real; there is a record of Yulia Tzakova graduating from there two years ago, and Buschekov was able to track down professors and classmates who verified that she did, in fact, attend classes.

Did the Ukrainians recruit her at the university, or did they plant her there? It's not out of the question that she's been working for them since her teens. Agents rarely get recruited that young, but it does happen.

"How long have you been doing this?" I ask when she's nearly done with her sandwich. Her pale cheeks have a bit of color in them now, and she looks less shaky. "Spying for Ukraine, that is?"

Instead of answering, Yulia takes a sip of water, puts down her glass, and looks straight at me. "May I use the restroom, please?"

My hands tighten on the table. "Yes—when you answer my question."

She doesn't blink. "I've been doing it for a while," she says evenly. "Now, may I please pee in the toilet? Or should I do it here?"

The rage smoldering within me flares brighter, and I give in to it. In an instant, I'm next to her, grabbing her by her hair and yanking her to her feet. She cries out in pain, her hands clutching at my wrist, but I don't give her a chance to start fighting. In less than two seconds, I have her folded over the table, her arm twisted behind her back and her face pressed against the table surface. The plate with the remnants of the sandwich slides off the table, shattering on the floor, but I don't give a fuck.

She's going to learn an important lesson right now.

"Say that again." I lean over her, trapping her naked body underneath me. I can hear her fast, shallow breathing, feel the curve of her ass pressing into my crotch, and my cock hardens as dark sexual images invade my mind. In this position, all I need to do is open my fly, and I'll be inside her.

The temptation is almost unbearable.

"Since I was eleven." Her voice is thin, muffled against the table. "I've been doing it since I was eleven."

Eleven? Stunned, I release her and step back. What kind of agency recruits a child?

Before I can digest her revelation, she scoots off the table and faces me. "Please, Lucas." Her face is pale again, her lips trembling. "I really need to go to the restroom."

Fuck.

I grab her arm. "You have five minutes," I warn as I march her back to the bathroom. "And do not lock the door. I have the key."

She nods and disappears into the bathroom, her half-dry hair streaming down her slender back.

Shaking my head, I go back to the kitchen to clean up.

I don't want her to cut her bare feet on the shards of the broken plate.

CHAPTER EIGHTEEN

❖ YULIA ❖

My knees shaking, I collapse against the closed bathroom door and try to calm my frantic breathing. What nearly happened in that kitchen shouldn't have freaked me out so much, but it was too close to before . . . too close to that dark place I've fought so hard to escape. The position—on my stomach and helpless, with a man who's determined to punish me on top—had been all too familiar, and I panicked.

I panicked like that fifteen-year-old I thought I'd buried.

Perhaps it wouldn't have been so bad if it had been someone else—anyone else. I could've put up that steel mental wall, the one that kept me sane before. If fear and disgust were all I felt for Lucas, it would've been easier.

If I hadn't had those stupid fantasies about him in prison, it would've been less devastating.

Taking deep breaths, I force myself to straighten away from the door and use the toilet. I have only a couple of minutes before Lucas returns for me, and I can't afford to waste them this way. As I wash my hands and brush my teeth, I stare in the mirror, trying to convince myself that I can do this—that I can withstand whatever punishment he chooses to dole out, even if it's of a sexual variety.

"Your time's up." His deep voice startles me, and I realize I've been just standing there, letting the water run. "Come out."

Panic floods my veins. "Just a second," I call out.

I'm not ready for this. I'm not ready for *him*. For the first time in weeks, I've eaten a normal meal and had a shower, and somehow that makes it worse. Because now that I feel semi-human, I'm keenly aware of my nakedness and how much I am at the mercy of a man who wants to hurt me.

My heart pounding, I scan the bathroom. Lucas wouldn't be stupid enough to leave a weapon lying around, but I don't need much. My gaze falls on the plastic toothbrush I just used, and I grab it. Using both hands, I snap the handle in half. As I'd hoped, one side ends up sharp and jagged, and I clutch it tightly, concealing it in my right hand.

Taking another deep breath, I open the door and step out. "All done," I say, hoping he can't hear the strain in my voice.

"Let's go." Lucas grabs my left arm, and I stumble, on purpose this time. He turns to steady me, and in that moment I strike upward with my makeshift weapon, aiming for his kidney. I shut off the part of my brain that cringes at the thought of hurting him, the part where those fantasies still live, and I let my training take over.

He twists at the last moment, his reflexes razor sharp, and I graze his torso instead of stabbing him. The broken toothbrush catches on his shirt, forcing me to let go of it, but I don't let that stop me. He's still holding my arm, so I drop to the floor, letting my full weight hang on that arm, and kick up with my right leg. My foot connects with his jaw, the impact sending a shock of pain through me, but he reels back—which gives me the split second I need to twist free of his hold.

Scrambling to my feet, I sprint for the kitchen, desperate to grab a knife, but before I can take more than two steps, he tackles me from behind. I manage to turn, half-rolling as we land on the carpet, and my elbow slams into his hard stomach. The impact makes my arm go numb. He continues rolling without so much as a grunt, and a moment later has me pinned down, his hands capturing both of my wrists and lifting them above my head at the same time as his powerful legs anchor mine to the floor.

I can't move. I'm once again helpless underneath him.

Breathing hard, I stare up at him, my insides squeezing with dread as I wait for his retaliation. Our fight aroused him; I can feel the hard bulge in his jeans against my naked stomach. Or maybe he's still hard from earlier.

Either way, I know how he's going to punish me.

He's also breathing heavily, his chest rising and falling above me. I can see the rage burning in his pale eyes—rage and something far more primal.

To my shock, a tiny tendril of heat snakes through me, my mind transposing the horror of my current predicament with the stunning pleasure of that night. I lay underneath him then, too, and my body doesn't seem to understand that it was different.

That the man on top of me doesn't only want my body.

He wants revenge.

He lowers his head, and I freeze, scarcely breathing as his lips brush my left ear. "You shouldn't have done that," he whispers, the damp heat of his breath burning my skin. "I was going to give you more time, let you get stronger, but no more . . ." His mouth presses against my neck, and I feel his tongue flicking over the delicate area, as though tasting it. "You've used up all my patience, beautiful."

I shudder, trying to arch away from that hot, wicked mouth, but I have nowhere to go. He's all around me, his muscular body large and heavy on top of mine. The brief burst of energy I felt after my meal is gone, my strength nonexistent after weeks of deprivation. Exhausted, I stop struggling—and realize that the tendril of heat is expanding in my core, making me slick with unwelcome need.

"Lucas, please." I don't know why I'm begging. I just tried to wound him; he won't show me mercy ever again. "Please, don't do this." My body's irrational response should've made this easier to bear, but it just highlights my helplessness, my complete lack of control. I can't face this with him. It would destroy me. "Please, Lucas . . ."

He shifts on top of me, his mouth still hovering near my ear. "Don't do what?" he murmurs, transferring both of my wrists into one of his large palms. Moving his free hand, he wedges it between us, his fingers slipping between my thighs to find my sex. "This?" His thumb presses on my clit as his index finger penetrates me.

I jerk at the invasion, the heat inside morphing into a pulsing ache. My nipples tighten, and I feel myself getting even slicker, my body eager for an act that would leave my soul in pieces. "Don't. Please don't." Tears, stupid, pathetic tears, come, and I can't contain them. They spill out and roll down my temples, making me burn with embarrassment at my weakness. "No, please . . ." His finger advances deeper into me, and the old memories crowd in, taking me back to that dark, suffocating place. My breathing turns into frantic pants, my voice rising in pitch. "Please, Lucas, don't!"

To my surprise, he stills, and then with a curse, he rolls off me, rising fluidly to his feet. "Get up," he snarls, grabbing my arms to pull me up. As soon as I'm vertical, he drags me into the living room and pushes me onto the couch, gritting out, "If you move a muscle . . ."

Dazed, I watch as he disappears around the corner and reappears a moment later carrying a chair and a coil of rope. He places both in the middle of the room. I haven't moved—I'm shaking too hard for that—and I don't put up any resistance as he picks me up, deposits me into the chair, and binds my arms behind my back, securing them against the chair's sturdy wooden frame. Then he uses additional rope to tie my ankles to the legs of the chair, leaving them spread apart.

When he's done, he stands up and stares at me. The bulge in his jeans is still present, but the heat in his eyes has cooled, turning them into familiar slivers of ice.

"I'll be back in a few minutes," he says harshly. "When I return, you better be ready to talk."

And before I can respond, he strides out of the room, leaving me tied up, naked, and alone.

CHAPTER NINETEEN

❖ LUCAS ❖

I enter the bathroom and close the door in a controlled motion, making sure it doesn't slam too hard. Control—that's what I need right now.

Control and distance from *her*.

My cock is like a spike in my jeans, my balls so full I feel like I could blow any second. I've never come so close to fucking a woman and then stopped.

I've never denied myself something I wanted so badly.

She had been right there, stretched out underneath me, her long, slender body naked and vulnerable. I could've fucked her any way I chose, taking my rage out on her delicate flesh while slaking the hunger plaguing me for so long.

Instead, I let her go.

Son of a fucking bitch.

I stare in the mirror, seeing the fury and frustration on my face. She wanted me—I felt how wet she was, how her body was responding to me—and I still let her go.

Despite my body's burning need, I couldn't bring myself to rape her.

Disgusted with my weakness, I look away, running my hand over my short hair. Rape is no worse than the crimes I've committed in recent years. In Esguerra's service, I've killed and tortured both men and women, and I've felt no qualms. Taking Yulia should've been the easiest thing in the world—I've dreamed of fucking her every night over the last two months—yet I stopped myself.

I stopped myself because the terror in her voice had been real, and I couldn't ignore it.

Gritting my teeth, I lift my shirt and examine my ribcage. There's no blood where Yulia's weapon grazed me, but there is an angry red scratch. She had probably been aiming for my kidney. If I hadn't been fast enough, I would be bleeding out in hellish pain on that floor—assuming she didn't slit my throat immediately. As it is, my jaw throbs where her foot struck me, reminding me how treacherous—and dangerous—she is.

It would've been smarter to leave her with the Russians.

No. As soon as the thought crosses my mind, my entire body tenses in rejection. Now that I finally have her in my possession, the idea of someone else tormenting her is unbearable. Everything inside me screams that she's mine—mine to fuck, mine to punish in any way I choose.

Nobody else will lay hands on her ever again.

Unzipping my jeans, I pull out my engorged cock and close my fist around it. Squeezing my eyes shut, I imagine that I'm inside her and it's her inner walls gripping my dick so tightly.

With the pornographic images filling my mind, it takes less than a minute for me to come, my seed spurting into the clean white bowl of the sink.

CHAPTER TWENTY

❖ YULIA ❖

I don't know how long it takes me to realize that the reprieve is real, but eventually I calm down enough to stop shaking.

He didn't go through with it.

He didn't force me.

I still can't believe it. I know how hard he was—I felt it. There was no reason for him to show me mercy. I'm not some woman he picked up in a bar; I'm the enemy who just tried to injure him. He should've gloried in my pathetic begging and used the weakness I revealed to break me completely.

That's what I would've expected him to do, at least.

Lowering my head, I stare at my naked legs, trying to understand why he stopped. Lucas Kent is not a novice to this life—far from it. According to his file, he joined the United States Navy right after high school and entered the SEAL training program several months later. There wasn't much in that file on his assignments—only that they were usually classified and extremely dangerous missions—but the reason for him leaving was listed.

It was a murder charge eight years into his service. The man holding me captive killed his commanding officer and disappeared into the jungles of South America. There's a four-year gap in the file after that, but eventually, Lucas Kent resurfaced as Esguerra's trusted and extremely deadly second-in-command.

A tingle runs down my arms, and some sixth sense makes me look up.

Two pairs of dark eyes are watching me from the window, one huge and fringed by thick lashes, and the other slightly almond-shaped.

It's two young women, I realize as the owner of the thick lashes ducks out of sight, leaving me staring at the braver intruder. The remaining girl is about my age and looks Colombian, her bronzed, round face framed by smooth dark hair. She's pretty—and extremely curious about me, judging by her arrested stare.

I don't have time to register more because a second later, she ducks and disappears too.

Confused, I continue staring at the window, waiting, but they don't return. Instead, I hear footsteps and turn my head to see Lucas entering the room with another chair.

Placing it in front of me, he sits down on it and crosses his arms in front of his chest. "All right, Yulia." His gaze is hard as it travels down my naked body and then returns to my face. "Why don't you begin by telling me your story."

My reprieve is over.

Trying to remain calm, I moisten my lips. "May I please have some water?" I'm thirsty—and desperate to put off the interrogation for as long as possible.

He doesn't move. "Talk and I'll give it to you."

I swallow, noting the implacable set of his jaw. "What do you want to know?" Perhaps there are some basics I can share with him, just like I shared with the Russians. I can admit to being a spy for the Ukrainians—he already knows that much—and I can give him a little bit of my background.

Maybe that information will buy me some time without pain.

"You said you started at eleven." He watches me coldly, without so much as a hint of the lust that burned between us. "Tell me about them—the people who recruited you."

So much for hoping I can stall him with innocuous revelations.

"I don't know much about them," I say. "They would send me on assignments; that's all."

His eyes narrow. He knows I'm lying. "Is that right?" His voice is deceptively soft. "And was enrolling in Moscow State University an assignment?"

"It was." There's no point in denying it. "They falsified my documents and enrolled me in the university so I could live in Moscow and get close to key people in the Russian government."

"Get close how?" He leans forward, and I see something dark flash in his pale eyes. "How exactly did they want you to carry out your assignment, beautiful?"

I don't answer, but I can see that he knows. How else does a young woman insinuate herself into top government circles?

"How many?" Lucas's voice is sharp enough to slice me into pieces. "How many did you have to fuck to 'get close'?"

"Three." Two lower-level officials and one of Buschekov's friends—which is how I got the job as Buschekov's interpreter. "I had to sleep with three of them." I stare directly at Lucas, ignoring the ball of shame lodged deep in my chest. "Esguerra would've been the fourth, but I ended up with you instead."

His eyes narrow further, and my pulse spikes with cold fear. I don't know why I'm taunting him like this. Getting Lucas angry is a bad idea. I need to be pacifying him, buying myself more time. It doesn't matter that the contempt on his face is like a knife stabbing into my liver.

An actual knife would be much, much worse.

He stands up abruptly, looming over me, and I try not to flinch as I tilt my head back to meet his gaze. His eyes glint at me, rage flickering in their blue-gray depths again. For a moment, I'm convinced he's going to hit me, but he grips a fistful of my hair instead, forcing my head to arch back more.

"Did you want them?" His fingers tighten in my hair, making my eyes sting at the pain in my scalp. "Did your pussy cream for them too?"

"No." I'm telling the truth, but I can see that he doesn't believe me. "It wasn't like that with them. It was just something I had to do." I don't know why I'm trying to convince him. I don't want him to know that he was in any way special, but at the same time, I can't bring myself to lie about this. "It was my job."

"Just like I was your job." He stares down at me, and I catch a glimpse of the dark lust lurking underneath his anger. "You gave me your body to get information."

I don't deny it, and I see his chest expanding as he draws in a breath. I brace myself for hurtful words of condemnation, but they never come. Instead, his painful hold on my hair eases a fraction, as though he realizes my neck can't stay bent like that.

"Yulia . . ." There is a strange note in his voice. "How old were you when you slept with the first one of the three?"

I blink, caught off-guard by the question. "Sixteen."

Or at least that was when our relationship began. Boris Ladrikov, a short, slightly balding member of the State Duma, had been my first boyfriend, and our affair lasted for the better part of three years. He introduced me to all the important people, including Vladimir, who had become my next assigned lover.

"Sixteen?" Lucas repeats, and I notice a muscle ticking near his ear. He's furious, and I have no idea why. "How old was your target?"

"Thirty-eight." I don't know why Lucas is asking all these irrelevant questions, but I'm happy to answer them for as long as it keeps him away from more important topics. "He thought I was eighteen; the identity I assumed was two years older."

I expect Lucas to drill me on this some more, but to my surprise, he releases my hair and steps back.

"That's enough for now," he says, and I catch that odd note in his voice again. "We'll resume this in a bit."

Without saying another word, he turns and leaves the room. A minute later, I hear the front door open and close, and I know I'm alone again.

CHAPTER TWENTY-ONE

❖ LUCAS ❖

A child. She had been a fucking child when they planted her in Moscow and forced her to sleep with sleazy government assholes.

The rage blasting through me feels hot enough to incinerate my insides. It had taken every ounce of my self-control to conceal my reaction from Yulia. If I hadn't left the house when I did, I would've put my fist through a wall.

The impulse is still with me an hour later, so I hammer the sandbag in front of me, channeling my fury into each blow. I can see the other men giving me inquiring looks; I've been at it for the past forty minutes without so much as a water break.

"Lucas, you crazy gringo, what's gotten into you?" A man's voice breaks my concentration, and I spin around to see Diego standing there. The tall Mexican is grinning, his teeth flashing white in his bronzed face. "Shouldn't you be saving some of that energy for your prisoner?"

"Fuck you, pendejo." Annoyed at the interruption, I grab the water bottle off the floor and take a swig. I normally like Diego, but right now I'm tempted to use him as my punching bag. "My prisoner is none of your fucking business."

"I helped deliver her here, so she's kind of my business," he objects, but the grin leaves his face. He can tell I'm in a mood. "She's the bitch who caused that crash, right?"

I wipe the dripping sweat off my forehead. "What makes you say that?" I'd been under the impression that only Esguerra, Peter, and I knew of Yulia's involvement.

Diego shrugs. "We got her from a Russian prison, and everyone knows the Ukrainians were behind it. It just seemed to fit. Plus, it seemed kind of personal for you, so . . ." His voice trails off as I give him a hard look.

"Like I said, she's none of your fucking business," I say coldly. The last thing I want is to discuss Yulia with the other men. What should've been the easiest thing in the world—revenge—has turned into a mess of epic proportions. The girl tied to the chair in my living room is not what I thought she was, and I have no fucking clue what to do about that.

"Yeah, okay, no worries." Diego grins again. "Just tell me: did you fuck her already? Even with the prison smell, I could tell she's a hot piece—"

My fist slams into his face before he finishes speaking. It's not a conscious action on my part; the fury filling me is simply too explosive to contain. He stumbles back from the force of my blow, and I follow, leaping and tackling him to the ground. My leg protests the sudden movement, but I ignore the pain, raining blow after blow on Diego's shocked face.

"Kent, what the fuck?" Steely hands grab my arms and drag me off my victim, resisting my attempts to throw them off. "Calm down, man!"

"What's going on here?" Esguerra's voice is like a splash of icy water on the flames of my rage. As my mind clears, I realize that Thomas and Eduardo are holding my arms while our boss is standing a dozen feet away, at the entrance of the training gym.

"Just a little disagreement." I manage to keep my voice steady despite the bloodlust still surging through me. Seeing that I'm no longer fighting them, Thomas and Eduardo release me and step back, their expressions carefully neutral.

Knowing I need to say something, I turn to the guard I assaulted. "Sorry, Diego. You caught me at a bad time."

"Yeah, no kidding," he mutters, getting to his feet with some effort. His nose is bleeding, and his left eye is already swelling up. "I've got to put some ice on this."

He hurries out of the gym, and Esguerra gives me a questioning look.

I shrug, as though the problem is too minor to explain, and to my relief, Esguerra doesn't pursue it. Instead, he informs me about a call with our Hong Kong supplier later this evening—he thinks it's a good idea for me to be present—and then heads back to his office, leaving me to shoot beer cans with the guards and try not to think about my captive.

CHAPTER TWENTY-TWO

❖ YULIA ❖

I don't know how long I sit there, trying to find a comfortable position on the hard chair, but eventually, a quiet rapping on the window draws my attention. Startled, I look up and see the girl who was watching me before—the one with the rounded face. She's standing outside, her nose pressed to the glass as she stares at me. I don't see her friend, so she must've come alone this time.

"Hello?" I call out, unsure whether she speaks English or would even be able to hear me through the glass. "Who are you?"

She hesitates for a second, then asks, "Where's Lucas?" Her voice is barely audible through the window, but I can tell that her English is of the American variety, with only a trace of a Spanish accent.

"I don't know. He left a little while ago," I say, studying her as thoroughly as she's studying me. It's not a fair exchange; all I see of her is her head, while she's looking at me in my birthday suit. Still, I note her regular features and full lips, filing the information away in my mind in case I need it later.

Who is she? Could she be Lucas's girlfriend? There was no mention of significant others in his file, but Obenko wouldn't know about Lucas's relationships on this estate. For all I know, my captor could have a wife and three kids here. A pretty young girlfriend is a no-brainer; Lucas is a virile, highly sexual man who'd have no trouble attracting women, even in a place as remote as this compound.

The more I consider it, the more it makes sense to me. This, right here, is why he didn't fuck me earlier.

It wasn't because of my pleas—it was because he didn't want to be unfaithful.

"What do you want?" I ask the girl, trying to ignore the irrational sense of betrayal at this realization. She doesn't seem disturbed at seeing me naked and tied up, so she obviously knows what her boyfriend is up to. "Why are you here?"

She opens her mouth as though to respond, but ducks out of sight instead. A moment later, I hear the front door opening and realize why.

Lucas is back.

A hum of awareness flutters through me as I hear his footsteps. He enters the room, stopping directly in front of me, and I see that his tan skin is glowing with perspiration. His sleeveless shirt is plastered against his muscular chest, a V of sweat visible in the middle. He looks powerfully, uncompromisingly male, and as I meet his icy gaze, I become cognizant of a heated ache between my legs.

As unbelievable as it is, I want him.

With effort, I tear my eyes away from his face, afraid he'll realize what I'm feeling. Nothing about my interactions with him makes sense. I just realized he has a girlfriend, and even if he didn't, how can I want a man I fear? And why hasn't he hurt me yet?

My gaze falls on his knuckles, and I tense as I see bruises there.

He just beat someone up.

I want to ask him about it, but I stay silent and look down at my knees. He's still angry—I can sense it— and I don't want to provoke him. I also don't bring up the girlfriend, though I'm dying to confront him about it. For some reason, the dark-haired girl didn't want him to know she was spying on me, and I don't want to sell her out for now.

I need whatever tiny advantage I can get.

"Are you hungry?" Lucas asks, and I look up, surprised by the question.

"I could eat," I say cautiously. I'm actually starving, my body demanding sustenance after weeks of nonstop hunger, but I don't want him to use that against me. I also really have to pee—a fact I've been trying not to focus on too much.

He stares at me, then nods, as though coming to a decision. Turning, he disappears down the hallway to the bathroom, and then I hear water running. Is he taking a shower?

Three minutes later, he reappears, dressed in a pair of black cotton shorts and a fresh T-shirt. His muscular neck is gleaming with droplets of water, and he smells like the body wash I used earlier, confirming my guess about the shower.

Crouching in front of me, he deftly unties my ankles and then walks around to untie my arms. "Let's go," he says, grabbing my elbow to pull me to my feet. "You can use the bathroom, and then I'll feed you."

He leads me to the bathroom, and I walk alongside him, too shocked to think about another escape attempt. "Go on," he says, giving me a push when we get to the bathroom, and I step inside, deciding not to question my good fortune.

As I wash my hands, I see a new, unbroken toothbrush sitting on the counter. For a second, I'm tempted to repeat my earlier stunt, but I decide against it. If I couldn't get him with the element of surprise, I certainly won't be able to overpower him now that he's aware of my capabilities.

Besides, he said he would feed me, and my stomach is doing cartwheels at the mere thought of food.

"Hands," Lucas says, grabbing my wrists as soon as I step out of the bathroom, and I open my palms, showing him that they're empty. He gives me an approving nod. "Good girl."

I raise my eyebrows at his odd behavior, but he's already leading me to the kitchen.

"Sit," he says, pointing at a chair, and I obey, watching as he takes out the same ingredients he used at lunch and begins making two sandwiches. As he works, I quickly scan the kitchen, trying to locate anything that could be used as a weapon. To my disappointment, I don't see a rack of knives or anything along those lines. The countertops are empty and clean, with the exception of the sandwich makings. He's not wearing a gun either; he must have all his weapons stashed somewhere else, like in his car.

"Here," he says, putting a plate in front of me, and I notice that it's paper, not ceramic like the one that broke earlier. The knife that he used to spread the mayo is plastic too. He's being cautious around me now. I have no doubt that if I searched through the drawers, I'd find something, but Lucas would be on me before I so much as opened a drawer.

My hands may be untied, but escape is as impossible as ever.

I run my tongue over my dry lips. "May I please have—"

"Water? Here you go." He pours water from the sink into a paper cup, places it in front of me, and sits down across the table with his own sandwich.

I have a million questions for him, but I make myself drink my water and eat most of my sandwich before I give in to the impulse. The last thing I want is to upset him and lose out on this meal.

Finally, I can't wait any longer. "Why are you doing this?" I ask as he finishes his food. My stomach is full to the point of bursting, and I can feel myself getting stronger as my body absorbs the calories. "What do you want from me?"

Lucas looks up, his features taut, and I realize he was just staring at my breasts—which are visible through my long hair. Heat climbs up my neck, and my nipples tighten, responding to the unconcealed desire in his eyes. I've been naked in front of him all day, and I'm getting desensitized to it, but that doesn't mean the situation isn't intensely sexual. As I hold his gaze, it dawns on me that part of the reason for his silence during dinner must've been the distraction of my unclothed body.

He still wants me, and I don't know if the knowledge terrifies or excites me.

"Tell me about them," he says abruptly. "Tell me about the people who recruited you, who made you do this."

And here it is: the true reason he's being nice to me. He's playing good cop to the Russians' bad one, the savior to their villain. It's so close to my fantasies that I want to cry. Except he's not interested in saving me; he wants to get answers—answers that I can't and won't give.

"What happened that day?" I ask instead. This question has been plaguing me ever since I learned that he and Esguerra are alive. "How did you survive?"

Lucas's jaw hardens, and the desire in his gaze fades. "You mean with the plane crash?"

"So there *was* a plane crash?" I hadn't been sure, though I figured his desire to make me pay meant that *something* had happened.

Lucas leans forward, his hands crushing his empty paper plate. "Yes, there was a crash. Didn't your superiors keep you informed?"

I fight the urge to flinch at the renewed fury in his voice. "They did, but I thought they might've had wrong information."

"Because we survived."

I nod, holding my breath.

He stares at me for a second, then stands up and walks around the table. "Let's go," he says, grabbing my arm again. "We're done here."

And dragging me back to the living room, he ties me up in the chair and leaves again, the front door slamming loudly behind him.

CHAPTER TWENTY-THREE

❖ LUCAS ❖

As Esguerra discusses the latest transportation concerns with our Hong Kong supplier, I sit silently, my attention only partially on the video call. I don't understand how one young woman can tie me into knots like this. One minute I want to take care of her, get her strong and healthy, and the next I'm torn between fucking her and killing her on the spot.

A child prostitute.

That's essentially what they made her. They took her at eleven, trained her, and set her loose in Moscow at sixteen with instructions to get close to the highest circles of Russian government.

Just thinking about it makes me sick. I don't know what infuriates me more: that they did this to her, or that she was involved in the plane crash that killed forty-five of our men and left three more burned beyond recognition.

How is it possible to hate someone and want to avenge the wrongs done to her at the same time?

"Thank you for your time, Mr. Chen," Esguerra says, uncharacteristically polite, and I see the wizened old man on the screen nodding as he parrots back the words. It's important to observe the niceties in that part of the world, even when dealing with criminals.

As soon as Esguerra disconnects, I get up, impatient to get back to Yulia. "I'll see you tomorrow," I say, and he nods, still working on his computer.

"See you," he says as I walk out.

It's dark when I step outside—dark, warm, and humid. Esguerra's office is a small building near the main house, which is a bit of a hike from the guards' quarters, where I reside. I could've driven here, but I enjoy walking, and after sitting still for two hours, I'm eager to stretch my legs and clear my mind.

Before I take a dozen steps, I hear a woman calling my name and turn to see Esguerra's maid, Rosa, hurrying across the wide lawn. She's holding what looks like a covered pot against her chest.

"Lucas, wait!" She sounds out of breath.

I stop, curious to find out what she wants. I vaguely recall Eduardo talking about her. He might've been dating her at the time. From what he said, she was born on this estate; her parents worked for Juan Esguerra, my boss's father. I've seen her around and exchanged greetings with her a number of times, but I've never really spoken to the girl.

"Here," she says, stopping in front of me and handing me the pot. "Ana wanted you to have this."

"She did?" Surprised, I take the heavy offering. The aroma seeping through the lid is rich and savory, making my mouth water. "Why?"

Esguerra's housekeeper occasionally sends some cookies or extra fruit to the guards, but this is the first time she's singled me out like this.

"I don't know." For some reason, Rosa's rounded cheeks turn pink. "I think she just made some extra soup, and Nora and the Señor didn't want it."

"I see." I don't see, but I'm not about to argue with what smells like a delicious meal. "Well, I'll gladly eat it if they don't want it."

"They don't. It's for you." She gives me a hesitant smile. "I hope you like it."

"I'm sure I will," I say, studying the maid. She's pretty, with lush curves and sparkling brown eyes, and as I watch her flush deepen under my gaze, it dawns on me that the middle-aged housekeeper might not have been the one behind this.

Rosa's interested in me. I'm suddenly sure of that.

Doing my best to conceal my discomfort, I wish her a good night and turn away. A couple of months ago, I would've been flattered and gladly accepted the invitation evident in the girl's shy smile. Now, however, all I can think about is the long-legged blonde waiting for me at home and the dirty, savage things I want to do to her.

"Bye," Rosa calls out as I resume walking, and I give her a neutral smile over my shoulder.

"Thanks for the soup," I say, but she's already hurrying back to the house, her maid's black dress billowing around her like a shroud.

* * *

As soon as I get home, I put the pot in the refrigerator and then go to the living room. I find my prisoner exactly where I left her: tied up in the chair in the middle of the room. Yulia's head is lowered, her long blond hair veiling most of her upper body. She doesn't move as I approach, and I realize she must've fallen asleep.

Crouching in front of her, I begin untying her ankles, trying to ignore my reaction to her nearness. With her legs bound apart, I can see the tender folds between her thighs, and I recall with sudden vividness how her pussy tasted—and felt around my cock.

Fuck.

I look down at my hands, determined to focus on my task. It doesn't help. As my fingers brush over her silky skin, I notice that her feet are long and slender, like the rest of her. Despite her height, her build is delicate, her ankles so narrow I can encircle each one with my thumb and index finger.

It would take no effort at all to break those fragile bones. The thought cuts through my haze of lust, and I seize upon it, welcoming the distraction. That's what I need: to think of her as an enemy, not as a desirable woman. And as an enemy, she'd be easy to torment. With just a bit of pressure, I could snap her feet in half. I know, because I've done it. A couple of years ago, a Thai missile manufacturer double-crossed us, and we retaliated by killing his entire family. The man's wife tried to hide her husband and teenage sons, but we tortured their location out of her, breaking every bone in her legs in the process.

We haven't had trouble in Thailand since.

That's what I should do with Yulia: hurt her, make her reveal her secrets, and then kill her. That's what Esguerra expects me to do.

That's what I'd planned to do after I had my fill of her.

Her leg twitches, tensing in my grasp, and I look up to find Yulia awake, her blue eyes locked on my face.

"You're back," she says quietly, and I nod, rendered mute by a brutal spike of renewed lust. My cock, already semi-stiff, turns into an iron rod in my shorts, and I realize that my right hand is sliding up her inner calf, as though of its own accord. Higher, higher . . . I can feel her tensing even more, sense her breathing changing as her pupils expand, and I know she's scared.

Scared and maybe something else, judging by the color creeping up her face.

Unable to resist the dark compulsion, I let my hand continue on its journey, my fingers trailing over the pale curve of her knee and the softness of her inner thigh. Her leg muscles are so tightly bunched they vibrate under my touch, and under the veil of her hair, her nipples harden, drawing into taut pink buds.

Her throat works as she swallows. "Lucas—"

I don't hear what she's about to say because at that moment, my phone buzzes loudly in my pocket.

Son of a bitch.

Livid with frustration, I yank my hand away from Yulia's thigh and pull out my phone. Glancing down, I see a message from Diego.

Potential problem at North Tower One.

I want to throw the phone against the wall, but I resist the urge. Instead, I get up and walk to my office, so Yulia wouldn't overhear me.

Taking a breath to calm myself, I call Diego.

"What is it?" I bark as soon as he picks up. "What's so important?"

"We detained a trespasser near the north border. He says he's a fisherman, but I'm not so sure."

I tamp down my anger. Diego did well to alert me, even if his interruption came at a shitty time. "All right. I'll be there in fifteen minutes."

I return to the living room and swiftly untie Yulia, doing my best to ignore my raging erection. "Do you need the bathroom?" I ask, pulling her to her feet, and she nods, looking bewildered.

"Let's go then." I drag her down the hallway and practically shove her into the restroom. "Be quick about it."

She comes out five minutes later, her face freshly washed and her breath smelling like toothpaste. I check her hands to make sure they're empty, and then I lead her to the bedroom. Keeping a careful eye on her, I grab a blanket and throw it on the floor near the foot of the bed. Then I reach into the nightstand drawer, take out a coil of rope I'd prepared earlier, and tell Yulia, "Get down on the blanket."

She freezes, and I see her staring at the rope I'm holding.

"Get down," I repeat, reaching for her. "On the blanket. Now."

She tenses as I pull her toward the blanket, and for a second, I'm sure she's going to try to fight me. Instead, she complies stiffly, folding her long legs underneath her.

"Lie down." I release her arm to press down on her shoulder. My dick throbs at the feel of her soft skin, and I have to inhale deeply to fight the urge to take her before I go. With the way I'm feeling, I wouldn't need more than a couple of minutes to blow my load, and the temptation to spread open her legs and fuck her is all but impossible to resist. If I didn't want more than a rough quickie, I would already be inside her.

"Lucas." Her lips tremble as she looks up at me. "Please, I—"

"Lie the fuck down. Now," I bark, losing my patience. If I have to force her down, I *will* take her.

Her face pale, Yulia obeys, stretching out on the blanket. As soon as she's horizontal, I kneel beside her, grab her wrists, and raise them above her head. Careful not to cut off her circulation, I wrap the rope tightly around her wrists and tie the other end of it on the leg of the bed. Then I repeat the maneuver with her ankles and the other leg of the bed, ignoring her stiffness. The end result is her stretched out on her side on the blanket, ankles and wrists tied to the opposite sides of the bed.

Getting up, I view my handiwork. With the bed as heavy as it is, Yulia is even more securely tied than she was in the chair—and she's in a better position to sleep if the trespasser situation takes longer than I expect.

Before I leave, I take a pillow and bend down to stuff it under her head. Her hair is all over her face, so I brush the silky blond strands away, trying to ignore the lust pounding through me. She stares up at me, her eyes like deep blue pools, and I almost groan when her tongue flicks out to wet her lips.

"I'll be back soon," I say, forcing myself to straighten and step away from her.

And before I can change my mind about the quickie, I exit the room and head over to North Tower One.

CHAPTER TWENTY-FOUR

❖ YULIA ❖

My pulse racing, I hold my breath as I listen to the sound of Lucas's departing footsteps. He'll be back soon, he said. Does that mean he went to take a shower, or did he leave to go somewhere? No matter how much I strain, I can't hear the front door opening, but that doesn't mean anything. The bedroom is probably too far away from the entrance.

After a few more minutes of silence, I shift on the blanket, trying to ease the strain in my shoulders. With my hands tied to one leg of the bed and my ankles to the other, I can't move more than a couple of centimeters in any direction, and the stretched-out position is only a shade more comfortable than sitting in the chair.

Growing frustrated, I test my bonds. As expected, there's no give in them, and the wooden king-sized bed is so heavy it might as well be welded to the floor. Every pull on the rope makes it cut into my skin, so I stop tugging on it.

Inhaling slowly, I try to relax, but I'm too anxious.

Where is Lucas? Why did he leave me here like this? When he got the rope and told me to get down on the blanket, I was sure he was going to force me, girlfriend or no girlfriend. I could see his erection, feel the intense hunger in his touch, and it was only the knowledge that it would be infinitely worse if I fought that made me comply with his orders.

If I did as he demanded, I hoped he wouldn't be as rough.

Except he didn't touch me. He just tied me to the bed and left me lying here on the blanket. He even gave me a pillow, as though my comfort matters to him.

As though I'm not someone he ultimately plans to kill.

Another few minutes tick by with no sign of Lucas, and I decide that he did leave the house after all. It must be because of that text message he got. Is it work-related or personal? Does it have something to do with that mysterious girlfriend of his? She knows I'm here. She's seen me sitting in his house naked. Could she have called Lucas to her because she suspects something's going on between us? Because she doesn't want her boyfriend toying with his captive like this?

Irrationally, the thought makes my insides twist. I don't know why I care that Lucas has a girlfriend. We're not in a relationship, at least not in a romantic sense. He brought me here to torment me, to make me pay for what I've done. If anyone has a claim on him, it would be that girl, not me.

I'm the other woman—the one he may want, but will never love.

Closing my eyes, I try to relax again. Exhaustion presses down on me like a layer of bricks, but for some reason, sleep refuses to come. The draft from the air-conditioning is cold on my bare skin, and my shoulders ache from having my arms extended up like that. As ridiculous as it is, a small part of me wishes that Lucas were here—that I were even now lying in his hard embrace.

The fantasy is so alluring that I give into it, like I did in that prison. In my dream, none of this is real. Lucas doesn't hate me. There was no plane crash, and we're not on opposing sides. He's just holding me, kissing me . . . making love to me.

In my dream, he's mine and I'm his—and there's nothing keeping us apart.

CHAPTER TWENTY-FIVE

❖ LUCAS ❖

By the time I get to the guard tower, Diego and the others have strung up the trespasser in a small shed nearby. It's pitch-black outside, and there's no electricity in the shed, so I bring a battery-operated lantern with me to inspect the intruder.

As I shine the light on him, I see that he's an average-looking Colombian man, likely in his early thirties. His clothes look cheap and rather dirty—though that could be from struggling with our guards. He's also gagged, likely to prevent him from annoying the guards with his pleading.

I step back and turn to Diego. The young Mexican is sporting a mean black eye—a reminder of my earlier outburst over Yulia. For a moment, I consider apologizing more sincerely, but decide that now's not the time. "Where did you find him?" I ask instead.

"He was by the river," Diego says, keeping his tone low. "He had a boat, and he claims he was fishing."

"But you don't believe him."

"No." Diego glances at the guy. "His boat doesn't have a scratch on it. It's brand new."

"I see." Diego's right to be suspicious. Few fishermen around these parts can afford a new boat. "All right. Ungag him, and let's see what he says."

* * *

It's two in the morning by the time the trespasser finally breaks. I don't enjoy torture as much as Esguerra does, so I let the guards have a go at the guy first. They pummel him, breaking a few ribs, and then I ask him what he's doing here. He tries to lie, claiming he came to the estate by accident, but after I do a few rounds with my switchblade, he begins to sing and tells us all about his employer, a powerful drug lord from Bogotá.

"Do these *cabrons* never learn?" Diego says in disgust when the man's speech devolves into sobbing pleas for mercy. "You'd think they'd know better than to try this shit. Sending this joker to find holes in our security—could they be any stupider?"

"They could." I step toward the blubbering man and slice my knife across his throat, putting him out of his misery. "They could try attacking us here."

"True." Diego steps back to avoid the spray of blood. "Do you want his body shipped to his *patrón* or taken to the incinerator?"

"The incinerator." I wipe the switchblade on my shirt—it's so bloody that an extra stain is nothing— and close the knife before putting it away. "Let his boss wonder."

"Okay." Diego motions to the two other guards, and they drag the body out of the shed. The place will need to be cleaned, but that's a task for the next shift. I wait for the new guards to arrive and give them those instructions before heading out to my car.

Diego walks out beside me, so I ask, "Need a ride?"

"Sure. I was going to walk, but a ride sounds good." He shoots me a grin. "Get myself to bed faster."

"Yeah." Before we get in the car, I take out a rolled-up towel I keep for these occasions and spread it on the driver's seat. Diego isn't as dirty as I am, so I let him get in the passenger seat as is.

It's a short drive, but Diego manages to talk my ear off on the way. He's hyper, like some guys get after a kill. It's as if he needs to reinforce that he's alive, that it's not his body that's about to be incinerated out there. I know how he feels because a version of the same excitement is humming in my veins. It's not as extreme as it was with my first few kills—you can get used to anything, even taking lives—but I still feel sharply alive, all my senses heightened by the proximity of death.

"Listen, man," Diego says when I stop in front of his barracks building, "I just want to say I didn't mean anything earlier today with that girl of yours. You were right—it's none of my business."

"She's not my girl." As soon as the words leave my mouth, I know them to be a lie. Yulia may not be "my girl," but she's mine.

She's been mine from the moment I laid eyes on her in Moscow.

"Yeah, sure, whatever you say." Grinning, Diego opens the door and jumps out. "See you tomorrow."

He shuts the door, and I drive off. Loose gravel shoots out behind my car as I floor the gas, filled with sudden impatience.

I've waited long enough.

It's time to claim what's mine.

* * *

Before I go into the bedroom, I take a long shower, washing off all traces of blood and dirt. The warm water takes some of the edge off, but the dark thrum of adrenaline is still there as I step out of the stall and towel off, my cock hardening with anticipation.

I don't bother to get dressed before I leave the bathroom. The air is cool on my still-damp skin as I walk down the hallway, and my heartbeat quickens as I picture Yulia lying there, naked, tied up, and completely at my mercy. I've never wanted a woman in that position before, but everything about my prisoner brings out my basest instincts. I want her bound and helpless.

I want her to know she can't get away.

It's dark in the bedroom when I step in, so I reach for the light switch. When the bedside lamp comes on, I see Yulia there, stretched out on the blanket in front of me. Her naked body is long and sleek as she lies on her side, her back toward me. Even after her weight loss, her ass is nicely curved, and her pale skin looks like alabaster against the dark blanket. She doesn't move as I approach, and I see that she's asleep, her eyes closed and her lips slightly parted. Her plump, round breasts move with her steady breathing, her nipples soft and pink in her repose.

The lust that's been building all day roars back, more violent than ever. Kneeling beside her, I run my hand over the side of her body, stroking her from shoulder to mid-thigh. Even bruised in a few places, her skin is gorgeous, so soft and smooth it makes me want to taste her all over.

Giving in to the urge, I lean over her, trapping her between my arms, and lower my head to take her nipple into my mouth. It immediately contracts, hardening as I suck on it, and I feel her tensing underneath me, the rhythm of her breathing changing as she wakes up.

Lifting my head, I look down at her, meeting her gaze. There's fear in her eyes, but there's also something more—something that turns me on unbearably.

Desire.

Slowly, using every ounce of willpower to control myself, I trail my right hand over her waist and hip. She doesn't make a sound, but I see her eyes darkening as my hand moves lower to cup the firm, round curve of her ass. Her skin is cool and smooth to the touch, her flesh resilient as I lightly squeeze her ass cheek. She feels good, so fucking good that my cock is all but ready to explode, and my hand shakes with lust as I move it lower, slipping my fingers under the curve of her ass and between her thighs.

Yes, that's it. A savage triumph fills me as I reach her folds and feel the wetness at the rim of her opening. Her pussy's ready for me, just like it was the first time I touched her. Still holding her gaze, I push my finger into her tight heat and feel her shudder as she suppresses a soft gasp.

"You want me, don't you?" My voice is low and hoarse. "You want *this*." I find her clit with my thumb and press on it, watching her reaction. She seems to have stopped breathing, her eyes enormous in her thin face as she stares up at me.

"Say it." I curl my finger inside her and put more pressure on her clit. "Tell me you fucking want this."

She swallows, her pale throat moving, and I feel her pussy squeezing my finger as a long shudder ripples through her. "Lucas, please . . ."

"Fucking say it," I grit out, but she shuts her eyes, turning her face away from me. She's breathing fast now, her chest expanding and contracting in a frantic rhythm, and I feel her muscles clenching as I push a second finger into her, stretching her tight channel.

She's fighting me, denying me.

My hunger turns dark, lust intermingling with rage and frustration. How fucking dare she do this to me? She's mine—her body's mine to do with what I will. I don't have to give her a choice. She's my prisoner, my spoils of war, and I've been more than patient with her.

"Look at me." Keeping my hand on her sex, I rise up on my knees and grab her jaw with my other hand, forcing her to face me. "Don't play games with me," I growl when she opens her eyes. "You'll lose, do you understand me?"

She blinks, and I feel her inner muscles rippling around my fingers. She's dripping wet, her body welcoming my touch. "Yes."

"Yes, what?" It's all I can do to keep talking instead of fucking her right then and there. My thumb moves over her clit, forcing a gasp out of her. "Yes, what?"

"Yes, I—" She sucks in a breath, her voice shaking. "I understand."

"Good. Now stop lying and answer the fucking question." I curl both fingers inside her, wringing another ripple out of her. "Do you want me?"

Her nod is faint, almost imperceptible, but it's enough.

I release her face and withdraw my fingers from her pussy, my balls ready to burst. I'm tempted to take her right on this blanket, but I've been imagining her in my bed all these weeks, and that's where I want her this time.

Too impatient to bother with the knots in the rope, I get up and go to the laundry room, where I left my bloodied clothes. Thirty seconds later, I return with my switchblade.

Approaching Yulia's legs, I open the knife. Her eyes widen with sudden fear, but I just cut through the rope, freeing her ankles.

"Lie still," I order, getting up to walk around her. A second later, her arms are free too. Not wanting a weapon near her, I go to the other side of the room and put the knife into the top drawer of my dresser before turning to face her.

Yulia's already on her knees, about to get up, but I don't give her a chance. Closing the distance between us, I bend down and lift her up against my chest. I know she can get on the bed herself, but I need to touch her, to feel her. I can see the pulse beating in her throat as I place her on the white sheets, and my lust intensifies.

Mine. She's mine.

The words are a primal drumbeat in my mind. I've never felt so possessive about a woman, have never wanted to claim one so badly. The desire is purely visceral, a need that's as dark and ancient as the urge to kill. I've already had her that one night in Moscow, but it's not enough.

It's nowhere near enough.

Watching her, I reach into the bedside drawer and pull out a foil packet. Ripping it with my teeth, I take out the condom and roll it onto my throbbing cock. Her gaze follows my fingers, and I see her body tensing even more. With fear, with lust? I don't know, and I'm past the point of caring.

"Come here," I order, climbing onto the bed. I don't know what I expect when I reach for her, but what happens isn't it.

The moment I touch her, Yulia wraps her arms around my neck and presses her lips to mine.

CHAPTER TWENTY-SIX

❖ YULIA ❖

I don't know what makes me kiss Lucas at that moment, but as soon as our lips meet, my anxiety melts away, replaced by aching need. I want him—this hard, confusing man who is my captor.

With my fantasies fresh in my mind, I want him more than I fear him.

The panic I felt earlier today is absent, the dark memories quiescent as he bears me down to the mattress, his hands sliding into my hair. I arch against him, and he deepens the kiss, his tongue invading my mouth and exploring it hungrily. He tastes like heat and raw passion, like my dreams and my nightmares.

He consumes me, and I consume him in return, my hands moving frantically over his muscular back, his neck, his short hair. I know he'll most likely kill me in the not-too-distant future—I know the hands cradling my head might one day crack my skull—but at this moment, none of that matters.

I'm living solely in the present, where his touch is bringing me pleasure instead of pain.

His lips drift over to my ear, and I feel his teeth grazing my neck before he sucks on the tender skin. My entire body erupts in goosebumps, the pleasure sharp and electrifying as his right hand slides down my side, traveling over the curve of my waist and hip before delving between our bodies to find my sex. Unerringly, his fingers hone in on my clit, and the ache inside me intensifies, the tension becoming unbearable.

I cry out his name, shocked by the intensity of the sensations, but it's too late. I'm already coming, my body having been poised on the edge too long.

He pets me through the shattering waves of pleasure, his fingers stroking my folds until my orgasm ends, and then he grabs my leg and drapes it over his hip, opening me wide. His cock presses against my inner thigh, thick and unyielding, and a tendril of fear invades me again as I meet his glittering gaze.

"I'm going to fuck you," he says, his voice low and guttural. "You're mine, do you understand me? Mine."

Stunned, I attempt to process the claim, but in that moment, Lucas kisses me again and my eyes drift shut, my ability to think evaporating. His body is a warm steel cage on top of me, his scent and taste overwhelming my senses. I can't take a breath without inhaling him, can't feel anything but the devouring force of his mouth and the hardness of his erection at the entrance to my body.

I clutch at his sides, my nails digging into his skin, and then I feel it—his thick cock pushing into me, penetrating me. His left hand tightens in my hair, preventing me from turning away from his mouth, and I can't even cry out as he stretches me, invading my body as if it's his right. He goes deep, so deep it should hurt, and it does—except there's pleasure too, pleasure and a strange kind of relief.

Relief that in this moment, I truly belong to him.

When he's in all the way, he lifts his head, letting me catch my breath, and I open my eyes, meeting his gaze once more. His lips are shiny from kissing me, and his sun-burnished skin is drawn tight over his harshly beautiful features. I can feel him lodged inside me, the heat of him burning me from within, and my body softens for him, embracing him with more wetness.

"Yulia," he whispers, staring down at me, and I know that he feels it too, this pull, this visceral connection between us. He may have all the power, but in this moment, he's as vulnerable as I am, caught in the grip of the same madness.

I don't know whether he realizes it too, but suddenly, his jaw hardens, his gaze growing cold and shuttered. Without saying another word, he reaches down with his left hand to grab one of my wrists and pin it above my head. Next, he repeats the maneuver with his right hand, leaving me stretched out underneath him, unable to move or touch him in any way.

Leaving me helpless under a man who wants to punish me.

"Lucas, wait," I whisper, feeling the dark prickles of panic, but it's too late. Holding my wrists above my head, he begins to move inside me, his eyes glinting with icy fury. His thrusts are hard, merciless, stealing my breath and wringing pained cries from my throat. He's not making love; he's taking my body, claiming it as brutally as any conqueror.

I begin to fight him then, the panic spreading as the old memories flood in, but there's nothing I can do. I'm pinned, invaded, and the man above me has no mercy. His body takes mine, over and over again, and I feel myself sliding into that cold, dark place, the one from which I fought so hard to emerge. The lines between the present and the past blur, and I hear Kirill's cruel, taunting voice, smell the suffocating stench of his cologne as he crushes me into the floor. The horror begins to engulf me, but before I'm completely lost, Lucas transfers my wrists into one of his big hands and reaches between us with the other, finding my clit once more. His touch is skilled, unerring, and the stunning pleasure wrenches me back into the present, making me aware of the tension building within me again.

Squeezing my eyes shut, I try to twist away, to escape, but there's nowhere to go. There's only his cock inside me and his fingers on my clit, pain and pleasure tangling together in a vicious erotic spiral. There was never pleasure with Kirill, never anything but awful pain, and the shock of the dual sensation keeps me grounded in the moment, reminding me that the man on top is not my trainer.

It's Lucas, another man who hates me.

Except my body doesn't know that, doesn't realize that the way he touches me shouldn't cause me pleasure. Despite the roughness of his thrusts, Lucas's fingers on my clit are gentle, and the pleasure intensifies, chasing away the darkness. Gasping and panting, I arch up, frantic pleas tearing from my throat, and he presses harder on my clit, pushing me to that sharp, volcanic edge.

"Come for me, beautiful," he rasps out, lowering his face to my neck, and to my shock, I feel myself peaking. Explosive ecstasy wells up and radiates out to every cell in my body, all of my muscles quivering with sensations as I spasm around his thick cock.

Stunned, I cry out his name, and at that moment, I hear his breathing changing, a low groan rumbling in his chest. His hand tightens around my wrists as he thrusts deeply one last time and halts, his hips moving in a circular, grinding motion. I feel his cock pulsing within me, and I know he came too.

Desperately sucking in air, I turn my head to the side, unwilling to face him or the confusing jumble of feelings in my chest. I'm shattered, undone by both the pain and the pleasure. He's still inside me, his cock only marginally softer than before. I feel the stickiness of sweat gluing our bodies together, hear the harsh bellows of his breathing, and strange, unwelcome tears burn my eyes.

If I had any doubts about the reality of what's happening, they're gone. This act, this soul-tearing thing that happened between us, impresses upon me more than ever the fact that Lucas is alive.

He's alive, and I'm his prisoner.

The tears threaten to spill out, and I squeeze my eyelids tighter, determined to prevent that from happening. I can't allow myself the luxury of crying. Whatever this means, whatever Lucas has in store for me, I have to bear it. I have to be strong because this is only the start.

My captivity is just beginning.

Bind Me

Capture Me: Book 2

213

PART I: HIS CAPTIVE

CHAPTER ONE

❖ YULIA ❖

Prisoner. Captive.

With Lucas's heavily muscled weight pinning me to the bed, I feel that reality more acutely than ever. My wrists are restrained above my head, and my body is invaded by a man who just showed me both heaven and hell. I can feel Lucas's cock softening inside me, and my eyes burn with unshed tears as I lie there, my face turned away to avoid looking at him.

He took me, and once more, I let him. No, I didn't just let him—I embraced him. Knowing how much my captor hates me, I kissed him of my own accord, giving in to dreams and fantasies that have no place in my life.

Giving in to my desire for a man who's going to destroy me.

I don't know why Lucas hasn't done it yet, why I'm in his bed instead of strung up in some torture shed, broken and bleeding. This is not what I expected when Esguerra's men brought me here yesterday and I realized that the man whose death I thought I caused was alive.

Alive and determined to punish me.

Lucas stirs on top of me, his heavy weight lifting slightly, and I feel the cool breeze from the air conditioning on my sweat-dampened skin. My inner muscles tighten as his cock slips out of me, and I become aware of a deep soreness between my legs.

My throat constricts, and the burn behind my eyelids intensifies.

Don't cry. Don't cry. I repeat the words like a mantra, focusing on keeping the tears under control. It's harder than it should be, and I know it's because of what just transpired between us.

Pain and pleasure. Fear and lust. I never knew the combination could be so devastating, never realized that I could soar right after being plunged into the abyss of my past.

I never imagined I could come mere moments after remembering Kirill.

Just thinking of my trainer's name makes the knot in my throat expand, the dark memories threatening to well up again.

No, stop. Don't think about that.

Lucas shifts again, lifting his head, and I exhale in relief as he releases my wrists and rolls off me. The prickling sensation behind my eyes recedes as I take in a full breath, filling my lungs with much-needed air.

Yes, that's it. I just need some distance from him.

Gulping in another breath, I turn my head to see Lucas get up and remove the condom. Our eyes meet, and I catch a hint of confusion in the blue-gray coolness of his gaze. In the next moment, however, the emotion is gone, leaving his square-jawed face as hard and uncompromising as ever.

"Get up." Lucas reaches for me and grabs my arm. "Let's go." He drags me off the bed.

I'm too shaky to resist, so I just stumble along as he marches me down the hallway.

A few moments later, he stops in front of the bathroom door. "Do you need a minute?" he asks, and I nod, grateful for the offer. I need more than a minute—I need an eternity to recover from this—but I will settle for a minute of privacy if that's all I can get.

"Don't try anything," he says as I close the door, and I take his warning to heart, doing nothing more than using the toilet and washing my hands as quickly as I can. Even if I could find something to fight him with, I don't have the strength right now. I'm drained, both physically and emotionally, my body aching nearly as much as my soul. It was too much, all of it: the brief connection I thought we had, the way he suddenly became cold and cruel, the memories combined with the devastating pleasure.

The fact that Lucas took me even though he has that other girl, the dark-haired one who spied on me from the window.

My throat closes up again, and I have to choke back a sob. I don't know why this thought, of all things, is so painful. I have no claim on my captor. At best, I'm his toy, his possession. He'll play with me until he gets bored, and then he'll break me.

He'll kill me without a second thought.

You're mine, he said as he was fucking me, and for a brief moment, I thought he meant it. I thought he felt as drawn to me as I am to him.

Clearly, I was wrong.

A thin film of moisture veils my vision, and I blink to clear it from my eyes. The face staring back at me from the bathroom mirror is gaunt and starkly pale. Two months in the Russian prison took their toll on my appearance. I don't even know why Lucas wants me right now. His girlfriend is infinitely prettier, with her warm complexion and vibrant features.

A hard knock startles me.

"Your minute's up." Lucas's voice is harsh, and I know I can't delay facing him any longer. Taking a breath to calm myself, I open the door.

He's standing at the entrance, waiting for me. I expect him to lead me back, but he steps into the bathroom instead.

"Get in," he says, pushing me toward the shower. "We're going to wash up."

We? He's coming in with me? My insides clench, heat spreading over my skin at the image, but I obey. I don't have a choice, but even if I did, the memory of my showerless weeks at the Moscow prison is still horribly fresh in my mind.

If my captor wants me to take five showers a day, I'll gladly do so.

The shower stall is big enough to accommodate both of us, the glass enclosure clean and modern. In general, everything about Lucas's house is clean and modern, completely different from the tiny Soviet-era apartment in Moscow where I used to reside.

"Your bathroom is nice," I say inanely when he turns on the water. I don't know why I choose this topic of all things, but I need to distract myself somehow. We're in the shower, naked together, and even though we just had sex, I can't stop staring at him. His sharply defined muscles bunch with every movement, and his heavy sac hangs between his legs, where his semi-hard cock is glistening with traces of his seed. He's not the only man I've seen naked, but he's by far the most magnificent.

"You like the bathroom?" Lucas turns to face me, letting the water spray hit his broad back, and I realize

I'm not the only one aware of the sexual charge in the air. It's there in the heavy-lidded gaze that travels over my body before returning to my face, in the way his big hands curl, as if to stop themselves from reaching for me.

"Yes." I try to keep my tone casual, as though it's not a big deal that we're standing here together after he fucked my brains out and sent my emotions into a tailspin. "I like the simplicity of your decor."

It makes for a nice change from the complexity of the man himself.

He stares at me, his pale eyes more gray than blue in this light, and I see that unlike me, he's not willing to be distracted. He wanted us to take a shower together for a reason, and that reason becomes obvious as he reaches for me and pulls me under the water spray with him.

"Get down." He accompanies the order with a hard push on my shoulders. My legs fold, unable to withstand the force of his hands pressing down, and I find myself on my knees in front of him, my face at the level of his groin. His broad back deflects most of the water spray, but the droplets still reach me, forcing me to close my eyes as he grips my hair and pulls my head close to his hardening cock.

"If you bite me . . ." He leaves the threat unsaid, but I don't need to know the specifics to understand that such action wouldn't go well for me. I want to tell him that the warning isn't necessary, that I'm too shattered for battle right now, but he doesn't give me a chance. As soon as my lips part, he thrusts his cock in, going so deep that I almost choke before he takes it out. Gasping, I brace myself on the steely columns of his thighs, and he pushes back in, slower this time.

"Good, that's a good girl." His grip in my hair eases as I close my lips around his thick shaft and hollow out my cheeks, sucking on him. "Exactly like that, beautiful . . ." Bizarrely, his words of encouragement send a spiral of heat through my core. I'm still wet from our fucking, and I feel that slickness as I press my thighs together, trying to contain the ache within.

I can't possibly want him again. My sex is raw and swollen, my insides tender from his harsh possession. I also remember that encroaching darkness, the memories that came so close to sucking me in. Being with a man like this—when I'm completely in his power and he wants to punish me—is my worst nightmare, yet with Lucas none of that seems to matter.

I'm still turned on.

His fingers fist in my hair as he thrusts into my mouth, developing a rhythm, and I do my best to relax my throat muscles. I know how to give a good blow job, and I use that skill now, cupping his balls with both hands as I create suction with my lips.

"Yes, that's it." His voice is thick with lust. "Keep going."

I obey, squeezing his balls tighter as I take him even deeper into my throat. Strangely, I don't mind giving him this pleasure. Though I'm on my knees, I feel more in control now than I have at any moment since my arrival this morning. I'm *letting* him do this, and there's power in that, though I know it's mostly an illusion. I'm his prisoner, not his girlfriend, but for the moment, I can pretend that I am, that the man thrusting his cock between my lips regards me as something more than a sexual object.

"Yulia . . ." He groans my name, adding to the illusion, and then he thrusts in all the way and stops, spurting thick jets of cum into my throat. I focus on breathing and not choking as I swallow, my hands still cradling his tightly drawn balls.

"Good girl," he whispers, letting me get every drop, and then he strokes my hair, his touch as gentle as I've ever felt. I should've found his approval humiliating, but I revel in the small tenderness, soaking it up with desperate need. I feel tired, so tired that all I want to do is stay like this, with him stroking my hair as I drift off into nothingness.

All too soon, he helps me to my feet, and I open my eyes when the water spray starts hitting me in the chest instead of my face. Lucas doesn't speak, but when he pours body wash into his palm and applies it to my skin, his touch is still gentle and soothing.

"Lean back," he murmurs, stepping behind me, and I lean on him, resting my head against his strong shoulder as he washes my front, his big hands soaping my breasts, belly, and the tender place between my legs. He's taking care of me, I realize dreamily, my mind beginning to drift as I close my eyes to enjoy the attention.

All too soon, I'm clean, and he steps back, directing the spray at me to rinse me off. I sway slightly, my legs barely able to hold me up as Lucas turns off the water and guides me out of the shower.

"Come, let's get you into bed. You're about to fall over." He wraps a thick towel around me and picks me up, carrying me out of the bathroom. "You need sleep."

He brings me to the bedroom and lowers me to the bed.

I blink at him, my thoughts slow and sluggish. He's not going to tie me up on the floor next to the bed?

"You're going to sleep with me," he says, answering my unspoken question. I blink at him again, too tired to analyze what all of this means, but he's already taking a pair of handcuffs out of his nightstand drawer.

Before I can wonder about his intentions, he snaps one handcuff around my left wrist and attaches the second one to his own. Then he lies down, stretching out behind me, and curves his body around mine from the back, draping his cuffed left arm over my side.

"Sleep," he whispers in my ear, and I comply, sinking into the warm comfort of oblivion.

CHAPTER TWO

❖ LUCAS ❖

Yulia's breathing evens out almost immediately, her body turning boneless as she falls asleep in my embrace. Her hair is wet from the shower, the moisture seeping into my pillow, but it doesn't bother me.

I'm too focused on the woman in my arms.

She smells like my body wash and herself, a unique, delicate scent that still somehow reminds me of peaches. Her slender body is soft and warm, the curve of her ass cushioning my groin. My body hums with contentment as I lie there, but my mind refuses to relax.

I fucked her.

I fucked her, and it was once again the best sex I've ever had, surpassing even that time with her in Moscow. When I entered her, the intensity of the sensations took my breath away. It didn't feel like sex—it felt like coming home.

Even now, remembering what it was like to slide into her tight, warm depths makes my cock twitch and my chest ache with something indefinable. I don't want this with her, whatever "this" is. It should've been so simple: fuck her, get her out of my system, and then punish her, extracting information from her in the process. She killed men I'd worked and trained with for years.

She nearly killed *me*.

The idea that I can feel anything but hatred and lust for Yulia infuriates me. It took everything I had to ignore the softness in her gaze and treat her like the prisoner she is—to fuck her roughly instead of making love to her. I knew I was hurting her—I felt her struggling as I drove mercilessly into her—but I couldn't let her know how she affects me.

I couldn't give in to this insane weakness.

Except I did exactly that when she sucked my cock without a hint of protest, milking me with her mouth like she couldn't get enough. She gave me pleasure after I treated her like a whore, and that damnable need came over me again.

The need to hold her and protect her.

She knelt in front of me, her wet, spiky lashes fanning across her pale cheeks as she swallowed every drop of my cum, and I wanted to cradle her, to take her in my arms and make her promises I should never keep. I settled for washing her, but I couldn't bring myself to tie her up and make her sleep on the floor— just like I couldn't bring myself to truly hurt her earlier.

What a fucking mess. She's been here less than twenty-four hours, and the fury that's burned inside me for two months is already beginning to cool, her vulnerability getting to me like nothing else. I shouldn't care that she's weak and starved, that her body is a shadow of its former self and her blue eyes are ringed with exhaustion. It shouldn't matter to me that she was recruited at eleven and sent to work as a spy in Moscow at sixteen.

None of those facts should make a difference to me, but they do.

Fucking hell.

I close my eyes, telling myself that whatever it is I'm feeling is temporary, that it will pass once I've had my fill of her.

I tell myself this even though I know I'm lying.

It's not going to be that simple, and I should've known it.

* * *

A strange noise startles me out of deep sleep. My eyes spring open, all traces of sleepiness gone as adrenaline rockets through me. I tense, preparing for a fight, and then I recall that I'm not alone.

There's a woman lying in my arms, her left wrist handcuffed to mine.

I exhale slowly, realizing the noise came from her. She shifts restlessly, and I hear it again.

A soft whimper that ends as a choked cry.

"Yulia." I place my left hand on her shoulder, bringing her arm up with it. "Yulia, wake up."

She twists, struggling with sudden ferocity, and I realize she's not awake yet. She's half-crying, half-gasping, and yanking at the handcuffs with all her strength.

Son of a bitch.

I grab her left wrist to stop her from hurting us both and roll on top of her, using my weight to immobilize her. "Calm down," I whisper in her ear. "It's just a dream."

I expect her to stop struggling then, to wake up and realize what's going on, but that's not what happens.

She turns into a wild animal instead.

CHAPTER THREE

❖ YULIA ❖

"*It's your fault, bitch. It's all your fault.*"

A heavy body presses me into the floor, cruel hands tearing at my clothes, and then there's pain, brutal, searing pain as he thrusts into me, telling me that it's my punishment, that I deserve to pay.

"Don't!" I scream, fighting, but I can't move, can't breathe underneath him. "Stop, please stop!"

"Calm down," he whispers in my ear in English. "Just calm the fuck down."

The incongruity of Kirill speaking English jolts me for a second, but I'm in too much of a panic to analyze it fully. The pain of the violation and the shame are like a vise crushing my chest. I'm suffocating, spinning into the cold darkness, and all I can do is fight, scream and fight.

"Yulia. Fuck, stop that!" His voice is deeper than I remembered, and he's speaking English again. Why is he doing that? We're not in training right now. The oddity nags at me, and I realize it's not the only thing that's strange.

He's not wearing cologne either.

Confused, I still underneath him and realize I'm not actually in pain.

He's on top of me, but he's not hurting me.

Reality shifts and realigns, and I remember.

Kirill was seven years ago. I'm not in Kiev—I'm in Colombia, captive of another man who wants to punish me for what I've done.

"Yulia." Lucas's quiet voice is near my ear. "Can I let you go?"

"Yes," I whisper into the pillow. My muscles are trembling from overexertion, and my breathing is labored, as if I've been running. I must've been fighting Lucas instead of the phantom in my nightmare. "I'm fine now. Really."

Lucas rolls off me, and I feel a tug on my left wrist, where the handcuffs still join us. My skin underneath the metal is stinging and raw. I must've been yanking on the shackle during the fight.

He stretches away from me, and a second later, a soft light comes on, illuminating the room. The sight of the clean white walls serves as additional proof that I was dreaming and Kirill is nowhere near me.

Lucas reaches into the nightstand and extracts a key to unlock the handcuffs. When he puts the key back in the drawer, I automatically note its location, though my teeth are already beginning to chatter. I haven't had a nightmare this strong and realistic in years, and I've forgotten how bad it can be.

Lucas turns to face me. "Yulia." His gaze is somber as he reaches for me. "What happened?"

I let him draw me into his lap, so I can feel the heat of his body on my frozen skin. I can't stop trembling, the shadow of the nightmare still hovering over me. "I—" My voice cracks. "I had a bad dream."

"No." He tilts my chin up with one hand, forcing me to look him in the eyes. "Tell me why you had this dream. What happened to you?"

I clamp my lips shut, fighting an illogical urge to obey that quiet command. Something about the way he's holding me—almost like a parent comforting a child—makes me want to confide in him, tell him things I've only shared with the agency therapist.

"What happened?" Lucas presses, his tone softening, and I feel a swell of longing, a desire for the connection I imagined between us before. Except maybe I didn't imagine it. Maybe there's something there.

I so badly want there to be something there.

"Yulia." Curving his palm over my jaw, Lucas strokes my cheek with his thumb. "Tell me. Please."

It's that last word that breaks me, coming as it does from a man so hard and domineering. There's no anger in the way he's touching me, no violent lust. It's true that he hurt me earlier, but he also gave me pleasure and some semblance of tenderness afterwards. And right now he's not demanding answers from me—he's asking.

He's asking, and I can't refuse him.

Not while I feel so lost and alone.

"All right," I whisper, looking at the man I dreamed about for the last two months. "What do you want to know?"

CHAPTER FOUR

❖ LUCAS ❖

"How old were you when it happened?" I ask, moving my hand to the back of her neck to massage the tense muscles there. Yulia's body is shaking as I hold her in my lap, and a fresh surge of rage knots my insides.

Someone hurt her, badly, and I'm going to make that person pay.

"Fifteen," she answers, and I hear the catch in her voice.

Fifteen. I force myself to remain still and not give in to the volcanic violence boiling within me. I'd suspected it was something like that. Her voice as she screamed had been high-pitched, almost childish, the words tumbling out in either Russian or Ukrainian.

"Who was he?" Keeping my voice even, I continue my little massage. It seems to be soothing her, easing some of her trembling. Her face color matches my white sheets, her blue eyes dark in the dim light of the bedside lamp. She might be twenty-two, but at this moment, she looks impossibly young.

Young and incredibly fragile.

"His name—" She swallows. "His name was Kirill. He was my trainer."

Kirill. I make a mental note of that. I'll need his last name to mobilize a search, but at least I already have something. Then the second part of what she said sinks in.

"Your trainer?"

She averts her gaze. "One of them. His specialty was hand-to-hand combat."

Motherfucker. A fifteen-year-old girl—hell, even a grown man—wouldn't have stood a chance.

"And the people you work for allowed this?" The rage creeps into my voice, and she flinches, almost imperceptibly. Not wanting to frighten her, I take a deep breath, trying to regain control. She's still looking away from me, her eyes trained on some spot to the left of me, so I slide my hand into her hair and gently cup her skull, bringing her attention back to me.

"Yulia, please." With effort, I even out my tone. "Did they sanction this?"

"No." Her lips curl with bitter irony. "That's the thing. They didn't."

"I don't understand."

She laughs, the sound raw and full of pain. "They should've just sanctioned it. Then he wouldn't have been angry like that."

My blood feels both hot and icy. "Tell me."

"He started coming on to me when I turned fifteen, right after I got my braces off." Her gaze drifts away from mine again. "I was an ugly child, you see—tall, skinny, and awkward—but when I grew up, I looked better. Boys started liking me, and men began noticing me as well. It happened almost overnight."

"And he was one of the men."

She nods, returning her attention to me. "Yes. He was one of the men. It wasn't a big deal at first. He'd hold me a little longer on a mat, or he'd make me practice a move a few extra times so he could touch me. I didn't even realize he was interested, not until—" She stops abruptly, a tremor running over her skin.

"Not until what?" I prompt, trying to remain calm enough to listen.

"Not until he cornered me in the locker room." She swallows again. "He caught me after a shower, and he touched me. All over."

Motherfucking piece of shit. I want to kill the man so badly I can taste it.

"What happened then?" I force myself to ask. It's not the end of the story, I can tell that much.

"I reported him." A shudder runs through Yulia's slim body. "I went to the head of the program and told him about Kirill."

"And?"

"And they fired him. They told him to go away and have nothing to do with me ever again."

"But he didn't."

"No," she agrees dully. "He didn't."

I take a breath and brace myself. "What did he do to you?"

"He came to the dormitory where I lived, and he raped me." Her voice is flat, and her gaze slides away from me again. "He said he was punishing me for what I did."

The words knock the breath out of me. The parallels don't escape me. I, too, planned to use sex as punishment, sating my lust on her body and showing her how little she meant to me at the same time.

In fact, that's what I did earlier tonight, when I took her roughly, ignoring her struggles.

"Yulia . . ." For the first time in years, I feel the bitter lash of self-hatred. No wonder she panicked when I had her pinned on the hallway floor. "Yulia, I—"

"The doctors said I was lucky the other trainees found me when they did," she continues, as though I hadn't spoken. "Otherwise, I'd have bled out."

"Bled out?" A swell of rage tightens my throat. "The fucker hurt you that badly?"

"I was hemorrhaging," she explains, her face oddly calm as she meets my gaze again. "It was my first time, and he was rough. Very rough."

The motherfucking bastard's death will be slow. Very slow. I picture myself using some of Peter Sokolov's techniques on the trainer, and the fantasy steadies me enough that I can ask evenly, "What is his last name?"

Yulia blinks, and I see some of her unnatural calm dissipating. "His name doesn't matter."

"It matters to me." I clasp her shoulders, feeling the delicacy of her bones. "Come on, sweetheart. Just tell me his name."

She shakes her head. "It doesn't matter," she repeats. Her gaze hardens as she adds, "*He* doesn't matter. He's dead. He's been dead for six years."

Fuck. So much for that fantasy.

"Did you kill him?" I ask.

"No." Her eyes glitter like shards of broken glass. "I wish I had. I wanted to, but the head of our program sent an assassin for him instead."

"So they deprived you of vengeance." I know most people would be glad that a young girl didn't get a chance to commit murder, but I've never believed in turning the other cheek. There's a certain satisfaction in revenge, a sense of closure. It doesn't undo the past, but it can help one feel better about it.

I know, because it helped *me*.

Yulia doesn't respond, and I realize I've hit a sore spot. She resents them for this, this agency she refuses to speak about—this "head of the program," who should've protected her from the trainer to begin with.

Would she give them up if I asked her about them now? She's raw and vulnerable after reliving her painful past. I would be a real bastard to take advantage of that. Except if I do, I could have the information I need, and I wouldn't have to hurt her.

I would keep her safe, and nobody would hurt her ever again.

Yesterday, I would've pushed the thought aside, dismissing it as a weakness, but no more. I have been lying to myself all these weeks, and it's time to admit it. I won't be able to torture her. When I try to picture myself using my knife on her the way I did on that trespasser, my stomach turns. Even before her nightmare, I couldn't bring myself to treat Yulia like I would a real prisoner, and now that I know how much she's already suffered, the idea of causing her more pain makes me physically ill.

Reaching a decision, I say quietly, "Tell me about the program." This is my best chance to get the required information, and I have to use it, even if it means exploiting Yulia's vulnerability. Still holding her gaze, I move one of my hands to her nape and rub it gently. "Who are the people who recruited you?"

She freezes on my lap, and I see a flash of pain contort her features before they smooth into a beautiful mask. "The program?" Her voice sounds cold and distant. "I don't know anything about it."

And pushing me away, she leaps off the bed and sprints out of the room.

CHAPTER FIVE

❖ YULIA ❖

I run down the hallway, my bare feet silent on the carpet. Betrayal is a bitter, oily slime coating my tongue.

Fool. Idiot. Dura. Debilka. I castigate myself in two languages, unable to find enough words to cover my stupidity. How could I have trusted Lucas for even a second? I know what he wants from me, but I still gave in to that stupid longing, to fantasies that should've died out the moment I realized he was alive.

The man I dreamed about in prison has never been anything but a figment of my imagination.

The interrogation technique he used on me is beyond basic. Step one: Get close to your enemy and understand what makes her tick. Step two: Lend a sympathetic ear and pretend like you care. It's the oldest trick in the book, and I fell for it.

I had been so starved for human warmth I let an enemy see into my soul.

"Yulia!" I can hear Lucas running after me, but I'm already by the bathroom. Darting in, I close the door and lock it, then lean against it, hoping to keep him from breaking it down for at least a few moments.

"Yulia!" He bangs his fist on the door, and I feel it shaking, echoing the quaking of my body. I feel cold again, the chill from the nightmare returning. Why did I tell Lucas about Kirill? I never trusted anyone but the agency therapist with the full story. Obenko knew, of course—he was the one who ordered the hit on Kirill—but I never spoke about it with him.

Outside mandated therapy sessions, I never spoke about it with anyone until Lucas.

"Yulia, open this door." He stops banging, his tone turning calm and cajoling. "Come out, and we'll talk."

Talk? I want to laugh, but I'm afraid it'll come out as a sob. When I was first recruited, the agency therapist expressed a concern that I wouldn't be sufficiently detached for the job, that losing my family at a young age made me susceptible to emotional manipulation. It was a weakness I've worked hard to overcome, but apparently not hard enough.

A tender touch, a show of anger on my behalf, and I turned to putty in Lucas Kent's hands.

"Yulia, there's nothing in that room for you. Come out, sweetheart. I won't do anything to you, I promise."

Sweetheart? A spark of anger ignites in me, chasing away some of the icy chill. How much of an idiot does he think I am?

Stepping back, I turn and unlock the door. Lucas is right: there's nothing in this bathroom for me but self-recriminations and bitterness. I can't change what happened. I can't take back the fact that I trusted a man who desires nothing more than revenge.

What I can do, however, is turn the tables.

When the door opens, I look up at Lucas and let the tears stinging my eyes finally fall.

CHAPTER SIX

❖ LUCAS ❖

She stands in the doorway, looking so beautiful and vulnerable that my heart squeezes in my chest. Her eyes are glittering with tears, and as I reach for her, she wraps her arms around her naked torso in a defensive gesture.

"No, come here, sweetheart." I unwrap her arms and pull her toward me, doing a quick visual scan of her hands to make sure she's not concealing a weapon. No matter how fragile Yulia appears, I can't forget that she's a trained agent who's already tried to kill me.

To my relief, she's unarmed, so I fold my arms around her, pressing her against my chest. "I'm sorry," I whisper, stroking her hair. "I'm so sorry."

The feel of her bare skin against mine makes my body stir again, and I have to focus to ignore the press of her nipples against my chest. I don't want to get distracted by lust, not after what I've just learned.

I know I'm being irrational. It shouldn't matter that she's been abused. Some of the most twisted individuals I know have had a rough past, and I've never been inclined to cut them any slack. If they fucked up, they paid. Nobody gets a free pass with me, yet that's precisely what I'm planning to give her.

My one-eighty turn is so sudden I want to laugh at myself. She's been here less than twenty-four hours, and my plans for her have already gone up in smoke. I suppose I should've expected this, given that I haven't been able to get Yulia out of my mind for the last two months, but the intensity of my need and the inconvenient feelings that came with it still blindsided me.

She killed dozens of our men and nearly killed me.

The thought that always enraged me now brings up only echoes of my former fury. She was doing her job, carrying out the assignment she'd been entrusted with. I've always known it was nothing personal, but that didn't matter to me before. An eye for an eye—that's the way Esguerra and I have always operated. You cross us, you pay.

Except I don't want to make Yulia pay anymore. She's been through enough, first at the Russian prison, then at my hands. Instead of her, I'll focus my vengeance on the ones who are truly responsible: the agency that gave her that assignment.

"Let's go back to bed," I say, pulling back to gaze down at Yulia. She's stopped trembling, though her face is still wet with tears. "It's early."

She gives a curt shake of her head. "No, I can't sleep. I'm sorry, but I just can't."

"All right." The sun's already starting to come up, so I figure it's not a big deal. "Do you want something to eat?"

She extricates herself from my hold and takes a step back. "Another sandwich?" Her voice still sounds shaky, but there's a tiny note of amusement there too.

"I have soup," I say, trying to keep my eyes off her slim, naked body.

She blinks. "What kind of soup?"

"I'm not sure. I forgot to look inside the pot before putting it in the fridge. It's something from Esguerra's house. His maid gave it to me last night."

A small, surprising smile curves Yulia's lips. "Really? Do they also feed you scraps from their table?"

"No." I chuckle at her not-so-subtle jab. "I wish they would, though. Esguerra's housekeeper is amazing in the kitchen, and I can't cook worth shit."

Yulia arches her delicate eyebrows. "Seriously? *I* can."

"Oh?" I find myself enjoying the unexpected banter. "Did they teach you that in spy school?"

"No, I taught myself some basic recipes when I first arrived in Moscow. I was living off a student stipend, so I didn't have a lot of money for eating out. Later on, I discovered I liked cooking, so I started experimenting with more advanced recipes."

The reminder of the fucked-up nature of her job kills my lighter mood. "You weren't getting a salary?"

"What?" She looks taken aback. "No, of course I was. It was being deposited into my bank account in Ukraine. I just couldn't use those funds—I had to live like a student, else I wouldn't have passed the Kremlin's background checks."

Of course. Undercover living at its finest.

"All right," I say, forcing my tone to lighten. "Let's try the soup for now. Maybe later you can show me your cooking skills."

* * *

The soup Rosa gave me is delicious, filled with mushrooms, rice, beans, and chunks of lamb. As we eat, I observe Yulia, wondering what the hell I'm going to do with her now. Keep her naked and tied up in my house forever?

To my shock, the idea holds a certain dark appeal. For the first time, I understand why Esguerra kept his wife, Nora, on his private island for the first fifteen months of their relationship. It's as secure and isolated as one can get—a perfect place for a woman who may not necessarily want to be there.

If I had an island, I'd keep Yulia there, with nothing but her long blond hair to cover her.

Her spoon clinks against her ceramic bowl—I don't have paper plates for soup—and I tense, my gaze jumping to her hand. She's just eating, though, her attention seemingly focused on her meal.

Despite her calm demeanor, I don't relax. She's going to try something, I'm sure of it. I may have decided against making her pay, but that doesn't mean I trust Yulia or expect her to trust me. Even if I told her I no longer plan to punish her, she wouldn't believe me. Given a chance, she'd escape in a heartbeat, and the fact that she's being so docile worries me. It's a good thing I took the precaution of stashing all weapons from my house in the trunk of my car; it would've been too risky to have guns around when I let her eat untied like this.

Naked and untied.

I try not to get distracted by the sight of her nipples peeking through the veil of her hair, but it's impossible. Under the table, my cock feels like it's made of stone. I took the time to throw on a pair of cut-offs and a T-shirt before leading Yulia to the kitchen, but I didn't give her any clothes, and I'm starting to think that keeping her undressed like this is not such a good idea.

As if sensing my thoughts, Yulia tucks her hair behind her ear, causing it to shift and mostly cover her breasts. I let out a sigh of relief and resume eating as my arousal slowly subsides.

"You know, you never told me what happened that day with your plane," she says midway through her soup, and I see that her blue eyes are trained on my face, studying me. Once again, I'm reminded that I'm up against a skilled professional. She might've seemed fragile after her nightmare, but that doesn't mean she doesn't have a deep reservoir of strength.

She must have it, else she couldn't have done her job after that brutal attack.

"You mean after they shot the missile at us?" I push my empty bowl aside. The fact that she can talk so calmly about the crash brings back some of my anger, and it's all I can do to keep my voice even.

Yulia's hand tightens around her spoon, but she doesn't back down. "Yes. How did you survive it?"

I take a deep breath. As much as I hate talking about this, I want her to know what happened. "Our plane was equipped with an anti-missile shield, so it wasn't a direct hit," I say. "The missile exploded outside our plane, but the blast radius was so wide that it damaged our engines and caused the back of our plane to catch fire." Or at least that's the theory our engineers have come up with based on the remnants of the plane. "We crashed, but I was able to guide us to a cluster of thin trees and bushes. They softened our landing somewhat." I pause, trying to keep my fury under control. Still, my voice is hard as I say, "Most of the men in the back didn't survive, and the three who did are still in the hospital with third-degree burns."

Her face whitens as I speak. "So was your boss at the front with you?" she asks, putting down her spoon. "Is that how the two of you survived?"

"Yes." I take another breath to battle the memories. "Esguerra came into the pilot's cabin to talk to me right before it happened."

Yulia's forehead creases with tension. "Lucas, I—" she begins, but I raise my hand.

"Don't." My voice is razor sharp. If she starts lying right now, I may not be able to control myself.

She freezes and looks down at the table, instantly falling silent. I can feel her fear, and I force myself to take another breath and unclench my hands—which had unconsciously curled into fists on the table.

When I'm sure I'm not going to snap, I continue. "So yeah, we were both at the front, and we survived," I say in a calmer tone. "Esguerra was nearly killed afterwards, though. Al-Quadar sniffed out that he was in a hospital in Tashkent, not far from their stronghold, and they came for him."

Yulia's head jerks up, her eyes wide. "The terrorists got your boss?"

"Just for a couple of days. We got him back before they did too much damage." I don't go into the details of the rescue operation and how Esguerra's wife risked her life to save him. "His eye was the main casualty."

"He lost an eye?" She looks stunned, and her reaction awakens the old seedling of jealousy in me.

"Yes." The word comes out sharp. "But don't worry—he got an implant, so he's still as pretty as ever."

She falls silent again, looking down at her bowl. It's still half-full, so I say gruffly, "Eat. Your soup is getting cold."

Yulia obeys, picking up her spoon. After a few spoonfuls, however, she looks up at me again.

"He must hate me a lot," she says softly. "Your boss, I mean."

I shrug. "Not as much as he hates Al-Quadar. Or I should say, *hated* Al-Quadar."

She blinks. "They're gone?"

"We wiped them out," I say, watching her reaction. "So yes, they're gone."

She flinches, so subtly that I would've missed it if I hadn't been staring at her. "The whole organization? All their cells?" She sounds incredulous. "How is that possible? Weren't governments worldwide hunting them for years?"

"They were, but governments are always . . . constrained." I smile grimly. "When you're trying to be better than the thing you're hunting, it's hard to do what it takes. They have their hands tied by laws and budgets, by public opinion and democracy. Their constituents don't want to see stories on the news about children killed in drone strikes or terrorists' families abused during interrogations. A little waterboarding, and everyone's up in arms. They're too soft for this fight."

"But you and Esguerra are not." Yulia puts down her spoon, her hand unsteady. "You're willing to do what it takes."

"Yes, we are." I can see the judgment in her eyes, and it amuses me. My spy is still an innocent in some ways. "The Al-Quadar stronghold in Tajikistan was one of the last big cells remaining, and from there, it was just a matter of finding the few that were still scattered around the world. It wasn't difficult once we threw all our resources at it."

She stares at me. "I see."

"Eat your soup," I remind her, seeing that she's not eating again.

Yulia picks up her spoon, and I get up to get myself another bowl. By the time I return to the table, I see that she has nearly finished her portion.

"Do you want more?" I ask, and she shakes her head, once again letting me catch a glimpse of her nipples.

"I'm full, thank you."

"Okay." I force myself to start eating instead of staring at Yulia's breasts. When I look up again, she has her knees drawn up and her arms wrapped tightly around them. It makes me wonder if she saw the lust on my face and was reminded of her nightmare.

Thinking about that—about what happened to her at fifteen—infuriates me all over again. I want to dig up Kirill's corpse and shred it into pieces. I know it's ironic as hell that I'm outraged over a rape when I've done things most people would deem a thousand times worse, but I can't be rational about this.

I can't be rational about *her*.

"So, Lucas, what made you decide to work here?" Yulia asks, dragging me out of my thoughts, and I realize she's trying to feel me out, to understand me better so she can manipulate me. I can deflect her question, but she was open with me earlier, so I figure I owe her some answers.

A little honesty will do no harm.

"Esguerra pays well, and he's fair to his people," I say, leaning back in my chair. "What else can one ask for?"

"Fair?" Yulia frowns. "That's not your boss's reputation. 'Ruthless' is how most people would describe him, I think."

I chuckle, inexplicably amused by that. "Yeah, he's a ruthless bastard, all right. However, he generally keeps his word, which makes him fair in my book."

"Is that why you're loyal to him? Because he keeps his word?"

"Among other reasons." I also appreciate Esguerra's loyalty to his own. He's taken care of the people on this estate after his parents' death, and I admire that. But all I say is, "A seven-figure salary helps for sure."

Yulia studies me, and I wonder what she sees. An amoral mercenary? A monster? A man just like Kirill? For some reason, this last bit bothers me. I may not be much better, but I don't want her to see me that way.

I don't want to feature in her nightmares.

"So when did you meet Esguerra?" she asks, still in her information-gathering mode. "How did you end up working for him?"

"They didn't tell you that?" I imagine she must've been briefed extensively on my boss, since he was her original assignment. And possibly on me, since I accompanied him.

"No," Yulia replies. "That wasn't in either of your files."

So she did study up on us. "What *was* in my file?" I ask, curious.

"Just the basics. Your age, where you went to school, that sort of thing." She pauses. "Your discharge from the Navy."

Of course. I shouldn't be surprised she knows about that. "Anything else?"

"Not really." Yulia pauses again, then says quietly, "It didn't even mention whether you're married or otherwise attached."

A peculiar warmth unfurls in my chest. Pushing my empty bowl aside, I lean forward to rest my forearms on the table. "I'm not," I say, answering the question she didn't pose. "In fact, I haven't been with anyone but you since Moscow."

Yulia gives me an unreadable look. "You haven't?"

"No." I don't bother explaining how I've been too obsessed with her to think about any other woman.

Getting up, I take the bowls to the sink, then turn to face her. "Let's go, beautiful. Breakfast is over."

CHAPTER SEVEN

❖ YULIA ❖

As Lucas leads me to the living room, I reflect on what I just learned. What Lucas told me about Al-Quadar fits perfectly with the information in Esguerra's file. Lucas's boss is merciless with his enemies, and I'm one of them.

By all rights, I should've already been killed in some gruesome way, yet I'm alive, fed, and unharmed. Now that I'm thinking more clearly, I realize Lucas's decision to manipulate me emotionally rather than torturing me physically is a stroke of unbelievable luck. My feelings may be wounded, but my body is whole, some minor soreness aside. I have no doubt that he's playing me, but it's possible that at least some of his game is real.

It's possible that his desire for me is temporarily stronger than his hate.

I tested that theory when I came out of the bathroom, first by showing vulnerability, then by being subtly friendly. When my captor seemed to respond well to that, I brought up the plane crash, a topic that had provoked him before. The fact that he didn't attack me—that he actually conversed with me, telling me some of his story—is beyond encouraging.

It means that some of the sympathy he displayed earlier may be genuine.

Feeling hopeful, I glance at Lucas as he walks beside me. He has a fresh coil of rope in his hands, and when we stop in front of the chair where he had me tied before, I do my best to assume a vulnerable expression.

"Do you really need me naked?" I ask, letting my eyes glisten with tears. It's easy to bring them up; my emotions are still ricocheting from hurt to anger to lingering longing for comfort. "It's cold when the air conditioning comes on."

He hesitates, and I give him a desperate, pleading look. I'm only half-acting. It's a small thing, clothes, but being dressed would make me feel more human. More importantly, though, Lucas granting me this request would mean that my strategy of playing on *his* emotions is working.

"All right," he says, giving in as I hoped. "Come with me." Leaving the rope on the chair, he takes my arm and brings me to the bedroom.

"Here," he says, handing me a T-shirt. "You can wear this for now."

Trying to hide my ecstatic relief, I accept the piece of clothing and pull it over my head, noting the heat in Lucas's eyes as he watches me do so. It's a man's shirt—*his* shirt—and it's long enough to cover me to mid-thigh.

"All right, let's go," he says when I'm dressed, and leads me back to the chair. As he ties me up, I look at his big, sun-darkened hands looping the rope around my ankles and wonder if he's feeling the same electric tingle that I am. It's fucked up that I still want him, but it may also aid me in escape.

It may help propagate this new, more amicable dynamic between us.

When he's done tying me up, Lucas stands up and says, "I have to get some things done. I'll be back in a few hours."

"Okay, sure," I say, keeping a poker face.

With a lingering glance at me, Lucas departs, and I let my relieved smile break across my face.

* * *

After a while, my ebullient feeling fades, replaced by a combination of boredom and discomfort. The chair is hard under my butt, and the ropes bite into my skin every time I try to change my position. The minutes begin to stretch, passing by slowly and monotonously. I keep looking at the window, waiting for the mystery girl to return, but she doesn't. There's only an occasional lizard running over the window screen.

Sighing, I look down and ponder the other tidbit that gave me hope. If Lucas didn't lie, my dark-haired visitor wasn't his girlfriend.

He doesn't have a girlfriend at all.

The knowledge is like a balm to my ragged feelings. I don't know why it matters to me whether Lucas is single, married, or hooking up with a dozen women, but the fact that he's not cheating on that girl with me makes me feel better about last night. I didn't wrong another woman. Whatever's going on with me and Lucas is just between the two of us. Nobody else is going to get hurt.

Of course, I have to allow for the possibility that he lied, that this is all part of his interrogation technique, but I'm inclined to believe him on this. There are no signs of a woman's presence in his house: no decorations or picture frames, no hair dryers or feminine products in the bathroom.

This place is a bachelor residence, right down to the almost-bare fridge, and if I hadn't been so terrified and exhausted yesterday, I would've noticed that obvious fact.

Yawning, I look at the window again. Another lizard runs by. I watch it and wonder what it's like out there, in the jungle beyond these walls. Every part of me aches to be out there, to feel the warm sun on my skin and hear the singing of birds. The small glimpse I got yesterday hadn't been enough.

I want to be outside.

I want to be free.

Soon, I promise myself, shifting in the hard chair. I now understand the game Lucas is playing, and I can play along. I'll be his sex doll for as long as he lusts after me, and I'll seem weak and open. I'll tell him everything except the information he seeks, and I'll let him think that he's prying the secrets out of me, that his soft interrogation is working. This way, he won't resort to harsher methods for a while, and I'll use this time to formulate a real escape plan, something more promising than a desperate attack with a broken toothbrush.

I'll also work on building a bond with Lucas.

Lima Syndrome. That's what they call the psychological phenomenon where the captor sympathizes with the captive so much that he releases said captive. I studied it during training, as there was a high probability I'd be captured one day. Lima Syndrome is not as common as its inverse, Stockholm Syndrome, where the captive falls for his or her captor, but it does occur. I'm not foolish enough to think that I'll be able to get Lucas to release me, but it's possible that I could get him to lower his guard and do little things that would make my escape easier.

Like letting me wear clothes.

Yawning again, I watch yet another lizard scurry across the window, and I imagine that I'm small and green. Small enough to slip out of my bonds and slither through the vents. If I could do that, I'd be the best spy in the world.

It's a silly thought, but it comforts me, taking my mind off what awaits me if my plan fails. My eyelids grow heavy, and I don't fight it. As I nod off, I dream of little green lizards and my baby brother, who's laughing and chasing them around a jungle park.

It's my most joyful dream in years.

* * *

"Yulia."

I wake up instantly, my heart jumping, and look up.

Lucas is back—and he's not alone. In addition to my captor, there is a short, balding man standing in front of me, his brown eyes regarding me with a detached curiosity. His clothes are casual, but the bag in his hands appears to be a medical kit.

My stomach drops. I was wrong about Lucas waiting to use the harsher methods.

Before I can panic, the short man smiles at me. "Hello," he says. "I'm Dr. Goldberg. If you don't mind, I'd like to examine you."

Examine me?

"To make sure you're not injured," the doctor explains, undoubtedly reading my confused expression. "If you don't mind, that is."

Right, okay. I take a deep breath, my fear easing. "Sure. Go right ahead." I'm tied to a chair wearing nothing but Lucas's T-shirt, and the man is asking if I'd mind a doctor's examination? What would he do if I said I minded? Apologize for the intrusion and go away?

Apparently oblivious to the sarcasm in my voice, the doctor turns to Lucas and says, "I'd like the patient to be untied, if possible."

Lucas frowns, but kneels in front of me and begins working on the rope around my ankles. Glancing at the doctor, he says tersely, "I'm going to stay here. She's creative with household items."

"But—"

At a hard look from Lucas, the doctor falls silent. Lucas finishes untying my ankles and moves around me to undo my hands. I wiggle my feet surreptitiously, restoring circulation, and think longingly about the bathroom.

I don't know how long I've been tied up, but my bladder's convinced it's been forever.

"I need to pee," I tell Lucas, figuring I have nothing to lose by being honest. "Would it be okay if I went to the bathroom before the examination?"

Lucas's frown deepens, but he gives a curt nod. "Let's go," he says when he's done with the rope. Grabbing my arm, he pulls me up, his grip as rough as upon my arrival. Startled, I nearly stumble as he drags me down the hallway, the gentleness of this morning nowhere in sight.

My anxiety returns. Was I wrong about him, or did something happen? Does this examination have something to do with it?

Before I can analyze my captor's alarming behavior, he pushes me into the bathroom and says harshly, "You have one minute and not a second longer."

And on that note, he slams the door shut.

CHAPTER EIGHT

❖ LUCAS ❖

When I bring Yulia back into the living room, Goldberg has her stand while he feels her pulse and listens to her breathing with a stethoscope. "Good, good," he mutters under his breath, jotting down something in his notebook.

He bends down to look at a big bruise on her knee, and Yulia shoots me an anxious glance. I can see that she wants answers, but I don't give her any reassurance.

I don't want the doctor to know how much I've softened toward my captive.

After a minute, Goldberg stops and gives Yulia a smile. "Just a few scrapes and bruises," he says cheerfully. "You're underweight and a little malnourished, but a few good meals should fix that. Now, I'd like to take some blood if you don't mind. Please, have a seat."

He points toward the couch, and Yulia glances at me again.

"Sit," I bark, doing my best to ignore the distressed look that steals over her face as she complies.

Goldberg pulls on a pair of latex gloves and takes out a syringe with an attached vial. "This won't be too bad," he promises. I wonder if he's trying to compensate for my harsh manner. He's not usually this gentle with the guards—though, granted, none of them have Yulia's fragile beauty.

She doesn't wince or make a sound as the needle sinks into her skin, her expression one of stoic endurance. I, on the other hand, have to fight an irrational urge to tear Goldberg away from her.

I hate to see someone hurting her, even if it's the doctor I brought here myself.

"All done," Goldberg says, taking the needle out and pressing a small sterile pad to the wound. "I'll take this to my lab for analysis. Now, one last thing . . ." He gives me an imploring look, and I respond with a curt shake of my head.

I'm not leaving him alone with Yulia; he'll have to do the exam with me present.

Goldberg sighs and turns his attention back to her. "I have to perform a gynecological examination," he says apologetically. "To make sure you're okay."

"What?" Yulia's eyes widen. "Why?"

"Just do it." I make my voice as hard as I can. I'm not about to explain that I'm worried I hurt her last night with my roughness. She had been wet, but that doesn't mean I didn't tear her or bruise her internally.

Her face is bright pink as she lies down on the couch, obeying Goldberg's instructions. As the doctor pulls up her shirt and takes out a speculum, I force myself to stand still instead of ripping into the man for touching her. Goldberg is gay, but seeing his hands on her still awakens something savage in me—something that makes me want to murder any man who touches what's mine.

The exam takes less than a minute. I watch Yulia carefully to make sure she doesn't lash out at the doctor, but she lies still, her knees bent and her eyes trained on the ceiling. Only her hands betray her agitation; they're clenched into white-knuckled fists at her sides.

When Goldberg is done, he carefully pulls down Yulia's shirt and steps away. "All done," he says, addressing us both. "Everything seems fine. The IUD is in place, so you have nothing to worry about."

IUD? I frown at the doctor, but he's already explaining, "An intrauterine contraceptive device. Birth control."

"I see." I give Yulia a speculative glance. If she's protected and the doctor determines she's clean, I could fuck her without a rubber.

My cock twitches with instant arousal.

She sits up on the couch, staring straight ahead, and I see that her cheeks are still flaming with color. I want to embrace her and assure her that everything's okay, that I didn't do this to humiliate her, but now is not the time.

As far as the doctor knows, she's a prisoner I despise, and I have to treat her as such.

* * *

After thanking Goldberg, I usher him out and return to the living room, where Yulia is still sitting on the couch. Her face is back to its normal porcelain shade, but her eyes are glittering brightly. She's upset—I can feel it, even though her expression is outwardly calm.

"Yulia." As I approach, she looks away, her hair rippling down her back in a golden cloud. "Yulia, come here."

She doesn't respond, even when I reach for her and pull her up, forcing her to stand and face me. She also doesn't look at me, her eyes focused on something just beyond my right ear.

Aggravated, I grip her jaw, turning her face so she has no choice but to meet my gaze. "I needed to make sure you're okay," I say harshly. It still bothers me on some level that I feel this way about her, that I want to heal her and keep her safe instead of hurting her. It's a weakness, this obsession of mine, and I can't help the anger that seeps into my tone as I say, "You could've had internal injuries."

Her eyes narrow. "Bullshit. You just wanted to make sure you don't have to wear a condom."

Her accusation is so close to my earlier thought that I wonder for a second if I said it out loud.

Something must've shown on my face because Yulia lets out a short, bitter laugh. "Yeah, exactly."

"That's not why—" I cut myself off. I don't owe her any explanations. If I want to have her examined so I can fuck her without a rubber, that's my prerogative. I may no longer plan to torture her, but that doesn't mean I've forgotten what she's done. By her own actions, she's placed herself in this situation, and now she's mine.

I own her, for better or for worse.

"I'm clean," I say instead. A better man would undoubtedly leave her alone after what she told me, but I'm not that man. I want her too much to deny myself. "I had all my blood work done after the crash, and I'm completely safe."

Her jaw clenches. "Congratulations."

The sarcasm that drips from her voice sets my teeth on edge and arouses me at the same time. Everything about the girl is a contradiction designed to drive me mad. Compliant yet defiant, fragile yet strong. One minute I want to break her, make her acknowledge that she needs me, and the next I want to wrap her in a cocoon and make sure nothing bad can ever touch her again.

The only thing I don't want to do is let her go.

"Lucas." She sounds anxious as I draw her toward me. "Wait, I—"

I cut her off by slanting my mouth across hers. Cupping the back of her head with one hand, I wrap my other arm around her waist, drawing her flush against me. My balls tighten as my stiff cock pushes against her flat stomach, my ever-present lust for her flaring uncontrollably. I sweep my tongue across her lips, feeling their plush softness, and then I push into her mouth, invading the deliciously warm depths. She moans in response, her hands clutching at my sides, and I drink in the small sound, feeling her slender body softening and melting against mine.

Fucking hell, I want her. Every inch of her, from head to toe. It's wrong, it's fucked up, it's inconvenient, but I can't stop myself. The hunger burns inside me, overpowering whatever scruples I still possess. I know I'm a bastard for coercing her after what she's been through, but I can't stay away. Maybe if she didn't want me, it would be different, but she does. Even through two layers of clothing, I can feel her hard nipples pressing against my chest, can taste the sweetness of her response as her tongue coils eagerly around mine. She's not pushing me away—if anything, she's trying to get closer—and the mindless craving overtakes me, the savage in me taking control.

I don't know how we end up on the couch, but I find myself propped up on one elbow on top of her, her T-shirt bunched around her waist as I slide my free hand down her body to cup her sex. She's already wet, her folds slick and hot as I push two fingers into her, stretching her for my cock. At the same time, I grind the heel of my palm against her folds, putting pressure on her clit. Her inner walls spasm around my fingers as she moans my name, her neck arching and her nails raking down my back, and I know I can't wait any longer.

Pulling my fingers out, I unzip my pants to free my aching erection, and push into her wet heat.

It's like entering heaven. Somewhere in the back of my mind, a warning bell rings, reminding me about a condom, but I'm too far gone to withdraw. The clasp of her body is sheer perfection, so silky and tight that I can't stop myself from plunging in all the way, as deep as I can go. She cries out, arching underneath me, and I lower my head to kiss her, capturing the sound as I take in her taste and scent, reveling in the sensory pleasure of possessing her, of taking her for my own.

Mine, she's mine. The satisfaction the thought gives me is deep and primal, having nothing to do with logic and reason. I've fucked dozens of women without ever wanting to claim them, but that's precisely what I want to do with her. Fucking Yulia is about more than just sex.

It's about tying her to me, binding her so tightly she'll never be able to leave.

Lifting my head, I stare down at her, my cock throbbing deep inside her body. Her eyes are closed, her parted lips are swollen from my kisses, and her skin is glowing with warm color.

She's the sexiest fucking thing I've ever seen, and she's mine.

"Yulia."

She opens her eyes, and I realize I spoke her name out loud. Her gaze is unfocused, her pupils dilated as she stares up at me. She looks dazed, overcome by the same need that's incinerating my insides, and the sight tempers my savage lust, filling me with a peculiar tenderness.

Lowering my head, I take her mouth again, swallowing her needy moan as I begin to thrust in and out, moving slowly so I can feel every inch of her tight warmth. I've never had sex bareback before, and the sensations are incredible. Her pussy is soft and silky, a slick, delicate sheath that appears to have been made just for me. Her inner walls clasp me, embracing me with creamy moisture as I slide in and out, and I focus on the soft clues of her breathing to gauge her response.

The primitive, possessive hunger that gripped me earlier is still there, but now it's reined in by the need to please her, to make her feel at least a fraction of the ecstasy she gives me. Continuing to thrust in a slow, steady rhythm, I move my mouth from her lips to her neck and nibble on the tender skin there. At the same time, I slide my hand under her shirt and gently squeeze her breast.

"Lucas. Oh God, Lucas . . ." My name is a breathless plea on her lips as I scrape my teeth over her neck and catch her nipple between my fingers, twisting it lightly. She's writhing with need now, her slim legs wrapping around my hips to draw me in deeper as her hands clutch at my sides. I can feel her quivering, her body wound as tightly as a spring, and I pick up my thrusting pace, sensing that she's close.

When her orgasm hits, it's like a quake that reverberates through my body. She tenses, arching beneath me with a cry, and her inner muscles ripple around my cock, the squeezing pressure so strong that it hurls me over the edge. My balls tighten, and then the orgasm sweeps through me, the pleasure dark and intense, shattering in its raw power.

Groaning, I thrust deeper into her and hold her tightly as my cum bursts out into her hot, spasming depths.

CHAPTER NINE

❖ YULIA ❖

Breathing hard, I lie under Lucas, my heart pounding in the aftermath of the devastation that is sex with my captor.

Why is it always like this with him, with this difficult, dangerous man who hates me? I'm far from inexperienced. It's true that I've survived sex at its ugliest, but I've also known its more pleasant variations. My second assignment—Vladimir Vashkov, a trim forty-something FSB liaison—prided himself on being a good lover, and he introduced me to real orgasms, teaching me about arousal and pleasure. I thought I was able to handle anything a man could throw at me in bed, but clearly I was wrong.

I can't handle Lucas Kent.

Maybe it would've been better if he had taken me roughly again. Lust—pounding, punishing lust—is what I expected when he reached for me. And it's what he gave me at first, kissing me by force, using my body's reaction to override my defenses. I was prepared for that after the last time, but I wasn't prepared for his gentleness.

I didn't expect him to treat me like I matter.

"Yulia." He lifts his head, gazing down on me, and my cheeks heat up as our eyes meet. With the fog of lust receding, I become aware that he's still deep inside me—and that I'm holding him there, my legs wrapped so tightly around his hips that he can't move.

My flush intensifying, I unlock my ankles and lower my legs. I also change my grip on his sides to push him away instead of holding on to him. I can't play Lucas's game right now. It feels too real.

He leans down to brush a kiss on my lips and then carefully disengages from me. As he pulls out, I feel a warm, sticky wetness between my thighs.

His seed.

He fucked me without a condom after all.

Irrational bitterness seizes me, chasing away the remnants of my post-coital glow.

"You should've waited for the blood test," I say, pulling my shirt down as Lucas pushes away from me and stands up, getting off the couch. Squeezing my legs together, I give him a hard look. "I have AIDS and syphilis, you know."

"Do you now?" He sounds more amused than worried as he puts away his cock and zips up his jeans. His eyes gleam as he looks at me. "Anything else? Maybe gonorrhea?"

"No, just herpes and chlamydia." I smile at him sweetly, propping myself up on one elbow. "But you'll learn all of that soon, when the test results come back. Now, may I please have a towel or a tissue? I wouldn't want to soil your nice carpet."

To my disappointment, he doesn't rise to my bait. Instead, he laughs and disappears into the kitchen, only to return a second later with a paper towel. "Here you go," he says, handing it to me. Then he watches with undisguised interest as I sit up and wipe away the wetness on my thighs, doing my best to keep my shirt down as I do so.

"Good job," he says when I'm done. "Now, are you hungry? I think it's time for a second breakfast."

I frown, more than a little frustrated that he's being so calm. I don't know why I want to yank at a tiger's tail, but I do. I hate what he did to me; that impersonal doctor's examination had been humiliating and dehumanizing. And then to come up with that bullshit excuse about potential internal injuries, as though I couldn't see straight through him.

As though I don't know that I'm his sex doll for as long as he cares to play with me.

"I'm not hungry," I say, but right away realize I'm lying. My body is desperate for calories after being starved for so long. "Wait, no, actually—"

Before I can finish my sentence, I hear a faint buzzing sound and see Lucas reaching into his pocket. He pulls out his phone, looks at it, and lets out a quiet curse.

"What is it?" I ask, but he's already grabbing my arm and pulling me off the couch.

"Esguerra needs me," he says, leading me down the hall. "Use the restroom if you need to, and then I have to tie you up again. We'll eat when I return."

And just like that, he's my unfeeling captor once more.

CHAPTER TEN

❖ LUCAS ❖

Julian Esguerra is already in his office when I step in, the flatscreen monitors on the wall displaying news from all over the world. I take note of the Bloomberg one, where a reputable economist is forecasting another market crash.

It may be time to catch up with my investment manager.

I walk past a large oval conference table and approach Esguerra's wide desk, which is populated with several computer screens. He's on the phone, so he gestures for me to take a seat in one of the high-end leather chairs. I do so and wait for him to wrap up his conversation. Given the mention of Israeli border security, I'm guessing he's talking with his contact at the Israeli intelligence agency, the Mossad.

After a minute, Esguerra hangs up and turns his attention to me. "How's the interrogation going?" he asks. "Any progress so far?"

"A little," I say with a shrug. "Nothing worth mentioning yet." I don't usually keep secrets from my boss, but I don't want to discuss Yulia with him until I figure out the best way to approach the topic. Out of everyone on the estate, he's the only one with the power to take her away from me—which means I need to tread carefully.

Esguerra's harsh reputation is well deserved.

"Good." He seems satisfied with my answer. "Now, on to the reason I wanted you here . . ."

"An urgent security matter, you said."

"Yes." He leans back, interlocking his hands behind his head. "Nora and I will be taking a trip to the States to visit her family. I'm going to need you to make sure we—and they—are fully protected for the duration."

"You're going to visit your wife's parents? In Oak Lawn?" I'm convinced I must've misheard him, but he nods.

"We'll be there for two weeks," he says. "And I want the security to be top-notch."

"All right," I say. I'm fairly certain Esguerra's lost his mind, but it's not my place to say so. If he wants to enter a country where he's technically wanted by the FBI and spend two weeks with the parents of a girl he kidnapped, married, and impregnated, that's his business.

My job is to ensure he can do it safely.

"The new recruits are already far in their training, so we can take some of the more experienced guys with us," I say, thinking out loud. "Two dozen should probably suffice."

"That sounds about right. Also, I want armored vehicles for all of us, and a good supply of ammo."

I nod, already thinking through the logistics of that. Some would say Esguerra's being paranoid—bulletproof cars are hardly a necessity in the Chicago suburbs—but I don't blame him for being cautious. Al-Quadar may have been squashed for now, but there are plenty of others who'd love to get their hands on him and his pretty young wife.

"I'll make the arrangements," I say, even as my chest tightens at the realization of what this trip will mean.

For two whole weeks, I'm going to be separated from my captive.

"How long do you think it'll take to set everything up?" Esguerra asks. "Nora should be done with her exams in about a week and a half."

"I'm guessing about two weeks." Two weeks during which I'll still have Yulia. "Procuring the cars and all the weapons will take some time, especially if we don't want to set off any alarms at the FBI or CIA."

"Good thinking. We definitely don't want that." Unlocking his hands from behind his head, Esguerra leans forward. "All right. Two weeks should be good. Thanks."

I incline my head and stand up so I can leave and start making calls, but before I can turn away, Esguerra says, "Lucas, there's one more thing."

I stop, my attention caught by an unusual note in his voice. "What is it?"

"I don't know if you're aware of this, but my wife and her friend saw Yulia Tzakova in your house yesterday morning. Nora mentioned it to me today."

"What?" That's the last thing I expected him to say. "Why were Nora and her friend—Wait, what friend?"

"Rosa, our maid," Esguerra says. "They've become close in recent months. I have no idea what they were doing over there, but you need to make sure your house is secure." He pauses and gives me a grim look. "I don't want Nora exposed to anything disturbing in her condition. Do you understand me?"

"Perfectly." I keep my voice even. "I'll keep an eye out for any visitors, I promise."

And the next time I see Esguerra's maid, I'm going to have a little talk with her.

CHAPTER ELEVEN

❖ YULIA ❖

"Hey."

A quiet rapping on the window draws my attention. Startled, I look up and see the dark-haired young woman from before—the one I thought was Lucas's girlfriend.

"Hey," she repeats, pressing her nose against the window. "What's your name?"

"I'm Yulia," I say, deciding I have nothing to lose by talking to the girl. At least I'm not naked this time. "Who are you?"

"Yulia," she repeats, as though committing my name to memory. "You're the spy who caused the plane crash." She says that as a statement, not a question.

I look at her silently, letting none of my thoughts show. I have no idea who she is or what she wants from me, and I'm not about to say anything that would get me in trouble.

She nods, as if satisfied by my non-response. "Why did Lucas bring you here?"

Instead of answering, I say, "Who are you? What do you want?"

I expect her not to answer either, but she says, "My name is Rosa. I work over at the main house."

Her name sounds familiar. I frown, and instantly, it comes to me. Lucas mentioned a Rosa this morning. She must be the one who gave Lucas that pot of soup.

"What do you want?" I ask, studying the girl.

"I don't know," she surprises me by saying. "I just wanted to see you, I guess."

I blink. "Why?"

"Because you killed all those guards and almost killed Lucas and Julian." Her expression doesn't change, but I hear the tightness in her voice. "And because for some reason, Lucas has you in his house instead of strung up in the shed, where they take traitors like you."

So I'm right to be cautious. The girl hates me for what happened—and possibly has a thing for Lucas. "Do you like him?" I ask, deciding to be blunt. "Is that why you're here?"

She flushes brightly. "That's none of your business."

"You're here to look at me, which makes it my business," I point out, amused. The girl looks to be only a little younger than me, but she seems so naïve it's as if decades separate us instead of years.

Rosa stares at me, her brown eyes narrowed. "Yes, you're right," she says after a moment. "I shouldn't be here." Turning quickly, she ducks out of sight.

"Rosa, wait," I call out, but she's already gone.

* * *

At least two hours pass before Lucas returns, and my stomach is painfully hollow by then. According to the clock on the wall, it's one in the afternoon when the front door opens—which means my early breakfast of Rosa's soup was nearly seven hours ago.

Despite my hunger, a prickle of awareness dances over my skin as Lucas approaches, walking with the athletic, loose-limbed gait of a warrior. Like yesterday, he's wearing a pair of jeans and a sleeveless shirt, and his body looks impossibly strong, his well-defined muscles flexing with each movement. I'm again reminded of an ancient Slavic hero—though a Viking raider comparison would likely be more apt.

"Let me guess," he says, kneeling in front of me. His blue-gray eyes glint at me. "You're starving."

"I could eat," I say as he unties my ankles. I could also use a form of entertainment that doesn't include watching lizards, and a more comfortable chair, but I'm not about to complain about such minor things. After my stint in the Russian prison, my current accommodations are positively luxurious.

Lucas chuckles, rising to his feet, and walks around me to free my arms. "Yeah, I bet you could." His big hands are warm on my skin as he undoes the knots. "I can hear your stomach rumbling from here."

"It does that when I don't eat," I say, an inexplicable smile tugging at my lips. I try to contain it, but it breaks through, the corners of my mouth inexorably tilting upwards.

It's bizarre. I can't possibly be genuinely happy to see him, can I?

It's because he's about to feed me, I tell myself, managing to wrestle the smile off my face by the time Lucas removes the rope and tugs me to my feet. It's because I'm subconsciously associating his arrival with good things: food, restroom, not being tied up. Even orgasms, as unsettling as those may be.

It's only my second day here, but my body is already becoming conditioned to regard my captor as a source of pleasure, much like Pavlov's dogs learned to salivate at the sound of a bell. I know that one day soon Lucas may hurt me, but the fact that he hasn't so far has gone a long way toward soothing my fear of him.

There's no point in being terrified if torture and death aren't imminent.

"Come," Lucas says, his fingers an unbreakable shackle around my wrist as he leads me to the kitchen. "We still have some soup, and I can make us a sandwich."

"All right," I say. I'm hungry enough to eat wallpaper, so the sameness of the meals is not a problem. Still, as we stop in front of the table, I can't help offering, "Do you want me to try making something for dinner? I really *can* cook."

He releases my wrist and looks at me, his lips curving slightly. "Oh, yeah. You and knives. I could see that working out." He pulls out a chair for me. "Sit down, baby. I'm going to make those sandwiches."

Baby? Sweetheart? It's all I can do not to react as he takes out the sandwich ingredients and pours soup into bowls. It's a small thing, those pet names, but it's a reminder of what passed between us earlier.

Of the way he caught me at my weakest and tried to make me crack.

Lucas turns away, focusing on microwaving the soup, and I take a calming breath. This is not worth getting agitated about. The invasive doctor exam, yes, but not this. I need to be playing along, acting like I'm starting to trust him. That way, when I slowly open up to him, it will be believable.

The emotional bond between us will feel real.

"So," Lucas says, placing one soup bowl in front of me, "how is it that you speak English so well? You don't have an accent." He takes a seat across from me, his pale eyes regarding me with impassive curiosity.

And so the gentle interrogation begins.

I blow on my soup to cool it down, using the time to gather my thoughts. "My parents wanted me to learn English," I say after swallowing a spoonful, "so I took extra classes, beyond what they taught us in school. It's easy not to have an accent if you learn a language as a child."

"Your parents?" Lucas raises his eyebrows. "Were they preparing you to be a spy?"

"A spy? No, of course not." I eat another spoonful, ignoring the ache of old memories. "They just wanted me to be successful—to get a job in some international corporation or something along those lines."

"But they were okay with you being recruited?" He frowns.

"They were dead." The words come out harsher than I intended, so I clarify in a calmer tone, "They died in a car crash when I was ten."

He sucks in a breath. "Fuck, Yulia. I'm sorry. That must've been rough."

He's sorry? I want to laugh and tell him he has no clue, but I just swallow and look down, as if the subject pains me too much. And it does—I'm not acting this time. Talking about the loss of my parents is like picking at a barely healed scab. I could've lied, made up a story, but that wouldn't have been nearly as effective. I want Lucas to see me this way, real and hurting. He needs to believe I'm someone he can crack without resorting to brutality or torture.

He needs to see me as weak.

"Are you—" He reaches across the table to touch my hand, his fingers warm on my skin. "Yulia, are you an only child?"

Still looking at the table, I nod, letting my hair conceal my expression. My brother is the one piece of my past Lucas can't have. Misha is too closely associated with Obenko and the agency.

Lucas withdraws his hand, and I know he believes me. And why wouldn't he? I've been completely truthful with him up until now.

"Did any of your relatives take you in?" he asks next. "Grandparents? Aunts? Uncles?"

"No." I raise my head to meet his gaze. "My parents didn't have any siblings, and they had me in their mid-thirties—really late for their generation in Ukraine. By the time the accident happened, I had one grandfather who was dying of cancer, and that's it." It's the truth once again.

Lucas studies me, and I see that he already knows the answer to what he's about to ask. "You ended up in an orphanage, didn't you?" he says quietly.

"Yes. I ended up in an orphanage." Looking down, I force myself to resume eating. My stomach is in knots, but I know I need food to regain my strength.

He doesn't ask me anything else while we finish the soup, and I'm grateful for that. I hadn't expected this part to be so difficult. I thought I'd gotten past it after all these years, but even a brief mention of the orphanage is enough for the memories to flood in, bringing with them the old feelings of grief and despair.

When we're done with the soup, Lucas gets up and washes our bowls. Then he pours us two glasses of water, makes the sandwiches, and places my portion in front of me.

"Is that where they recruited you? At that orphanage?" he asks quietly, taking his seat, and I nod, purposefully not looking at him. We're getting too close to the topic I can't discuss with him, and we both know it.

I hear him sigh. "Yulia." I look up to meet his gaze. "What if I told you that I want the past to be the past?" he asks, his deep voice unusually soft. "That I no longer plan to make you pay for following orders and just want to find the ones truly responsible—the ones who gave you those orders?"

I stare at him blankly, as though trying to process his words. I had expected this, of course. It's the logical next move. First, sympathy and caring—some of it genuine, perhaps—then an offer of immunity if I give up my employers. Bringing me to his house, washing me, feeding me—it was all leading up to this. Only sex wasn't part of the equation; the intimacy between us is too raw, too powerful to be staged.

He fucked me because he wanted me, but everything else is part of the game.

"You're going to let me go?" I say, sounding appropriately incredulous. Only a total idiot would fall for his non-promise, and hopefully, Lucas doesn't consider me quite that stupid. He'll have to work to convince me that I can trust him—and during that time, I'll be working on getting him to lower his guard.

To my surprise, Lucas shakes his head. "I can't do that," he says. "But I can promise not to hurt you."

I run my tongue over my suddenly dry lips. This is not what I was expecting; freedom is always the carrot dangled in front of prisoners. "What exactly are you saying?"

He holds my gaze, and my heartbeat accelerates at the dark heat in his eyes. "I'm saying that I want you, and that if you tell me about your associates, I'll keep you safe from them—and from anyone else wishing to harm you."

My insides twist with an unsettling mix of fear and longing. "I don't understand. If you're not going to let me go . . ."

He looks at me silently, letting me draw my own conclusion.

My pulse is a rapid drumbeat in my ears as I pick up my glass of water, noting with a corner of my eye that my hand is not entirely steady. I gulp down the water, more to buy myself time than out of any extreme thirst. Then I force myself to put down the glass and look at him.

"You're offering me protection in exchange for sex," I say, my voice wavering slightly.

Lucas inclines his head. "You could think of it like that."

"What about your boss?" I can't believe this turn of conversation. "Isn't he expecting you to hack me into pieces, or whatever it is you typically do to make people talk? Isn't that why he had me brought here?"

"*I* had you brought here, not Esguerra."

I gape at him, caught off-guard once more. "What?"

"I wanted you." Lucas leans forward, resting his forearms on the table. "We had that one night, and it wasn't enough. It's true that I wanted to punish you for what happened, but even more than that, I wanted *you*." His voice roughens. "I wanted you in my bed, on the floor, up against a wall, any fucking way I could get you."

"You brought me here for sex?" This goes beyond anything I could've imagined. "You took me out of prison so you could *fuck me*?"

His gaze darkens. "Yes. I told myself I did it for revenge, but it was to get you."

"I—" Unable to sit still, I stand up, no longer the least bit hungry. My voice is choked as I say, "I need a minute."

On shaky legs, I walk over to stand by the kitchen window. The sun outside is bright over exotic tropical vegetation, but I can't focus on the natural beauty in front of me. I'm too stunned by Lucas's revelations.

Is he telling me the truth, or is this just another attempt to throw me off-kilter and get answers? A startlingly different interrogation technique that uses our mutual attraction as the base? I'm used to men wanting me, but this is something else entirely.

What Lucas is saying indicates a degree of obsession that would be frightening if it were real.

As I stand there trying to come to grips with his revelations, I hear his footsteps. The next moment, his large hands grip my shoulders. He's already aroused; I feel his erection pressing into my ass as he draws me against his hard body.

"This doesn't have to be bad for you, beautiful." His breath is warm on my cheek as he bends his head and brushes his lips against my temple. "You could be safe here, with me."

A tremor of treacherous arousal ripples through me, my nipples tightening under my shirt. "How?" I whisper, closing my eyes. His chest is hard, sculpted muscle under my back, his strength terrifyingly seductive. It's as if he's tapped into my deepest desires—into my longing for safety in his embrace. "How can you promise that when your boss could have me killed in an instant?"

"He won't touch you." Lucas's powerful arms fold around me, restraining and comforting all at once. "I won't let him. Esguerra owes me, and you're the favor I'm going to collect."

"Lucas, this—" My head falls back onto his shoulder as he nuzzles my ear, the bulge in his jeans pressing into me more insistently. "This is insane."

"I know." His voice is a rough growl in my ear. "You think I don't fucking know that?" Releasing me, he spins me around and grips my hips, pulling me to him again. Startled, I open my eyes to see savage need tightening his features. He drags me to the right and presses me against the wall next to the window, his lower body pinning me in place. "You think I haven't told myself that a million times?" His cock presses into my stomach as his gaze burns into me. His pupils are dilated, and there's a vein throbbing in his forehead.

He's not acting.

Far from it.

My breath hitches, arousal mixing with a primitive feminine fear. The man in front of me is not about to listen to reason—and my body may not want him to.

"Lucas." Fighting the drugging pull of his nearness, I wedge my hands between us and press my palms against his chest. "Lucas, I think we need to talk—"

"You want to talk about this?" He rocks his hips in a crude, suggestive motion, his cock thrusting against my lower belly through two layers of clothing. His hand catches my jaw, holding my face immobile as he leans in, his lips hovering centimeters from mine. I freeze in anticipation, my heart hammering, and at that moment, a flicker of motion catches my attention.

Startled, I glance toward the window and see a flash of dark hair ducking out of sight.

"What is it?" Lucas's tone is sharp as he registers my distraction. Following my gaze, he looks at the window and lets out a low curse before releasing me and stepping toward it.

As he leans closer to the glass, I slip around him, putting the table between us. My body is thrumming with heat, but I'm glad for the reprieve. I need to digest what Lucas told me, and I can't do that while he's fucking my brains out.

The untouched sandwich on the table draws my attention. I'm no longer hungry, but I pick up the sandwich and bite into it just as Lucas turns to face me, his lips a thin, hard line.

"Who was that?" I ask, my words muffled by a mouthful of food. I need time, and this is the only way I can think of to extend my reprieve. Chewing determinedly, I wave my sandwich at the window. "Did someone come see you?"

His jaw muscle flexes. "No. Not exactly." Lucas stalks around the table and takes a seat on the other side, his pale eyes boring into me. "You saw someone out there. Who was it?"

I swallow, the sandwich dry and tasteless in my mouth. "I don't know. I only saw the person's hair from the back," I say truthfully. What I don't say, however, is that I have a very good reason to suspect who the owner of that hair might be.

"Male? Female?" Lucas presses. "Hair long? Short?"

I deliberately take another bite of the sandwich and chew it as I mull his question over. "A woman," I say when I can speak again. He wouldn't believe me if I pretended not to notice something so obvious. "Hair in a bun, and I think she was wearing a dark dress."

Lucas nods, as if I confirmed his suspicion. "All right," he says, his expression smoothing out.

Then he picks up his own sandwich and starts eating it, watching me the entire time.

CHAPTER TWELVE

❖ LUCAS ❖

We finish the meal in silence, the air across the table thick with sexual tension. As I watch Yulia consume the last crumbs of her meal, my cock strains in the tight confines of my jeans, throbbing painfully.

If Rosa hadn't chosen that unfortunate moment to play stalker, I would already be inside Yulia, nailing her against the wall.

I shocked my prisoner. I can see it in the heightened color of her cheeks and the way her gaze slides away from mine. Did she believe me? Did she realize I was being sincere? The solution to the dilemma of what to do with her came to me as I was walking home, and I knew instantly that was the only way.

I'm going to do exactly as my instincts demand and keep Yulia.

Once, such an action would've been unimaginable. When I was in high school, if someone told me that I would so much as think about holding a woman against her will, I would've laughed. Even when I was in the Navy, long after I knew I was capable of doing whatever the job required without a flicker of remorse, I still clung to the morals of my childhood, trying to resist the pull of darkness within myself. It was only when I became a wanted man that I fully understood my nature and the extent of my willingness to cross lines I once viewed as sacred.

Keeping Yulia for my own is nothing in the grand scheme of things, and it's certainly better than the fate I originally planned for her.

"So how exactly would this work?" she asks, finally breaking the silence. Her eyes lock on my face. "You're going to keep me tied up in the chair all day and handcuffed to you all night?"

I smile at her, anticipation sizzling through my veins. "Only if that turns you on, beautiful. If not, I think we can work out a better arrangement." I'm already thinking of the tracker implants Esguerra used on his wife. I could do something similar with Yulia, making sure at least one of the trackers is implanted where it would be all but impossible to remove.

First, though, I'll need to make sure the agency she works for is wiped out; otherwise, Yulia could use their resources to disappear, trackers or not.

"You'll untie me?" Her eyes are wide as she stares at me. "And let me go outside?"

"I will." Once her agency is destroyed and I have the trackers in her, that is. "But you need to tell me about your employers first. Who is the head of the program?"

She doesn't answer me. Instead, she rises to her feet and carries both of our empty paper plates to the garbage can in the corner. I watch her, making sure she doesn't try anything, but she just throws out the plates and returns to the table.

Stopping next to her chair, she looks at me. "How do I know I can trust you? Once I tell you what you want to know, you could just kill me."

"I could, but I won't." I get up and approach her side of the table. Stopping in front of her, I run my knuckles over the soft skin of her cheek. "I want you too much for that."

The color in Yulia's face deepens. "So, what? You're going to spare me because you want to fuck me?" There's disbelief mixed with derision in her voice. "Do you always let your dick decide who lives and who dies?"

I chuckle, not the least bit offended. "No, beautiful. Just when he's this insistent."

In fact, I can't remember ever being swayed from my course of action by a woman. I've always enjoyed sex and female companionship, but the need for it has never been a ruling force in my life. My last longer-term relationship—a three-month affair in Venezuela—was before I started working with Esguerra, and I haven't thought about that girl in years. My more recent encounters have been more along the lines of a one-night stand, or at best, a few days of casual fun.

Yulia gives me a dubious look, her eyebrows arching, and I can't wait any longer. She's mine, and I'm going to do what my body's been clamoring for during the past hour.

"Let's go," I say, my fingers closing around her slender arm. "I think it's time we commenced our arrangement."

* * *

She's silent as I lead her into the bedroom, her long, sleek legs drawing my attention as we walk. I suppose I'll need to get her some clothes of her own soon, but for now, I like seeing her in my shirt, as baggy as it is on her slim frame.

I know that by the moral standards of my childhood, what I'm doing to her is wrong. She's my prisoner, and I'm not giving her any choice in this. I'm coercing her into a relationship she may not want, despite her physical response and seeming willingness to accept my touch. It would be tempting to justify my actions by telling myself that her job makes her fair game for such treatment, but I know better.

She was forced into this life by circumstances beyond her control, and I'm a cruel bastard for taking advantage of her.

As I strip off Yulia's shirt, pulling it over her head, I wait for my conscience to rear up, but all I'm cognizant of is a powerful craving for her. The things I've done in the past eight years—the things I've had to do to survive—rid me of whatever morals my family managed to instill, ripping away the layer of civilization that had always been skin-deep. The man who stands before Yulia now bears no resemblance to the boy who left his upper-middle-class home sixteen years earlier, and my conscience remains dormant as I drop the shirt on the floor and rake my gaze over my captive's naked body.

"Lie down," I tell her, my voice roughening with lust. "I want you on your back."

She hesitates, and I wonder if she's going to fight me after all. It would be pointless—even at her full strength, she'd be no match for me—but I wouldn't put it past her to try something anyway.

To my relief, she doesn't. Instead, she climbs onto the bed and lies down, watching me.

I approach her, my cock swelling even more. Though Yulia is still overly thin, her body is gorgeously proportioned, with a tiny waist, feminine hips, and high, round breasts. Her bright golden hair is like a halo on the pillow, framing a face that appears to be straight out of some fashion magazine. With her finely drawn features, thickly lashed eyes, and perfect skin, she's almost too pretty to fuck.

"Almost" being the key word.

Still, I rein in my savage lust. I don't want to hurt her. She's had too much of that, at my hands and at those of others. Just thinking about that—about other men touching her—makes me murderous with fury.

If a man ever lays a hand on Yulia again, he'll pay with his life.

Climbing onto the bed, I throw my knee over her thighs and cage her between my arms. I'm determined to control myself this time, so I hold myself raised on all fours without touching her. Her chest is rising and falling with shallow breaths as she stares up at me, and I know she's nervous.

Nervous and aroused, judging by her erect nipples and flushed skin.

"You're gorgeous," I murmur, bending over one of those tender nipples. She doesn't move, but I can feel the tension in her body as I press my mouth to the pink aureola. The nipple contracts further at my touch, and I close my lips around the taut peak, sucking on it gently. She gasps, her hands curling into fists at her sides, and her eyes close, her head arching back on the pillow.

"Yes, utterly gorgeous," I whisper, turning my attention to the other nipple. It tastes like her, like warm feminine skin and peaches. After I suck on it, I blow cool air over the distended bud and am rewarded with a small moan.

I move on to the rest of her breasts then, nibbling and sucking on the plump, delicate flesh, touching her with nothing but my mouth. Her body is a sensuous feast, every curve, dip, and hollow silky-soft, her scent intoxicating. Even with the lust raging inside me, I can't help lingering over the underside of her breasts, her ribcage, her navel . . . Moving lower, I taste the tender flesh at the top of her slit, and then push my tongue between her pussy folds.

She cries out, tensing, and I feel her hands on my head, her nails digging into my scalp as I find her clit and press my tongue against it. She's wet—I can taste her arousal—and the uniquely female flavor sends a surge of blood straight to my cock. My balls tighten, drawing close to my body, and my arms tremble with the urge to grab her and thrust inside her, to take her as I've been dying to do since the interruption in the kitchen.

"Lucas." The word is a breathless gasp as she twists underneath me, her hips rising in a silent plea as her nails rake over my hair. "Oh, God, Lucas . . ."

Ruthlessly tamping down my own need, I focus on her, using my mouth to keep her on the edge without sending her over. I lave every inch of her pussy with my tongue, then capture her labia in my mouth and suck on the tender folds, knowing the pulling motion will squeeze her clit. Her cries grow louder, her nails sharper on my skull, and I fist my hands in the sheets to keep from reaching for her. I want to give her this pleasure first, make her feel some of the hunger that consumes me around her.

"Lucas!" She's thrashing now, her heels digging into the mattress on each side of me, and I know she can't bear much more. Sliding my hand between her thighs, I push two fingers into her and suck on her clit at the same time.

Her back bows as she cries out, and I feel her clenching on my fingers, her flesh rippling around me in release. I wait just long enough to feel her contractions begin to ease, and then I move up her body. Holding myself up on my elbows, I push her legs apart with my knees and line my cock up against her opening.

"Yulia." I wait for her to open her eyes, her gaze still dazed and unseeing, and then I give in to my own desperate need, driving into her in a single deep thrust. She gasps, her hands moving up to clutch my sides, and I'm finally lost. Mindless lust descends on me, and I begin pounding into her, taking her hard and fast.

Vaguely, I'm aware that her legs fold around my hips and she starts matching me thrust for thrust, but I'm too far gone to slow down. She's wet, soft, and tight around me, her inner muscles squeezing my cock, and the tension that builds inside me is uncontrollable, volcanic. It grows and intensifies, my heartbeat roaring in my ears, and then the sensations finally crest, the orgasm hitting me with brutal intensity. Grasping her tightly, I groan as I jet my seed into her body in a series of long, draining spurts.

To my shock, she cries out again, and I feel her tightening around me once more, her body spasming in her second climax. My cock jerks with an answering aftershock, and then I collapse to the side, pulling her to lie on top of me.

There are no thoughts in my mind except one.

I'm never letting her go.

CHAPTER THIRTEEN

❖ YULIA ❖

"You fucked me without a condom again," I say when I can find the breath to speak. I'm lying next to Lucas, my head resting on his shoulder as I wait for my galloping heartbeat to slow.

My captor chuckles, the sound a masculine rumble in his chest. "Oh, yes. I forgot about your million diseases. Well, you'll be glad to hear that I got the test results back from Goldberg, and you only have crabs."

"What?" Horrified, I jerk to a sitting position, but he's already laughing, deep guffaws escaping his throat as he sits up as well.

"You asshole!" Furious, I grab a pillow and smack him with it, wishing it had a brick inside it. "That's not funny!"

Laughing even harder, Lucas grabs me and wrestles me back down to the mattress, rolling on top of me to hold me in place. With maddening ease, he captures my wrists, pinning them above my head as he subdues my kicking legs with his powerful thighs. "Actually," he says, grinning, "I thought it was hilarious."

"Oh, really?" Unable to throw Lucas off, I use the only weapon I have left. Lifting my head, I sink my teeth into the muscular junction between his shoulder and neck.

"Ouch! You little animal." Transferring my wrists into his left hand, he fists my hair with his right, pulling my head down on the mattress. To my annoyance, he's still grinning, not the least bit fazed by the red mark my teeth left on his skin. "You shouldn't have done that."

"Is that right?" Despite my helpless position, the old memories are dormant, leaving me free to focus on my anger. "Why's that?"

"Because"—he lowers his head, bringing his mouth close to my ear—"you made me want you." And raising his head to meet my gaze, he nudges his hardening cock against my thigh, leaving no doubt of his meaning.

Incredulous, I stare at him, seeing the now-familiar glow of heat in his wintry eyes. "Are you kidding me? Again?"

"Yes, beautiful." His mouth curves in a darkly carnal smile as he wedges his knee between my thighs, forcing them open. "Again and again."

* * *

It's well over an hour before I'm able to take refuge in the bathroom and gather my scattered thoughts. My body is sore and aching, worn out by the endless orgasms, and the residue of sex is crusted on my thighs. After I take care of my most pressing needs, I turn on the shower to take a quick rinse.

Before I can get in, the door opens and Lucas steps in, still fully nude. "Good idea," he says, glancing at the running water. "Let's go in."

Horrified, I gape at my insatiable jailer. "You can't possibly."

He grins, white teeth flashing. "I could, but I won't. I know you need a break. Come here, baby." Grasping my arm, he pulls me into the stall. "It's just a shower, I promise."

He's true to his word, his big hands soaping me without lingering more than a few moments on my breasts and sex. Even so, I'm aware of a slow heated pulse between my thighs as he washes me thoroughly, his fingers sliding between my folds and up into the crevice of my ass. Shocked, I clench my buttocks as the tip of his finger presses into that hole, and he lets out a soft laugh, releasing me when I push at him.

"All right, I can wait," he says agreeably, and I turn away, my stomach roiling at the knowledge that it's only a matter of time before he takes me that way too, regardless of my thoughts on the matter.

Thankfully, Lucas finishes washing himself quickly and steps out of the stall. "Come out when you're ready," he says as he towels off, and then he's gone, leaving me alone in the shower.

Exhausted, I slump against the wall, letting the water beat down on my chest. My nipples are painfully sensitive, as is my swollen, aching sex. Prior to meeting Lucas, I had no idea that pleasure could be so draining, that it could take everything out of me, both physically and mentally. I can't resist him, and it has nothing to do with the fact that he's my captor.

Even if I were free, I'd never be able to deny him.

Protection in exchange for sex. The words circle through my mind, filling me with a confusing mix of outrage and longing. Is it possible he meant it? Did he really bring me halfway across the globe to be his sex toy?

It seems ridiculous—except I felt the strength of his desire for me. Even now, my body aches from his relentless passion. Would Lucas really do that? Let bygones be bygones and simply keep me if I tell him about my agency? When I was thinking of establishing a bond with him earlier, I was hoping to buy myself some time without pain and a shot at escape before I'm killed. However, if what he says is true, my not-so-terrible captivity could go on indefinitely—or at least until Esguerra demands my head on a platter.

No matter what Lucas says about favors owed, I don't believe his boss will spare me forever. Sooner or later, Esguerra will want to get his pound of flesh, and then I'm dead. And even if, by some miracle, Lucas really can protect me, he won't do so for long.

He'll throw me to the wolves once he realizes I'm not going to give him the answers he seeks.

Straightening away from the wall, I turn off the water and step out of the stall. As I towel off, I try to figure out if this turn of events changes anything and decide that it doesn't.

All it means is I've gotten incredibly lucky.

I will have time to plan my escape.

CHAPTER FOURTEEN

❖ LUCAS ❖

When Yulia comes out of the bathroom, I give her a clean T-shirt to wear and take her back to the living room, my body humming with the bone-deep satisfaction only sex with her can bring.

"Do you like to watch TV?" I ask as I tie her ankles to the chair. I can't remember the last time I felt so relaxed and content. Soon, I'll get the answers I need, and I'll be able to give her more freedom.

For now, the least I can do is alleviate her probable boredom.

"TV?" Yulia gives me a bewildered look. "Sure. Who doesn't?"

"Any preferences? Shows? Movies? News channels?"

"Um, anything, really."

"Okay." Finished with the rope, I turn her chair to face the large television on the opposite wall. "How about *Modern Family*? It's light and funny. Have you seen it?"

"No." She's staring at me like I've sprouted green whiskers.

"Okay, then." Suppressing a smile, I turn on the TV and select the first season of the show from the files I've stored on there. "I have some work to do before dinner, but this should keep you entertained."

"Sure," she says, looking so adorably confused that I can't help myself. Bending down, I press a kiss to her parted lips, swallowing her startled gasp. The delicious warmth of her mouth makes my cock twitch, and I force myself to straighten and step back before I get carried away.

As unbelievable as it is, I want Yulia again.

Inhaling deeply, I turn away, determined to regain control. "I'll see you soon," I tell her over my shoulder and stride out of the house.

As much as I'd like to spend all day fucking my prisoner, there's work to be done.

* * *

I spend the first couple of hours in Esguerra's office, ironing out the logistical details of his Chicago protection with him and the guards I'm planning to bring with us. There's a lot to coordinate, as Nora's parents will need extra protection during and after our visit, in case some of Esguerra's business associates decide that using his in-laws as leverage is a good idea. It's doubtful—everyone knows what happened to Al-Quadar when they tried it with his wife—but it's always good to be cautious.

Some people's stupidity verges on suicidal.

Just as we're about to finish, Esguerra's wife walks in. Her dark eyes widen when she sees us all sitting there. "Oh, I'm sorry. I didn't mean to interrupt—"

"What is it, baby?" Esguerra rises to his feet and comes toward her, his eyebrows drawn together in a worried frown. "Is everything okay? How are you feeling?"

Nora shoots me and the guards an embarrassed look before turning her attention to her husband. "I'm fine. Everything's fine," she says hurriedly. "I wanted to ask you about something, but it can wait."

"Are you sure?" Esguerra's voice softens, as it often does when he speaks to his petite wife. "I can step out—"

"No, please don't. Really, it's not important." Rising on tiptoes, she presses a quick kiss to his jaw. "I'm going to be by the pool. Come find me when you're done."

"All right." Nora steps out and Esguerra gazes after her, frowning. I can see that he wants to follow her, but doesn't want to seem even more obsessed with her than we already know him to be. If he were anyone else, the guards would rib him about this for weeks to come. Instead, we all keep our faces expressionless as our boss returns to the table.

It doesn't take long to finish hammering out the security logistics. As soon as we're done, the guards return to their duties, and Esguerra heads out to find his wife, leaving me alone in his office to catch up on a couple of emails. I decide to use this opportunity to video call our Hong Kong supplier and procure the tracker implants for Yulia. To my disappointment, the old man informs me that he's only going to be able to get them to me in two weeks—exactly when we'll be in Chicago.

"Is there any way you can do it sooner?" I ask, not liking the idea of leaving Yulia unsecured for so long, but the man just shakes his head.

"No, I'm afraid not. The ones Mr. Esguerra got that time were a prototype, and we'll need to manufacture the ones for you from scratch. The coating is highly specialized, so it will have to be custom-ordered—"

"Never mind. I understand." I'll just have to assign some trustworthy men to watch over my prisoner in my absence. "Thank you for your time, Mr. Chen."

Disconnecting from the video call, I get up and exit Esguerra's office.

There's one more thing I have to take care of today.

* * *

Ana, Esguerra's middle-aged housekeeper, opens the door for me.

"Hello, Señor Kent," she says in her accented English. "Are you looking for Señor Esguerra? He just went upstairs to take a shower."

"No, I'm not looking for him." I smile at the older woman. "May I come in?"

"Of course." She steps back, letting me into a large, luxurious foyer. "Nora is by the pool. Would you like to speak to her?"

"No, actually." I pause, looking around before glancing back at the housekeeper. "Is Rosa here? I'd like to ask her something."

"Oh." Ana seems startled, but recovers quickly, saying, "Yes, she's in the kitchen, helping me with dinner. Come, this way." She leads me through a set of double doors and past a wide curving staircase.

When we enter the kitchen, I'm greeted by a mouthwatering smell of roasted garlic. Rosa herself is standing next to a gleaming sink with her back turned to us, cutting up vegetables.

"Rosa," Ana calls out to the girl. "You have a visitor."

The maid turns toward us, and I see her brown eyes widen as a flush spreads across her face. "Lucas."

"Hello, Rosa," I say, keeping my tone neutral. "Do you have a minute?"

She nods and quickly wipes her hands on a towel. "Yes, of course." A bright smile appears on her lips. "What can I do for you?"

I turn to look at the housekeeper, but Ana is already hurrying away, having correctly deduced that I want privacy.

"Thank you for the soup," I say, deciding to ease into it. "It was excellent."

"Oh, good." Her smile widens. "I'm so glad you enjoyed it. It's my mother's recipe."

"Wait." I frown. "You made it, not Ana?"

Rosa turns beet red. "I did—I'm sorry I lied to you earlier. It was just that—"

"Rosa," I interrupt, holding up my hand. I want to spare the girl any unnecessary awkwardness. "Thank you. It was a wonderful soup, but I'd rather you didn't make it again for me. Or anything else for that matter, all right?"

She looks like I just slapped her across the face. "Of c-course," she stammers. "I'm sorry, I—"

"And I need you to stay away from my house," I continue, ignoring the tears pooling in the girl's eyes. I'd sooner face a dozen terrorists than do this, but I have to drive the point home. "It's not safe for you. My prisoner is dangerous."

"I just—"

"Look," I say, feeling like I was just cruel to a child, "you're a beautiful girl, and very sweet, but you're much too young for me. You're what, eighteen, nineteen?"

Rosa's chin lifts. "Twenty-one."

"Right." It strikes me that she's only a year younger than Yulia, but I've never thought of the Ukrainian spy as being too young for me. Still, I continue without missing a beat. "I'm thirty-four. You should find someone closer to your own age. A nice guy who'll appreciate you."

"Of course." To my surprise, the maid regroups, pulling herself together with startling composure. Her tears dry up, and she gives me a steady smile, though a flush still colors her cheeks. "You don't have to worry, Lucas. I won't bother you anymore."

I frown, unsure whether I can take her at face value, but she's already turning away, her attention on the vegetables once more.

PART II: THE BREAKING

CHAPTER FIFTEEN

❖ YULIA ❖

Over the next week, Lucas and I settle into an uneasy routine. He has sex with me every chance he gets—which is at least a couple of times at night and once during the day—and we eat all of our meals together in the kitchen. The rest of the time I spend watching TV while tied to the chair, or sleeping cuffed at Lucas's side.

"Do you think it would be possible for me to read something?" I ask after two days of binging on TV shows. "I love books, and I miss reading them."

"What kind of books?" Lucas appears unusually interested.

"All kinds," I answer honestly. "Romance, thrillers, science fiction, nonfiction. I'm not picky—I just love the feel of a book in my hands."

"All right," he concedes, and the next day, he takes me to a small room next to the bedroom. Like the rest of his home, it's sparsely furnished. However, it's much cozier, boasting a desk, three tall bookshelves filled with books, and a plush armchair next to a bay window that faces the forest.

"Is this your library?" I ask, surprised. I've always thought of my captor as a soldier, someone more interested in guns than books. It's easier to imagine Lucas wielding a machete than peacefully reading in this room.

"Of course it's mine." Leaning against the door frame, he gives me an amused look. "Who else's would it be?"

"And you've read all of these?" I approach the shelves, studying the titles. There must be hundreds of books there, many of them mysteries and thrillers. I also see a number of biographies and nonfiction works that range from popular science to finance.

"Most of them," Lucas replies. "I tend to order in bulk, so I always have something new to read when I have downtime."

"I see." I don't know why I'm so shocked to discover this aspect of him. I've always suspected that Lucas is keenly intelligent, but somehow I've let myself buy into the stereotype of a hardened mercenary, a man whose life revolves around weapons and fighting. The fact that he went straight from high school to the Navy only added to that impression.

I underestimated my opponent, and I need to be careful not to do that again.

Stopping in front of the bay window, I turn to look at him. "When did you manage to acquire all these books?" I ask. "I thought you spent a few years on the run after you left the Navy."

Lucas's gaze hardens for a second, but then he nods. "Yes, I did. I keep forgetting how much you know about me." He crosses the room to stand in front of me. "I got most of these books within the past year, after Esguerra decided we should make this compound our permanent home. Before that, we were traveling all over the world, so I kept a few dozen of my favorites in storage. And before that, I didn't own many belongings at all—made it easier to move around."

"But that's not what you want anymore," I guess, studying him. "You want to own things, to have a home."

He stares at me, then lets out a bark of laughter. "I suppose. I never thought of it that way, but yeah, I guess I got a little tired of never sleeping in the same bed twice. And owning things?" His voice deepens as his gaze travels over me. "Yeah, there's something to that. I like having *things* I can call my own."

My cheeks heat up as I look away, pretending I'm interested in the view outside the bay window. Lucas's extreme possessiveness hasn't escaped my notice. I know my captor believes he owns me, and for all intents and purposes, he does. He controls every aspect of my life: what I eat, when I sleep, what I wear, even when I go to the bathroom. When I'm not tied up, I'm with him, and for much of that time, we're in bed, where he does whatever he pleases with me.

If I didn't want him as intensely as he wants me, it would be hell.

"Yulia . . ." Lucas's voice holds a familiar heated note as he steps behind me. His big hand gathers my hair to move it to one side, exposing my neck. Leaning down, he kisses the underside of my ear and slides his free hand under the man's shirt I'm wearing as a dress. Delving between my legs, he finds my sex, and I can't suppress a moan as he penetrates me with two fingers, stretching me for his possession.

And for the next hour, as Lucas fucks me bent over the arm of the chair, books are the furthest thing from our minds.

* * *

After that time in the library, the quality and variety of my entertainment improves. Instead of watching TV all day, I spend a portion of my alone time reading by the bay window. I also gain the concession of a more comfortable seat and having my hands handcuffed in the front—that way, I can actually hold and read a book. Every morning after breakfast, Lucas secures me to the armchair with ropes, leaving my handcuffed hands just enough range to turn the pages, and I read there until lunch, at which point he comes to feed me and let me stretch my legs.

"You know, I'm not a dog who uses the bathroom on a schedule," I dare to complain one day. "What if I really have to go, and you're not home?"

To my relief, he doesn't point out how spoiled I've become. Instead, later that day, he gives me a small device that resembles an old-fashioned pager.

"If you press this button, I'll get a text," he explains. "And if I can, I'll come to you. Or send someone else to help you."

"Thank you," I say, feeling genuinely grateful and increasingly hopeful.

Maybe one day he really will let me go, or at least give me enough freedom to enable my escape.

Of course, I know I can't rely on that. Every day, Lucas spends a portion of the mealtimes interrogating me, and even though I've successfully stonewalled him thus far, I'm afraid he'll eventually lose patience and resort to more surefire methods of extracting information.

It hasn't been that long, and I can already feel his frustration growing.

"You don't owe them a damn thing," he says furiously when I refuse to talk about the agency for the fifth time. "They took you when you were a fucking child. What kind of bastards send a sixteen-year-old to a corrupt city like Moscow and tell her to sleep her way to government secrets? Fuck, Yulia"—he slaps his palm on the table—"how can you be loyal to those motherfuckers?"

How, indeed. I want to scream at him, tell him that he doesn't understand anything, but I remain silent, looking down at my plate. There's nothing I can say that won't expose Misha to danger and ruin his life. My loyalty is not to Obenko, the agency, or even Ukraine.

It's to my brother—the only family I have left.

To my relief, Lucas lets my non-response slide, ultimately changing the topic to the plot of a post-apocalyptic thriller I read that day. We discuss it in great detail, as we frequently do with books and movies, and we both agree that the author did a good job of explaining why the scientists couldn't prevent the Gray Goo from taking over the world. The meal concludes on an amicable note, but my determination to escape is reinforced.

Eventually, Lucas will get fed up with my silence, and I don't want to be around when he does.

CHAPTER SIXTEEN

❖ YULIA ❖

As I plan my escape, I realize that I'm faced with three major obstacles: the fact that I'm tied up when Lucas is not around, the military-level security of the compound, and Lucas himself. Any of those three would be enough to contain me, but when all three are combined, escape is all but impossible.

On the surface, it shouldn't be difficult. When Lucas is home, he usually keeps me untied, letting me eat at the table and even do a few stretches and body-weight exercises to keep fit. However, he always keeps a watchful eye on me during those times, and I know I won't win in a physical battle with him. Even if I managed to grab a knife, he'd probably wrestle it away from me before I could inflict a serious injury. A gun would be a different matter, but I haven't seen anything more deadly than a kitchen knife inside the house. I know Lucas usually carries weapons—I saw him with an assault rifle that first day—but he must leave them in the car or some other location outside.

Contrary to appearances, I'm more likely to escape when he's not around.

To that end, every time Lucas ties me up, I test the rope to see if he left some slack in it, and every time, I discover he didn't. The bonds are always just tight enough to keep me restrained without cutting off my circulation. I don't want to leave betraying marks on my skin, so I don't tug at the rope too hard. Even if I managed to get free, I'd still need to get past guard towers and through a jungle patrolled by Esguerra's men and high-tech drones—assuming Lucas didn't catch me before I got that far.

For me to stand a chance, I need my captor far away, and I need to know the patrol schedule.

I begin by trying to get the latter out of Lucas when we're lying in bed, relaxed and satisfied after a lengthy sex session.

"How did you get this?" I ask as I trace my fingers over a bruise on his ribcage. "The compound wasn't attacked, was it?"

My concern is only partially feigned; the idea of Lucas getting hurt in any way bothers me. He seems invulnerable, every inch of his body packed with hard muscle, but I know that won't save him from a bomb or a gun. In his line of work, life expectancy is much shorter than average—a fact that makes me sick with worry when I dwell on it too much.

"No, nobody would attack the compound," Lucas says, a smile curving his lips. "I got this bruise in training, that's all."

"I see." Acting on some irrational impulse, I press a small kiss to the injured area before looking up to meet his gaze. "Why wouldn't someone attack the compound? Doesn't your boss have a lot of enemies?"

"Oh, he does." Lucas's eyes darken as he slides his hand into my hair and guides me lower, toward his stomach. "But they would be suicidal to come here. The security is too tight. And now"—he pushes my head toward his rising erection—"I want something else that's tight."

Hiding my disappointment, I close my lips around his cock and apply the strong suction he likes.

Lucas is too smart to give me the security details I need—which means I'll have to figure out something else.

* * *

As the days drag on without me getting any closer to a viable escape plan, I console myself with the knowledge that I'm using the time to recover from my ordeal at the Russian prison and rebuild my strength. Between sitting most of the day and consuming every bite of food—no matter how boring—Lucas puts in front of me, I'm steadily putting on weight, my body regaining the curves it lost during my weeks of near-starvation. By the time I've been in Lucas's house nine days, I'm no longer a skeleton—and I'm desperate for something other than sandwiches and cold cereal with milk.

"You know, you seriously should let me try cooking," I say after yet another sandwich for lunch. "I can make omelets, soup, chicken, lamb, mashed potatoes, salad, rice, dessert—anything you want, really. If you don't trust me with a knife, you can help me by cutting things up. I'll just add seasoning and things like that. You'll be perfectly safe—unless you store rat poison in your kitchen."

He laughs, making me think he's going to ignore my offer, but that afternoon, he brings in several boxes of food, including all kinds of fruits and vegetables, two types of fresh fish, several whole chickens, a dozen lamb chops, and an entire collection of spices.

"Where did all of this come from?" I ask, eying the bounty in astonishment. There's enough in those boxes to feed five people—assuming one knows how to prepare it all, of course.

"Esguerra gets weekly deliveries, so I took some for us," Lucas says. "I figure it's time to test your cooking skills."

I can't conceal my startled joy. "You'd trust me to cook?"

"I'd trust you to direct me." He grins. "You'll sit there"—he points at the kitchen table—"and tell me exactly what to do. I'll follow your orders, and who knows? Maybe I'll learn something."

"Okay," I agree, more than a little excited by the prospect of ordering Lucas about. "I can do that. Let's start by putting everything away, and tonight, we'll make lamb chops with garlic-dill potatoes and green salad."

CHAPTER SEVENTEEN

❖ LUCAS ❖

As I peel potatoes and chop garlic under Yulia's guidance, she lounges in the kitchen chair, her blue eyes bright with amusement.

"You know you don't have to take half the potato off with the skin, right?" Grinning, she glances at the pile of mangled potatoes on the counter. "Haven't you ever done this before?"

"No," I say, doing my best not to cut too deeply into my current root vegetable. It's harder than it seems. "And now I know why."

"They didn't make you peel potatoes in the Navy?"

"No, that's a thing of the past. We had private contractors who handled the mess halls."

"I see. Well, you need a potato peeler," she says, crossing her long legs. "Like with everything else, a specialized tool helps."

"A peeler. Got it." I make a mental note to order one. I also do my best to keep my eyes off those bare, distracting legs. Four days ago, I finally got Yulia some clothes of her own, but they're of the skimpy summer variety, and I'm now realizing my mistake.

In a white midriff-baring top and tiny jean shorts, Yulia's no-longer-starved body is impossible to ignore.

"Okay, that's enough potatoes, I think," she says, getting up. Her flip-flops—the only shoes I got her—make a slapping noise on the tile floor as she comes toward me. "Now we need to take the garlic, mix it with dill, salt, and pepper, and place everything on a frying pan. You have oil, right?"

"Oil. Check." I grab a bottle of olive oil from a cabinet to my left. "Do I pour it over the potatoes?"

She props her hip on the edge of the countertop. "You're kidding me, right?"

I frown, not appreciating the mockery.

She bursts out laughing. "Lucas, seriously. Have you never fried anything in your life?"

"Nothing that was edible afterwards," I grudgingly admit. "I may have tried it once or twice and given up."

"Okay." Yulia manages to stop laughing long enough to explain, "You pour oil into the *frying pan.*

No, not so much—" She seizes the bottle from me before I can pour out more than a quarter of its contents. Laughing hysterically, she grabs a paper towel and dips it in the oil, mopping up the excess. "We're not deep-frying the poor potatoes," she explains when she's able to talk again.

"All right," I say, watching as she picks up the potatoes and the garlic and deposits everything into the oiled pan. Her movements are fast and sure, her slim hands moving with graceful economy.

She wasn't lying when she said she knows what she's doing.

"I wish we had fresh dill," she says, grabbing one of the bottles from the spice rack. "But I think the dried one will also work. Next time, if you like this dish, do you think you could get us some fresh herbs?"

"Sure." *Fresh herbs.* I make another mental note. "I can get us anything."

"Great. Now if you don't mind, I'll season this myself. The potatoes won't be any good if you dump the entire salt shaker in." She looks like she's about to start laughing again.

"Be my guest," I say, moving the knife I used to peel the potatoes behind me. "This mess is all yours."

And for the next half hour, I watch as Yulia whirls around the kitchen, humming under her breath. She seasons and fries the potatoes, bathes lamb chops in some kind of marinade, and washes greens for the salad. She's practically vibrating with excited energy, and for the first time, I realize how little I've seen this side of her—how subdued she usually is in my presence.

It's not surprising, of course. Though I haven't hurt her, she's my prisoner, and I know she still doesn't trust me. No matter how much I push for answers, she either changes the topic or refuses to respond. It frustrates me, but I force myself to remain patient.

Once Yulia realizes I truly don't intend to harm her, she'll hopefully see the light and give up the people who fucked up her life. For now, all I can do is keep her reasonably comfortable—and restrained—until the trackers I ordered arrive.

"All done," she says when the oven alarm goes off. Smiling brightly, she bends to take out the lamb chops, and my cock hardens at the sight of her ass in those tiny shorts.

If the lamb didn't smell so delicious, I would've dragged Yulia to bed right then and there.

As it is, while she carries the dish to the table, I have to take several deep breaths to control myself. It's ridiculous. I've always had a strong sex drive, but around Yulia, I'm like a randy teenager watching his first porn. I want to fuck her all the time, and no matter how often I take her, the desire doesn't diminish.

If anything, it grows stronger.

It takes a few more breaths before my erection subsides enough for me to help her set the table. By then, Yulia's got the salad arranged prettily in a bowl and the frying pan with the potatoes sitting on a neatly folded towel in the middle of the table. I presume the latter is to keep the hot pan from burning the table surface—a clever solution my parents' housekeeper used as well.

Finally, we both sit down to eat.

"Yulia, this is amazing," I say after demolishing half of my plate in under a minute. "The best I've had in a long, long time."

She gives me a happy smile and picks up her lamb chop. "I'm glad you like it."

"Like it? I love it." I can't remember the last time I had a meal this satisfying. The savory potatoes are perfect with the rich lamb and the crisp, lemony greens of the salad. "If I could eat this three times a day, I would."

Yulia's smile widens. "Good. I thought about making dessert too, but I figured we'll be too full from this. We'll just have some grapes instead."

"Whatever you say," I mumble through a mouthful of potatoes. "It's all good."

She laughs and digs into her own food. We eat in easy, companionable silence, and when most of the food is demolished, I put away the leftovers and wash the dishes. I do it automatically, without thinking, and it's only when I sit down to eat the grapes that it strikes me how content I feel.

No, more than content.

I'm fucking happy.

Between the meal, Yulia's bright smile, and the anticipation of taking her to bed, I'm thoroughly enjoying this evening. And it's not just today, I realize as I grab a handful of grapes.

This past week, ever since I decided to keep Yulia, has been my happiest in recent memory.

"So, Lucas," Yulia says before I can digest the revelation, "tell me something . . ." Her soft lips twitch with a poorly suppressed smile. "How did you get this far in life without ever peeling a potato?"

I pop a grape into my mouth as I consider her question. "I suppose I had a pampered upbringing," I say after swallowing the grape. "We had a housekeeper, so neither of my parents did any chores, and they didn't force me to do them. Later on, when I was in the Navy, we ate whatever was served to us, and after that . . ." I shrug, recalling the hardscrabble days of camping out in the jungle with small groups of men as lawless and desperate as myself. "I guess I just saw food as sustenance. As long as I didn't go hungry, I didn't think about it much."

"I see." She eyes me thoughtfully. "What made you decide to leave home? It's a big leap to go from a family with a housekeeper to enrolling in the Navy."

"I suppose it was." My parents certainly thought I'd gone insane. "It just seemed like the right thing to do at that point in my life."

"Why?" Yulia seems genuinely puzzled. "You don't have a draft in the United States. Did you feel called to defend your country?"

I chuckle. "Something like that." I'm not about to tell her about the thug I killed in that Brooklyn subway station, or the sick rush I got from seeing his blood spill over my hands. She already fears me; she doesn't need to know I became a killer at seventeen.

"That's very admirable of you," Yulia says, and I can hear the skepticism in her voice. "Very self-sacrificing."

"Yeah, well, someone had to do it." I bite on another grape, letting the cold, sweet juice trickle down my throat. I want her to drop this topic, so I add, "Just like someone had to be a spy, right?"

Predictably, she clams up, her face assuming the shuttered expression she always wears when I get too close to that subject. "Would you like some tea?" she asks, rising to her feet. "I saw there was some Earl Gray in one of those boxes."

I lean back in my chair, watching her. "Sure." I can count on one hand the number of times I've had tea, but I got it because I remembered Yulia drinking it at the Moscow restaurant where we first met. "I could go for a cup."

She puts on some water to boil and readies two cups for us, her movements as graceful as usual. Everything about her is graceful, reminding me of a dancer.

"Did you ever do ballet?" I ask as the thought occurs to me. "Or is that a stereotype about Eastern European girls?"

Yulia turns to face me with a cup in each hand. "It *is* a stereotype," she says, her tense expression fading. "In my case, though, it's true. My parents had me take ballet lessons from the time I was four. They thought it would help me overcome my shyness."

"You were shy as a child?"

"Very." She walks back to the table. "I wasn't a cute kid—far from it. Other children often mocked me."

"Really? I can't imagine you as anything but beautiful." I accept the cup Yulia hands to me. "How does one go from a not-cute kid to the hottest woman I've ever seen?"

Warm color sweeps over her high cheekbones. "I'm not exactly Helen of Troy." She sits down, cradling her cup. "My mom was pretty, though, so I think I got some of her genes. They just kicked in later, after I went through puberty. Oh, and braces helped, too." She gives me a wide smile that shows off her straight white teeth.

"Yeah, I'm sure," I say wryly. "Total ugliness to total gorgeousness, just like that."

She shrugs, blushing again, and I have a sudden mental image of her as that shy child.

"I bet you *were* cute," I say, studying her. "All that blond hair and big blue eyes. You just didn't realize it.

That's why they took you from the orphanage, isn't it? Because they saw your potential?"

Yulia stiffens, and I know I ventured too close to the forbidden subject again. My mood darkens as I reflect on the fact that over the last several days, I've made zero progress with her. She may smile at me, cook for me, and willingly take me into her body, but she still doesn't trust me one bit.

"Yulia." I move my tea to the side. "You know this can't go on forever, right? You're going to have to talk to me one day."

She looks down into her cup, her body language all but screaming for me to back off.

"Yulia." Holding on to my temper by a thread, I get up and walk over to pull her to her feet. Holding her arms, I stare into her mutinous gaze. "Who are they?"

She remains silent, her thick eyelashes lowering to conceal her thoughts.

"Why won't you tell me about them?"

She doesn't answer, her eyes trained somewhere on my neck.

My grip on her arms tightens, and she flinches, tensing in my hold. Realizing I'm inadvertently hurting her, I force myself to unlock my fingers and drop my hands. I'm getting angry, which is not good. The fact that I'm not willing to torture her means I have to gain her trust to get answers, and this is not the way to do it.

Taking a breath to regain control, I lift my hand and tuck her hair behind her ear, being careful to keep the gesture gentle and nonthreatening. "Yulia." I stroke her cheek with the back of my fingers. "Sweetheart, they don't deserve your loyalty. They ruined your life. What they did to you was wrong, don't you see that? I told you I'll protect you—from them and from anyone else who wants to harm you. You don't have to be afraid to talk to me. I'm not going to turn on you once I have this information—you have my word on that."

Her eyelashes sweep up as she meets my gaze. "So what are you going to do if I tell you about them? What's going to happen to the agency?"

I suppress my pleased smile. This is the closest she's come to giving in. "We're going to take care of them."

"The way you took care of Al-Quadar?" Her eyes are wide with what appears to be curiosity and hope. "You'll wipe them out?"

"Yes, you'll be safe from them. By the time we're done, nobody connected to the organization will be around to hurt you." I intend my words as a reassurance, a promise of better things to come, but as I speak, I see color leaching from Yulia's face.

She steps out of my reach, her lashes descending to hide her gaze again, and a sudden suspicion stirs within me.

"Yulia." I catch her arm as she turns away. Spinning her around to face me, I stare at her pale face. "Are you protecting them? Are you protecting someone there?"

She doesn't say anything, but I can see the tension on her face, the fear that she's trying so hard to hide.

This goes beyond simple loyalty to an employer, beyond concern for coworkers.

She's terrified for them—like someone would be for a person one loves.

Stunned, I release her arm and step back. I don't know why this possibility never occurred to me. I'd been so hung up on the idea that they fucked up her life, I never wondered whether there might be someone Yulia cares about in Ukraine.

Whether she might have a lover who's not an assignment.

* * *

I spend the rest of the evening functioning on autopilot. Esguerra and I have another late-night call with Asia, so I tie Yulia up in my office, letting her read while I take care of business. She's unusually wary around me, watching me like I might attack her at any moment, and her fear adds to the rage bubbling deep within my chest. It takes everything I have to hand her a book and walk out of the room without grabbing her and demanding answers.

Without resorting to violence that I can't and won't use on her.

As I listen to our Malaysian suppliers argue over the quality of the latest batch of plastic explosives, I try to keep my thoughts from straying to my captive, but it's impossible. Now that the idea is lodged in my mind, I can't push it away.

A lover. A man Yulia cares about and wants to protect.

The mere thought of that fills me with murderous fury. Who is he? Another operative from her agency? Someone she met during her training, perhaps? It's not out of the question. She would've been very young when she met him, but girls that age fall in love all the time. He could've been another trainee, someone she felt close to because they shared the same experiences. Or he might've been older—an instructor or an already-trained agent. Kirill couldn't have been the only one who noticed the ugly duckling blossoming into a swan.

The more I think about it, the more likely it seems. They could've met during her training and continued their romance later on. Just because Yulia's job involved getting close to men for information doesn't mean she couldn't have had a genuine relationship on the side. And if she did have one, another agent would've been the most logical choice for a lover. Someone from her organization would've understood her profession, forgiven her for doing what she had to do.

Accepted that she let me fuck her while she was in love with *him*.

The pencil I've been toying with during the call snaps in my hands, the crack startlingly loud in the pause during the conversation. Esguerra lifts his eyebrows, shooting me a cool glance, and I force my hands to unclench from the broken pieces of the pencil.

I can't give in to this anger. I can't allow myself to lose control. I need to figure out a new strategy, something that doesn't rely on Yulia ultimately trusting me.

If I'm right about her lover, she'll never give me the answers I seek.

She'll protect her agency because he's part of it.

* * *

Yulia is still reading when I step into my office, her blond head bent over the open pages of a Michael Crichton techno-thriller. She's holding the book on her lap—the only position the ropes securing her to the armchair allow.

At the sound of my entry, she looks up, her gaze filled with wariness. She's expecting me to push for information, and her fear is like gasoline on the flames of my fury.

Far be it from me to disappoint my prisoner.

"Why are you protecting them?" I cross the room and stop in front of her. My voice is cold, though the anger coursing through my veins is hot enough to burn. "What do they mean to you?"

Yulia's gaze drops to my stomach. "I don't know what you're talking about."

"Don't lie to me." I crouch in front of her, so we're at the same eye level. Extending my hand, I grip her jaw and force her to look at me. "You don't want us to go after your agency. Why?"

She's silent as she holds my gaze.

"Is there someone there you're protecting?"

Her eyes widen slightly, and I catch a glimpse of panic in their blue depths. "No, of course not," she says quickly.

She's lying. I know she is, but I play along. "Then why won't you talk to me?"

"Because they don't deserve your vengeance." Her words tumble out, fast and desperate. "They were just doing their job, protecting our country."

"So it's all about patriotism for you? Is that what you're telling me?"

"Of course." A pulse is throbbing visibly in her throat. "Why else would I do this?"

"Maybe because they took you when you were a fucking child." My hand tightens on her jaw. "Because the only choice they gave you was to whore for them or rot in the orphanage."

Yulia flinches at my harsh words, her eyes filling with tears, and I stop, fighting a swell of rage. Realizing my fingers are digging into her skin, I unclench my hand and lower it to my lap. My palm immediately curls into a fist, and she shrinks back against the chair, as if afraid I'll hit her.

I relax my hand with effort. "Yulia." I manage to moderate my tone. "They're fucking monsters. I don't know why you can't see it."

She closes her eyes, and I see a tear trickling down her cheek. "It's not that simple," she whispers, opening her eyes to look at me again. "You don't understand, Lucas."

"No?" Unable to resist, I raise my hand and wipe the streak of wetness off her face. My touch is almost gentle, the worst of my violent anger receding at the sight of her tears. "Then explain it to me, beautiful. Make me understand."

"I can't." Another tear escapes, undoing my work. "I'm sorry, but I can't."

"Can't or won't?" There's only one reason I can think of for her continued silence. My suspicions were correct. Yulia has someone there she's protecting— someone she can't tell me about because she knows what will happen if I learn of his existence.

Because she knows he'll die at my hand.

She doesn't answer my question. Instead, she says quietly, "May I please use the restroom? I really have to go."

I stare at her, my fury deepening. In less than five days, I'm going to Chicago, and I'm still no closer to getting real answers.

I will never get any closer for as long as she loves him.

As I look at her tear-streaked face, an idea comes to me, one I would've once dismissed as too cruel. Now, however, with this new knowledge fueling my rage, I can't see any other way. I can't keep Yulia locked up in my house forever; at some point, I'll have to give her more freedom, and when I do, I need to be certain there's nowhere she can run and hide.

I need to make sure she can't go back to *him*.

Reaching into my pocket, I take out my switchblade and cut through her ropes while she watches me, pale and visibly terrified.

Schooling my face into a hard, impassive mask, I take hold of her slim arm and pull her to her feet. "Let's go," I say, my voice like ice.

As I lead her down the hallway, my resolve firms.

It's time for the gloves to come off.

One way or another, Yulia is going to talk tonight.

CHAPTER EIGHTEEN

❖ YULIA ❖

My pulse hammers with anxiety as we walk silently to the bathroom. I can feel Lucas's anger. It's different from what I've seen from him before—colder and more controlled. He's both furious and resolved, and that frightens me more than if he had just exploded at me.

He lets me go into the bathroom alone as usual, and I close the door behind me, leaning against it to gather my thoughts and calm my frantic heartbeat. The food I ate at dinner is like a brick in my stomach. I haven't felt the bite of terror in over a week, and I've forgotten how powerful it can be.

He lied. He lied when he promised not to hurt me. I could see the dark intent on his face, feel the barely restrained violence in his touch.

He's going to do something to me tonight—something terrible.

Feeling sick, I use the toilet and wash my hands, going through the motions despite my panic. The knowledge of Lucas's betrayal is like a spear through my chest. In the beginning, I suspected he may be playing me, but as the days went on, I slowly began to lose my natural distrust of him, to believe that the bizarre domesticity of our arrangement might continue for some time.

To hope he truly won't hurt me.

Dura. Dura, dura, dura. The Russian word for fool is like a jackhammer in my skull. How could I have been such an idiot? I know what Lucas is. I see the demons that drive him. My captor is a man who walked away from a good, safe home to embark on a life of danger and violence, and he didn't do it out of love for his country.

He did it because it's his nature—because he needed to find an outlet for the darkness within.

I've known others like him. My instructors. Obenko himself. They all share this trait, this inability to be part of a peaceful society and abide by its laws. It's what makes them so good at their jobs—and so dangerous.

When conscience is nonexistent, it's easy to do what needs to be done.

"Yulia." A knock on the door startles me, and I realize I've just been standing there, absorbed in thought. "Are you done?" Lucas's deep voice breaks my paralysis, and I spring into action, my fear drowned under a wave of adrenaline.

"Almost," I call out, raising my voice to be heard over the running water. "Just need to wash my face."

Leaving the faucet on to mask the sounds of my movements, I kneel and open the cabinet under the sink. There, among extra toilet paper rolls and tubes of toothpaste, is the object I hid for just such an eventuality.

It's a small metal fork I snitched from the kitchen two days ago, slipping it into my shorts pocket while Lucas was washing the dishes. He'd left it inside the kitchen drawer that holds napkins and other small items, likely without realizing it was there. I took it while getting fresh napkins for the table and hid it here, hoping I'd never need to use it.

Well, I need it now. The little fork is not much of a weapon, but it's sturdier than a plastic toothbrush.

Ignoring the part of me that revolts at the idea of injuring Lucas, I take the fork, slip it into the back pocket of my shorts, and close the cabinet.

I can't allow him to break me.

My brother's life depends on it.

* * *

Lucas takes me to the bedroom, once again leading me there without speaking. I don't make the mistake of jumping him as soon as I come out—I won't catch him by surprise the second time. Instead, I walk as calmly as I can, trying not to focus on the little fork burning a hole in my pocket. I know Lucas always looks at my hands, so I keep them loose and relaxed at my sides, fighting the instinct that screams to protect myself, to strike *now*.

"Strip," Lucas says, stopping in front of the bed. His pale eyes are hooded as he releases my arm and steps back. I can feel the hunger within him. It's dark and potent, despite the cold anger evident in the hard lines of his face.

This won't be a tender lovemaking session. He's going to hurt me.

It takes everything I have to reach for the edge of my short tank top and pull it up over my head, baring my breasts to his gaze. My throat is so tight I can scarcely breathe, but I drop the tank top and face him without flinching. The worst thing I can do is show him how terrified I am—and how desperate.

"The rest," Lucas prompts when I pause. His expression is unchanging, but I see the growing bulge in his jeans. "Get it all off—or I will." His arm muscles flex, betraying his impatience.

I force my lips into a teasing smile. "Oh, yeah?" Slowly, very slowly, I reach for my zipper, praying that my hands don't shake. "And how exactly are you going to do that?"

At my challenge, Lucas's nostrils flare and he does precisely what I counted on.

He reaches for me and hooks his fingers through the top of my shorts, yanking me against his hard body. I gasp playfully, as if excited by his roughness, and while he's distracted, I slip my right hand into my back pocket, grab the fork, and strike.

In a blur of motion, my hand flashes toward his face, the fork targeting his eye at the same time as my knee jerks up, aiming for his balls. Each injury might disorient him for a few crucial moments, and the two together should give me enough time to run.

It should've worked—with any other man, it would've worked—but Lucas is not like any other man. As fast as I am, he's even faster. In a split second, he jerks back. The fork grazes his cheekbone and my knee hits his inner thigh, and then he's on me, twisting my right arm behind my back in a swift, merciless motion. His fingers squeeze my wrist, making my hand go numb. The fork slips out of my fingers, and in the next instant, I'm on my stomach on the bed, his big body pinning me down. I can feel his erection throbbing against my ass, sense the rage and lust radiating from him, and the old fear flares, the memories washing over me in a sickening tide.

No. Please, no. I can't move, can't breathe. I'm pinned, helpless as rough male hands rip away my clothes. The man on top of me wants to punish me, to hurt me. I struggle, but I can't do anything, and the dark panic engulfs me, sends me spinning out of control.

"No, please, no!" I'm scarcely aware of my screams and cries, of the pleas that tear from my throat. All I can feel are his hands dragging my shorts down my legs and his knees digging into my thighs to hold me restrained. There's no tenderness in his touch, nothing but raw, vengeful lust, and the terror is all-consuming as his fingers invade my body, thrusting in violently as I scream and sob in pain.

"Stop, please stop!" It's no longer Lucas on top of me, no longer the man who gave me pleasure. It's the brutal monster of my nightmares, the one who ripped me apart body and soul. The edges of my consciousness recede, spiraling into the past. "Don't! Please stop!"

The monster doesn't stop, doesn't listen. "Who am I?" he growls, his fingers relentless. "What is my name?"

"No, stop!" I thrash under him, mindless with fear. I don't understand what he's saying, what he wants from me. I need to get away. I need him to release me. "Let me go!"

"Tell me my name, and I'll stop." There's something wrong with that statement, something that should give me pause, but I can't think, can't concentrate on anything but the dark, swirling terror.

"Let me go!"

His fingers push in deeper, his voice hard and cruel. "Tell me my name."

"Kirill!" I scream, desperate for any hope, no matter how slim. I'd do anything, say anything to make him stop.

He doesn't stop. "My full real name."

"Kirill Ivanovich Luchenko!"

"Who am I?"

"My trainer!" The darkness consumes me, destroys me. "Please, stop!"

"Your trainer where?"

"At UUR!"

"What is UUR?" His body presses down on me, suffocating me with its weight. "What does it stand for, Yulia?"

"Ukrainskoye—" The oddity of it all finally penetrates my terror, and I freeze, my mind flitting in agony between the present and the past. It doesn't make sense. Everything is different, everything is wrong. The fingers inside me are rough, but they're not ripping me apart, and there's no cologne.

There's no cologne.

"What does it stand for?" the man repeats, and for the first time, I hear the strain in his familiar deep voice.

A voice that's speaking English.

No. Oh God, no. The realization is like an arrow puncturing my lungs.

It's not Kirill on top of me.

It's Lucas.

It's always been Lucas.

He made my nightmare come true, and I broke.

I told him everything.

CHAPTER NINETEEN

❖ LUCAS ❖

Yulia stills underneath me, her slim body wracked by violent tremors, and I know she's no longer there, in that old place of her terrors.

She's back here with me.

It should feel good, this victory. Her former trainer's name and the agency's initials are a solid lead. Our hackers will scour the net, and it's only a matter of time before they locate Yulia's bosses and her lover.

I've fulfilled the task I set out to complete.

Except for some reason, it doesn't feel like a victory. My chest aches dully as I withdraw my fingers from

Yulia's body, and there's an emptiness inside me, a void where rage and jealousy used to live.

I hurt her. Not much—maybe not at all, in the physical sense. She hadn't been totally dry, and I was careful not to injure her. But I hurt her nonetheless.

I took the horror of her past and used it to break her. Knowing her fear of sexual violence, I let her get scared enough to attack, and then I retaliated in the way she dreads most.

I recreated the conditions of her nightmare to bring back that terrified fifteen-year-old girl.

"Yulia." I move off her and sit up, the ache in my chest intensifying when she just lies there, trembling. Extending my hand, I gently stroke her back, unable to find the right words. Her skin is cold and clammy under my fingertips, her breathing unsteady. "Sweetheart . . ."

She twists away, her body contorting into a small ball of naked limbs. Her shorts are still around her knees, but she doesn't seem aware of that. She's just rolling up tighter and tighter, as if trying to make herself disappear.

"Come here, baby." I can't help reaching for her. She's stiff as I draw her into my lap, every muscle in her body rigid with tension. I know my touch is the last thing she wants right now, but I can't let her deal with this on her own.

Even knowing about her love for another man, I can't leave Yulia alone.

Her face is wet against my shoulder as I hold her, stroking her back, her hair, the sleek muscles of her calves. The peach scent of her skin teases my nostrils, but my lust for her is muted for the moment, leaving me free to focus on her comfort. With her knees drawn up to her chest, Yulia seems no bigger than a child, her entire body fitting on my lap. Her fragility weighs on me, adding to the heavy pressure around my heart. I don't know what to do, so I just hold her, letting my warmth soothe her chilled flesh. She doesn't pull away, doesn't fight me, and it's enough for now.

It has to be enough.

"I'm sorry," I murmur when her shaking begins to ease. The words probably sound as hollow to her as they do to me, but I persist, needing her to understand. "I didn't want to hurt you, but we had to move past this standoff. You would've never trusted me enough to tell me about UUR. And now it's over. It's done. I promised I wouldn't harm you if you talked, and I won't. It's going to be okay. Everything's going to be okay."

Once her lover is dead, she's going to be mine and mine alone.

Yulia doesn't say anything, but after a few more minutes, her breathing normalizes and her shaking stops. Even her skin feels warmer, though her body is still rigid in my embrace.

"Are you tired, baby?" I whisper, moving my hand over her back in small, soothing circles. "Do you want to go to sleep?"

She doesn't answer, but I feel her stiffening even more.

"Don't worry, I won't touch you," I say, guessing at the source of her tension. "We'll just go to sleep, okay?"

Still no response, but I'm not expecting any at this point. Cradling her against my chest, I get up and carry her to her side of the bed, then gently place her on top of the sheets. Yulia immediately rolls away from me, wrapping herself in the blanket, and I let her be while I take off my clothes and get the handcuffs.

Lying down beside her, I pull away the blanket and reach for her left wrist. "Come here, sweetheart. You know the drill."

She doesn't resist when I snap the handcuffs around her wrist and mine. It should've been uncomfortable to sleep like this, with our left wrists locked together, but I've gotten so used to it that it feels entirely natural.

As soon as I have Yulia secured, I pull her against my chest, holding her from the back. When my groin presses against her ass, I feel rough material against my bare cock and realize she managed to pull up her shorts while I was undressing. I consider letting her sleep like this, but after shifting a few times in search of a better position, I reach for the shorts' zipper.

"I'm just going to hold you," I promise, tugging the shorts down her legs while she lies rigid and unresisting. "You'll be more comfortable as well."

Kicking the shorts away, I pull her back into the spooning position, marveling at the perfect way her naked body fits into my arms. Before I met Yulia, I didn't get the appeal of cuddling with a woman, but now I can't imagine not holding her as I fall asleep.

Of course, normally I hold Yulia *after* sex, I realize as my cock stiffens against her ass. Sleeping is a lot easier after I've fucked her a couple of times.

Oh, well. I take a deep breath and picture myself crawling through the mud in the mountains of Afghanistan, with icy sleet soaking through my clothes. When that doesn't work, I think of my parents and the way they never touched or smiled at each other, substituting politeness for caring and mutual ambition for a family bond.

The latter memory does the trick, and my erection subsides enough for me to relax. As I sink into the soothing darkness of sleep, I dream of peach pies, angels with long blond hair, and a smile.

Yulia's bright, genuine smile.

CHAPTER TWENTY

❖ YULIA ❖

"*It's your fault, bitch. It's all your fault.*"

Dimly, I'm aware that the words are strangely distant, but the terror still engulfs me, pressing down on me like a smothering blanket. I can feel him over me, and I scream, struggling to avoid the violation, the awful pain.

"No, please, no!"

"Shh, baby, it's okay. You're just having a bad dream."

Strong arms tighten around me, pressing me against a hard, warm body, and the suffocating terror eases, the cruel voices receding. Sobbing with relief, I try to turn, to face the person holding me, but something hard tugs at my left wrist.

The handcuffs.

"Lucas?"

"Yeah, it's me." Warm lips brush my temple as a big hand smoothes back my hair. "I've got you. You're all right now. You're fine."

He's got me. Something should worry me about that statement, but at this moment, all I'm aware of is its seductive comfort. Lucas's powerful arms are around me, holding me, protecting me in the darkness, and the horror of the dream grows more distant, sinking back into the mire of the past.

There's no Kirill. There's just Lucas, and nobody can take me away from him.

"Baby, you've got to stop moving like that." His voice is hoarse, strained, and I realize I'm rocking against him in an attempt to burrow even deeper into his embrace. In the process, my ass is shimmying against his groin—with a predictable result.

The horror flickers distantly, the panic returning for a moment, and I try to turn again, to hide my face against his broad chest, but the handcuffs are in the way.

"Shh, it's okay. You're safe." There's a tug and a quiet *snick* as the key turns, unlocking the cuffs. "You don't have to be afraid. It's okay."

It's okay. The panic retreats, especially when I'm able to wrap my arms around Lucas's muscular torso and inhale his familiar scent. He smells like his body wash and warm male skin, like safety, strength, and comfort. Burying my face in his chest, I throw my leg over his hip, wanting to wrap myself around him like a vine, and I hear him groan as his hard cock presses into my belly.

Something about that should worry me too, but with my mind still wrestling with the dream, I can't figure out what. I just want him closer—as close as two people can possibly get.

"Fuck me," I whisper, slipping one hand between our bodies to cup his tightly drawn balls. "Please, Lucas, fuck me."

"You . . ." His voice sounds strangled. "You want me?"

"Yes, please, Lucas." I know it's pathetic to beg, but I need him. I need him to chase away the horror. "Please"—I grab his cock and try to align it with my sex—"please fuck me. Please."

"Yeah. Oh, fuck, yeah." He sounds incredulous as he rolls on top of me, his hips settling between my open thighs. "Whatever you want, beautiful. Whatever you fucking"—he thrusts in deep—"want."

We both groan when he's seated to the hilt, his thickness stretching me to the limit. I'm not as wet as usual, but it doesn't matter. The near-painful friction, the overwhelming force of his sudden entry—it's exactly what I need. This is not about sex or pleasure.

It's about being his.

"Yulia . . ." His voice is a tortured groan as he begins to move inside me. "Fuck, baby, you feel so amazing . . ."

"Yes." I wrap my legs around his muscular thighs, taking him even deeper. "Yes, just like that. Oh God, just like that."

He complies, his rhythm strong and steady, and I forget all about the initial discomfort. As he keeps thrusting, a wild heat ignites inside me, a need that's purely animalistic. I want him to fuck me so hard it hurts, to make me come so much I'll forget my own name.

I want his savagery to destroy my demons.

"Harder," I whisper, sinking my nails into his back. "Take me harder."

He tenses, a shudder running through his big body, and I feel his cock swelling even more. A low growl rumbles in his chest, and he picks up the pace, his muscled ass flexing under my calves as he jackhammers into me, each thrust so deep it almost cleaves me in two. It should be too much, too hard, but my body embraces him, the heat inside me blazing brighter with every bruising stroke. I can hear my own cries, feel the explosive pressure building, and all my fears evaporate, leaving nothing but scorching pleasure.

"Lucas!" I don't know if I scream his name, or if it's only in my mind, but at that moment, he lets out a hoarse cry, and I feel him jetting into me as white-hot ecstasy rips through my nerve endings. The orgasm is so powerful my entire body arches upward and white flecks appear at the edges of my vision. It seems to go on forever, one pulsing spasm after another, but eventually, the waves of pleasure recede, and awareness slowly returns.

Lucas is lying on top of me, his big body covered with sweat, but just as I register the heavy weight of his frame, he rolls off me, gathering me against him so that my head rests on his shoulder. We lie like that, both panting and too drained to move, and as my heartbeat begins to slow, the heavy lethargy of satiation steals over me.

"Sleep tight, baby," I hear him whisper as it pulls me under, and I close my eyes, knowing I'm safe.

I belong to Lucas, and he'll keep the bad dreams away.

* * *

"Morning, beautiful." A tender kiss on my shoulder wakes me up. "How about some tea?"

"What?" I pry open my eyelids and blink to clear the fog of sleep from my brain. I'm lying on my side, so I roll over onto my back and squint up at Lucas—who's standing next to the bed, already dressed and with what appears to be a steaming cup in his hand.

"Tea," he says. His hard mouth is curved into a smile. "I made some for you. I hope I didn't mess it up."

"Um . . ." My brain is still not fully functioning, so I sit up and try to make sense of what's happening. "You made me tea?"

"Hmm." Lucas sits down on the edge of the bed and carefully hands me the cup. "Here you go. I wasn't sure how long it should steep, but there were instructions on the box, so hopefully, it's right."

"Uh-huh." I take the cup from him and take a few sips. The tea is hot enough to burn my tongue, but the familiar taste of Earl Gray revives me, chasing away the cotton-candy fuzz in my mind. Slowly, in bits and pieces, it all starts coming back to me.

Lucas as Kirill. Telling him about UUR.

The cup tilts in my hand, hot liquid spilling onto my naked breasts.

Startled by the sudden pain, I look down and hear Lucas curse as he grabs the cup from me. He puts it on the nightstand before dabbing at my chest with a corner of the sheet. "Fuck. Yulia, are you okay?"

I stare at him, my skin growing cold despite the burn from the tea. "You want to know if I'm okay?" I remember everything now. The way he broke me. The way he held me afterwards. The nightmare. Clinging to him in the darkness.

Asking—no, *begging* him to fuck me.

Lucas's face tightens. "Did you get badly burned?"

"No." The chill within me deepens, numbing the sick terror flowing through my veins. "I didn't get burned."

Not by tea, at least.

Turning away, I lift the blanket, searching for the pair of shorts he kicked away when we were going to sleep. It's something to focus on, something to do. Besides, I need those clothes. They're a buffer, and I need that.

I need to cling to something to stay sane.

How could I have reached for Lucas after that awful dream, when just hours earlier he made it my reality? How could I have wanted a man who broke me in that manner? It's like I blanked out about what he did, suppressed it all in my desperate need for comfort.

In my weak, selfish neediness, I embraced the man who's going to destroy my brother.

"Yulia." Lucas reaches for me, but I twist away. My fingers finally close around the shorts, and I grab them before jumping off the bed on the other side. I know I have nowhere to go, but I can't let him touch me yet.

I'll shatter all over again.

"What are you doing?" he asks as I shimmy into the shorts and then get on all fours, looking for the top I dropped last night. "Yulia, what the fuck are you doing?"

Ah-hah, there. Ignoring his question, I grab the tank top—if the lacy-edged sports bra can even be called that. All the clothes Lucas got me are like that: casual, yet ridiculously sexy. They're better than nothing, though, so I pull on the tank top and get to my feet, doing my best not to look at him.

That seems to irritate him. In a second, he crosses the room and stops in front of me, his fingers closing around my arm.

"What the fuck, Yulia?" Lucas grips my chin with his free hand and forces me to look at him. "What game are you playing?"

"Me?" As I meet his gaze, a tiny ember of anger flickers in the ashes of my despair. "You're the game master, Kent. I'm just along for the ride."

His eyebrows snap together. "So last night was what? You going along for the ride?"

"Last night was a moment of insanity." That's the only way I can explain it to myself, at least. My voice is hard and bitter as I add, "Besides, what do you care? You have what you need."

"Yes, I do." His expression is unreadable. "I have enough to take down UUR."

A swirl of nausea makes me want to throw up. I don't know if Lucas senses it, but he lets go of my chin and steps back.

"You'll be fine," he says, his voice oddly strained. "I told you I'm not going to kill you or do anything to you once I got the information, and I won't. There's no reason for you to stress anymore. It's done."

I stare at him, struck by the fact that the idea of Lucas killing me didn't cross my mind either last night or this morning. I didn't think about what's going to happen to me at all. Somewhere along the way, I started believing that my captor doesn't want me dead.

I started trusting that his sexual obsession with me is real.

"Look," Lucas says when I remain silent, "things are going to get better. Once UUR is gone, I'll give you more freedom. You'll be able to walk around the estate on your own, go anywhere you please."

"Really?" Despite my despair, I almost laugh out loud. "And what makes you think I won't run?"

The corners of his lips pull up in a dark smile. "Because you wouldn't get far if you tried. I'm going to put some trackers on you."

My heart falters for a beat. "Trackers?"

Lucas nods, releasing my arm. "Esguerra's guys worked out a new prototype. For now, why don't I give you a small taste of what your future will be like and take you outside after breakfast? We'll go for a walk."

A walk outside. At any other point, I would've been ecstatic, but now, it's all I can do to interact with him in a semi-normal manner.

To act as if my whole world isn't about to come crashing down.

"Breakfast first, though," Lucas says when I remain frozen. "Let's go. I'll take you to the bathroom for your morning routine."

Bathroom. Breakfast. I want to scream that he's insane, that I can't possibly eat, but I keep my mouth shut and do as he says. I need to figure out what to do, how to fix the awful mess I've made.

"What kind of trackers are you talking about?" I force myself to ask as we walk to the bathroom. "Implants or the exterior kind?"

"Implants." Lucas stops in front of the bathroom door and looks at me. "Just a few to keep you safe."

And ensure he'd always know where I am.

"When are you going to put them on me?" I ask, trying to keep my voice steady. If the trackers are going to be as difficult to remove as I suspect, escape will be all but impossible.

"When I return from Chicago," Lucas says. "I have a two-week trip coming up in five days. Unfortunately, the trackers won't be here before then, so you'll need to be restrained for the duration."

"You're leaving?" My heartbeat kicks up with sudden hope. If he's going to be gone . . .

"Yes, but don't worry. I'll have a couple of guards I trust keep an eye on you." He smiles, as if reading my mind. "They'll make sure you're safe and comfortable."

And still here when I return.

The unsaid words hang in the air as I step into the bathroom and quietly close the door behind me. Lucas's plan to chain me to him should terrify me, but the nauseating fear I feel has nothing to do with my own fate.

If Esguerra's men come after UUR the way they've gone after other enemies, nobody connected to the agency will escape their wrath.

Obenko's entire family will be wiped out—and my brother along with them.

CHAPTER TWENTY-ONE

❖ LUCAS ❖

Yulia is silent and withdrawn as she makes us breakfast, and I have no doubt she's thinking about him—the man who holds her heart. She's probably wondering what's going to happen to him, beating herself up with the knowledge that she inadvertently betrayed him. I want to grab her and order her to put him out of her thoughts, but that would just make things worse. If she realizes I know about him, she might plead for his life, and I don't want that.

I'm going to kill the fucker no matter what, and I don't want her unnecessarily upset.

As it is, there's no sign of yesterday's joyous smile, no jokes or laughter as she moves about the kitchen, performing her task. With the fork incident fresh in my mind, I keep an extra-careful eye on her, making sure she doesn't conceal anything else. I suppose it's arrogant of me to let my prisoner walk around like this, untied and with access to things that could be used as weapons. I'm fairly sure I can contain her as long as I see her attack coming, but there's always a chance she might catch me off-guard one day.

She's dangerous, but like a challenging mission, that fact only excites me.

The breakfast Yulia makes is a simple one: an omelet with cheese and a bowl of strawberries for dessert. I could've theoretically made that, except my eggs would've been either rubbery or runny, and the cheese would've gotten burned on the edges of the frying pan. With Yulia, none of that happens. The omelet comes out light, fluffy, and perfectly cheesy, and even the strawberries taste better than I recall.

"This is amazing," I tell her as I devour my portion, and Yulia nods in a quiet acknowledgement of my thanks. Aside from that, she doesn't look at me or speak to me.

It's as if I don't exist.

Her behavior infuriates me, but I contain my anger. I know I deserve her silent treatment. I might not have hurt her physically, but that doesn't lessen the severity of what I did.

I tortured her, used her worst fear to break her.

Annoyed by the sharp prickle of guilt, I get up and wash the dishes, using the routine task to distract me from my churning thoughts. As far as I'm concerned, I'm doing Yulia a favor by getting her lover out of her life. It's clear that he's in no way worthy of her. He let her go to Moscow to sleep with other men, and he left her to rot in the Russian jail for two months. Agent or not, the man is a weakling, and she's better off without him. When Yulia came on to me last night, I thought that by some miracle she forgave me and decided to forget her lover, but now I see that was just wishful thinking on my part.

She'd been too traumatized to know what she was doing.

"Ready for the walk?" I say, approaching the table. Yulia is sipping her tea and still not looking at me. "I have a call in less than two hours, so if you want to come out, we should go now."

She gets up, still silent, and I see that her face is ashen. She's upset. No, more than upset—devastated.

The guilt bites at me again, and I push it away with effort. "Come here," I say, taking her hand. Her slender fingers are cold in my grasp as I lead her out of the kitchen. "We'll go out back."

The bedroom has a door that opens into the backyard, and I use that entrance now to avoid prying eyes. I don't want anyone seeing my prisoner outside and spreading rumors. Until I have something tangible to give Esguerra about UUR, I don't want to broadcast our relationship. My boss does owe me a favor, but it's better if it's a combo deal—the heads of our enemies alongside the news that I want to keep Yulia for my own.

"Sorry it's so hot," I say when we step out. It's only eight-thirty in the morning, but it's already like a steam bath. It'll probably rain within the next hour, but for now, the sky is clear with just a few white clouds. "Next time, we'll go earlier."

"No, this is fine," Yulia says, stopping in a clearing between the trees. Surprised, I glance at her and see that her face has a tinge of color now. As I watch, she closes her eyes and tilts her head back. She looks like a plant absorbing the sunlight, and I realize that's exactly what she's doing: basking in the sun, taking its warmth into herself.

"You like it here." I don't know why that surprises me. I suppose I pictured somebody from her part of the world being acclimated to the cold and hating the humid heat of the rainforest. "You like this weather."

She brings her head down and opens her eyes to look at me. "Yes," she says quietly. "I do."

"I'm glad." Squeezing Yulia's hand, I smile at her. "It took me a while to get used to it, but now I can't imagine living someplace cold."

She doesn't smile back, but her hand feels warmer in my hold as we resume walking, going deeper into the forest that borders the compound. Esguerra's estate is huge, extending for miles through the thick canopy of the rainforest. Back in the eighties, Juan Esguerra, Julian's father, processed vast quantities of cocaine here, but few traces of that remain now. The jungle has already swallowed up the old shack-style labs, nature reclaiming its turf with brutal swiftness.

"It's so beautiful here," Yulia says as we enter another clearing, and I see her looking at the tropical flowers that line a tiny pond a dozen feet away. She sounds oddly wistful.

I release her hand and turn to face her. "It's your new home." Reaching up, I tuck a strand of hair behind her ear. "Once everything is settled, you'll be able to come here whenever you want."

I intend that as a reassurance, a promise of good things to come, but her face tightens at my words, and I know she's worrying about her lover again.

Motherfucker. I wish the man was already six feet under, so she could move on from him.

Reminding myself to be patient, I drop my hand and say, "This is one of several nice places on this estate. There's also a pretty lake not too far away."

Yulia doesn't reply. She turns away and walks over to the pond. Her flip-flops are barely visible as she stands in the thick grass. The sight of the green stalks brushing her ankles makes me realize that I should get her some sneakers for these walks. There are snakes here, and all kinds of bugs. Wildlife, too—some guards have reported seeing jaguars on the grounds.

Suddenly concerned, I join Yulia at the pond and inspect the grass nearby. There's nothing particularly threatening, so I decide to let her be. She appears lost in thought as she gazes into the water, her smooth forehead creased in a faint frown. The sunlight makes her hair glow, and I notice for the first time that some of the strands are a near-white shade of gold, while others are a darker honey color. There are no roots showing, so her color must be entirely natural.

"Were your parents this blond?" I wonder idly, stepping behind her. Unable to resist, I gather her hair in my hands, marveling at its thickness. "You don't often see this shade with adults."

"My mom was." Yulia doesn't seem to mind my messing with her hair, so I indulge myself, running my fingers through the silky mass and then moving it to one side to expose her long, slender neck. "My dad's color was more of a sandy brown, a few shades darker than your hair. He was really light when he was a kid, though."

"I see." I lean down to breathe in her peach scent, but can't resist the urge to nuzzle the tender spot under her right ear. Her skin is warm and delicate under my lips, and as I graze my teeth over her earlobe, I hear her breath hitch. Instantly, desire spikes through me, my body hardening with need.

"Yulia . . ." I release her hair to cup her soft, round breasts. "I want you so fucking much."

She shivers, her lips parting on a silent moan as her head falls back against my shoulder and her eyes close. She might be upset about her lover, but she still wants me—that much is undeniable. Her nipples are stiff as they press into my palms through her tank top, and her pale skin is painted pink with a warm flush.

Last night wasn't an aberration after all. Yulia might not have forgiven me for my actions, but her body has.

Still kissing her neck, I bend my knees and tug her down to the grass with me. Turning her to face me, I stretch out on my back and have her straddle me, her hands braced on my shoulders. Yulia's eyes are open now, and she stares at me as I hold her hips and rock my pelvis upward, pressing my erection against her sex. Even through the layers of our clothing, it feels good to grind into her, especially when I see her blue eyes darken in response.

"Come here," I murmur, moving one hand up her back. Curving my fingers around her nape, I pull her head toward me and kiss her, swallowing her startled exhalation. She tastes like strawberries and herself, her tongue curling tentatively around mine as I deepen the kiss. I press her tighter against me, needing to get closer, but our clothes are in the way.

Growing impatient, I stop kissing her for a moment and move my hands down to grab the bottom of her tank top. With one smooth motion, I pull it off, exposing her gorgeous breasts—breasts that she immediately covers with her hands.

"Lucas, wait." Yulia casts an anxious glance behind us. "What if—"

"Nobody will bother us here." I reach for her shorts. "We're too far off the beaten path."

"But the guards—"

"The nearest guard towers are too far away to see us here." I unzip her shorts and roll over, stretching her out on the grass. Tugging her shorts down her legs, I add with a dark smile, "We're all alone, beautiful."

I take off my own clothes next, and Yulia watches me with a torn, almost tormented expression. I don't know if she feels like she's betraying him by wanting me, but I'm not about to put up with it. As soon as I'm naked, I cover her with my body and wedge my knees between her legs, spreading them open.

"Look at me," I order when she tries to close her eyes and turn her face away. Holding myself up on my elbows, I capture her face between my palms and repeat, "Look at me, Yulia." Her sex is less than an inch from the tip of my cock, and the lust is beginning to cloud my brain. Before I can take her, though, I need this from her.

I need to know she belongs to me.

Yulia opens her eyes, and I see tears swimming there. She blinks rapidly, as if trying to contain them, but they spill out, streaking down her temples. At the sight of them, something squeezes inside me, a strange ache awakening deep within my chest.

"Don't," I whisper, leaning down to kiss the moisture away. "Don't, sweetheart. It's okay. Everything's going to be fine." The taste of salt on my lips makes the ache intensify. "Don't cry. You're okay. I'm going to take care of you."

Her tears don't stop—they just keep coming—and I can't restrain myself. The hunger inside me is like a demon clawing its way to the surface. Taking her mouth in a deep kiss, I thrust into her and feel her slick flesh enveloping me, squeezing me so tightly that I shudder with violent pleasure.

She tenses underneath me, a raw, pained sound ripping from her throat, but I don't stop. I can't. The need to claim her is potent and primal, an instinct born in the mists of time. She was made for me, this beautiful, broken girl. She was destined to be mine. Still kissing her, I drive into her, again and again, as deep as I can go, and eventually, I feel her hands on my back as she embraces me, holding me close.

Binding me as tightly as I've bound her.

PART III: THE RIFT

CHAPTER TWENTY-TWO

❖ YULIA ❖

Over the next four days, we settle into a new routine. When I'm not tied up, I cook, we eat our meals together, and we go for early morning walks in the forest. And we fuck. We fuck a lot. It's as if the knowledge that we'll soon be separated makes Lucas even hungrier for me. He fucks me everywhere—the bedroom, the kitchen, up against a tree in the forest— and so frequently that by the end of the day, I'm raw and aching, my body sore and my soul torn by the knowledge that I'm sleeping with the enemy.

No, not that I'm sleeping with the enemy—that I'm enjoying it. No matter what I tell myself, no matter how much I try to resist, I unravel at the seams the moment Lucas touches me. Maybe if he hurt me again, it would be different, but he doesn't. His passion for me is forceful, even violent sometimes, but there's no anger or intent to harm in it. And often—far too often for my sanity—there's tenderness too.

It's as if he's beginning to care about me, to want me for something more than sex.

I try not to think about that—about his plans for me and the trackers he's going to use, shackling me to him while he destroys everything I hold dear. Lucas hasn't talked much about UUR, but from the little he let slip, I know he's already set things in motion with some hackers. There's a chance his search will set off alarms at the agency and they'll have time to go into hiding, but there's no guarantee of that. Obenko has never been up against an enemy as powerful and ruthless as the Esguerra organization, and there's a very real possibility he's outmatched.

If Lucas and his boss were able to take down Al-Quadar, it's only a matter of time before they'll do the same with my agency. I need to escape, or at least send them a message to warn them of what's coming, but Lucas is as careful with his phone and laptop as he is with his guns. Maybe one day, I'll be able to sneak into his office and crack the password on his computer, but I can't count on that.

There's only one way I can possibly save Misha now.

I have to tell Lucas about him.

It's a terrifying step for me. I don't trust my captor—he's already proven he'll use my vulnerabilities against me—but I don't see any other way. If I stay silent, Misha is as good as dead. I know I won't be able to talk Lucas out of vengeance on UUR, but maybe he'd be willing to use whatever influence he has with Esguerra to spare my brother.

Misha's normal life is already forfeit, but there's a chance I can keep him from getting killed.

Before approaching Lucas with my request, I decide to fix the rift between us, to make things go back to the way they were before he broke me. I do it subtly to avoid raising his suspicions, but by the evening after our first walk, I respond to him in full sentences, and by the next day, I act almost as if nothing happened. I go down on him in the shower, ask him what he would like me to make for dinner, and resume talking to him about the books I'm reading. I even tell him about my first horrendous experience at ballet, when a teacher said in front of the whole class that I have the neck of an ostrich—which, of course, led to the other kids calling me "Ostrich" for years.

Lucas laughs at that story, his light-colored eyes crinkling with amusement, and I smile at him, forgetting for a moment that he's my enemy, that I'm not doing this for real. It's shockingly easy to buy into my own act. When I'm not thinking about Misha's imminent fate, I truly do enjoy Lucas's company. For such a hard-edged man, my jailer is surprisingly easy to talk to—attentive and smart without being arrogant. Though Lucas never attended college, he's well versed in a number of topics and can speak intelligently about everything from world politics and the stock market to cutting-edge developments in science and technology.

"Where did you learn so much about investing?" I ask during a walk when the conversation turns to a finance book I read earlier this morning. Nassim Taleb's *The Black Swan* is a strongly worded criticism of risk management in the finance industry, and it surprises me to discover that it's one of Lucas's favorite nonfiction works.

"Both of my parents are corporate lawyers on Wall Street," he says. "I grew up with CNBC blaring in the background, and on my twelfth birthday, my father opened an investment account for me. You could say it's in my blood."

"Oh." Fascinated, I stop and stare at him. "Do you invest now?"

Lucas nods. "I have a good-sized portfolio. I don't manage it myself because I don't have time to do it properly, but the guy I use is good. He's actually Esguerra's manager as well. I'll probably visit him when we're in Chicago."

"I see." I don't know why I'm surprised. It makes sense. I know Lucas's background from his file. I guess I thought none of his upbringing rubbed off on him, but I should've known better, especially once I discovered all those books in his office.

"Do you keep in touch with them?" I ask. "Your parents, I mean?"

"No." Lucas's expression turns shuttered. "I don't."

His file said as much, but I'd wondered if that was a cover he concocted to keep his family safe. Apparently not. I'm tempted to ask more, but I don't want to pry—it's important to stay in my captor's good graces. For the rest of the walk, I let Lucas guide the conversation, and when we stop by the pond again, I sink to my knees and give him a blow job, using every skill I possess.

His happiness is my top priority these days.

* * *

The day before Lucas's departure, I decide it's time to tell him about Misha. For lunch, I prepare what I discovered is Lucas's favorite meal: roast chicken with mashed potatoes and apple pie for dessert. I also take special care to brush my hair until it's silky smooth, and wear a short white sundress—the nicest outfit he got for me. When we sit down at the table, I see Lucas devouring me with his eyes, and I know that in this at least, I pleased him.

Now I need to see how far his goodwill extends.

As we eat, I try to figure out the best moment to broach the subject. Will he be in the best mood before or after dessert? Should I let him finish his chicken, or is it okay to bring up my brother now? While I'm debating that, Lucas says conversationally, "I did some research on your hometown of Donetsk recently. Is it true that for most people there, their native language is Russian, not Ukrainian?"

I let out a relieved breath. This is as good a lead-in to this topic as any. "Yes, it's true," I say, smiling. "My family spoke Russian at home. I studied Ukrainian in school, but I'm actually more fluent in English than in Ukrainian."

Lucas nods, as if I confirmed something he suspected. "That's why they came to your orphanage, right? Because the kids there were already fluent in one of the languages they needed?"

It takes everything I have to keep smiling. The reminder of the orphanage and UUR takes away my appetite, even though we're getting closer to the subject I want to discuss. Moving my half-full plate aside, I say as calmly as I can manage, "Yes, that's why. I was a particularly good candidate because I also knew English."

"And because you're beautiful." Lucas's gaze cools unexpectedly. "Don't forget that part."

I gather my courage. "Maybe," I say carefully. "But they're not all bad people. In fact—"

Lucas holds up his hand, palm out. "Yulia, stop. I know what you're going to say."

Stunned, I stare at him. "You do?"

"You want me to spare one of them, right?" Lucas's eyes once again remind me of winter ice. "That's what all this"—he sweeps his hand in a gesture encompassing the table—"is about, isn't it? The dress, the food, the pretty smiles? You think I don't see right through you?"

I swallow, my heart beginning to race. "Lucas, I just—"

"Don't." His voice is as hard as the look on his face. "Don't humiliate yourself. It's not going to work. It's out of my hands."

My stomach fills with lead. "What do you mean?"

"Esguerra will never go for it, and I won't use up my currency with him on this."

I stand up, reeling. "But—"

"There's nothing more to discuss." Lucas gets up as well, his expression forbidding. "The only person from UUR who'll be spared is you."

I step around the table, my shock transforming into cold terror. Surely he doesn't mean this. "Lucas, please. You don't understand. He's innocent. He has nothing to do with this." I grab his hand, squeezing it in desperation. "Please, I'll do anything if you spare him. He's just one person. All you need to do is let him live—"

Lucas wrenches his hand out of my grasp, cutting off my plea. "I told you. There's nothing I can do for him." There's no pity on my captor's face, no hint of mercy. "Esguerra decides these matters, not me. You're shit out of luck, beautiful."

My vision darkens at the edges, blood pounding in my ears. "Please, Lucas—" I reach for him again, but he grabs my wrist and twists my arm upward, preventing me from touching him.

"Do not fucking beg for him." Squeezing my wrist painfully, Lucas pulls me to him, and I see scalding fury in the icy depths of his eyes. "You're lucky to be alive yourself. Don't you fucking get that? If you weren't such a hot lay—" He stops, but it's too late.

I hear his message loud and clear, and the fragile remnants of my fantasies turn to dust.

CHAPTER TWENTY-THREE

❖ LUCAS ❖

Yulia's eyes are enormous as she stares at me, her slender wrist caught in my grasp. She looks like I just tore her heart out, and something resembling regret cools the burning fog of rage surrounding me.

Releasing her wrist, I say in a calmer tone, "Yulia, that's not what I—"

"Why don't you just do it right now?" she interrupts, her gaze unflinching as she steps back. "Go ahead, kill me. You will anyway. When I'm no longer such a 'hot lay,' right?"

"No, of course not." My anger returns, only this time it's directed at myself. "I told you—you're safe with me."

"Not if your boss wants me dead." Her upper lip curls. "Isn't that what you just told me?"

"That's not what I meant." I curse myself ten ways to Sunday. Esguerra seemed as good of an excuse as any to stop her from pleading for her lover, but I should've realized how Yulia would interpret my words. "I promised you I'll protect you, and I'm going to keep that promise."

"Then why can't you protect *him*?" Her gaze fills with desperate hope as she comes toward me again. "Please, Lucas. He's an innocent—"

"Stop." I refuse to hear her beg for him. "I don't give a fuck about his guilt or innocence. I told you— one person only. That's the deal."

I expect Yulia to back down then, to accept that she lost, but she lifts her chin instead, her eyes like blue coals in her starkly pale face. "Then spare *him*. I want Misha to be that person, not me."

Misha. I file that name away even as my ribcage tightens with renewed fury.

She's ready to die for him—for her weakling of a lover.

"What you want doesn't matter." My words are as caustic as the jealousy burning my chest. "I decide who lives, not you."

She reacts like I just struck her. Her lips quiver, and she backs away, folding her arms around her middle.

"Yulia." I come after her, her pain cutting me like a blade, but she turns away to face the window as I approach. I lift my hand to lay it on her shoulder, but change my mind at the last moment. There's nothing I can do to make her feel better, except the one thing I'm not willing to promise.

I want this Misha dead, and I won't let her manipulate me into sparing his life.

Lowering my hand, I step back and survey Yulia's rigid figure. My captive is even more gorgeous than usual today, her short white dress making her look innocently sexy. With her hair streaming down her back in a sleek waterfall, she's temptation personified—and I know it's on purpose.

Like everything else Yulia has done over the last couple of days, her dressing up today is an attempt to save her lover.

The thought fills me with bitter anger. Turning away, I pack up the remainder of the meal and wash the dishes, using the time to cool down. Yulia doesn't move from her spot by the window, and when I approach, I see she's still deathly pale, her gaze distant and unseeing.

Steeling myself against an irrational urge to console her, I reach out to take her arm. "Let's go. " My voice is quiet. "I have to tie you up."

And holding her arm tightly, I lead Yulia to the library.

* * *

She doesn't say a word as I secure her in the armchair, making sure the ropes don't cut into her skin. When I'm done, I step back and look at her. "Which book do you want?"

She doesn't respond, her gaze trained on her lap.

"Yulia. I asked you a fucking question."

She glances up, her eyes dulled with pain.

"What do you want to read?" I repeat, trying not to let her obvious distress get to me. "Which book?"

She looks away, but not before I catch a glimmer of moisture in her eyes.

Fuck.

"All right, suit yourself." I grab a random thriller off the shelves and place it on her lap. "I'll be back before dinner."

Yulia doesn't acknowledge my words in any way, and I leave before the fury simmering inside me boils over.

CHAPTER TWENTY-FOUR

❖ YULIA ❖

I don't give a fuck about his guilt or innocence. It's out of my hands. If you weren't such a hot lay . . .

Lucas's words echo in my mind, replaying on a sickening loop over and over again. He had been so cold, so cruel. It was as if the last two weeks had never happened, as if our time together meant nothing to him.

My heart feels sliced into ribbons, the pain so vast it smothers me. I take in shallow breaths, trying to cope with the agony, but it just seems to grow and expand, sinking deeper into my chest.

I failed. I failed my brother. Everything I've done from the moment Obenko approached me at the orphanage has been for Misha, and now it will all be for nothing.

The man on whom I pinned my last hopes is a merciless monster, and I'm a gullible fool.

Don't humiliate yourself. It's not going to work.

Somehow Lucas knew about my brother. He knew I was going to ask him to spare Misha's life. He knew I was trying to soften him up all these days, and he let me.

He took everything I had to give, and then he drove a knife straight into my heart.

A bitter bubble of laughter escapes me as I think of the genius of his sadistic plan. I have to admit, Lucas Kent's idea of vengeance is exquisite. No physical torture would've hurt as much as his blunt refusal to save my brother.

My laughter turns into a sob, and I gulp it down, choking off the sound. Even to my own ears, I sound mad, hysterical. The agency therapist had been right. I'm not cut out for this job. I'm not like Lucas or Obenko.

I don't have what it takes to remain sufficiently detached.

"Your loyalty to your brother is admirable, but it's also your biggest weakness," Obenko told me a couple of months into my training. "You cling to Misha because he's a part of your past, but you can't have a past anymore. You can't have a family. You need to come to terms with that, or you won't be able to cope with this life. There will be times when you'll need to get close to people without letting them get close to you. You'll need to be in control of your emotions. Do you think you're capable of that?"

"Of course I am," I answered quickly, fearing he'd kick me out of the program and place my brother back in the orphanage. "Just because I love Misha doesn't mean I'd get attached to anyone else."

And I worked hard to prove that. I was friendly with the other trainees, but I didn't become friends with any of them. Same thing with the instructors. I kept my emotional distance from all of them. Even after the incident with Kirill, I did my best to deal with the trauma on my own.

I was such a good, diligent trainee that Obenko gave me the Moscow assignment less than a year after Kirill's assault.

Another sobbing laugh rises in my throat. I swallow the hysterical sound, but I can't control the tears that spill down my cheeks. I thought I was good at what I did. I smiled and flirted with my assigned lovers, but I never fell for them. Even with Vladimir, who taught me about sexual pleasure, I remained cool and detached. No one mattered to me except my brother.

No one until Lucas.

In my effort to get close to my captor, I opened myself up too much. I lost control of my emotions. I let a ruthless, treacherous man get close to me, and he used that closeness to devise the cruelest of all punishments.

He figured out the best way to destroy me.

CHAPTER TWENTY-FIVE

❖ LUCAS ❖

I have a shitload to do before we depart tomorrow morning, but I go to the gym because I can't focus on anything, my thoughts occupied by Yulia and the agony in her gaze.

As I pummel the sandbag, I try to push away images of her sitting there, so distant and wounded. She looked at me like I betrayed her—like I hurt her beyond belief.

The bag sways from side to side as I ram my fists into it, landing one hard blow after another. The idea of *her* feeling betrayed by *me* makes me want to beat someone to a pulp. What the fuck did she expect? That she'd give me a couple of blow jobs and I'd happily save her lover? That I wouldn't question her desire to spare this Misha's life?

An innocent, she called him, as if that would matter to me. As far as I'm concerned, the man deserves to die for nothing more than touching her. Add to that his being part of UUR, and he'll be lucky if I kill him quickly.

"Lucas. Hey, man. Are you almost done?"

Diego's question interrupts my mindless punching spree. Wiping sweat from my forehead, I turn to see the young Mexican standing there, his gloves already prepped. Behind him are a couple more guards waiting their turn.

Judging by the looks on their faces and the soreness in my knuckles, I must've been working off my anger for quite some time.

"It's all yours," I say, forcing myself to step away from the sandbag. "Go ahead."

As I leave the gym, I debate going back to my house to take a shower, but I'm not calm enough to face Yulia yet. So instead, I make my way to Esguerra's mansion to use the shower by the pool. He keeps a stash of T-shirts there in case of any unexpected bloody business, and I grab one of them to change into when I'm clean.

I rinse quickly, and as I'm pulling on my shorts and a fresh T-shirt, I catch a glimpse of a familiar dark-haired figure hurrying into the house.

Rosa.

I'd all but forgotten about the maid. She must've taken my words to heart, as I haven't seen her since our talk in Esguerra's kitchen. Hopefully, I didn't hurt the girl too badly, but it couldn't be helped. I didn't want her lurking anywhere near Yulia.

Feeling marginally calmer after my hard workout, I head to Esguerra's office for a call with the Israeli intelligence agency.

* * *

We spend the next two hours talking with the Mossad about the recent developments in Syria and the rest of the Middle East. As the call wraps up, I consider telling Esguerra what I've uncovered about UUR so far, but decide it's not the right time. I'll speak to him about Yulia and her agency when we return from Chicago. By then, I should have more concrete information, as the hackers are finally having some success sifting through the coded data in the Ukrainian government's files.

After the call is done, Esguerra and I go over last-minute logistics for tomorrow's trip.

"When we land, we're going to go straight to Nora's parents' house," Esguerra says. "They want to see her right away, even if it means a late dinner."

I'm long past wondering about the insanity of this trip, so I just say, "All right. I'll be with the guard detail tomorrow night to make sure everyone knows what they're doing."

"Good." Esguerra pauses for a second. "You know Rosa is coming with us, right?"

I actually didn't know that. "She is? Why?"

"Nora wants her company."

"Okay." I don't see how that changes anything. Unless . . . "Do I need to bring extra men to look out for her, or will she be with you and Nora most of the time?"

"She'll be with us." Esguerra seems vaguely amused. "All right, then, sounds like we're all set. I'll see you on the plane tomorrow."

"See you," I say, and head over to the guards' barracks for my meeting with Diego and Eduardo—the two guards I'm appointing as Yulia's jailers in my absence.

* * *

"Walk me through it again," I tell Eduardo after I give him and Diego the full list of instructions concerning my captive. "How many times will you visit my house to let her use the bathroom and stretch her legs?"

The Colombian rolls his eyes. "Three times in addition to releasing her during meals. We got it, Kent, I promise."

"And what will you do if she attempts to escape?"

"We'll restrain her, but not harm her in any way," Diego says, his lips twitching with amusement. "You've got to chill out, man. We understand. We're not going to touch a hair on her head other than to make sure she doesn't go anywhere. She's going to have her books, her TV shows, and yes, I'll take her out for a walk once a day."

"And we'll keep our mouths shut about the whole thing," Eduardo adds, parroting my exact words. "Nobody will hear a peep about your spy princess from us."

"Good." I give them a hard look. "And food?"

"We'll bring her products from the main house and let her cook them," Diego says, openly grinning now. "She'll be the most well-fed, well-entertained prisoner in existence."

I ignore his ribbing. "And at night?"

"I will shackle her wrist to the metal post you installed by the bed," Eduardo says. "And I will not lay a hand on her. It'll be as if she's a sack of potatoes—but a really important one," he adds quickly when my hand tightens into a fist. "Seriously, Kent, I'm just kidding. We're going to take good care of your girl, I promise. You know you can trust us."

I do know that. That's why I chose them for this task. Both guards have been working here for the past two years, and they've proven their loyalty. They might find my orders amusing, but they'll do as I say.

Yulia will be safe with them.

"Okay," I say, nodding at them. "In that case, I will see you both tomorrow morning. Be at my house at nine sharp."

And leaving the guards' barracks, I go to the training field to check on our new recruits.

CHAPTER TWENTY-SIX

❖ YULIA ❖

I don't know how much time passes before I get my tears under control, but by the time I open the book Lucas left for me, the sun is already setting outside. I stare at the words on the open page, but the text fades in and out, the letters jumbling together in front of my swollen eyes.

I failed my brother. Because of me, he's going to be killed.

I attempt to focus on the book, to push the devastating knowledge away, but it's all I can think about. Old memories press in, and I close my eyes, too tired to fight them off.

"Please watch your brother," my mother implores, her blue gaze filled with worry. "Check on him before you go to sleep, all right? He seemed a little feverish earlier, so if his forehead feels unusually warm, call us, all right? And don't open the door for anyone you don't recognize."

"I won't, Mom. I know what to do." I might be ten, but it's not the first time I've stayed alone with Misha while my parents rushed to my grandfather's sickbed. "I'll take good care of him, I promise."

Mom kisses me on the forehead, her floral perfume teasing my nostrils. "I know you will," she murmurs, stepping back. "You're my wonderful grown-up girl." Her face is tense with stress, but the smile she directs at me is full of warmth. "We'll be back as soon as your grandfather stabilizes a bit."

"I know, Mom." I smile back at her, unaware that my life is about to change forever. "Go to Grandpa. I'll watch over Misha, I promise."

And I tried to do exactly that. When the policemen came to our apartment the next morning, I didn't let them in until they showed me pictures of my parents' bodies in the morgue, broken and bloodied from the car crash. I insisted that my brother stay with me when Child Services tried to separate us, claiming that a two-year-old shouldn't attend his parents' funeral. And when Vasiliy Obenko approached me at the orphanage a year later, offering to have his sister and her husband adopt Misha if I joined his agency, I didn't hesitate.

I told the Head of UUR I'd do anything if he gave my brother a normal, happy life.

Opening my eyes, I try to focus on the book again, but at that moment, a flash of movement in my peripheral vision catches my attention. Startled, I look up and see a dark-haired woman standing in the middle of Lucas's library.

Rosa, I realize, my pulse jumping.

"What are you doing here? How did you get in?" I can't hide the undertone of panic in my voice. My hands are handcuffed, and I'm bound to the chair with a thick layer of ropes. If she means to harm me, I can't stop her.

Rosa holds up a key ring. "In the main house, we have a spare key for every building in this compound, private houses included."

I don't see any weapons on her, which is somewhat reassuring. "Okay, but why are you here?" I ask in a calmer tone.

"I wanted to see you," she says. "Tomorrow, we're leaving for two weeks. Going to Chicago to visit Nora's family."

"Nora's family?"

"Señor Esguerra's wife," Rosa clarifies.

I frown in confusion. I now recall that Nora is the name of the American girl Esguerra kidnapped and married. Lucas didn't tell me the reason for his upcoming trip, but I assumed it was business-related. I had no idea Lucas's sadistic boss has any kind of relationship with his in-laws.

"Anyways," Rosa continues, "I wanted to see you in person before I left."

My confusion intensifies. "Why?"

Rosa steps closer. "Because I don't think you belong here." Her hands are locked together in front of her black dress. "Because this isn't right."

"What isn't right?" Does she want me strung up in some torture shed like she'd implied before?

"You. This whole thing." Her brown eyes regard me steadily. "It's wrong that Lucas has you here like this. That he's leaving you with Diego and Eduardo. They're good guys, both of them. They like to play poker."

"Poker?" I'm completely lost.

Rosa nods. "They play with the guards on North Tower Two. Every Thursday afternoon from two to six."

"They do?" My heartbeat kicks up again. Is Rosa telling me what I think she's telling me?

"Yes," she says evenly. "It's not a problem because the drones patrol the perimeter around the estate, and there are heat and motion sensors everywhere. Anything approaching the border of the estate, no matter how small or big, gets scanned and examined by our security software, and the guards get alerted if the computer thinks there's a problem."

My pulse is now a frantic drumbeat. "I see." *Anything approaching,* she said. That means the computer disregards things heading in the other direction. "How far is the northern border of the estate from here?"

Rosa hesitates, and I kick myself for being too blunt. She clearly wants to pretend she's just chatting with me, and whatever information I glean is something she's giving by accident.

"Two and a half miles," she finally says, and I exhale in relief. I didn't scare her off after all. "There's a river that marks that border," she continues, dropping all pretense. "Farther to the west, a small road crosses the river. It goes all the way north to Miraflores. Occasionally, we get some deliveries via that route." She pauses, then adds, "The next delivery is scheduled for Thursday at three p.m."

"Thursday at three," I repeat, hardly able to believe my luck. "As in, this Thursday afternoon. The day after tomorrow."

She nods. "We're getting some food items brought in."

"Okay." My mind is racing, sifting through the potential obstacles. "What about—"

"I have to go now," Rosa says, stepping even closer. "Lucas will be home soon." She brushes her fingers over the book I'm holding, and her hand touches mine for a second. "Bye, Yulia," she says quietly before turning and hurrying out of the room.

Stunned, I look down and see two small objects on top of my book.

A razor blade and a hairpin.

CHAPTER TWENTY-SEVEN

❖ LUCAS ❖

It's after eight by the time I get home. To my relief, Yulia is calmly reading in her armchair when I step into the library.

"Sorry it took so long," I say, approaching the chair to untie her. "You must be starved—not to mention, needing the restroom."

She looks up at me, and I see that her eyes are slightly reddened, as if she's been crying. She doesn't say anything, but I don't expect her to. I have a strong suspicion tonight's dinner won't be a particularly chatty affair.

Bending down, I untie her and help her out of the armchair, ignoring the way she stiffens at my touch.

"Come. It's getting late." Determined to maintain control of my temper, I lead her to the bathroom.

I wait as Yulia uses the restroom, and then I bring her to the kitchen. I was hoping she'd make dinner despite being upset, but she just sits down at the table and stares straight ahead.

"All right," I say, not letting my irritation show. "You can sit if you want. I'll heat up some leftovers."

She doesn't respond, doesn't even move as I set the table and prepare everything. Luckily, the chicken and mashed potatoes she made for lunch taste great even when warmed up in the microwave.

Given Yulia's withdrawn state, I half-expect her not to eat, but she digs into the food the moment I set the plate in front of her.

I guess her hunger is stronger than her anger with me.

We demolish the chicken in silence; then I cut us each a slice of apple pie for dessert. I'm about to put Yulia's slice on her plate when she startles me by saying, "None for me, thanks. I'm full."

"All right." I conceal my pleasure at having her speak again. "Do you want any tea?"

She nods and rises to her feet. "I'll get it."

With those graceful, efficient movements I've come to know, she makes us each a cup and brings them over. Placing one cup in front of me, she sits down across the table and blows on her tea to cool it down. I do the same before taking a sip. The liquid is hot and slightly bitter, but not unpleasant. I can almost see why Yulia likes it so much.

We don't speak as we drink our tea, but the silence doesn't feel quite as strained as before. It gives me hope that this evening won't be a total disaster.

When we're done with the tea, I take care of the cleanup while Yulia sits and watches me, her expression unreadable. Does she hate me? Wish she could stab me with the nearest fork? Hope I never return from this trip?

The thought is more than a little unpleasant.

Pushing it aside, I finish wiping the counters and approach Yulia. "I arranged for two guards to watch over you in my absence," I say. "Diego and Eduardo. You've already met Diego—he's the one who carried you off the plane."

"Yes, I remember him." Yulia's voice is quiet as she rises to her feet. "He seems like a decent-enough guy."

"He is—and so is Eduardo." I stop in front of her. "They'll take good care of you."

"Jail me, you mean," she says evenly, looking up at me.

"Whatever you wish to call it." I lift my hand to pick up a lock of her hair. "They'll make sure you have everything you need."

She nods and takes a small step back, her silky strands sliding out of my fingers. "All right."

"Come." I catch her wrist before she can step out of my reach. "Let's go to bed. I have to wake up early."

She stiffens, but allows me to lead her to the bathroom without an argument. I let her in there to take a quick shower—I showered earlier, so I don't need one—and then I take her to the bedroom. As we enter the room, my cock rises in anticipation and erotic images fill my mind.

Fighting off the sudden surge of lust, I stop next to the bed and turn to face Yulia. Releasing her wrist, I frame her face with my palms, smoothing errant strands of hair back with my thumbs. She doesn't move, just gazes at me mutely, her blue eyes large and shadowed in her delicate face.

"Yulia . . ." I don't know what I can say to her, how I can fix the situation, but I have to try. The thought of leaving for two weeks while things are so strained between us is unbearable. "It doesn't have to be this way," I say softly. "It can be . . . better."

She blinks, as if startled by my words, and I see a fresh sheen of moisture in her eyes. "What are you talking about?" she whispers, her hands coming up to curl around my wrists. "Isn't this what you wanted? To hurt me? To punish me?"

"No." I let her pull my hands away from her face. "No, Yulia. I don't want to hurt you, believe me."

Her eyebrows draw together as she releases my wrists. "Then how can you—"

"I don't want to discuss this anymore. It's done. We're going to move past this. Do you understand me?" My words come out unintentionally harsh, and I see her flinch as she takes a step back.

I take a deep breath. The jealousy is still festering inside me, but I'm determined not to let it spoil our last night together. Forcing myself to move slowly and deliberately, I pull off my T-shirt and drop it on the floor, then remove my shoes, shorts, and underwear. Yulia watches me, her cheeks turning a soft shade of pink as her gaze falls on my growing erection. To my relief, I see the hardened peaks of her nipples through the white material of her dress.

She might hate me, but she still wants me.

"Come here." Unable to hold off any longer, I reach for her, clasping her slim shoulders. She's stiff as I pull her toward me, but I see the pulse throbbing at the base of her throat. She's far from immune to me, and I intend to use that.

One way or another, tonight Yulia won't be thinking of her lover.

I bend my head, wanting to taste her soft lips, but at the last moment, she turns her head and my mouth grazes her jaw instead. I feel her shudder, and then she twists out of my grasp altogether and backs away. Her chest is heaving and her face is flushed, her eyes glittering as she stares at me.

"I can't—" Yulia's voice cracks. "I can't do this, Lucas. Not after—"

"Stop." The unwanted jealousy returns, the pit of my stomach burning with anger as I come after her. "I told you I don't want to discuss this."

She keeps backing away. "But—"

"Not another word." Her back meets the dresser, and I close the remaining distance between us, trapping her there. Placing my palms on the dresser on both sides of her head, I lean closer, breathing in her delicate scent. Every dark fantasy I've ever had slides through my mind, and my voice roughens as I whisper in her ear, "I've had enough of this. You're mine now, and it's time you learned what that means."

CHAPTER TWENTY-EIGHT

❖ YULIA ❖

The damp heat of Lucas's breath on my ear makes me quiver, my thighs clenching convulsively to contain the growing ache between them. The treachery of my body adds to the tumult in my mind. I thought I'd have to force myself to endure his touch, but revulsion is the last thing I'm feeling.

Even knowing he's a heartless monster, I can't stop wanting Lucas.

His mouth trails over my jaw as he holds me caged against the dresser, and my heart rate accelerates as the hard length of his cock presses against my belly. "Don't," I whisper, my hands bunching into fists at my sides. I can feel the warmth of his powerful body surrounding me, pressing in on me, and my stomach twists with a combination of fear, shame, and longing.

"Please . . . let me go."

Lucas ignores my words, moving his right hand to my shoulder. Hooking his fingers under the strap of my dress, he pulls it down. His mouth is now on my neck, teasing and nibbling, and my arousal intensifies as his hand slips into the bodice of my dress and cups my breast, the rough edge of his thumb rasping over my nipple.

Heat blooms low in my core, my arousal intensifying even as self-loathing fills my chest. I don't want to feel this for my cruel captor. I'm not fighting him because I can't risk jeopardizing my upcoming escape, but I shouldn't be enjoying this.

I shouldn't desire the man who plans to kill my brother.

As if reading my thoughts, Lucas lifts his head to gaze down at me. There's lust in his pale gaze and something else—something dark and intensely possessive.

"No, beautiful," he murmurs, his hand still on my breast. "I'm not letting you go."

I begin to respond, but he lowers his head and slants his mouth across mine. His left hand grips my nape, holding me still, and his right hand moves down to pull up the skirt of my dress. In one yank, he rips off my thong. I hardly register the act; his kiss is too ravenous, too consuming. His lips and tongue steal my breath away, and it takes everything I have to remember why I shouldn't want him. Desperate, I splay my palms on the dresser behind me to keep myself from reaching for him. It's a small victory and one that doesn't last long. Still devouring my mouth, Lucas turns around, dragging me along, and begins backing me toward the bed.

The backs of my thighs hit the edge of the bed, and then I'm on my back, my dress hiked up above my waist and Lucas bending over me. His face is taut with hunger, his eyes glittering. Before I can recover from the kiss, he grips my knees, spreading them wide, and moves off the bed to crouch between my open legs.

"No, please, not this." I try to scramble backwards, but Lucas holds me tight, pulling me closer to the edge of the bed. His lips twitch with an ironic half-smile—he understands why I don't want this pleasure—and then he buries his head between my thighs and swipes his warm, wet tongue along my slit.

The lash of pleasure is almost brutal. My entire body arches up as he latches on to my clit and begins sucking on it in soft, rhythmic pulls. Gasping, I try to close my legs, to move away from the erotic torment, but Lucas's grip is unbreakable and his rhythm doesn't falter. I can feel the slickness of my arousal seeping out, and my nipples draw tight as unbearable pressure builds inside me, intensifying with every moment.

He picks up the tempo of his sucking motions, his lips squeezing my clit with every pull, and a stifled cry escapes my throat as I feel the orgasm approaching. *My brother's killer . . .* The words whisper through my mind as my body begins to contract in release.

"No, stop!" Without thinking, I jackknife to a sitting position and twist to the side with all my strength, breaking his grip on my thighs. The suddenness of my resistance catches Lucas off-guard, and I manage to scramble on my knees almost all the way across the bed before he leaps after me, his fingers closing around my ankle at the last second.

Acting on instinct, I turn and kick at him, aiming for his face, but he jerks to the side, causing my kick to miss. Before I can try again, he catches my other ankle and drags me across the bed toward him.

"What the fuck, Yulia?" Controlling my flailing legs with his knees, Lucas pins me down and captures my wrists to stretch my arms wide at my sides. His face is rigid with fury, his eyes narrowed into slits. "Are you that crazy about him?"

I stare at him, breathing hard. My body is throbbing with frustrated arousal, and a toxic cocktail of fear, adrenaline, and anger is boiling in my chest. Fighting Lucas was a stupid move on my part, but coming in his arms would've been a horrible betrayal of my brother. "Of course I am," I bite out, unable to restrain myself. "What the fuck did you expect?"

Lucas's fingers tighten around my wrists. "He's nobody to you now." Rage glitters in his eyes. "Nobody. You belong to *me*, understand?"

I gape at my captor, uncomprehending. How can he expect me to forget my brother? I know Lucas is possessive, but this demand borders on insanity.

Before I can gather my thoughts, Lucas's face hardens. Moving swiftly, he drags my right arm over my body, joining my right wrist with the left one. I end up on my side, my wrists held in his left hand as he reaches over me for the nightstand, his heavy weight crushing me into the mattress. Air rushes out of my compressed lungs, but a moment later, he lifts himself up, relieving the pressure on my ribcage. Holding my wrists with his left hand, Lucas looms over me, his lower body pinning mine in place—and in his right hand, I see the reason for his action.

He grabbed a coil of rope from the nightstand.

A chill dances over my skin, my desire dampened by a spike of fear. "What are you doing?" The words come out in a frantic, pleading whisper. "Lucas, you don't need to do this. I won't fight anymore."

But it's too late. He's already winding the rope around my wrists, and the old anxiety rises up, choking me with memories of Kirill. The paralyzing terror of the past rushes toward me, but at that moment, Lucas leans down and whispers in my ear, "I'm not going to hurt you—but I will make you forget him."

I draw in a shaking breath, his words providing the modicum of reassurance I need to stay in the present. Not that my anxiety is lessened in any way; what he's doing and saying is more than a little mad. I begin to struggle again, desperate to get away, but he's too strong. Ignoring my attempts to throw him off, Lucas ties the rope tightly around my wrists and reaches down to grab my ankles. As he does so, his weight briefly lifts off my legs, and I manage to kick him in the side before he seizes my ankles.

"Oh no, you don't." His voice is a low growl as he drags my ankles up, folding my body in half. I strike out with my bound hands, but I don't have much leverage, and the blow glances off his shoulder as he squeezes my calves in the crook of his muscular arm. With his hands free, he loops the other end of the rope around my ankles. His motions are swift and sure, utterly merciless. In a matter of seconds, he has me trussed up like a turkey, my ankles and wrists tied together in front of my body. With my dress flipped up and my underwear gone, my lower body is completely exposed.

The vulnerability of my position propels my heart rate so high I feel dizzy. Blood pounds in my ears in a thundering roar as Lucas forces my bound wrists and ankles up above my head, stretching my hamstrings to their limits. He secures the rope to the metal pole he installed by the bed and moves down my folded-in-half body. His hands grip my quivering thighs, and I see him looking at me—at my wide-open pussy and ass.

"What are you doing?" I can scarcely breathe through the growing panic in my chest. "Lucas, what are you doing?"

He looks up to meet my gaze, his eyes burning with savage heat. "Whatever I want, baby. Whatever I fucking want."

And lowering his head between my legs, he latches onto my clit again.

CHAPTER TWENTY-NINE

❖ LUCAS ❖

The taste of her is intoxicating, unbearably erotic. Her pussy is dripping with cream, and the heated feminine scent of her makes my cock weep with pre-cum. I want to thrust into her, feel her slick tightness cradling me, but I also want something else—something Yulia's withheld from me thus far.

First, though, I need to finish what I started. Ignoring the lust burning in me, I suck on her clit using the same rhythm that brought her to the edge of climax before. I felt her beginning to spasm before she started fighting, and I know I would've had her in another second. She panicked—probably because she doesn't want to betray *him*—but I'm not about to stand for it.

She's going to come tonight, again and again, until her lover is nothing but a distant memory.

It takes less than a minute to bring Yulia to the brink this time; she's already primed, her pink flesh swollen and sensitized from my earlier ministrations. She pleads with me, begging me to let her go, but I persist until I feel her pussy rippling under my tongue and hear her cry out in release.

Then I begin again, sliding my finger into her spasming channel to stimulate her as I lick her clit. She comes hard and fast, her juices coating my hand, and I go for the third one, even though my cock is ready to burst.

"No more," she moans as I push two fingers into her wet heat, finding the spot inside that drives her wild. "Please, Lucas, no more . . ."

But I'm not done yet. I'm far from done. Using the two fingers to fuck her, I close my lips around her clit again. My fingers drill her hard and fast, and her cries grow in volume with every second. I feel her inner walls contracting in another orgasm, but I don't stop. I keep going until I feel her come again—and then I scoop out the abundant moisture from her pussy and smear it on the tiny opening of her asshole.

She doesn't react at first, just lies there with her face flushed and her eyes closed as she attempts to catch her breath. With her ankles tied to her wrists and her pussy wet and swollen, she's the epitome of helpless sensuality. Bondage isn't normally my thing, but restraining Yulia is different. It's not about kink; it's about possession.

After tonight, she'll have no doubt that she's mine.

When her asshole is sufficiently lubed, I press the tip of my finger to the tight opening, watching her reaction. The one time I touched her ass in the shower, she tensed, and I realized she either has a problem with anal sex or is new to it. I hope it's the latter, but I suspect it might be the former.

Sure enough, as my finger pushes in the first quarter of an inch, Yulia's ass cheeks clench, and her eyes fly open. "Don't." Her voice is strained. "Please don't."

"Was it your trainer?" I keep my finger where it is, neither pressing forward nor retreating. "Did he hurt you this way too?"

She stares at me, her chest heaving, and I see her mouth tremble before she presses her lips together. She doesn't say anything, but I don't need a verbal confirmation.

The motherfucker did hurt her like this—and she's afraid I will too.

Something squeezes painfully inside me. I don't deserve her trust, but a part of me wants it. It's a desire that directly contradicts my primitive need to subdue her, to keep her at any cost.

Even as I hold her bound and helpless, I don't want her fearing me—not that way, at least.

"I won't hurt you," I say quietly, holding Yulia's gaze. The savage hunger pounding through me dies down to a muted roar as I withdraw the tip of my finger. "I promise you that."

She shudders with relief, her eyes closing, and I lower my head again, licking her pussy with gentle swipes of my tongue. Her flesh is pliant, still soft and wet. I know she's nowhere near an orgasm now, and I don't try to give her one. Instead, I soothe her with my lips and tongue, giving her undemanding pleasure. I do this for what feels like hours, and eventually, I feel the remnants of terrified tension leave her body.

Continuing to lick her, I move my mouth lower, to her creamy slit, and dip my tongue inside, tasting her there. She tenses in a different way, a moan escaping her lips, and I capitalize on her growing arousal by carefully rubbing her swollen clit with my fingers. She's moaning in earnest now, and I move my tongue even lower, to the tight ring of muscle between her ass cheeks.

Yulia stiffens for a second, but I just lick her there, tonguing her back opening and rubbing her clit until she's panting and gasping, her hips rocking in an instinctive rhythm. I can sense that she's on the verge, and I ruthlessly push her over, pinching her clit with a firm, steady pressure.

Her body tightens, and I feel the ring of muscle pulsing and spasming under my tongue as she cries out in release. I lick her one last time, depositing as much saliva as I can, and then, using the distraction of her orgasm, I push my finger in again. It slides in easily before her body clamps down on it, and I keep it there, letting her adjust to the sensation as I sit up and shift closer, pressing my groin against her lower body.

Her eyes are wide and dazed-looking, her lips parted as she stares at me, her chest rising and falling with panting breaths.

"I won't hurt you," I repeat, keeping my finger inside her as I use my free hand to guide my cock to her pussy. "This is as far as we'll go today."

Yulia doesn't respond, but her eyes close, her teeth sinking into her lower lip as the tip of my cock enters her tight, slick heat. With my finger buried in her ass, I can actually feel my cock pushing into her, stretching her inner walls as I go deeper, and I groan at the exquisite pleasure of it, my balls tightening with explosive need.

"Yes, baby, that's it. Let me in deeper . . ." I'm barely cognizant of what I'm saying, my voice a feral rumble in my chest as her pussy sucks me in, engulfing my entire length. "Oh, fuck, yeah, just like that . . ."

She cries out as I brace myself on the bed and begin thrusting, no longer able to restrain myself. Being inside her is paradise, and I never want to leave. If I had my way, I'd fuck Yulia forever. But all too soon, the pleasure intensifies, turning into razor-sharp ecstasy, and I feel the boil of incipient orgasm in my balls. My thrusting pace picks up—I'm all but jackhammering into her now—and I hear her cries growing louder, mixing with my own grunting groans. My vision blurs, my entire body seizing with intolerable tension, and through the hammering roar of my heartbeat, I hear Yulia scream and feel her inner muscles clamp down on my cock and my finger.

Dimly, I realize she's coming, and then my own climax is upon me, my cum spurting out into her as my cock jerks uncontrollably, again and again.

CHAPTER THIRTY

❖ YULIA ❖

I'm dazed and shaking, my heart rate somewhere in the stratosphere as Lucas slowly withdraws his finger from my ass and pulls out of me. I'm so out of it I barely notice when Lucas unties me, lifts me into his arms, and carries me out of the room.

It's not until the water spray hits me that I realize we're standing together in the shower, his arms wrapped around me from the back to prevent me from collapsing. My leg muscles are quivering from being stretched for so long, and my body is throbbing in the aftermath of his dual invasion. Lucas is kissing my neck as he holds me in front of him, and I'm letting him, my head resting on his shoulder as warm water cascades over our bodies.

"Relax, beautiful." His voice is a soft rumble in my ear as I attempt to pull away. His arms tighten around me, holding me in place. "We're just going to take a nice shower together, that's all."

I know I should protest, push him away, but I don't have the strength to fight him anymore. Maybe I never did—because fighting Lucas means fighting myself as well. Something perverse in me is drawn to this cruel, dangerous man, has been drawn to him from the very beginning.

Seeing that I'm no longer trying to pull away, Lucas makes sure I'm steady on my feet and carefully loosens his grip.

"Let me wash you," he murmurs, reaching for a bottle of body wash, and I stand like an obedient child as he lathers my whole body, washing me from head to toe. His soapy hands go everywhere, even into the place his finger invaded earlier, and I close my eyes, giving myself up to his gentle ministrations.

I'll despise myself for this tomorrow, but tonight, I want his tenderness. I crave it.

He kept his promise not to hurt me. I'm still vaguely surprised by that. When Lucas tied me up, I thought he'd do something horrible to me—and when he started touching my ass, I became sure of it. But other than the slight burn of the initial entry, his finger hadn't hurt, and his tongue there had felt . . . interesting. The sensations had been strange and foreign, but nothing like the terrible pain Kirill had inflicted on me that day.

The water spray stops, and I open my eyes, realizing Lucas turned off the shower.

"Come, baby." He guides me out of the shower stall and wraps a fluffy towel around me before briskly drying himself. "Let's go to bed," he says, stepping toward me. "You're falling asleep on your feet."

He picks me up again, and I don't protest as he carries me back to the bedroom. Even after the shower, I feel like I'm about to fall over. The orgasms Lucas forced on me have depleted me both emotionally and physically, and there's nothing I want more than sleep.

Sleep will be my escape for the rest of the night, and tomorrow, my tormentor will leave.

He'll be gone, and if Rosa gave me good information, so will I.

The thought should fill me with joy, but as Lucas places me on the bed and handcuffs us together, happiness is the last thing I'm feeling. Even now, a part of me mourns the fantasy—the man I'd begun falling for before he shredded my heart.

* * *

Lucas wakes me up in the middle of the night by thrusting into me, his thick cock invading me from the back. I gasp, my eyes popping open at the sudden intrusion. I'm not as wet as before, but it doesn't matter. My body responds to him instantly, my core flooding with liquid heat as he begins driving into me. There's no finesse to this fucking, no attempt to make it anything but what it is.

A hard, basic claiming.

Our left wrists are still cuffed together, and the room is pitch black. I can't see anything; I can only feel as he holds me against him, his arm a steely band around my ribcage. His hips hammer into me, and I take him in, unable to do anything else. My breathing quickens, heat rippling over my skin in waves, and my inner muscles begin to tighten.

"Tell me you're mine." Lucas's hot breath washes over my neck. "Tell me you belong to me."

"I—" The intensity of the sensations overwhelms my sleep-fogged brain. "I'm yours."

"Again."

"I'm yours." I gasp as his cock hits a spot inside me that ups the heat to a volcanic burn. "I'm yours."

"Yes, you are." He moves his left hand to my sex, dragging my wrist along with it. "You're mine and no one else's."

"Yes, no one else's . . ." I don't know what I'm saying, but with his fingers touching my clit, I don't care. Everything about this feels surreal, like some kind of a sex dream. I can feel Lucas's muscled body surrounding me as his cock pumps into me, and the volcanic heat grows, burning away all thought and reason. Dazed, I cry out as the sensations crest, and then I'm coming, my inner muscles clamping around his hard shaft.

Lucas groans too, and I feel his big body tensing and shuddering behind me. The warmth of his seed floods me, and my sex spasms with aftershocks, sparks of residual pleasure sizzling along my nerve endings.

Breathing hard, I close my eyes, feeling his chest rise and fall against my back as his cock slowly softens inside me. I know I should get up and clean up, or at least reach for a tissue, but I'm too relaxed, too drained by the pleasure. I don't want to do anything but lie in Lucas's arms. He seems to be equally unwilling to move, and my lids grow heavy as my thoughts begin to drift. All my fears and worries feel unreal, distant from this moment and from us. In some faraway world, we're enemies and he's my captor, but I'm no longer in that brutal place.

I'm here, warm and safe in my lover's embrace.

The veil of darkness wraps around me, and as I sink deeper into the haze of dreams, I hear him say softly, "I'm sorry, Yulia. Do you hate me?"

"Never," I whisper to my dream Lucas. "I love you. I'm yours."

And as sleep drags me under, I feel him kiss my temple and hold me tighter, as if afraid to let me go.

428

CHAPTER THIRTY-ONE

❖ LUCAS ❖

Yulia's breathing takes on the steady rhythm of sleep, but I'm wide awake, my heart pounding heavily in my chest. Did she mean it? Did she know what she was saying?

Did she know it was *me* she was saying it to?

I want to shake her awake and demand answers, but I resist the impulse. I don't know what I would do if Yulia told me it was Misha she was dreaming about. The mere thought of it burns me like acid. If I found out she meant the words for him . . .

No. I can't go there. I don't want Yulia looking at me like I'm a monster again.

Tightening my arm around her ribcage, I brush my lips across her temple and close my eyes, trying to relax. It was most likely a slip of the tongue, something she mumbled by accident, but even if there's some truth to her words, why should I care? Sex is what I want from her, sex and a certain basic companionship.

Just because I want Yulia doesn't mean I need her love.

Forcing my breathing to slow, I will sleep to come, but the thought that she might love me is like a splinter in my brain. No matter how hard I try, I can't seem to let it go—or to suppress the warm sensation that accompanies the idea.

It's an illogical reaction on my part. I know better than anyone how meaningless those words are. My parents used "I love you" as a platitude, as something to say to each other and to me at social functions. It was part of the glossy façade they presented to the public, and I've always known not to take them at face value. Same with the women I've slept with: more than one of them had used the words casually, throwing them out like one might say "hello" and "goodbye." There's absolutely no reason for me to latch onto this one mumbled phrase from Yulia—a phrase that might not have even been meant for me.

Unless it had been meant for me. Is that possible? It wouldn't be casual for Yulia, that much I'm sure of. Given the circumstances, if she did fall in love with me, she'd resist letting me know for as long as possible—

which means she probably didn't realize what she was saying.

Fuck. Clearly, I can't let the matter rest. If Yulia loves me, I need to know, so I can stop obsessing about it.

Sitting up, I lean over her and turn on the bedside lamp.

She doesn't so much as twitch at my movements. Her lips are slightly parted, and her lashes form dark crescents on her pale cheeks. With her face relaxed in sleep, she looks impossibly young—an innocent worn out by my harsh demands.

I watch her for a few moments, then reach for the light and turn it off. Lying down, I mold my body against her slender form from the back and breathe in the sweet, peach-tinted scent of her hair.

Soon, I promise myself as I close my eyes. When I return from Chicago, I'll question her and find out the truth.

My captive's not going anywhere, and two weeks is not that long to wait.

* * *

The chirping of my phone alarm drags me out of deep sleep. Suppressing the urge to crush the offending object, I reach for the nightstand on my right and turn off the alarm. Yawning, I take out the key I keep in that drawer and turn back to face Yulia—who woke up from my movements this time and is regarding me with a sleepy, half-lidded gaze.

"Hi, beautiful." Unable to resist, I unlock the handcuffs and pull her into my lap. She's soft and pliant, her skin deliciously warm as I hold her against me, and I have to fight the urge to throw her down for one last fuck. "I have to go," I murmur instead, kissing the top of her head. There are so many things I want to say to her, so many questions I want to ask about last night, but I settle for saying, "Be good with Diego and Eduardo, okay?"

She tenses slightly, but I feel her nod against my chest.

"Yulia, about last night . . ." I slide my fingers into her hair and gently pull on it, needing to see her face, but she refuses to meet my gaze, her eyes trained somewhere on my chin.

I sigh and decide to let it go. Now is not the time to get into what Yulia may or may not have said to me when she was half-asleep. "I'll miss you," I say softly instead.

Her lips tighten, her gaze dropping even lower, and I remind myself to be patient. I can wait two weeks. Brushing another kiss over the crown of her head, I reluctantly shift her off my lap and get up, doing my best to keep my eyes off her naked curves.

Diego and Eduardo will be here in ten minutes, and I still need to shower and get dressed.

CHAPTER THIRTY-TWO

❖ YULIA ❖

"Yulia, you've already met Diego, and this is Eduardo," Lucas says, gesturing toward two young guards. "They'll be watching you in my absence."

I prop my hip against the kitchen table and nod at the two dark-haired men, keeping my expression carefully neutral. Diego is taller than Eduardo, but they're both muscular and in good shape. Handsome in their own way, though I much prefer Lucas's fierce, Viking-raider looks.

"Hello," I say, figuring I have nothing to lose by playing nice.

"Hi, Yulia." Diego grins at me, showing even white teeth. "I have to say, you look much . . . cleaner today."

His grin is contagious, and I find myself smiling back at him. "Showers have been known to do that," I say wryly, and he laughs out loud, throwing his head back. Eduardo chuckles too, but when I sneak a glance at Lucas, I see that his face is dark, his eyebrows pulled together into a frown.

Is he jealous of the guards he himself chose?

"You remember my instructions, right?" Lucas snaps, glaring at the two men, and I realize that he's indeed displeased with them. "All of them?"

"Yes, of course," Eduardo says quickly. Diego's grin disappears, and both guards stand up straighter. "You have nothing to worry about," the shorter man adds.

"Good." Lucas gives them a hard look before turning to me. "I'll see you in two weeks, okay?" he says in a softer tone, and I nod, trying to avoid meeting his pale gaze.

I have a terrible suspicion my dream last night might not have been entirely in my imagination.

Lucas pauses for a second, as if he wants to say something, but then he just turns and leaves, walking out of the kitchen. A few seconds later, I hear the front door close.

My captor is gone.

"So," Diego says cheerfully, bringing my attention back to him. He's grinning again, his arms crossed over his broad chest. "What's for breakfast?"

* * *

I make an omelet for myself and the two guards, being careful not to do anything suspicious. They may seem friendly, but I don't mistake their smiles for anything but an amicable mask.

Nice guys don't work for illegal arms dealers, and these two have a good reason to hate me—if they know about my role in the plane crash, that is.

"So, Yulia," Eduardo says, gobbling down his omelet with evident gusto, "how did you learn to cook like this? Is that a Russian thing?"

"I'm Ukrainian, not Russian," I say. Though the difference in my hometown region is slight, I prefer to think of myself as belonging to the country of my employers. "And yes, it's somewhat of an Eastern European 'thing.' Many people there still regard cooking as a necessary skill for a woman."

"Oh, it's necessary, all right." Diego forks the last bite of his omelet into his mouth and glances longingly at the empty frying pan. "Should be mandatory, as far as I'm concerned."

"Sure. Just like cleaning, laundry, and taking care of the kids, right?" I give the two men a syrupy-sweet smile.

"If a woman looked like you, I'd do the laundry," Eduardo says with apparent seriousness. "But cleaning . . . I guess help with that would be nice."

I laugh, unable to help myself. The guy's not even trying to conceal his chauvinistic views.

"I think what Eduardo's trying to say is that Lucas is a lucky guy," Diego says diplomatically, kicking the other guard under the table. "That's all."

"Right." I suppress the urge to roll my eyes. "I'm sure that's it."

"You bet." Diego winks at me and gets up to throw out his paper plate. "Eduardo's just spoiled," he explains, returning to the table. "First his *mamacita* babied him, then his ex-girlfriend."

"Shut up," Eduardo mutters, glowering at Diego. "Rosa didn't baby me. She was just good at domestic things."

"Rosa?" My ears perk up at the familiar name.

"Yeah, she's Esguerra's maid," Diego says. "Sweet girl. Way too good for this guy here"—he jerks his thumb toward Eduardo—"so she dumped his ass months ago."

"Oh, I see," I say, trying not to appear too interested. If Rosa had dated Eduardo at some point, that explains how she knows about their poker games. "Does Esguerra have many servants?"

"Not really," Eduardo answers, getting up to throw out his empty plate. He's frowning; I guess the memory of being dumped by Rosa is not a pleasant one. "We should get going," he says abruptly, then glances at me. "Are you almost done with your food, Yulia?"

I nod, consuming the remnants of my omelet. "Yes." I carry my plate to the garbage and dump it, then wash the frying pan and place it on a paper towel to dry. "All done."

"Good." Diego smiles at me, his dark eyes gleaming. "Then go use the restroom, and we'll take you on your morning walk."

* * *

As the two men lead me on a brisk stroll through the forest, I decide they most likely don't know about my involvement in the plane crash that killed their colleagues. Or if they do, they're excellent actors. They banter with me as easily as they do with each other, their manner friendly and relaxed. They don't seem like killers—except I see the guns stuck in the waistband of their jeans.

If they're ordered to plant a bullet in my brain, I'm sure neither one will hesitate to do so.

Our walk takes about twenty minutes, and then they bring me back to Lucas's house.

"All right, chica," Diego says, leading me to Lucas's library. "Your boyfriend said this is your usual spot. Grab whatever book you want, and then we have some work to do."

"Boyfriend?" Startled, I look at the guard. "You mean, Lucas?"

Diego grins. "That's the one. Unless you have more than one around here?"

I bite back a denial and grab a book at random. Lucas is definitely *not* my boyfriend, but if that's what they think, it could play to my advantage.

It could also explain why the two guards are being so nice to me, I realize as I walk over to the armchair. It's generally smart to show respect to the girlfriend of one's boss—even if that girlfriend is to be handcuffed and tied up most of the time.

Sitting down, I place the book on my lap, take a deep breath, and extend my wrists toward Diego. "Go ahead. I'm ready."

CHAPTER THIRTY-THREE

❖ LUCAS ❖

Our flight to Chicago is uneventful. Esguerra stops by the pilot's cabin every couple of hours to check on things, but for the most part, he stays in the main cabin with his wife and Rosa, who's accompanying them on this trip.

"Nora is still sleeping," he says, stopping by again an hour before we land. His dark eyebrows are drawn into a worried frown. "Do you think this is normal, to sleep this much?"

"Pregnant women need a lot of rest, or so I've heard," I say, concealing a smile. Esguerra's acting like no woman has ever carried a baby before. "I'm sure it's fine."

He nods and disappears back into the cabin. Probably to watch over Nora, I think with amusement before turning my attention back to the controls.

After the crash, I'm leaving nothing to chance.

We land at a small private airport just outside Chicago, where an armored limo is waiting for us on the runway. I've sent most of the guards ahead of us, and they've scrubbed this airport top to bottom, so I know it's safe. Still, I automatically scan our surroundings for danger before walking over to the limo and getting into the driver's seat.

One can never be too careful in our line of work.

As I drive the limo to Nora's parents' house, my thoughts turn to Yulia. Esguerra is in the back with Nora and Rosa, and everything is quiet on the road, so I decide to use this time to call Diego.

"How's it going?" I ask as soon as the guard picks up.

"Well, let's see . . ." He sounds like he's on the verge of laughing. "For breakfast, she made an amazing omelet. For lunch, she fed us the best chicken I've ever had, and for dinner, she's grilling pork chops and baking a chocolate cake. So I'd say it's going pretty well. Oh, and we took her for a walk this morning."

"She's behaving? No escape attempts?"

"Are you kidding me? Your girl's a model prisoner. She even taught us a few swear words in Russian at lunch. Like *yob tvoyu mat'*—"

"Excellent." I grit my teeth, battling a swell of irrational jealousy. I know I can trust these two guards, but it still bothers me that they seem to be getting so chummy with my captive. Loyal or not, they're still men, and I know how easy it is to get obsessed with Yulia. "Don't forget to handcuff her to the bedside pole at night."

"You got it, man."

"Good." I draw in a deep breath. "And, Diego, if you or Eduardo so much as lay a finger on her—"

"We would never." The young Mexican sounds insulted. "She's yours, we know that."

"All right." I force myself to relax my grip on the wheel. "Call me if anything comes up."

And disconnecting, I turn my attention back to the road.

* * *

Esguerra's dinner with his in-laws passes without an incident until Frank, Esguerra's CIA contact, decides to pay us a visit. He insists on speaking with Esguerra, so I call my boss outside after first making sure our snipers are in position.

If the US agency decides to double-cross us tonight, they'll have a battle on their hands.

Fortunately, Frank doesn't seem to be suicidal. He sends his car away and goes for a walk with Esguerra. I follow at a small distance, keeping my hand on the gun inside my jacket. They don't go far, just to the nearest park and back.

"What did they want?" I ask Esguerra when Frank's black Lincoln pulls away.

"For us to stay the fuck out of their country," Esguerra explains. "Apparently, the FBI is going apeshit—Frank's words, not mine. They're worried about why we're here. Plus, there's the whole matter of Nora's abduction."

"Right. So what did you tell him?"

"That we're not here on business, and that we'll leave when we're good and ready. Now if you'll excuse me, I have a family dinner to get back to." He disappears back into the house, and I head to the limo, shaking my head in disbelief.

My boss has balls, I have to give him that.

* * *

It's late by the time Esguerra's dinner is over. Fortunately, it's not a long drive to Palos Park, a wealthy community where Esguerra bought a mansion on my recommendation.

"It'll be more secure than a hotel," I told him when we began planning the trip two weeks ago. "This specific house is particularly good because it's fenced in and has an electronic gate, not to mention a long driveway—optimal for privacy."

When we pull up to the mansion, Esguerra, Nora, and Rosa go inside while I check in with the guards to make sure they're properly positioned and know what to do in case of emergencies. It takes me over an hour, and by the time I finally enter the house, I'm more than ready to hit the sack. First, though, I need to grab a bite to eat; the two energy bars I ate in the car were a shitty substitute for dinner.

I clearly got spoiled by Yulia's cooking.

"Oh, hi, Lucas," Rosa says when I enter the kitchen. Her cheeks flush as she looks at me. I must've caught her on her way to bed, because she's wearing long pajamas and cradling a cup of steaming milk. "I didn't realize you were still up."

"Yeah, I had to do some last-minute security checks," I say, suppressing a yawn. "Why are you awake?"

"I couldn't sleep. Too many new impressions, I guess." Her full lips curve in a wry smile. "I've never flown before—or been to America."

"I see." Battling another yawn, I make my way over to the fridge and open it. It's fully stocked already—I made the arrangements for food delivery myself—so I grab some cheese and a loaf of bread to make myself a sandwich.

"Do you want me to make you something?" Rosa offers, watching me uncertainly. "I can whip up something in a minute."

"It's nice of you to offer, thanks, but you should go to sleep." I slap a slice of cheese on a piece of bread and bite into the dry sandwich. "I'm sure you'll have plenty of cooking to do tomorrow," I say after I chew and swallow.

"Yeah, well, that's my job." She shrugs, then adds, "Though you're probably right—I think Señor Esguerra is hoping to impress Nora's parents tomorrow night."

"Hmm-mm." I finish the rest of the sandwich in three bites and put the cheese back in the refrigerator. "Have a good night, Rosa," I say, turning to leave.

"You too." She watches me walk out of the room, her expression oddly tense, but I'm too tired to wonder about what's on her mind.

When I get to my room, I take a quick shower and fall into bed. Surprisingly, sleep doesn't come right away. Instead, I lie awake for several minutes, tossing and turning on a king-sized mattress that feels cold and far too empty.

It's been less than a day, and I already miss Yulia.

Two weeks, I tell myself. I just need to get through the next two weeks. Then I'll be home, and Yulia will be in my arms every night again.

CHAPTER THIRTY-FOUR

❖ YULIA ❖

I stare at the dark ceiling, unable to close my eyes despite the late hour. It's strange being in Lucas's bed without him . . . feeling the cold steel of the handcuffs anchoring me to the bedside pole instead of to his wrist. I've gotten used to sleeping tucked into his large warm body, and even with the blanket drawn up to my chin, I feel cold and exposed as I lie there alone, trying to relax enough to go to sleep.

Diego and Eduardo have been good jailers so far. They adhered to the routine Lucas must've laid out to them, letting me eat, stretch, use the restroom, and read in the comfortable armchair. They also kept me company at mealtimes, though I suspect the food I cooked had a lot to do with that. By the time our dinner was over, I decided that I like both of them—as much as it's possible to like mercenaries whose job is to keep you captive. Rosa was right about them being good guys; under different circumstances, we might've been friends.

I hope Lucas won't punish them too harshly for my escape—assuming I succeed tomorrow, that is.

Thinking about tomorrow chases away whatever little sleepiness I was beginning to feel. To alleviate my anxiety, I mentally go over the details of my plan again. It's simple: Right after lunch, I'll use the tools Rosa gave me to free myself and make a run for the northern border of the estate, where the guards at North Tower Two might be distracted with their poker game. Diego and Eduardo will be at that poker game, so they won't come looking for me until after six p.m. By then, I'll be on the delivery truck—which, hopefully, will be far away from Esguerra's compound at that point.

If all goes well, tomorrow evening I will no longer be Lucas Kent's prisoner.

I should be excited, but instead, there's a hollow ache in my chest. The dream from last night—if it was a dream—is still painfully vivid in my mind. For a brief moment, I forgot who we are, what passed between us, and I told Lucas something I didn't know myself until that moment.

"Do you hate me?" he asked, and like an idiot, I said I loved him.

I admitted my terrible, irrational weakness to a man who's hurt me with every weapon I've given him.

Maybe I didn't say the words out loud. Maybe it *was* a dream—or, more precisely, a nightmare. Except if that's the case, why did Lucas bring up last night when he was telling me goodbye? Why did he say that he'll miss me?

Groaning, I turn onto my side and punch the pillow with my free hand. I must be sick, or at least brainwashed by my captivity. I can't be in love with a man who intends to destroy my brother.

I can't be the idiot who's fallen for a killer with an ice rock instead of a heart.

I'll miss you.

His deep voice whispers through my mind, and I squeeze my eyelids together, trying to shut it out. Whatever I'm feeling, whether it's love or temporary insanity, will pass once I'm far away from here.

I have to believe that, so I can focus on my escape.

* * *

Breakfast and lunch drag by with agonizing slowness. By the time Diego and Eduardo tie me to the armchair and leave, I'm ready to jump out of my skin. I hope they couldn't tell how anxious I am; I did my best to act normal, but I don't know if I succeeded.

After I hear the front door close behind them, I sit quietly for a few minutes, making sure they're not coming back. When I'm satisfied that my jailers are gone, I begin to move. My heart is beating in a fast, desperate rhythm, and my palms are sweating as I carefully reach into the chair cushions for the items Rosa gave me.

I fish out the hairpin first. With the ropes securing my upper arms to the chair, my range of motion is limited, but I manage to stick the pin into the lock of the cuffs. I'm far from an expert lock picker, but they taught us this during training, so after a few failed attempts, I succeed in opening the cuffs.

The razor blade is next. With my hands no longer stuck together, I wedge the tiny blade under the ropes around my upper arms and saw through them. It's not an easy task—I'm bleeding from several cuts by the time I'm done with one thick rope—but I'm determined, and ten minutes later, I've sawed through enough ropes to be able to wiggle out of the chair.

Step one of the plan complete.

Next, I rush to the kitchen and grab two water bottles and a few energy bars I found in one of the cabinets. I don't expect to be in the jungle for long, but it's best to be prepared. At this time of day, the heat could dehydrate me in a matter of hours. I also take the sharpest kitchen knife I can find and slip the razor blade and the hairpin into the pocket of my shorts, just in case. I put the food and the knife in a backpack I find in Lucas's closet, and then I head for the door in Lucas's bedroom—the one that leads to the backyard and the jungle beyond.

Holding my breath, I open the door and scan the area. There's no sign of the guards, and all I hear are the usual nature noises.

So far, so good.

I step outside and close the door behind me. A wave of humid heat washes over me, making my clothes stick to my skin. I was right to take those water bottles. I'll have to go north for two and a half miles and then west along the river to reach the dirt road Rosa mentioned, and I'll need to drink on the way.

Taking a breath to steady my nerves, I head toward the trees behind the house. My sneakers—the footwear Lucas got me for our walks—make almost no noise as I enter the thick jungle, and I exhale in relief as the canopy of trees closes over my head, concealing me from any potential eyes in the sky.

Now I need to get to the border and locate the road by which the delivery truck will be leaving the estate at some point after three p.m.

Sweat gathers under my arms and drips down my back as I walk briskly, trying not to step on any insects or snakes. Thin tree, thick tree, a cluster of bushes, a fallen log—these landmarks are how I track my progress. Focusing on my immediate surroundings helps me not think about the drones that might be hovering overhead or the guard towers I'll have to pass on my way to the border. Rosa told me North Tower Two is the one where the guards play poker, but I have no idea how I'll distinguish between that tower and some other one.

If there's a North Tower Two, there must be a North Tower One, and if I stumble upon the wrong tower, I'm screwed.

After a half hour, I take out the first bottle and gulp down most of the water, then wipe the sweat off my face with the bottom of my shirt. Even in the shorts and skimpy tank top I'm wearing, the heat is difficult to bear.

Just a little longer, I tell myself. It can't be that far to the river now. I just need to reach it and then follow it west until I get to the road.

It's at most another half hour of walking.

"Alto!"

At the harshly yelled Spanish command, I freeze, instinctively raising my hands. The water bottle falls out of my nerveless fingers. *Oh, shit. Shit, shit, shit.*

The male voice barks another command at me, and I turn around slowly on the assumption that that's what he told me to do.

A dark-haired musclebound man is standing a couple of meters in front of me, his M16 pointed at my chest. He's dressed in camouflage pants and a sleeveless shirt, and I see a radio hanging on his hip.

It's one of the guards. He must've been patrolling the forest and spotted me.

I'm so, so fucked.

Glaring at me, the guard says something in Spanish, and I shake my head. "Sorry." I moisten my parched lips. "I don't speak much Spanish."

The young man's glower deepens. "Who are you? What are you doing here?" he says in heavily accented English.

"I'm—" I swallow, feeling sweat trickling down my temples. "I'm staying with Lucas."

"Lucas Kent?" The guard looks confused for a moment; then his dark eyes widen. "You are the prisoner."

"Um, kind of. But now I'm his guest." I attempt a shaky smile as I slowly lower my hands to my sides. "You know how that goes."

An understanding look comes over the guard's face. "You are his *puta*."

I'm pretty sure he just called me a whore, but I nod and widen my smile, hoping it looks seductive rather than frightened. "He likes me," I say, pulling my shoulders back to thrust my braless breasts forward. "You know what I mean?"

The man's gaze slides from my face to my sweat-dampened tank top. "Sí." His voice is slightly hoarse. "I know what you mean."

I take a step toward him, keeping the smile on my face. "He's away," I say, making sure to roll my hips. "Went on a trip with your boss."

"With Esguerra, yes." The man seems hypnotized by my breasts, which sway with my movement. "On a trip."

"Right." I take another step forward. "I got bored sitting at home."

"Bored?" The guard finally manages to tear his gaze away from my chest. His eyes are slightly glazed as he looks at my face, but his weapon is still pointed at me. "You should not be out here."

"I know." I purposefully bite my lower lip. "Lucas lets me go out into the backyard. There was a pretty bird, I followed it, and I got lost."

It's the stupidest story ever, but the guard doesn't seem to think so. Then again, the fact that he's staring at my lips like he wants to eat them may have something to do with that.

"So, yes, maybe you can point me back to his house," I continue when he remains silent. I risk another tiny step toward him. "It's very hot today."

"Yes." He lowers his weapon and takes hold of my left arm. "Come. I will take you there."

"Thank you." I smile as brightly as I can and jab my right hand up, ramming the heel of my palm into the underside of his nose.

There's a crunching noise, followed by a spray of red. The guard stumbles back, reflexively clutching his broken nose, and I grab the barrel of his M16, kicking at his knee as I yank the assault rifle toward me.

My foot connects with his knee, but the man doesn't let go. Instead, he releases his nose and grips the weapon with both hands, pulling it—and me—toward him.

He may not be as well trained as Lucas, but he's still much stronger than me.

Realizing I only have seconds before he wrestles me to the ground, I stop pulling and push the gun toward him instead, causing him to lose his balance for a moment. At the same time, I kick upward between his legs as hard as I can.

My sneaker meets its target: the guard's balls. A choked gasp escapes the man's throat, followed by a high-pitched scream as he bends at the waist. His face turns sickly pale, and his grip on the gun loosens for a second—which is all the time I need.

Jerking the heavy weapon out of the guard's hands, I swing it at his head.

The rifle makes a loud *thud* as it meets his skull. The impact of the collision sends a shock of pain through my arms, but my opponent drops like a stone.

I have no idea if he's unconscious or dead, and I don't waste time checking. If there are other guards in the vicinity, they might've heard his scream.

Clutching the M16, I begin running.

Tree. Bush. A gnarled root. An ant hill. The tiny landmarks blur in front of my eyes as I run, my breath rattling loudly in my ears. Every couple of minutes, I glance behind me for signs of pursuit, but none are evident, and after a few minutes, I risk slowing down to a jog.

Where the hell is that river? Two and a half miles is about four kilometers; it shouldn't take this long to get there.

Before I have a chance to wonder if Rosa might've lied, the ground in front of me suddenly slopes downward at a sharp angle. I skid to a stop, barely managing to avoid tumbling down the incline, and through the thick tangle of bushes in front of me, I see a shimmer of blue below.

The river.

I'm at the northern border of Esguerra's compound.

My breath whooshes out in relief. I start forward to get a closer look—and freeze again.

Less than a hundred meters to my left is a guard tower.

The trees had obscured it from my view.

I back up and crouch behind the nearest tree, desperately hoping the guards didn't spot me yet. When I don't hear shouts or gunshots, I risk peeking out to look at the tower again.

The structure is tall and ominous, looming over the forest. At the top is a solid square enclosure with slits instead of windows, and around the enclosure is an open-air walkway. I don't see any guards on the walkway, but they're all probably inside, hiding from the stifling heat in the shade. There are no markings on the structure. It could be North Tower Two, or it could be some other one. There's no way for me to know.

I'll be passing right by it if I head west, and if the guards inside the enclosure look outside, I'll be caught in an instant.

For a moment, I consider turning back and trying to locate the road when I'm farther south, out of sight of this guard tower, but I decide against that. There could be more towers there. Plus, Rosa said the security software focuses on things *approaching* the estate. That means the computer might flag anything moving south from this point.

I have to either cross the river here, or turn west now and attempt to find the road where it intersects with this river.

I look at the river. With the thick bushes blocking my view, I can't tell how wide or deep it is. It could easily have a strong current or, since it's the Amazon rainforest, be teeming with crocodiles. If I were a particularly strong swimmer, I'd risk it, but crossing jungle rivers wasn't a big part of my training.

I glance at the tower again. Still no guards on the walkway. Could they be playing poker inside?

I vacillate between my two options for a minute, debating the pros and cons of each, but ultimately, it's the position of the sun that helps me make my decision. It's moving lower in the sky, signifying that the afternoon is wearing on. I don't have a watch, so I don't know the time, but it's probably getting close to three p.m.

If I don't locate the road soon, I risk missing the delivery truck, and then it won't matter if the guards in the tower spot me or not. Once Diego and Eduardo realize I'm missing, I'll be found in a matter of hours if I'm still in this jungle on foot.

Trying to steady my shaking hands, I place the M16 on the ground. I'm much more likely to get shot if I'm visibly armed, and one assault rifle won't help me against guards who are better armed and have the protection of the enclosure.

With one last look at the river, I leave the shelter of my tree and head west, toward the tower.

Thin tree. Thick tree. Root. Bush. A cluster of wild flowers. I stare at the plant life as I walk, the fear like icy fingers clawing at my chest. The tower looms closer—I can see it in my peripheral vision now—and I focus on not looking at it, on moving slowly and deliberately, just one foot in front of another.

Thick tree. Another thick tree. A small ditch that I have to jump over. My heart feels like it might leap out of my throat, but I keep moving, keep not looking at the tower. It's parallel to me, then slightly behind me, and I still keep my gaze trained ahead and walk at the same measured pace.

My skin crawls and the back of my neck tingles as I cross a small clearing, but there are still no shouts or gunfire.

They don't see me.

This must be North Tower Two.

I risk picking up my pace slightly, and when I glance back a couple of minutes later, the tower is no longer visible.

I stop and lean against a tree trunk, my knees going weak with relief.

I made it past the tower without getting shot.

When my frantic heartbeat slows a little, I force myself to straighten and keep going.

I don't know how long it takes before I reach the road, but the sun is hovering lower in the sky when I find it. The road is not much—it's just an unpaved path cutting through the jungle—but at the point where it meets the river, it widens onto a sturdy wooden bridge.

I stop and listen, but all is silent. No sounds of a car approaching, no signs of the guards.

I turn onto the bridge and start walking. Immediately, I realize I was right not to try crossing the river at the earlier location. The river is wide, and both banks are steep, almost cliff-like. Even if I made it across, I would've had trouble climbing up the other side.

I keep walking, and soon the bridge—and Esguerra's compound—is behind me. I try to keep to the tree line as much as I can while staying by the road. I don't want to be spotted by any drones that might be patrolling the area, but I can't chance missing the returning delivery truck.

I walk for what feels like hours before I finally hear the rumble of a car engine.

This is it.

I take out the knife I stole from Lucas's kitchen and stick it into the waistband of my shorts, covering the handle with the bottom of my tank top. I hope I won't have to use the knife, but it's best to be prepared.

Ignoring the frantic hammering of my pulse, I step out onto the road and wait for the vehicle to approach.

It's a van, not a truck as I supposed. It stops in front of me, and the driver—a short middle-aged man with darkly bronzed skin—jumps out, staring at me in surprise. He asks something in Spanish, and I shake my head, saying, "Tourist. I'm an American tourist, and I got lost. Please help me."

He looks even more surprised and says something in rapid-fire Spanish.

I shake my head again. "Sorry, I don't speak Spanish."

He frowns and looks around, as if expecting a translator to jump out from the bushes. When nothing happens, he shrugs and motions for me to follow him to the car.

I climb into the passenger seat next to him, making sure to keep my hand close to the knife at my side. The delivery man could be Esguerra's employee, or he could be a civilian who just happens to deliver food to an arms dealer's estate.

Either way, if he tries anything—or attempts to call anyone—I'm ready.

The driver starts the car, and the van begins moving, heading north on the dirt road. After a few minutes, the man puts on some music and starts humming along under his breath. I smile at him and move my hand off the knife handle.

I made it.

I escaped.

Now I can warn Obenko and save my brother.

"Goodbye, Lucas," I whisper soundlessly as the van bumps along the unpaved road, carrying me away from my captor.

Carrying me away from the man I love.

SNEAK PEEKS

Thank you for reading! If you would consider leaving a review, it would be greatly appreciated.

Lucas & Yulia's story concludes in *Claim Me (Capture Me: Book 3)*. If you'd like to be notified when the book is out, please sign up for my new release email list at www.annazaires.com.

If you haven't read Nora & Julian's story, I encourage you to try *Twist Me*. All three books in that trilogy are now available.

Additionally, if you liked this book, you might enjoy Mia & Korum's story, another trilogy of mine that is already complete.

Finally, if you like audiobooks, please be sure to check out this series and our other books on Audible.com.

And now please turn the page for a little taste of *Twist Me, Close Liaisons,* and some of my other works.

EXCERPT FROM *TWIST ME*

Author's Note: *Twist Me* is a dark erotic trilogy about Nora and Julian Esguerra. All three books are now available.

* * *

Kidnapped. Taken to a private island.

I never thought this could happen to me. I never imagined one chance meeting on the eve of my eighteenth birthday could change my life so completely.

Now I belong to him. To Julian. To a man who is as ruthless as he is beautiful—a man whose touch makes me burn. A man whose tenderness I find more devastating than his cruelty.

My captor is an enigma. I don't know who he is or why he took me. There is a darkness inside him—a darkness that scares me even as it draws me in.

My name is Nora Leston, and this is my story.

* * *

It's evening now. With every minute that passes, I'm starting to get more and more anxious at the thought of seeing my captor again.

The novel that I've been reading can no longer hold my interest. I put it down and walk in circles around the room.

I am dressed in the clothes Beth had given me earlier. It's not what I would've chosen to wear, but it's better than a bathrobe. A sexy pair of white lacy panties and a matching bra for underwear. A pretty blue sundress that buttons in the front. Everything fits me suspiciously well. Has he been stalking me for a while? Learning everything about me, including my clothing size?

The thought makes me sick.

I am trying not to think about what's to come, but it's impossible. I don't know why I'm so sure he'll come to me tonight. It's possible he has an entire harem of women stashed away on this island, and he visits each one only once a week, like sultans used to do.

Yet somehow I know he'll be here soon. Last night had simply whetted his appetite. I know he's not done with me, not by a long shot.

Finally, the door opens.

He walks in like he owns the place. Which, of course, he does.

I am again struck by his masculine beauty. He could've been a model or a movie star, with a face like his. If there was any fairness in the world, he would've been short or had some other imperfection to offset that face.

But he doesn't. His body is tall and muscular, perfectly proportioned. I remember what it feels like to have him inside me, and I feel an unwelcome jolt of arousal.

He's again wearing jeans and a T-shirt. A gray one this time. He seems to favor simple clothing, and he's smart to do so. His looks don't need any enhancement.

He smiles at me. It's his fallen angel smile—dark and seductive at the same time. "Hello, Nora."

I don't know what to say to him, so I blurt out the first thing that pops into my head. "How long are you going to keep me here?"

He cocks his head slightly to the side. "Here in the room? Or on the island?"

"Both."

"Beth will show you around tomorrow, take you swimming if you'd like," he says, approaching me. "You won't be locked in, unless you do something foolish."

"Such as?" I ask, my heart pounding in my chest as he stops next to me and lifts his hand to stroke my hair.

"Trying to harm Beth or yourself." His voice is soft, his gaze hypnotic as he looks down at me. The way he's touching my hair is oddly relaxing.

I blink, trying to break his spell. "And what about on the island? How long will you keep me here?"

His hand caresses my face, curves around my cheek. I catch myself leaning into his touch, like a cat getting petted, and I immediately stiffen.

His lips curl into a knowing smile. The bastard knows the effect he has on me. "A long time, I hope," he says.

For some reason, I'm not surprised. He wouldn't have bothered bringing me all the way here if he just wanted to fuck me a few times. I'm terrified, but I'm not surprised.

I gather my courage and ask the next logical question. "Why did you kidnap me?"

The smile leaves his face. He doesn't answer, just looks at me with an inscrutable blue gaze.

I begin to shake. "Are you going to kill me?"

"No, Nora, I won't kill you."

His denial reassures me, although he could obviously be lying.

"Are you going to sell me?" I can barely get the words out. "Like to be a prostitute or something?"

"No," he says softly. "Never. You're mine and mine alone."

I feel a tiny bit calmer, but there is one more thing I have to know. "Are you going to hurt me?"

For a moment, he doesn't answer again. Something dark briefly flashes in his eyes. "Probably," he says quietly.

And then he leans down and kisses me, his warm lips soft and gentle on mine.

For a second, I stand there frozen, unresponsive. I believe him. I know he's telling the truth when he says he'll hurt me. There's something in him that scares me—that has scared me from the very beginning.

He's nothing like the boys I've gone on dates with. He's capable of anything.

And I'm completely at his mercy.

I think about trying to fight him again. That would be the normal thing to do in my situation. The brave thing to do.

And yet I don't do it.

I can feel the darkness inside him. There's something wrong with him. His outer beauty hides something monstrous underneath.

I don't want to unleash that darkness. I don't know what will happen if I do.

So I stand still in his embrace and let him kiss me. And when he picks me up again and takes me to bed, I don't try to resist in any way.

Instead, I close my eyes and give in to the sensations.

* * *

All three books in the *Twist Me* trilogy are now available. Please visit my website at www.annazaires.com to learn more and to sign up for my new release email list.

EXCERPT FROM *CLOSE LIAISONS*

Author's Note: *Close Liaisons* is the first book in my erotic sci-fi romance trilogy, the Krinar Chronicles. While not as dark as *Twist Me* and *Capture Me*, it does have some elements that readers of dark erotica may enjoy.

* * *

A dark and edgy romance that will appeal to fans of erotic and turbulent relationships . . .

In the near future, the Krinar rule the Earth. An advanced race from another galaxy, they are still a mystery to us—and we are completely at their mercy.

Shy and innocent, Mia Stalis is a college student in New York City who has led a very normal life. Like most people, she's never had any interactions with the invaders—until one fateful day in the park changes everything. Having caught Korum's eye, she must now contend with a powerful, dangerously seductive Krinar who wants to possess her and will stop at nothing to make her his own.

How far would you go to regain your freedom? How much would you sacrifice to help your people? What choice will you make when you begin to fall for your enemy?

* * *

Breathe, Mia, breathe. Somewhere in the back of her mind, a small rational voice kept repeating those words. That same oddly objective part of her noted his symmetric face structure, with golden skin stretched tightly over high cheekbones and a firm jaw. Pictures and videos of Ks that she'd seen had hardly done them justice. Standing no more than thirty feet away, the creature was simply stunning.

As she continued staring at him, still frozen in place, he straightened and began walking toward her. Or rather stalking toward her, she thought stupidly, as his every movement reminded her of a jungle cat sinuously approaching a gazelle. All the while, his eyes never left hers. As he approached, she could make out individual yellow flecks in his light golden eyes and the thick long lashes surrounding them.

She watched in horrified disbelief as he sat down on her bench, less than two feet away from her, and smiled, showing white even teeth. No fangs, she noted with some functioning part of her brain. Not even a hint of them. That used to be another myth about them, like their supposed abhorrence of the sun.

"What's your name?" The creature practically purred the question at her. His voice was low and smooth, completely unaccented. His nostrils flared slightly, as though inhaling her scent.

"Um . . ." Mia swallowed nervously. "M-Mia."

"Mia," he repeated slowly, seemingly savoring her name. "Mia what?"

"Mia Stalis." Oh crap, why did he want to know her name? Why was he here, talking to her? In general, what was he doing in Central Park, so far away from any of the K Centers? *Breathe, Mia, breathe.*

"Relax, Mia Stalis." His smile got wider, exposing a dimple in his left cheek. A dimple? Ks had dimples? "Have you never encountered one of us before?"

"No, I haven't," Mia exhaled sharply, realizing that she was holding her breath. She was proud that her voice didn't sound as shaky as she felt. Should she ask? Did she want to know?

She gathered her courage. "What, um—" Another swallow. "What do you want from me?"

"For now, conversation." He looked like he was about to laugh at her, those gold eyes crinkling slightly at the corners.

Strangely, that pissed her off enough to take the edge off her fear. If there was anything Mia hated, it was being laughed at. With her short, skinny stature and a general lack of social skills that came from an awkward teenage phase involving every girl's nightmare of braces, frizzy hair, and glasses, Mia had more than enough experience being the butt of someone's joke.

She lifted her chin belligerently. "Okay, then, what is *your* name?"

"It's Korum."

"Just Korum?"

"We don't really have last names, not the way you do. My full name is much longer, but you wouldn't be able to pronounce it if I told you."

Okay, that was interesting. She now remembered reading something like that in *The New York Times*. So far, so good. Her legs had nearly stopped shaking, and her breathing was returning to normal. Maybe, just maybe, she would get out of this alive. This conversation business seemed safe enough, although the way he kept staring at her with those unblinking yellowish eyes was unnerving. She decided to keep him talking.

"What are you doing here, Korum?"

"I just told you, making conversation with you, Mia." His voice again held a hint of laughter.

Frustrated, Mia blew out her breath. "I meant, what are you doing here in Central Park? In New York City in general?"

He smiled again, cocking his head slightly to the side. "Maybe I'm hoping to meet a pretty curly-haired girl."

Okay, enough was enough. He was clearly toying with her. Now that she could think a little again, she realized that they were in the middle of Central Park, in full view of about a gazillion spectators. She surreptitiously glanced around to confirm that. Yep, sure enough, although people were obviously steering clear of her bench and its otherworldly occupant, there were a number of brave souls staring their way from farther up the path. A couple were even cautiously filming them with their wristwatch cameras. If the K tried anything with her, it would be on YouTube in the blink of an eye, and he had to know it. Of course, he may or may not care about that.

Still, going on the assumption that since she'd never come across any videos of K assaults on college students in the middle of Central Park, she was relatively safe, Mia cautiously reached for her laptop and lifted it to stuff it back into her backpack.

"Let me help you with that, Mia—"

And before she could blink, she felt him take her heavy laptop from her suddenly boneless fingers, gently brushing against her knuckles in the process. A sensation similar to a mild electric shock shot through Mia at his touch, leaving her nerve endings tingling in its wake.

Reaching for her backpack, he carefully put away the laptop in a smooth, sinuous motion. "There you go, all better now."

Oh God, he had touched her. Maybe her theory about the safety of public locations was bogus. She felt her breathing speeding up again, and her heart rate was probably well into the anaerobic zone at this point.

"I have to go now . . . Bye!"

How she managed to squeeze out those words without hyperventilating, she would never know. Grabbing the strap of the backpack he'd just put down, she jumped to her feet, noting somewhere in the back of her mind that her earlier paralysis seemed to be gone.

"Bye, Mia. I will see you later." His softly mocking voice carried in the clear spring air as she took off, nearly running in her haste to get away.

* * *

If you'd like to find out more, please visit my website at www.annazaires.com. All three books in the Krinar Chronicles trilogy are now available.

EXCERPT FROM *THE THOUGHT READERS* BY DIMA ZALES

Author's Note: If you'd like to try something different—and especially if you enjoy urban fantasy and science fiction—you might want to check out *The Thought Readers*, the first book in the *Mind Dimensions* series that I'm collaborating on with Dima Zales, my husband. But be warned, there is not much romance or sex in this one. Instead of sex, there's mind reading. The book is now available at most retailers.

* * *

Everyone thinks I'm a genius.

Everyone is wrong.

Sure, I finished Harvard at eighteen and now make crazy money at a hedge fund. But that's not because I'm unusually smart or hard-working.

It's because I cheat.

You see, I have a unique ability. I can go outside time into my own personal version of reality—the place I call "the Quiet"—where I can explore my surroundings while the rest of the world stands still.

I thought I was the only one who could do this—until I met *her*.

My name is Darren, and this is how I learned that I'm a Reader.

* * *

Sometimes I think I'm crazy. I'm sitting at a casino table in Atlantic City, and everyone around me is motionless. I call this the *Quiet*, as though giving it a name makes it seem more real—as though giving it a name changes the fact that all the players around me are frozen like statues, and I'm walking among them, looking at the cards they've been dealt.

The problem with the theory of my being crazy is that when I 'unfreeze' the world, as I just have, the cards the players turn over are the same ones I just saw in the Quiet. If I were crazy, wouldn't these cards be different? Unless I'm so far gone that I'm imagining the cards on the table, too.

But then I also win. If that's a delusion—if the pile of chips on my side of the table is a delusion—then I might as well question everything. Maybe my name isn't even Darren.

No. I can't think that way. If I'm really that confused, I don't want to snap out of it—because if I do, I'll probably wake up in a mental hospital.

Besides, I love my life, crazy and all.

My shrink thinks the Quiet is an inventive way I describe the 'inner workings of my genius.' Now that sounds crazy to me. She also might want me, but that's beside the point. Suffice it to say, she's as far as it gets from my datable age range, which is currently right around twenty-four. Still young, still hot, but done with school and pretty much beyond the clubbing phase. I hate clubbing, almost as much as I hated studying. In any case, my shrink's explanation doesn't work, as it doesn't account for the way I know things even a genius wouldn't know—like the exact value and suit of the other players' cards.

I watch as the dealer begins a new round. Besides me, there are three players at the table: Grandma, the Cowboy, and the Professional, as I call them. I feel that now almost-imperceptible fear that accompanies the phasing. That's what I call the process: phasing into the Quiet. Worrying about my sanity has always facilitated phasing; fear seems helpful in this process.

I phase in, and everything gets quiet. Hence the name for this state.

It's eerie to me, even now. Outside the Quiet, this casino is very loud: drunk people talking, slot machines, ringing of wins, music—the only place louder is a club or a concert. And yet, right at this moment, I could probably hear a pin drop. It's like I've gone deaf to the chaos that surrounds me.

Having so many frozen people around adds to the strangeness of it all. Here is a waitress stopped mid-step, carrying a tray with drinks. There is a woman about to pull a slot machine lever. At my own table, the dealer's hand is raised, the last card he dealt hanging unnaturally in midair. I walk up to him from the side of the table and reach for it. It's a king, meant for the Professional. Once I let the card go, it falls on the table rather than continuing to float as before—but I know full well that it will be back in the air, in the exact position it was when I grabbed it, when I phase out.

The Professional looks like someone who makes money playing poker, or at least the way I always imagined someone like that might look. Scruffy, shades on, a little sketchy-looking. He's been doing an excellent job with the poker face—basically not twitching a single muscle throughout the game. His face is so expressionless that I wonder if he might've gotten Botox to help maintain such a stony countenance. His hand is on the table, protectively covering the cards dealt to him.

I move his limp hand away. It feels normal. Well, in a manner of speaking. The hand is sweaty and hairy, so moving it aside is unpleasant and is admittedly an abnormal thing to do. The normal part is that the hand is warm, rather than cold. When I was a kid, I expected people to feel cold in the Quiet, like stone statues.

With the Professional's hand moved away, I pick up his cards. Combined with the king that was hanging in the air, he has a nice high pair. Good to know.

I walk over to Grandma. She's already holding her cards, and she has fanned them nicely for me. I'm able to avoid touching her wrinkled, spotted hands. This is a relief, as I've recently become conflicted about touching people—or, more specifically, women—in the Quiet. If I had to, I would rationalize touching Grandma's hand as harmless, or at least not creepy, but it's better to avoid it if possible.

In any case, she has a low pair. I feel bad for her. She's been losing a lot tonight. Her chips are dwindling. Her losses are due, at least partially, to the fact that she has a terrible poker face. Even before looking at her cards, I knew they wouldn't be good because I could tell she was disappointed as soon as her hand was dealt. I also caught a gleeful gleam in her eyes a few rounds ago when she had a winning three of a kind.

This whole game of poker is, to a large degree, an exercise in reading people—something I really want to get better at. At my job, I've been told I'm great at reading people. I'm not, though; I'm just good at using the Quiet to make it seem like I am. I do want to learn how to read people for real, though. It would be nice to know what everyone is thinking.

What I don't care that much about in this poker game is money. I do well enough financially to not have to depend on hitting it big gambling. I don't care if I win or lose, though quintupling my money back at the blackjack table was fun. This whole trip has been more about going gambling because I finally can, being twenty-one and all. I was never into fake IDs, so this is an actual milestone for me.

Leaving Grandma alone, I move on to the next player—the Cowboy. I can't resist taking off his straw hat and trying it on. I wonder if it's possible for me to get lice this way. Since I've never been able to bring back any inanimate objects from the Quiet, nor otherwise affect the real world in any lasting way, I figure I won't be able to get any living critters to come back with me, either.

Dropping the hat, I look at his cards. He has a pair of aces—a better hand than the Professional. Maybe the Cowboy is a professional, too. He has a good poker face, as far as I can tell. It'll be interesting to watch those two in this round.

Next, I walk up to the deck and look at the top cards, memorizing them. I'm not leaving anything to chance.

When my task in the Quiet is complete, I walk back to myself. Oh, yes, did I mention that I see myself sitting there, frozen like the rest of them? That's the weirdest part. It's like having an out-of-body experience.

Approaching my frozen self, I look at him. I usually avoid doing this, as it's too unsettling. No amount of looking in the mirror—or seeing videos of yourself on YouTube—can prepare you for viewing your own three-dimensional body up close. It's not something anyone is meant to experience. Well, aside from identical twins, I guess.

It's hard to believe that this person is me. He looks more like some random guy. Well, maybe a bit better than that. I do find this guy interesting. He looks cool. He looks smart. I think women would probably consider him good-looking, though I know that's not a modest thing to think.

It's not like I'm an expert at gauging how attractive a guy is, but some things are common sense. I can tell when a dude is ugly, and this frozen me is not. I also know that generally, being good-looking requires a symmetrical face, and the statue of me has that. A strong jaw doesn't hurt, either. Check. Having broad shoulders is a positive, and being tall really helps. All covered. I have blue eyes—that seems to be a plus. Girls have told me they like my eyes, though right now, on the frozen me, the eyes look creepy—glassy. They look like the eyes of a lifeless wax figure.

Realizing that I'm dwelling on this subject way too long, I shake my head. I can just picture my shrink analyzing this moment. Who would imagine admiring themselves like this as part of their mental illness? I can just picture her scribbling down *Narcissist,* underlining it for emphasis.

Enough. I need to leave the Quiet. Raising my hand, I touch my frozen self on the forehead, and I hear noise again as I phase out.

Everything is back to normal.

The card that I looked at a moment before—the king that I left on the table—is in the air again, and from there it follows the trajectory it was always meant to, landing near the Professional's hands. Grandma is still eyeing her fanned cards in disappointment, and the Cowboy has his hat on again, though I took it off him in the Quiet. Everything is exactly as it was.

On some level, my brain never ceases to be surprised at the discontinuity of the experience in the Quiet and outside it. As humans, we're hardwired to question reality when such things happen. When I was trying to outwit my shrink early on in my therapy, I once read an entire psychology textbook during our session. She, of course, didn't notice it, as I did it in the Quiet. The book talked about how babies as young as two months old are surprised if they see something out of the ordinary, like gravity appearing to work backwards. It's no wonder my brain has trouble adapting. Until I was ten, the world behaved normally, but everything has been weird since then, to put it mildly.

Glancing down, I realize I'm holding three of a kind. Next time, I'll look at my cards before phasing. If I have something this strong, I might take my chances and play fair.

The game unfolds predictably because I know everybody's cards. At the end, Grandma gets up. She's clearly lost enough money.

And that's when I see the girl for the first time.

She's hot. My friend Bert at work claims that I have a 'type,' but I reject that idea. I don't like to think of myself as shallow or predictable. But I might actually be a bit of both, because this girl fits Bert's description of my type to a T. And my reaction is extreme interest, to say the least.

Large blue eyes. Well-defined cheekbones on a slender face, with a hint of something exotic. Long, shapely legs, like those of a dancer. Dark wavy hair in a ponytail—a hairstyle that I like. And without bangs—even better. I hate bangs—not sure why girls do that to themselves. Though lack of bangs is not, strictly speaking, in Bert's description of my type, it probably should be.

I continue staring at her. With her high heels and tight skirt, she's overdressed for this place. Or maybe I'm underdressed in my jeans and t-shirt. Either way, I don't care. I have to try to talk to her.

I debate phasing into the Quiet and approaching her, so I can do something creepy like stare at her up close, or maybe even snoop in her pockets. Anything to help me when I talk to her.

I decide against it, which is probably the first time that's ever happened.

I know that my reasoning for breaking my usual habit—if you can even call it that—is strange. I picture the following chain of events: she agrees to date me, we go out for a while, we get serious, and because of the deep connection we have, I come clean about the Quiet. She learns I did something creepy and has a fit, then dumps me. It's ridiculous to think this, of course, considering that we haven't even spoken yet. Talk about jumping the gun. She might have an IQ below seventy, or the personality of a piece of wood. There can be twenty different reasons why I wouldn't want to date her. And besides, it's not all up to me. She might tell me to go fuck myself as soon as I try to talk to her.

Still, working at a hedge fund has taught me to hedge. As crazy as that reasoning is, I stick with my decision not to phase because I know it's the gentlemanly thing to do. In keeping with this unusually chivalrous me, I also decide not to cheat at this round of poker.

As the cards are dealt again, I reflect on how good it feels to have done the honorable thing—even without anyone knowing. Maybe I should try to respect people's privacy more often. As soon as I think this, I mentally snort. *Yeah, right.* I have to be realistic. I wouldn't be where I am today if I'd followed that advice. In fact, if I made a habit of respecting people's privacy, I would lose my job within days—and with it, a lot of the comforts I've become accustomed to.

Copying the Professional's move, I cover my cards with my hand as soon as I receive them. I'm about to sneak a peek at what I was dealt when something unusual happens.

The world goes quiet, just like it does when I phase in . . . but I did nothing this time.

And at that moment, I see *her*—the girl sitting across the table from me, the girl I was just thinking about. She's standing next to me, pulling her hand away from mine. Or, strictly speaking, from my frozen self's hand—as I'm standing a little to the side looking at her.

She's also still sitting in front of me at the table, a frozen statue like all the others.

My mind goes into overdrive as my heartbeat jumps. I don't even consider the possibility of that second girl being a twin sister or something like that. I know it's her. She's doing what I did just a few minutes ago. She's walking in the Quiet. The world around us is frozen, but we are not.

A horrified look crosses her face as she realizes the same thing. Before I can react, she lunges across the table and touches her own forehead.

The world becomes normal again.

She stares at me from across the table, shocked, her eyes huge and her face pale. Her hands tremble as she rises to her feet. Without so much as a word, she turns and begins walking away, then breaks into a run a couple of seconds later.

Getting over my own shock, I get up and run after her. It's not exactly smooth. If she notices a guy she doesn't know running after her, dating will be the last thing on her mind. But I'm beyond that now. She's the only person I've met who can do what I do. She's proof that I'm not insane. She might have what I want most in the world.

She might have answers.

* * *

If you'd like to learn more about our fantasy and science fiction books, please visit Dima Zales's website at www.dimazales.com and sign up for his new release email list. You can also connect with him on Facebook, Google Plus, Twitter, and Goodreads.

ABOUT THE AUTHOR

Anna Zaires is a *New York Times, USA Today,* and #1 international bestselling author of sci-fi romance and contemporary dark erotic romance. She fell in love with books at the age of five, when her grandmother taught her to read. Since then, she has always lived partially in a fantasy world where the only limits were those of her imagination. Currently residing in Florida, Anna is happily married to Dima Zales (a science fiction and fantasy author) and closely collaborates with him on all their works.

To learn more, please visit www.annazaires.com.

9 781631 421709